Florence Adler
Swims Forever

~

Rachel Beanland

SIMON & SCHUSTER

New York   London   Toronto   Sydney   New Delhi

Simon & Schuster
1230 Avenue of the Americas
New York, NY 10020

This Simon & Schuster hardcover edition July 2020

SIMON & SCHUSTER and colophon are registered trademarks of Simon & Schuster, Inc.

For information about special discounts for bulk purchases, please contact Simon & Schuster Special Sales at 1-866-506-1949 or business@simonandschuster.com.

The Simon & Schuster Speakers Bureau can bring authors to your live event. For more information or to book an event contact the Simon & Schuster Speakers Bureau at 1-866-248-3049 or visit our website at www.simonspeakers.com.

Interior design by Carly Loman

Manufactured in the United States of America

10 9 8 7 6 5 4 3 2 1

Library of Congress Cataloging-in-Publication Data is available.

ISBN 978-1-9821-6026-5
ISBN 978-1-9821-3248-4 (ebook)

For my mother
Sara Hanstein Moyle

~

In memory of

my father
Samuel Boddie Moyle, III

and

my grandmother
Frances Katz Hanstein

June 1934

Gussie

Gussie Feldman didn't enjoy swimming but she did like to lie on the wet sand, in the shadow of Atlantic City's Steel Pier, and wait for the tiniest ripple of a wave to wash over her. If she positioned herself just so, her body rose with the incoming tide, and for a brief moment, she felt weightless.

She was lying in just such a manner, staring up at the bright blue sky, when her aunt Florence's face came into her field of vision. "I discovered a lovely note when I arrived home," Florence said. "I want to give my compliments to the artist."

Gussie grinned. She had devoted more than a quarter of an hour to writing the note, which she'd carefully positioned on the Oriental rug in the entryway of her grandparents' apartment, where Florence would be sure to see it. With her colored pencils, she had written in big, purple letters, *Dear Florence! And Anna. We are at the beach. Come have fun! Love, Gussie.* At the last minute, she decided she had not used enough exclamation marks, so she added three more after Florence's name but stopped short of allocating any to Anna. Maybe, if her grandparents' houseguest noticed she hadn't been awarded any, she'd decide to stay at the apartment.

"Do you want to be a mermaid?" Gussie asked Florence now, hoping to capitalize on her aunt's good mood. Sometimes, if Gussie asked sweetly, Florence would cross her legs at the ankles and pretend the two of them were merpeople, out for a swim around the Tongan Islands, which Gussie had read about in her picture book *Fairy Tales of the South Seas*.

"For a few minutes. Then I'm going to go out for a swim."

Florence lay down beside Gussie in the surf, and the two of them bumped against each other as the waves lapped at their ankles and hips and shoulders. When their skin touched, Gussie felt shy. It was always like this when her aunt returned home from college. It took time for Gussie to relearn Florence's face and the amount of space she took up in a room and the funny way she talked to Gussie like she was both a beloved child and a trusted grown-up.

"What do you think of Anna?" Florence asked as she propped herself up on her elbows and gave Anna a wave. It was a hot day and the beach was crowded with people, but Gussie spotted her right away.

"I think it's her fault I have to sleep on the sun porch."

Florence let out a loud cackle. "Nonsense. I spent my entire childhood begging your Nana and Papa to clear out that sun porch. Mainly so I could get away from your mother." She reached out and pinched Gussie in the ribs. "You're a lucky girl."

Gussie didn't know about any of that. The sun porch was fine—no tinier, in actual fact, than her bedroom in her parents' apartment. The room had a bank of windows that faced the ocean, and if she stood on her tiptoes, she could see beyond the pitched roofs of the homes that lined Virginia Avenue, all the way to the beach, where the blue-and-white umbrellas looked like tiny pinwheels. The view was nice but, on summer mornings, when the sun rose over the Atlantic Ocean and its long rays bored through the glass, the room became unbearably hot. In those moments, Gussie wished her grandparents had remained in their house on Atlantic Avenue for the summer.

"I wish we weren't in the apartment," she allowed herself to say out loud, since her grandparents were yards away in their beach chairs. In the summer months, Esther and Joseph rented out their house— just one block from the beach—to tourists and moved back into the apartment above the bakery, where, Esther reminded anyone who complained, the family had lived quite happily when Florence and her older sister, Fannie, were small.

"Do you know how many summers I spent wishing I weren't in that apartment?" Florence asked.

"How many?"

"God, I have no idea," she said, sending a small splash of water in Gussie's general direction. "It was a rhetorical question."

"What's *rhetorical* mean?"

Florence looked up at the sky and thought for a moment. "Something you say because it sounds good but not because you actually expect an answer from anyone."

"Then why say it?"

"Because it's better than saying nothing at all?" She squeezed a handful of wet sand through her fingers. "But when you put it like that, it makes me wonder if we shouldn't all just tell each other what we mean."

Gussie scrunched up her nose and grabbed at her own fistful of sand. What Florence seemed to forget was that, since Gussie was only seven, no one ever told her anything—one way or the other. Everything she'd ever learned about anything she had learned by keeping quiet and paying attention.

Take her mother's confinement, for instance. She first learned her mother, Fannie, was expecting another baby because she'd overheard her say something to Mrs. Kingman when they had stopped by her shop for a pair of stockings. She guessed the pregnancy was risky because she'd heard her grandfather warn her mother to be careful on several different occasions in recent months. And she knew Dr. Rosenthal had recommended strict bed rest at Atlantic City Hospital because her mother had repeated his prescription to Esther when she'd returned from a recent doctor's appointment.

There had been a good bit of debate between Gussie's mother and grandmother over what to do with Gussie while her mother was on bed rest. Remaining with her father, Isaac, had turned out to be out of the question. Gussie knew this because she had overheard Esther tell Fannie so in precisely those words. "Gussie remaining at your apartment is out of the question."

Gussie was sure her father would balk when he learned that her mother intended to send her to live with her grandparents for the summer but, as her mother's confinement neared, not a word was said about the plan, one way or the other. The day before Fannie was to be admitted to Atlantic City Hospital, she packed Gussie's summer clothes and bathing suit, some of her books, her jacks, and coloring pencils away in an old suitcase. The bag sat in the apartment's narrow hallway, a boulder that Isaac had to step over to get to the kitchen. When Gussie could no longer stand his silence on the subject, she begged, "Father, can't I stay with you? Here?"

"Gus-Gus," Isaac said, as if he were going to give her a straightforward response, "what in the world would we get into, knocking around by ourselves?"

Gussie had begun to wonder if her entire life might be rhetorical—no answers for any of it—when Florence pulled her back to the present, "Remember, knees and heels together. If you're a mermaid you can only move your feet. I mean, fins."

Gussie pushed off the sandy bottom and scooted through the waves, using her arms to steer and kicking her tail fiercely. Always, she was careful to keep her chin above water. "How do I look?" she called over her shoulder, but Florence wasn't watching her, wasn't even looking in her direction. Instead, she sat in the breaking waves, studying the shore.

Gussie circled back, waved a hand in front of Florence's face. "Let's pretend you're the mermaid in the glass tank at Steel Pier, and I'll swim from Australia to save you."

"Why do I need to be saved?" said Florence, who still looked very far away. "Don't I like my life at the Pier?"

"You want to be free to swim about in the ocean, silly."

Florence turned to face Gussie then, giving her niece her full attention. "Yes, you're quite right. I nearly forgot."

~

When Florence and Gussie returned to the chairs Joseph and Esther had rented, they found Anna sitting on a blanket, alone.

"Your parents went for a walk," Anna said to Florence, completely ignoring Gussie.

Florence motioned for a small, pleated bag, within arm's reach of Anna, and Anna passed it to her. As Florence rooted through it, a red bathing cap escaped. Gussie reached for it and handed it to Florence, who waved it away, one hairpin already in hand and three more in her teeth. While Florence pulled her short, brown hair away from her face, Gussie held the rubber cap in her lap, admiring it. Her aunt always had the prettiest things. Tiny stamped divots ran across the cap's surface in neat rows. Each one reminded Gussie of a starburst.

"Are bathing caps required at this beach?" Anna asked.

Florence mumbled something through her pursed lips but it was unintelligible on account of the pins, so Gussie answered for her. "Not anymore."

Anna exasperated Gussie but for no real reason. She was quiet and a little hard to understand but she was also perfectly nice, and even pretty—with dark brown hair, green eyes, and pale skin that was un-likely to get any darker if Anna continued to wear drab cotton dresses to the beach.

"My hair just gets in my eyes when I swim," Florence said after re-moving the last pin from her mouth.

"Very good," said Anna, but the word *good* came out sounding more like *gut*. Anna's English was close to perfect but her accent was heavy, and sometimes her words came out slowly, as if her sentences were a string of taffy. Often, Gussie didn't have the patience to wait on them. Gussie's mother had told her to be kind—that she should try to imag-ine what it must be like for Anna to be in a new place, so far from her parents, but Gussie wasn't inclined to be sympathetic.

Gussie heard a high-pitched whistle followed by a "heigh-ho!" and turned to watch Stuart Williams leap from the Boardwalk onto the hot sand.

"Have you abandoned your post?" her aunt shouted at him as he raced toward them and grabbed Florence up in a hug. Anna and Gussie stood to greet him, too.

Gussie thought Stuart was very handsome. He didn't look anything like the men in her family, or any of the men at the synagogue, for that matter. He had clear, blue eyes and short, blond hair, and in the summer months, his skin tanned to a golden brown. He wore the same blue suit that all the Atlantic City Beach Patrol lifeguards wore—a wool one-piece with a white belt and the letters *ACBP* stitched across his chest.

"Dan said you were here, so I had to come see the siren of the sea for myself." He rubbed the top of Gussie's head with his fist and extended a hand toward Anna. "I'm Stuart."

"Stuart, this is Anna from Germany," said Florence. "She's staying with my parents for the summer. Until she goes to college."

"Good to meet you, Anna from Germany," he said with a smile. "Where are you going to school?"

"New Jersey State Teachers College."

"Ah, in picturesque Trenton."

"He's a wisecrack. Don't pay him any attention," said Florence to Anna, conspiratorially. "Trenton's fine."

Stuart's eyes were shiny and bright. "When'd you get back?" he said, returning his attention to Florence.

Florence put a finger to her lips, as if she were doing a complicated arithmetic problem. "Three or four days ago?"

"And this is the first I'm seeing you? I'm outraged."

"I went looking for you at the States Avenue stand but they said you'd been booted down the beach."

He wagged his head in the direction of The Covington. "Long story. And one that's probably best told from the stern of a boat."

"Stuart coaches the Ambassador Swim Club in the off-season," Florence said to Anna. "Spent four years ordering me around."

"A lot of good it did," said Stuart.

"He's a monster," Florence said to Anna, which Gussie knew was not actually true. It bothered her when grown-ups said the opposite of what they meant.

"So, you're really going to do it?" he asked Florence when everyone's smiles had faded from their faces.

"I am."

"How's the training been going?"

"Fine, good. I'm in the pool all the time, so it's been good to get back in the ocean."

Gussie wondered if Anna even knew about Florence's plan. She was about to say something when Anna asked, "Is there a competition?"

"Just with myself," Florence said with a laugh.

"She's going to swim the English Channel," said Stuart.

Florence corrected him, "*Attempt* to swim the English Channel."

"Don't pretend to be modest," he said. "We can all see right through you."

Florence reached over, touched Anna's arm, and whispered, in a voice loud enough for everyone to hear, "Don't listen to him," and to Gussie's great surprise, Anna laughed. The noise was so foreign, Gussie didn't know quite what to make of it. Anna had arrived in Atlantic City in March—Joseph had driven up to Jersey City to collect her from the ferry terminal—and, in all that time, Gussie had never seen her eyes so much as twinkle.

Florence turned serious. "Stuart's actually been a big help."

"Might not want to give me too much credit until you make it across."

"How long does it take to swim the whole thing?" Anna asked.

"Trudy Ederle did it in a little over fourteen hours. I'm hoping to do it in under twelve."

"That's a long time in the water," said Anna.

Gussie was desperate to contribute to the conversation. "Florence says your tongue swells up like a balloon."

"Is that true?" said Anna.

Florence shrugged her shoulders. "Unfortunately, yes."

"She'll be great," said Stuart. "By the time I'm through with her this summer, she might as well fly across."

"Do you start in England or France?" Anna asked.

"France," said Florence. "Cape Gris-Nez. The tide's a little more forgiving if you swim toward Dover."

"So, will you go to France, too?" Anna asked Stuart.

Stuart looked as if he were about to say something but Florence cut him off. "Over my father's dead body. Both he and Mother think it would be completely improper."

"Once she gets to France, she's got Bill Burgess. He's world class. She won't need me."

"Not true," said Florence.

Something about the easy way Florence, Stuart, and even Anna talked made Gussie yearn to be a grown-up. As she watched them, she practiced resting a hand on her hip and using the other to make big, important gestures. Stuart crossed his arms at his chest, and she tried that, too, but it didn't feel as natural. Eventually, when he noticed she was mimicking him, he winked at her and she tied her arms in knots behind her back.

Stuart looked at his wrist but must have realized he wasn't wearing a watch. "I've got to get back. Meet me at the Kentucky Avenue stand tomorrow morning at six?" he said to Florence. "I'll tail you in the boat for a couple of hours."

Florence didn't say anything, just lifted her chin, which Gussie interpreted as a yes.

"It was nice to meet you," Anna said to Stuart as he prepared to depart.

"You too."

Gussie went to say her own good-bye but Stuart had already begun to jog back toward the Boardwalk.

"He seems nice," Anna said to Florence once he was well out of earshot. "And also completely in love with you."

"Stuart?" said Florence, as if she'd never entertained the possibility. "God, no. Now, where did I put my cap?"

Gussie, who'd had it the whole time, handed it to her begrudgingly.

"Do you mind watching Gussie until my parents get back?" Florence said to Anna as she stretched the rubber taut and yanked the cap over her hair.

Gussie couldn't help feeling annoyed. It had been her idea to go to the beach, and now she was stuck with Anna, who was unlikely to pretend to be a mermaid or much of anything else if she couldn't even be bothered to change into a proper bathing suit.

"You're swimming tomorrow morning. With Stuart." Gussie pleaded with Florence, in a last-ditch effort to redeem the afternoon. But her aunt wasn't hearing her. She just tucked the last wisps of her hair underneath the bathing cap, blew her a kiss, and headed off in the direction of the ocean.

Gussie watched as Florence waded into the water, past her knees and then her hips. She dove into the crest of a wave, and by the time Gussie could see her again, she was swimming. Florence reminded Gussie of the dolphins they sometimes spotted offshore, so graceful they barely looked like they were moving. She watched her for several more minutes, as she grew smaller and smaller. Eventually, all Gussie could make out against the horizon was Florence's red bathing cap, and then nothing at all.

~

Gussie was back in the water, eyes trained on the sky, when she heard three short whistles. She got her feet under her in time to watch one of the lifeguards in the stand nearest them run toward Garden Pier. There, two other lifeguards heaved a rescue boat into the waves.

"Gussie," Anna called. "Get out. Now."

It took a moment for Gussie to shake the water out of her ears. Had she heard her correctly? The beach seemed unnaturally quiet, as if she were watching a film with no sound.

She looked up the beach and watched as her grandparents ambled toward them.

"Where's Florence?" Esther asked in a loud enough voice to be heard over the sound of the breaking waves.

Anna responded. "She went for a swim."

"When?"

"Maybe an hour ago."

Gussie watched as her grandmother took in Anna and Gussie, then the small cluster of people who had gathered farther down the beach, then the boat hastening toward the horizon. Without warning, Esther took off down the beach at a run, Joseph following close behind. Gussie had never seen either of her grandparents run anywhere before, and she was surprised at how proficient they looked doing it.

She waded ashore, and Anna wrapped her in a towel, then led her in the direction of Garden Pier, too. By the time they reached Esther and Joseph, the rescue boat was so far from shore, it was difficult to make out what was happening. Gussie shielded her eyes with her hand, trying to see more clearly. It looked as if the vessel had stopped, and one or both of the lifeguards had jumped overboard.

"Is it her?" Esther whispered to Joseph in a voice loud enough for Gussie to hear.

"Who?" Gussie asked, but no one, including Anna, responded.

After several long minutes, the rescue boat began to grow larger again. Gussie could make out only one lifeguard rowing toward the shore. Where had the other one gone? It wasn't until the boat grew much closer that she saw the second lifeguard, bent over something in the bottom of the boat.

The boat plowed onto the wet sand, about a dozen yards from where the small crowd had gathered. Its oars clattered against the oarlocks and landed in the sand, and the men worked quickly to lift what could only have been a person from the bottom of the boat.

That's when Gussie saw it—the flash of color—and she looked at Anna to see if she'd seen it, too. Anna's hand moved to her mouth. The lifeguards lifted the body, pale and motionless, out of the boat and onto the sand but all Gussie could bear to look at was the red cap on her aunt's head. She covered her ears with her hands as the air filled with the sound of her grandmother's wails.

Esther

The Virginia Avenue Hospital Tent regularly treated sunburns, jelly-fish stings, and heatstroke but, if there had been patients who suffered from those ailments when the guards arrived at the tent with Florence, they were now long gone. Everyone on the small staff—beach surgeon, doctors, nurses—worked over a single cot in the far corner of the tent.

Esther could make no sense of the girl on the cot.

That the girl was her daughter.

That her daughter was not moving.

When Esther had arrived at the tent, she had been inclined to fight her way into the center of the commotion but Joseph nudged her toward a pair of canvas chairs. "Let's give them room to work," he said quietly, his face ashen.

She felt for the edge of a chair, could barely find it, then listened as the beach surgeon yelled instructions at the staff. How long had it been since Florence had been pulled from the water? Five minutes? Ten? Esther looked at her watch. It was half-past four. When had she heard the whistle blast? She hadn't thought to check the time.

"Keep going," Esther heard the beach surgeon say before he shouted at the assembled lifeguards. "Boys, form a line. We need you to cycle in and out."

"What are they doing?" Esther asked Joseph as she watched the first guard take over for the doctor who had previously been thumping on Florence's back.

"Giving compressions."

"Yes, but why the guards?"

"To relieve the staff," said her husband, whose eyes never left the cot. "They're getting tired."

Esther clutched her sides and put her head between her knees. How could they be tired? They'd scarcely been at this for any time at all.

After several more minutes had passed, she sat up and forced herself to watch, through tears that blurred her vision, as one guard after another beat on her daughter's back. Esther stared at the doctors and nurses and lifeguards for so long that they ceased to be individual people, morphing instead into an amalgam that pulsed to the beat of each round of compressions.

She nearly missed the beach surgeon tapping the guard on the shoulder, telling him to stop. "Help me turn her over," the beach surgeon said to one of the doctors who stood on the other side of the cot. His voice sounded garbled. The men looked at each other, with a kind of startled disappointment, and rolled Florence over, slowly, until she was faceup. They arranged her arms by her side. "Time of death," said the beach surgeon, looking at his watch and then at Esther, "five twenty-three."

~

Eventually, they came to take Florence away. A car pulled up along the Boardwalk and two men got out, carrying a wooden stretcher between them. Esther recognized one of the men as Abe Roth, who ran the Jewish funeral home.

"They can't take her!" Esther whispered to Joseph. "Please don't let them take her."

"Bubala, we will go with her. We won't let her be alone."

The men bowed their heads when they arrived at the cot where Florence rested.

"Joseph. Esther," Abe said. "I'm so very sorry."

Esther couldn't look at him. She kept her eyes on her daughter's pale cheeks, her purple lips.

"You're still over at Beth Kehillah?" Abe asked. He and his wife were members of Rodef Sholom, a conservative shul on Atlantic Avenue.

Joseph nodded.

"We'll give Rabbi Levy a call and let him know. He'll get the Chevra Kadisha over to our place. I assume you want the *Taharah* performed."

Esther's grandmother had been a member of the Chevra Kadisha in Wiesbaden, and her mother in Philadelphia. Still, Esther winced at the idea of women she barely knew touching her daughter's lovely, long limbs, washing away the salt water and the sand that clung to her arms and legs. Florence's arms had propelled her through the ocean but first they had propelled her across Esther's kitchen floor. They had been soft and dimpled and smelled of Pond's soap and talcum powder. Esther was the only one who had ever bathed her.

"Would you like me to say the *Vidui*?" Abe asked.

"What does she have to atone for?" Esther asked, her voice sharp. "She's twenty. My beautiful girl is just twenty."

"Esther," Joseph said quietly, his voice choked. To Abe, he said, "Please."

Abe began to chant the words as Esther sobbed into the wet silk of Florence's bathing suit. She imagined the Hebrew letters knitting together as they floated through the air, forming an invisible blanket that, when wrapped around Florence, would keep her safe. When Abe began the Shema, Joseph joined in, "Shema Yisrael, Adonai Elohenu Adonai Echad." *Hear O Israel, the Lord is our God, the Lord is One.* How many times had Esther heard this prayer? A thousand times? More? Had she ever considered what it meant? It was Joseph who was more connected to the old ways, Joseph who had grown up in the small shtetl of Lackenbach, where opportunities were scarce but Jewish law abounded.

Women were not obligated to say the Shema but, as Abe and Joseph continued their recitation, Esther began to mutter the words through her tears. Perhaps by saying this prayer, on this beach, on this day, Esther might shield her daughter from an unknown she could neither see nor imagine. She whispered, "Adonai Hu Ha'Elohim. Adonai Hu Ha'Elohim." *Adonai is God.*

∼

While the women of the Chevra Kadisha observed the ritual of *Taharah*, washing Florence's body and dressing it in the *tachrichim* they'd brought for the occasion, Esther and Joseph sat on a sofa in the front room of Roth's Funeral Home and spoke with Rabbi Levy.

The rabbi, whom the congregation had hired five years ago, was only adequate. He looked the part of a rabbi, with his graying beard and the spectacles he wore at the end of his nose, but in Esther's opinion, he had always been far more concerned with the profitability of the congregation's fund-raisers than with the spirituality of its members.

Rabbi Levy offered to secure a *shomer* for Florence—a congregant who would sit guard over her body throughout the night—but Joseph wouldn't hear of leaving his daughter with anyone.

"It will be a long night," said the rabbi. "Are you sure?"

"I'm her father," Joseph said, and the simple explanation made Esther feel proud to have married him, to have borne the children that made those three small words true.

Abe Roth had scoured the funeral home's closets and returned with a dark gray suit jacket and a mink fur stole. He handed the jacket to Joseph, who left it draped across his knees. Then he wrapped the stole, which smelled of mothballs, around Esther's shoulders. She thanked him and shuddered, involuntarily. For the first time, she realized she was still wearing her bathing costume.

Rabbi Levy asked Esther if her family would travel from Philadelphia, and she could feel herself growing annoyed. Her father had been dead for ten years, her mother for three. The rabbi had said *Kaddish* for both of them, repeatedly.

"No," she told him, refusing to elaborate.

"Is an afternoon service all right?"

Esther looked at Joseph, who had the same pronounced jaw as both his daughters. It had suited Florence but made Fannie look so serious, even as a young girl.

She whispered Fannie's name. Was this the first time, since Florence's death, that she had so much as thought of her surviving daughter? "Joseph," she said, louder this time, "Fannie."

Joseph rubbed his hands against the side of his face, as if he could no longer take in any new information.

There could be no funeral. Nothing public, anyway. "Fannie can't know."

"Is Fannie not well?" the rabbi asked.

He knew about last year's loss. Most of the congregation did. Fannie had carried the baby nearly to term, had been told by most of the women in the congregation, at one point or another, that she was carrying high and that the baby would be a boy. *Kena horah.* The fact that the baby *had* been a boy hadn't made it any easier for Fannie to return to the sanctuary on the High Holy Days.

"Fannie's expecting again," said Esther, her blood simmering beneath the surface of her skin. "She's been at Atlantic City Hospital for two weeks." Surely, she'd mentioned it to him. If she hadn't, someone on the women's committee had.

"When is the child due?" the rabbi asked.

"Not until August."

"And you want to keep this news from her?"

Esther looked at Joseph. "We can't risk her losing another baby." Her husband continued to stroke his face, his eyes unfocused. "You agree, don't you, Joseph? Joseph?"

"What?" he finally said.

"That we can't tell Fannie. Not when the pregnancy is already so precarious."

"What you're proposing will be extremely difficult," said the rabbi, looking across the room to Abe for support.

Esther considered all the different ways Fannie might learn that her sister was dead. The plan was not without risk. But what felt riskiest was telling Fannie the truth.

"We sit Shiva so we can have the time to look inward, to properly reflect on our loss. But we invite the community in because mourning is intensely lonely, and our friends and family can offer comfort." Rabbi Levy continued to talk long after Esther had stopped listening.

"What time is it?" she interrupted.

The rabbi consulted his pocket watch. "Half-past eight."

"Abe, is there a telephone I might use?"

He motioned down the hallway, "There's one in my office."

Joseph grabbed her by the arm as she stood, "Bubala?"

"I'm going to call Samuel Brody, over at the *Press*," she said. "We have to keep this out of the paper."

~

It was late when Rabbi Levy dropped Esther off at the apartment but, even in the dark, she recognized the young man sitting on her front stoop.

"Do you know him?" the rabbi asked.

"Yes."

The rabbi let the car run while he walked around to open Esther's door and help her out. "I'll collect you tomorrow at two."

She nodded, unable to take her eyes off Stuart, who was still in his ACBP uniform. When he stood the streetlamp illuminated his face, and she saw that he'd been crying.

The rabbi's car puttered away, and Esther motioned for Stuart to sit. Then she joined him. "Are Anna and Gussie upstairs?"

He shook his head. "When I got over here, Anna answered the door. I didn't believe it was true until I saw her face."

"How's Gussie?"

"Confused, I think."

Something about Florence's friendship with Stuart had never sat right with Esther. It was her experience that boys like him, whose fathers owned hotels on the Boardwalk and not shops north of Arctic Avenue, went away to college and usually to the sorts of schools she and Joseph lambasted. Schools like Princeton and Yale that had, in the last several years, implemented strict quotas and new admissions standards to keep their classrooms from swelling with too many Jewish students. That he had joined the Atlantic City Beach Patrol as a lifeguard, and cobbled together a coaching career in the off-season, struck Esther as a move designed to infuriate his father as much as anything else. His father was worth infuriating—The Covington Hotel was one of several hotels that refused Jewish guests—but sometimes Esther wondered if

Stuart's friendship with Florence was just another way to get under his father's skin.

It was Stuart who had encouraged Florence to apply to Wellesley; he had even taken the liberty of writing to Wellesley's swim coach, a Miss Clementine Dirkin, on Florence's behalf. Dirkin was apparently an icon in the Women's Swimming Association, and Stuart had argued—quite convincingly—that Florence needed to go to a school where women weren't relegated to synchronized swimming competitions, as was so often the case. At Wellesley, he promised, Florence would not just be swimming the 400, 800, and 1500 events but she'd be medaling in them.

Of course, it was Joseph, and not Stuart, who had taught Florence to swim. But for the last six years, ever since Florence had joined the Ambassador Club and then gone away to school, it was Stuart who had pushed her to swim faster and farther. He was always on the lookout for new races, always talking about the next big swim. Without Stuart, would Florence have swum the pageant swim? The solo swim around Absecon Island? Certainly, she wouldn't have set her sights on the English Channel. Were it not for him, Esther couldn't help but wonder, would her dear girl still be alive?

"I would have followed her in the boat."

"I know," she said, her voice as coarse as sandpaper.

"What was she doing out there on her own?"

Esther didn't know what to say, how to begin to admit that her daughter had acted rashly.

"Please," she said. "Don't."

Stuart wiped his eyes with the palms of his hands. "When will she be buried?"

"Tomorrow."

"That soon?"

"Jews don't wait."

Stuart studied his knees. "May I come?"

Her inclination was to tell him no, that the graveside service would be for family only. If Fannie couldn't be there, it seemed unfair for

Stuart to be. But Esther could imagine Florence chiding her for her bad behavior. It was obvious that Stuart loved Florence, and Esther found herself wondering if her daughter had known. Perhaps she had even loved him back. Sol and Frances Goldstein, who lived around the corner, had sat Shiva for their eldest daughter when she married a goy, and at the time, Esther hadn't so much as batted an eye. Treating a daughter who was alive and well—and even happy—like she was dead, all because she'd married outside the faith, felt suddenly preposterous.

"We'll go to Egg Harbor at two o'clock tomorrow afternoon."

"The City Cemetery?"

"No, Beth Kehillah."

A passing car backfired, and Esther jumped.

"One of the guards told you?" she asked.

"Word spread fast that there'd been a drowning at States Avenue."

"Does everyone know it was Florence?"

"Some of the guards do. Why?"

"We don't want Fannie to know," said Esther. "Not after what happened last summer."

"I see," said Stuart, although it was not entirely obvious to Esther that he did.

"Will you help?"

"I can talk to the guys if you want."

Esther considered the offer for a moment before she answered him, "Would you mind?"

~

A lamp was on in Gussie's room, and in the middle of the floor lay the canvas bag Esther had taken to the beach earlier that day. Alongside it was Florence's bag, a prettier, pleated tote. The bag's contents—a hairbrush, a towel, and several hairpins—spilled out onto the floor, and Esther stooped to pick up the items. When she had gathered them all, she allowed herself to let out a silent moan.

On the little cot, Anna and Gussie slept. The cot was barely wide enough for one of them. They fit side by side only because Anna had wrapped her arms around Gussie, tucking the small girl into the cave of her chest. Gussie's dark brown hair splayed out in all directions and her mouth hung open. In the last year, she had grown taller and lost much of her baby fat but, asleep, she still looked young.

Esther thought about waking Anna to remind her that she'd be more comfortable in a regular bed. If Anna had been Florence, she might have absentmindedly rubbed her back, grabbed one of her hands, and pulled her to her feet, enjoying that groggy moment when her adult daughter leaned into her, needing her. But Anna was not Florence, and Esther couldn't bear to have one more conversation than she absolutely needed to about the day's events. The telephone call she had to make to Isaac was going to take all the energy she had left.

The sun porch was hot and stuffy. One window sat open but Esther pushed open two more. It was too dark to see the beach two blocks away but she could hear the waves crashing against the shore. The perpetual movement of the ocean had always soothed her, particularly during times of trouble, but now the sound left her feeling outraged. That the ocean could take something so precious from her, without even stopping its dance to acknowledge her loss, seemed cruel.

Esther studied the young woman who cradled her granddaughter. She didn't like the feeling of being indebted to Anna, but she supposed she was nonetheless. Without being told anything, Anna had known to gather the family's things, remove Gussie from the beach, bring her back to the apartment, and offer her whatever comfort she could while Esther and Joseph attended to the business of saying good-bye to Florence. Anna had demonstrated the kind of sure-headedness that Esther had always hoped to instill in her own daughters.

Last fall, when Joseph had proposed bringing Anna to the United States, Esther had felt powerless to stop him. Anna was the daughter of a woman named Inez, someone Joseph now told her he had grown up alongside in Hungary but whom he had, interestingly, never once managed to mention in twenty-nine years of marriage.

Inez's letter, littered with German stamps, had arrived in the foyer of their Atlantic Avenue house like a small hand grenade last October.

Joseph was at the plant, so Esther had slid the envelope open, too curious about its contents to wait until he got home. She had been disappointed when she was unable to identify the sender's handwriting or interpret the signature, much less read the letter's contents, which were written in Joseph's native Hungarian.

When Joseph had finally arrived home and read the letter from start to finish, he gave Esther only the barest of translations. Inez's first husband had been killed in the war, and in the aftermath, Inez had moved from the embattled borderlands of Austria-Hungary to Vienna with Anna. There, she had met and married Paul, who was studying at the university. When Paul secured a teaching position in Berlin, they had moved to Prussia and eventually naturalized but everything was in jeopardy now that the Third Reich had come to power. Last summer, the family's citizenship had been revoked, and a few months later, Paul was let go from his position. As for Anna, she hadn't secured a spot at any of the German universities to which she'd applied the previous year, and it was Inez and Paul's sincere wish that she get out of Germany before things got any worse.

"What else does she say?" Esther had asked, glancing at the three-page letter, written in tight script.

"That's all," said Joseph, unable to meet her gaze, and Esther had known right away that he was lying. She could have summarized what Joseph had told her in five good sentences.

Over the next several months, Joseph helped Inez identify several American universities that might be good options for Anna. In some cases, he'd even written away for the application materials himself. Once Anna's application had been submitted to New Jersey State Teachers College, Joseph picked up the phone, calling anyone he knew with a connection to the school or its admissions director. Esther had thought Anna sounded smart enough to get into the school on her own merit, but Joseph told her he wanted to leave nothing to chance. Even when the acceptance came through, Joseph kept working, turning his full attention to helping Inez and Paul secure all the necessary documentation for Anna's student visa application. He offered to sponsor her, and when the visa was granted faster than expected, to put Anna up for the summer.

Esther told herself to be gracious, both about Anna's stay and the help she knew Joseph was now providing Inez and Paul, who were also eager to get out of Germany. The situation over there did indeed sound dire, and Esther knew several families at Beth Kehillah that were trying to help relatives, in Germany and elsewhere, immigrate to the United States.

The difference, Esther reminded herself, was that Anna wasn't a relative. She was barely even a friend. When Esther and Joseph had taken her to the Jewish Consumptive Relief Society's fund-raiser, back in April, it had been hard to know how to introduce her. *This is Anna, the daughter of an old friend of Joseph's*. Was that what Inez and Joseph had been to each other? Just old friends? Anytime Esther tried to bring up Inez, Joseph bristled.

Gussie coughed and turned over in her sleep, and Esther watched as Anna adjusted her own body to accommodate the little girl's.

"I'm home," Esther said aloud but Anna didn't answer. She breathed slowly in and out, her eyes closed, one arm stretched behind her head. What Esther wouldn't have given to be trapped in a sleep so deep that she couldn't be woken.

~

By a quarter to six the next morning, Esther was waiting in a chair outside the office of the hospital superintendent, Nellie McLoughlin. Esther had been inside the office once before, last summer, when they had needed to decide what to do with Fannie's baby, but this early in the morning, the first-floor office was shut up tight.

Esther wasn't one for putting women in charge of things, but it was hard to find a person in all of Atlantic City who didn't think McLoughlin was a skilled administrator and the right person for the hospital's top job. McLoughlin had run the hospital's nursing school for a decade and had played a large and visible role in the hospital's recent fund-raising campaign, which resulted in the construction of the new wing.

"Mrs. Adler," said a stiff voice that Esther realized belonged to a woman standing directly in front of her. She looked up from her lap to find Nellie McLoughlin, taller and more imposing than she remembered, staring down at her.

"Miss McLoughlin," said Esther as she stood on liquid legs.

"To what do I owe the pleasure of this early morning visit?" McLoughlin asked as she slid her key into the lock.

Esther waited until McLoughlin pushed the door open and turned on the office's overhead light before following her across the threshold, "Do you have a moment?"

"Certainly," McLoughlin said as she placed her handbag in an empty drawer of a tall filing cabinet, then unpinned her hat and set it inside the drawer as well. She gestured toward two chairs that sat across from a modest, metal desk. "Is everything all right with Fannie?"

"It's not Fannie," said Esther. "It's her sis—" She couldn't get the word out. The room was too hot. She yanked at the collar of her dress, tried to undo the top button. Couldn't do that either. "Sis." It was as if, with the utterance of this one little word, she had rediscovered that Florence was dead. Esther bent at the waist, unable to breathe. She could hear McLoughlin asking if she was all right, could feel a hand on her shoulder. Esther took a series of short breaths, tried to fill her lungs, but couldn't find enough air. She began to truly panic then, heard someone yelling for a nurse. Was it McLoughlin? This was not how she wanted this meeting to go.

"I'm fine," she tried to say as the room grew crowded with people. There was McLoughlin, a nurse, later a man in a white coat. She focused on the small floral pattern of her own dress. The flowers were pastel blue and yellow and pink, and they danced in front of her eyes.

"I'd recommend a sedative," Esther heard the man say. "Something to calm her down, let her rest for a while."

"Mrs. Adler," said McLoughlin. "Do you hear me?"

Esther nodded, tried to swim back up to the surface of her own consciousness. There was no time for any of this. She had to talk to McLoughlin, had to protect Fannie.

"I'm all right," she whispered.

"Can you sit up?"

Esther slowly raised her head from her knees, looked around the office, and eventually made eye contact with McLoughlin. She was mortified by her own behavior. "I'm sorry."

"You have nothing to be sorry for," said McLoughlin, leaning against the edge of her desk. "Tell me what's wrong."

Esther looked at the doctor who was standing just a few feet away from the two women, then looked back at McLoughlin. The superintendent nodded her head toward the door, and the doctor disappeared through it.

"Yesterday," Esther began. She didn't know what to say next. She breathed in and out, slowly. "Fannie's sister died."

McLoughlin sank into the chair beside Esther's. "I'm so sorry."

Esther began to cry in earnest now. It was so unlike her but all of her habits and predilections seemed entirely baseless now. How many more times in her life would she have to repeat that sentence or something similar? *Fannie's sister died. My younger daughter died. One of my daughters died when she was young.* If Esther lived until she was an old woman, she would still be explaining Florence's absence, trying to understand it herself.

"She drowned off States Avenue. Yesterday afternoon."

"No—"

Esther nodded her head, wiped at her wet cheeks with her hands.

McLoughlin handed her a handkerchief. "She was a very good swimmer, wasn't she?"

"Incredible," said Esther.

They sat together for quite some time, listening to the sounds of the hospital coming awake. A door opened and closed, a telephone rang in the distance, a pair of heels clicked up the stairs. Finally, McLoughlin spoke, "You're not here because you want my help telling Fannie."

Esther shook her head and blew her nose into the handkerchief. "I don't want to tell her anything."

"You're worried about an early labor?"

"Do you think I'm being irrational?"

"Not at all. It's a real risk. Particularly after last summer." McLoughlin stood and walked around to the other side of her desk, where she pulled open a drawer and removed a pad of paper. "So, let's figure out how to do this."

"I think we need to move her to a private room," said Esther. "Somewhere where we can keep better tabs on who comes and goes. Her father and I can pay the difference."

"How many people know about . . . Florence?" asked McLoughlin. Esther could tell she had been about to say something else, was about to use a less sanitized word like *drowning* or *death* and had stopped herself. Esther's confidence in McLoughlin grew.

"A lot of the lifeguards. The women in the Hebrew burial society."

"No one on the hospital staff?"

"Not to my knowledge. She was treated at the hospital tent at Virginia Avenue." McLoughlin scribbled something on the pad.

"And there's no announcement in the paper?" the superintendent asked.

Esther reached into her handbag, removed the morning's newspaper, and handed it to McLoughlin. Samuel hadn't managed to kill the story, only to soften its blow. On the front page was the headline GIRL DIES WHILE BATHING OFF STATES AV.

"Do they identify her?" McLoughlin said.

Florence was described as a local girl and a strong swimmer but was never named, thank God. "No," Esther whispered, "but an astute reader might very well figure it out."

McLoughlin skimmed the article, then began to write. On one sheet of paper, she listed the names of the doctors and nurses she planned to let in on the secret. "Lucky for us, the preceptors graduate tomorrow at noon. And the new class won't start until the end of the summer."

"Preceptors?"

"Students," said McLoughlin. "Doesn't matter. It's just fewer people who have to know."

On another sheet of paper, McLoughlin spelled out the accommodations the staff would make to limit Fannie's access to the outside world. They'd move her to a private room, of course, but they'd also remove the room's radio and limit Fannie's ability to visit the sun-room, where a telephone and a radio had been installed for the use of all the women on the ward.

"Can someone read her mail?" Esther asked.

It was the only request McLoughlin seemed to bristle at. "I'd prefer we just stop her mail entirely. We can deliver anything we receive to you, and you can decide what to do with it."

By the time they finalized the plan, it was half-past seven. McLoughlin tore the papers from the pad and folded them in half and then in quarters. "I'd better start my rounds or someone's going to put a copy of the *Atlantic City Press* on Fannie's breakfast tray."

Esther snatched up her handbag and stood to go. "I'll be by to visit later. After—"

McLoughlin eyed her mournfully. "Until then, you are not to worry. She's in good hands."

Esther knew she should thank McLoughlin, wanted to even, but when she went to say something, she found she had no words left.

～

Joseph arrived home an hour before the burial.

When he walked through the door, he looked pale and exhausted. His already thin hair was flat, his hazel eyes—normally bright and gleaming—had turned a sludge brown, and the dark circles under them looked unlikely to ever be erased. Esther wrapped her arms around him and they stood like that for a long time, not moving, barely breathing.

"Are you all right?" she finally asked.

"I can't," he said quietly as he unlocked her arms and moved toward the bedroom, where she had already laid his best suit out on the bed. She tried to swallow the rebuff, to remind herself that they each hurt in their own ways.

Isaac cut his arrival close, showing up at the apartment just a few minutes ahead of the rabbi. Gussie flew into his arms and refused to be put down, clutching his neck that much tighter every time he tried to release her. Ordinarily, Esther might have told her to stop being ridiculous but today she just sat quietly on the sofa and watched the scene unfold, her eyes watering as she thought about how Joseph had spent the last eighteen hours with his own daughter.

Esther couldn't believe that Isaac was really going to wear his beige sport coat to the burial. It had no lines to speak of and looked about as sharp as a paper bag on Isaac's tall frame. Were Fannie and Isaac's circumstances so dire, the salary Joseph paid Isaac so insufficient, that he couldn't have purchased something more appropriate this morning? A lightweight worsted suit in gray or blue would have been useful to own under any circumstance, and Sam Sloteroff would surely have given him a good price on it.

Despite the jacket, Isaac was a handsome man. He had a high forehead and a strong jaw and teeth that were unnaturally straight. At thirty-three, his dark hair was starting to recede, but Esther imagined that he'd remain an attractive man, even when it was gone.

Last evening, Esther had telephoned Fannie and Isaac's apartment three times before Isaac picked up. When he finally answered, near midnight, he had seemed out of breath, and Esther wondered briefly if he'd been drinking. He told her he'd been asleep, which explained the endless ringing and his hard breathing, but not his stoic reaction when she told him that Florence was dead. Isaac asked so few questions, demanded so few answers, that Esther found it difficult to believe he could have possibly heard her. He'd known Florence since she was twelve years old. Surely the duration of their relationship, if nothing else, demanded a real reaction.

It wasn't until she proposed keeping Florence's death from Fannie that Isaac seemed to come fully awake.

"What will we tell her?" he had asked, his voice unsteady.

"Nothing. Or rather, the ordinary things," said Esther. "That she's busy training to swim the Channel. That she's preparing for the trip to France."

"How long can we possibly keep that up?"

"Florence is set to leave on the tenth of July."

The line went quiet. *Was.* Florence *was* set to leave on the tenth of July.

"It feels wrong," said Isaac. "Not telling her. She'd want to know."

"Isaac," said Esther, not yet pleading but utterly prepared to, "you remember what it was like."

"We don't know what caused the early labor."

"Do you want to risk it? And possibly lose another son?" She was playing almost all of her cards now, even the ones she'd promised herself she wouldn't touch.

"So instead I should just lie to her for two months?"

"It's not lying," said Esther, weakly.

"What about Gussie? She'll be an accomplice in this? Or is she just going to be kept from her mother all summer?"

"No, of course not. She's a smart girl. We'll explain it."

"And the staff at the hospital? Surely some of them have already wandered in off the ward to give their condolences?"

"Very few people know. And I'll speak to Miss McLoughlin first thing in the morning."

The line fell quiet again. Esther could hear the slow in and out of Isaac's breathing.

"Isaac, please," Esther begged. "I've lost enough today."

Still, he didn't give.

Esther could stand it no longer. She played her final card.

"It would mean so much to Joseph."

Isaac owed his entire livelihood to Joseph. She knew it, Isaac knew it, and Isaac knew that she knew it. Without Adler's Bakery and the job Joseph had fashioned for him at the plant, their son-in-law would be nowhere.

"And if I go along with this," he asked, "what then?"

"After the baby is born, I can tell her."

When he didn't respond immediately, she held her breath, frightened she had said the wrong thing.

Finally, he said, "No, I'll tell her."

Esther swallowed hard, "That would be fine, too."

It was the following morning—after her visit with Nellie McLoughlin—before Esther felt she'd fully recovered from her conversation with Isaac. She returned home and made her way through the apartment, preparing the rooms for Shiva. She covered mirrors with sheets and poured out standing water from teakettles, watering cans, and washbasins. Anna tried to be helpful, unfolding and refolding bed linens and offering to drape the mirror above Florence's dressing table, so that Esther might avoid the room entirely.

Before Esther draped the mirror in her own bedroom, she studied her reflection. Her hair was gray and had been since the girls were small, but for years it hadn't mattered. Her face had looked young, and inside, she still felt like the nineteen-year-old girl who had once been so bold as to ask Joseph, a handsome young waiter at Chorney's Hotel, to go for a walk. Joseph and she had married and started the bakery, the girls had been born and grown up, Fannie had married and had Gussie, Florence had gone away to school, and the house had grown quiet again. How often had Esther remarked to Joseph, "I can't believe I'm old enough to have a married daughter" or "To think I'm a grandmother! How can this be?" Now, as she rubbed her hands against her temples, pulling the puffy skin around her eyes as tight as she could, she felt every one of the forty-nine years that had marched across her face. Esther threw a sheet over the mirror, disgusted with herself. Jews covered their mirrors during Shiva to prevent exactly this kind of shallow reflection.

"Should I lay anything out for the *seudat havra'ah*?" Anna asked.

"I don't think that will be necessary," said Esther. "I told Rabbi Levy I didn't want him to make any announcements to the congregation. No one will know to cook anything."

Anna opened her mouth to speak, then seemed to think better of it, and shut it again.

When Esther instructed Anna to keep Gussie at home during the burial, Anna surprised her and pushed back, asking if she might attend instead. Esther hadn't said a word in response, just looked at her long and hard. The girl had known Florence for, what, less than a week?

"Of course, I'll stay with Gussie if you prefer," said Anna, her eyes on the ground.

"Funerals are no place for children," said Esther.

Rabbi Levy arrived promptly at two, bearing a pair of scissors and a spool of thick, black ribbon. Esther showed him into the living room, where he invited Joseph, Isaac, Anna, and even Gussie to stand. "We'll perform the *Kriah* before we leave for the cemetery."

Nobody argued.

"In the Torah, Jacob tore his robes when he thought his son Joseph was dead," said the rabbi. "King David and his men did likewise when they heard about the deaths of Saul and Jonathan. Job, who grieved for his children, followed in the same tradition."

What Esther recalled about the story of Job was that his wife had gone crazy with grief over the loss of those children.

"It's traditional for children, parents, spouses, and siblings to wear torn clothes during the week of Shiva. Since Fannie cannot participate in this rite, it would be appropriate for Isaac to bear this burden," he said.

Isaac looked uncomfortable. Esther knew he had only the one jacket.

"Isaac will be back and forth to the hospital, visiting Fannie," said Esther. "Let's leave his jacket be."

"Cut mine, please," said Joseph, stepping forward.

Rabbi Levy took hold of Joseph's lapel and cut a deep gouge in the thick fabric. As he did so, he sang, "Boruch ato Adonai Elohenu Melech Ho'olom dayan ha'emet."

Scissors still in hand, the rabbi moved toward Esther.

"Not my clothes, please," she said quietly. "I'll take the ribbon."

He pursed his lips in judgment but reached into his pocket to remove a small, brass safety pin. As he fastened the ribbon to her blouse, he sang the blessing once more.

Esther could feel Gussie studying her, so she was not surprised when she heard her granddaughter's small voice: "Please may I have a ribbon, too?"

~

They made a small funeral party, Rabbi Levy at the wheel, Joseph beside him, and Esther and Isaac in the backseat of the rabbi's Pontiac coupe.

The drive to Egg Harbor Township was one that Esther rarely made. Joseph's trucks made deliveries in Pleasantville, Egg Harbor, and all the way to Cape May, but Esther rarely had reason to cross the Beach Thorofare.

When the car slowed on Black Horse Pike, Esther peered out her window and through the hemlocks that edged Beth Kehillah Cemetery. The property wasn't large, maybe a dozen acres of land that Egg Harbor's early Jewish settlers had consecrated when Absecon Island was little more than a railway depot with bathing houses for day-trippers from Philadelphia.

Two cars were parked near the entrance and beside them stood Abe and his son. And Stuart, who held a bouquet of flowers limp by his side, as if he'd purchased them and immediately regretted doing so. Such a goy, bringing flowers to a funeral. She tried to remind herself that he had no way to know.

Rabbi Levy pulled his car up behind Abe's and cut the ignition. When they were all out, Abe opened the rear door of his own car, and Esther found herself confronted with Florence's casket. She bit her lip and tasted blood.

"You'll carry it?" Abe asked the four men. They looked at each other and nodded.

"Not him," said Esther, pointing to Stuart.

Joseph's eyes widened.

"What?" she asked in a slightly incredulous tone. "He's not Jewish."

"I hardly think it matters now," Joseph sputtered, but not before Stuart took a large step backward and held up his hands, as if to say, *No, of course not.*

Neither Joseph nor Rabbi Levy was a young man, and it became obvious to Esther, some minutes later, as she watched them stumble under the weight of Florence's casket, that Stuart might have been a useful pallbearer. At the graveside, the men lowered the casket onto the pulley system Abe had rigged across the open grave.

Rabbi Levy removed a handkerchief from his breast pocket and wiped his brow. "With your permission, we'll begin," he said to Joseph, who looked at Esther for reassurance. She walked around the casket to the spot where her husband stood, took his hand, and nodded to Rabbi Levy, who began to read a familiar psalm. "He that dwelleth in the secret place of the most high shall abide under the shadow of the Almighty."

Scattered across the cemetery were the grave markers of infants—small squares of stone, the word CHILD chiseled across their fronts. No names, no dates. More often than not, a small lamb, cut from the same stone, rested atop the tiny monuments. Esther supposed the lamb was a symbol of innocence but it also struck her that he might be good company for children who had never learned to sleep through the night.

She looked across Florence's casket at the spot where Isaac stood. Did he notice the small markers? Wish for one for the baby he had lost? Fannie had pleaded for a burial for the child, had wanted a place to mourn, but Esther and Joseph told her, over and over again, that there was nothing to be done. The boy had lived just three weeks, and the rule was thirty days. At thirty days old, he would have been considered a human being under Jewish law and entitled to most, if not all, of their mourning rituals, including a burial in a Jewish cemetery and a small grave marker.

As things stood, Esther didn't know where the baby was buried, or if he had been buried at all. Fannie had begged her to find out the infant's whereabouts but Esther knew that Fannie didn't need a place to go and wallow. What she needed was to have another baby, to forget the whole sad business as quickly as possible. Surely Isaac agreed?

When the *El Malei Rachamim* had also been said, Rabbi Levy turned to Joseph once more, "Have you prepared a *hesped*?"

Joseph started to speak but no words came out. He tried again.

This time, he got as far as "My daughter was—" before his voice died. Esther could feel his hand shaking under hers. She grabbed hold of it with both her hands and squeezed it tight.

"You can try again," she whispered.

He choked. "I can't."

Rabbi Levy prompted her to continue in her husband's stead. "Esther, is there anything you'd like to say?"

"I'm not prepared . . ." she said, her voice trailing off. What was there to say? What could ever be enough?

"I could say something," Stuart said, stepping forward. "If it would be"—he eyed Esther cautiously—"proper."

Stunned by his chutzpah, Esther said nothing, which both Rabbi Levy and Stuart interpreted as acquiescence.

Stuart coughed, then cleared his throat. "I, um, thought Florence was a terrific girl. Er, we all did." His hands shook and Esther cringed as she watched him cover one with the other, then shove them both into his pockets instead.

"She was beautiful and smart and so funny she'd make you split your side. But the thing that always got me was—"

"Enough," Esther interrupted. All five men turned to look at her, shock registered on each of their faces. "I can't listen to this."

Joseph let go of her hand.

"Would you prefer I take over?" asked the rabbi.

"There is absolutely *nothing* to say." Esther looked Stuart in the eyes. His face had turned scarlet. "I'm sorry. Everything you said was, of course, true." Then she began to sob.

Shortly, Abe and his son cranked the winches, lowering the casket haltingly into the ground. Rabbi Levy picked up a nearby shovel, walked around to the foot of the grave where a pile of loose dirt sat waiting, and began the *K'vurah*. A shovelful of dirt landed on top of Florence's casket with a terrifying thud. He passed the shovel to Isaac, who in deference to Joseph, refused to replace any earth until Joseph had done so. In Joseph's hands, the shovel looked heavy enough to topple him. When Esther had not been looking, her husband, too, had grown old. Tears poured from his eyes as he heaved a shovelful of dirt into the abyss and then returned for another and another. Finally, when his brow was damp, he handed the shovel to her. Esther wiped her eyes and rubbed the wooden handle, warmed under Joseph's hands and worn smooth over years of use. The metal blade made a satisfying sound as she plunged it into the mound of dirt. Esther had always wondered how mothers buried children, and now she knew. One shovelful of dirt at a time.

Fannie

Fannie didn't even realize she'd dozed off until she felt a warm kiss on her forehead and opened her eyes to find her mother sitting on the edge of her hospital bed.

"How long have you been here?" Fannie asked, shaking the fog from her head.

"A little while."

"You should have woken me."

"I think not," said Esther.

"I feel like a sloth for sleeping in the middle of the afternoon." She yawned. "How's Gussie?"

"She's well," said Esther as she stood and walked over to the window. "Of course, she misses her mother."

Fannie doubted that. Gussie had Florence, who was far more fun. Three days ago, when Florence had brought Gussie to visit, it had been impossible to lure the girl out of her sister's lap.

"How do you like the new room? Isn't it lovely?" Fannie asked, waving at her new surrounds. She was appreciative of the south-facing window, clad in pretty, floral curtains. The furniture was the same as that of her old hospital room except that, in this room, the bed and dressing table were painted a chocolate brown. "Is it Father I've got to thank for this?"

"Yes, well," said Esther. "There was such a parade of women in and out of that room, we didn't know how you were getting any rest. And the visiting hours were atrocious."

"What does Pop care what the visiting hours are? He doesn't visit."

Esther gave Fannie her very best exasperated look. "It'd take more than decent visiting hours to get your father near a hospital."

"Well, it was very kind of him. When I woke up this morning and Dorothy told me they were moving me to a private room, I couldn't believe it. I must have asked her three times to check she had the right patient."

"Dorothy?" Esther asked, turning away from the window to study Fannie once more.

"Geller. She's a nurse on the obstetrics ward. A real busybody. Very short and squat with an extremely nasal voice. She went to school with Florence. Is always going on about it."

"Be careful or she'll hear you."

"I don't care if she does. You should have seen her fawning all over Florence the other day," said Fannie, giving her best Dorothy impression, "'What a feat, Florence! Swimming around the whole island! Whatever will you do next?'"

"Does she really talk like that?"

"Yes. And Florence was just soaking it up."

Her mother stared out the window. Was she even listening?

"What's Florence up to today? She didn't want to come with you?" Fannie asked, well aware that she was poking at her sister. Florence could hold a grudge as long as Fannie could, and Fannie knew she wouldn't come for a visit so soon after they'd had it out. Fannie was curious what Florence had told their mother, if anything, about her last visit. Did Esther know they'd argued?

Esther coughed. "She's out for a swim. With Stuart."

"All she ever does is swim."

Esther walked over to the dressing table and repositioned Fannie's hairbrushes and face cream, her back to Fannie, until the arrangement was to her liking. Florence must have already told Esther her side of the story, must have already won her allegiance. It was so obvious. Fannie's mother could barely make eye contact with her.

"All I suggested was that she postpone the trip, not cancel it. I would have thought she'd *want* to be close by."

"Of course she would. Does."

Esther began refolding an already folded blanket at the foot of the bed, neatening the corners and tightening the lines. Sometimes Fannie found her mother exhausting to be around. Esther was always busy, always moving. Both her house on Atlantic Avenue and the apartment above the bakery were neat as pins. She was a talented cook and an accomplished seamstress, too particular to hire help even after she and Joseph reached the point where they could finally afford it. Fannie didn't think she'd ever seen her mother pick up a magazine.

On Fannie's best days, she didn't accomplish half as much as her mother did. Fannie served Isaac and Gussie overcooked meat and mushy vegetables and could barely keep up with the dusting, let alone the laundry. In the evenings, when Isaac asked her how she'd spent her day, Fannie wanted to be able to rattle off a list of errands and other household achievements, but the truth was that entire afternoons passed in which she couldn't move from the sofa. Fannie so frequently felt overwhelmed—by what, exactly, she didn't know—that she had begun to wonder if she was even related to the girl she'd been before she married.

"Apparently, Florence doesn't want anything to do with me—or the baby," Fannie told Esther.

"Don't be ridiculous."

"Well, I don't understand why she'd choose to leave for France in July, knowing I'm due in August."

"Your sister loves you. She adores Gussie," said her mother, then she paused before adding, "and she'll adore this baby, too."

Without meaning to, Fannie began to cry. She cried so often these days, it was sometimes difficult to isolate the trigger.

"Fannie, dear."

"I don't know what's come over me. I think it's just being tucked away in the hospital like this. I know I'm missing all the fun out there," she said, waving at the window and all that the outside world contained.

Esther walked over to the bed, sat down heavily, and wrapped her arms around Fannie. She spoke softly into her daughter's hair, "You're missing nothing that won't wait."

❧

By the time Esther left the hospital, the sun was beginning to go down. Out Fannie's window, beachgoers were heading home to their dinners, and in another few hours, the Boardwalk would come alive with revelers. Fannie let out a long sigh, knowing it would be at least the next afternoon—if not longer—before she saw Isaac or anyone else for that matter.

On one hand, her hospital stay was a nice reprieve from domestic life. Fannie hadn't cooked or cleaned or shopped in more than two weeks. She'd read three books, all of them titles she'd been meaning to read since the previous summer.

On the other hand, Fannie didn't feel as if she were in control of her own life. The hospital staff poked and prodded her without approval or apology, she ate when her tray was brought in, and she saw her family and friends when they saw fit to visit. Then there was the biggest anxiety of all—that this hospital stay would do nothing to prevent another early labor.

Fannie strummed her fingers against her stomach. She might feel helpless but there was one thing she could do right now. She could settle this business with Florence.

Fannie's relationship with her sister had never been easy, not with seven years separating them. She had worked hard to be a good big sister but it often felt, to Fannie at least, as if she and Florence had had almost entirely separate childhoods. By the time Florence entered grade school, Fannie was through with it. By the time Florence was chasing the Pageant Cup, Fannie had quit swimming competitively. And by the time Florence had catapulted herself to Wellesley, Fannie felt even further away from her sister than the three hundred miles between them. She imagined how dull the details of her life must sound when Florence read her increasingly infrequent letters.

It wasn't just that Florence and Fannie were far apart in age. It was also that, by the accident of birth order, they had received two very different sets of parents. In 1907, when Fannie was born, Joseph and Esther had been busy trying to get Adler's Bakery off the ground. Joseph was always at the store, and since he could scarcely afford to pay himself a salary, let alone pay for staff, Esther was frequently behind the counter. Fannie spent her early years in the kitchen of Adler's, trying her best to stay out of the way of hot pans and scurrying feet. When Joseph began to hire bakers and bakers' assistants, one of their unacknowledged job duties was to keep his only child entertained. They'd give Fannie a small ball of dough and a rolling pin and put her to work.

Florence found a very different scene when she arrived in 1914. Esther was overjoyed at her arrival, having long given up the idea that she might conceive another child. The bakery was doing well, and with the exception of the year Joseph fought with the Allies on the Western Front, he encouraged Esther to remove herself to their upstairs apartment, where she could properly enjoy her daughter's infancy. Fannie would rush home from school to find Esther feeding Florence banana in her high chair or rocking her to sleep, and she'd join in wherever she could—remarking on Florence's squishy baby thighs or allowing Florence to gnaw on her own small fingers. Even now, at twenty years old, Florence was very much the baby of the family. If her mother had already sided with Florence, Fannie knew there was very little she could do to sway her. No, it would be better to sort this out with Florence directly.

Fannie threw back her blankets and got out of bed. For a moment, she felt light-headed—how many hours had it been since she'd stood up or moved around? She steadied herself, placing the palm of her hand flat against the mattress. When the spinning feeling stopped, she moved slowly across the room to the dressing table, where Dorothy had unpacked her belongings earlier that morning. She found her stationery and fountain pen in the top drawer and made her way back to the bed.

Fannie chewed on the lid of the pen for several minutes before she began.

Dear Flossie,

It seems odd to write a letter when you're not away at school, but already back in Atlantic City. I thought about wandering down the

*hall and asking to use the telephone but I'm not sure I trust myself
to get this out properly.*

*Your wanting to swim the Channel and my wanting to deliver a
healthy baby are not the same thing, and it hurt me tremendously
when you compared the two the other day. I know that they're both
things we want very much, but you must understand that if you
fail to accomplish your goal, you hop in a boat and come home. If I
fail, I will find myself holding another lifeless child in my arms.*

Fannie replayed their fight in her head. She had practically demanded, like a petulant child, that Florence remain at home until after
the baby was born, and when that hadn't worked, she'd made the mistake of reminding Florence that, by the age of twenty, she'd been a
married woman—somebody's wife.

"And look how well that's turned out," Florence said in a biting voice.
"Your marriage isn't exactly a ringing endorsement of the institution."

Fannie's pen hovered over the page. Should she try to defend her
marriage? Fannie's family had never warmed to Isaac, even in their very
early days together when he had tried harder to impress her parents
and sister. Fannie weighed her words, then decided that, maybe where
Isaac was concerned, it was best to say nothing at all.

*If swimming the Channel is what you want, then I want that
for you, too. I'm sorry I wasn't more generous when you visited.
Punish me if you must but don't stay away too long. There's
something about being tucked away inside this hospital that wears
on me—it's as if I'm trapped in another world. I can see the ocean
out my window but I can't hear or smell it.*

*Your Loving Sister,
Fannie*

When she was finished writing the letter, Fannie read it through
twice, then she folded the pages and stuffed them in an envelope. Just

as she did, Dorothy came in with her dinner tray, so she addressed the envelope in a flash—Florence Adler, Northeast Corner of Atlantic and Virginia Avenues, A.C.

"Dorothy, I wonder if you might be able to help me find a stamp?"

∼

By half-past ten, Fannie had given up on Dorothy. Nurses who worked the day shift clocked out at seven o'clock, and she had likely gone home for the night. Knowing her, she had put Fannie's request out of her mind the moment she'd left the room.

Fannie was awake, and a stamp was as solid an excuse as any to take a little stroll. The nurses tsked when she got out of bed, so she didn't try to make a habit of it, but it did feel good, every now and then, to stretch her legs. Fannie retrieved her slippers and robe and made her way out of the room and down the hall. She'd try the nurses' lounge, see if anyone had a stamp, and maybe take the newspaper if the women were finished reading it.

The obstetrics ward was quiet, save for the occasional sound of a baby's cry, and dark. The only source of light came from the end of the hallway, where the nursery and the nurses' lounge sat opposite each other.

Tonight she heard several hushed voices coming from the lounge. Was it a bad time to ask for something so immaterial as a stamp? Fannie hated to interrupt if there was important hospital business that had stolen the women's attention. She started to turn to go back to her room, but then she heard one of the nurses say, "It's just about the most tragic thing I've ever heard." Fannie stopped cold and listened harder, "Can you even imagine being the one to have to tell her?"

The quintuplets. Fannie hurried to the door of the lounge and peeked her head around the corner. "Is there any news?" she asked in a panic. Three nurses sat huddled together on a mohair sofa, smoking cigarettes. Fannie knew the names of two of them—Bette and Mary—and she'd seen the other one walk quickly past her room from time to time, always with what Fannie imagined to be great purpose. Perhaps she worked in the delivery room or the operating theater. All three women looked startled to see her. Bette balanced her cigarette in the ashtray the women shared, and jumped up to take Fannie's arm, "Are you all right? Why are you out of bed?"

Fannie thought she noticed the purposeful nurse dabbing at the corners of her eyes with her fingertips. "I thought I might borrow a stamp. Is there any news—"

The women looked at each other, stricken.

"—about the Dionne babies?"

Fannie watched as the women's faces rearranged themselves right in front of her.

"Yes! Yes!" said Mary, "The babies are all still alive! It's a miracle!"

Bette steered her into a rattan chair that sat opposite the sofa, "Here," she said, sliding a stack of magazines, a copy of the *Atlantic City Press*, and the ashtray farther down the coffee table. "Put your feet up at least."

"Cigarette?" asked the purposeful nurse, holding out a pack of Chesterfields.

"Yes, please," said Fannie, reaching forward to retrieve one.

Mary passed her a lighter. Fannie hadn't had a cigarette in more than two weeks, and how long had it been before that? Maybe the Newman party? She took a long draw. There was something about the cigarette that made the evening feel festive, like the women who sat across from Fannie might be friends and not hospital staff paid to change her linens and bring her meals.

"What's the latest on the babies?" Fannie asked, eyeing the paper.

Mary picked it up and rearranged it, handing the folded pages to Fannie. There, at the top of page twenty-one, was the headline TWO OF THE QUINTUPLETS ARE NOT SO WELL. The paper had devoted nearly two full columns to the five girls, born a little more than a week ago—two full months early—in Ontario, Canada.

Fannie couldn't let go of the story. According to the paper, in all of human history, only thirty cases of quintuplet births had ever been recorded. In not a single case had all the children lived. That these babies had managed to stay alive for more than a week was remarkable.

"Edith says it sounds like Marie's not doing so well," said Bette.

Fannie made note of the fact that Edith must be the name of the purposeful nurse. Then she asked, "Marie's the really tiny one?"

"Yes," said Edith.

"I love all their names—don't you?" said Mary.

Bette shook her head agreeably. "They're so French."

Fannie scanned the article. "It doesn't seem like the doctor's very optimistic."

The women clucked, and Fannie pressed her mouth into a frown of concern. The truth was that there was a small part of her—a tiny part of her really—that hoped something would go wrong with the quints. That one woman, who already had five children at home, should give birth to not one infant but five, and that they all might survive, made Fannie sick with jealousy.

The Dionne children had spent their first five days of life in a basket of blankets and hot-water bottles, positioned close to the stove. They were fed a mixture of breast milk, corn syrup, water, and rum, and when, on the fifth day, they had not yet died, they were moved to a donated incubator, not unlike the one in which Hyram had spent the final days of his life.

It wasn't as if Fannie were the first woman to ever lose a child. She knew that. If forced, she could probably list the names of a half-dozen women who had lost a baby in childbirth or shortly thereafter. There was Mildred Greenberg, whose husband drove for Adler's and Alice Cohen, who played bridge with Rachel Stern. Ethyl Kauffman and Gladys Rivkin. All of them got dressed each day, cooked and cleaned, shopped, and eventually had more babies. Fannie had run into Gladys in the lobby of the Warner Theatre, on a night when she and Isaac had gone to the pictures to see *I'm No Angel*. Fannie hadn't been able to pay attention to the film because she had spent so much time studying the back of Gladys's head, wondering how she managed to laugh at anything.

"I keep telling Dr. Rosenthal we should get a couple of those new incubators up here on the ward," said Edith.

Bette gave her a look but Edith didn't appear to notice. "It's ridiculous that a Boardwalk amusement has more success saving babies than a modern hospital."

"Fannie's baby spent some time at Couney's incubator exhibition last summer," said Bette. "Isn't that right, Fannie?"

Fannie nodded, perhaps too vigorously. "We moved him from the hospital to Couney's because we had hoped it would give him a better chance."

Edith leaned forward. "And did it?"

"No—"

Edith seemed disappointed, not necessarily because Fannie had lost her son but because the outcome undermined her argument that incubators were the future of medicine. She sank heavily into the sofa, leaned her head back as she took a long drag of her cigarette, and exhaled toward the ceiling.

A baby began to cry across the hall.

"I've got it," said Bette, stubbing out her cigarette in the ashtray. "Fannie, you care to join me or are you on your way back to bed?"

"Me?" Fannie asked, unsure if she had heard Bette correctly.

"Yes, you. Do you want to come feed a baby?"

"I'd love to," she said, putting down the paper and reaching across the table to extinguish her own cigarette in the now-crowded ashtray. She supposed the stamp could wait. She stood, said good night to Mary and Edith, and followed Bette across the hall, where more than a dozen bassinets lined both sides of the nursery. About half of them were filled with newborn babies. In the far corner, near the window, one infant had worked its arms free from its bunting and was squawking at the ceiling, all red in the face.

"That one's got a set of lungs on him," said Bette as she began preparing a bottle.

"May I?" asked Fannie, before reaching into the bassinet to pick him up.

"Oh sure."

The baby was big and round, and felt heavy in her arms—nothing like Hyram but probably something like how Gussie had felt, if she remembered correctly. Gussie had been longer and leaner at birth, but with cheeks that looked like plums. Fannie held the baby high, above the bulge of her stomach, and walked over to a rocking chair, where she sat down carefully.

"You won't break him. He's sturdy," said Bette as she handed Fannie a bottle.

Fannie put the small rubber nipple to the baby's mouth, and he latched immediately, sucking down the milky concoction with a ferocity that startled her. For three weeks last summer, she had prayed daily that her own son would swallow the droplets of formula that were placed on his tongue with a medicine dropper.

This was the first time Fannie had held a baby in her arms since Hyram died. Last fall she'd gone out of her way to avoid friends with small children, skipping Ellen Perlman's baby shower and the Hanukkah party at Beth Kehillah. Even after she found out she was pregnant again, she had let Anna take Gussie to the Baby Parade. Seeing all those infants in prams and wagons and rolling carts felt like too much. If Hyram had lived, he might have been among them, dressed up in his best gingham smock, gnawing on a cookie or perhaps a pretzel, and getting a good look at Atlantic City in all its resplendent excess.

The baby in Fannie's arms opened his eyes lazily, looked up at her briefly, and then shut them again. "He looks so healthy," she said, more to herself than to Bette.

Bette studied her for a moment before she said, "There's no reason to believe yours won't be."

∼

Isaac had been good about visiting Fannie the first week of her confinement, but in the last week or so, his visits had slowed considerably. Fannie knew he was busy with the bakery and Gussie, but the hospital wasn't far from their apartment, and she felt unsettled on the days he didn't stop by.

"Where have you been hiding, Mr. Feldman?" she asked him, when he tapped on her door early the following morning.

"Here and there," he said as he dragged the stool closer to the bed.

Visitor's hours didn't begin until nine. "How'd you get past the nurses?" Fannie asked as he planted a kiss on her forehead. She tried to breathe him in.

Isaac didn't offer her an explanation, just winked as he took a seat and crossed his legs at the knee. He was a handsome man, and Fannie knew he had to be popular with the nurses on the floor.

"Well?" she said, gesturing at the four walls that surrounded them.

"It's a nice room."

"Did Pop tell you he was doing this? I'm worried it must be very expensive."

"I'm sure it is. But your father can afford it."

Fannie cringed at the statement. Sometimes, when Isaac talked about money, she could feel herself growing pink around the neck. Her father never openly discussed his finances but Isaac was quick to remind her that only people with money could afford not to talk about it.

We *have* money, Fannie wanted to argue. But she knew that Isaac's obsession had less to do with the salary her father paid him than with the circumstances in which he'd been raised. Too often, he had gone without.

When Isaac started taking Fannie out, a million years ago now, he hadn't had two cents to rub together. He liked to promise her that, once he was a little more established, he'd be able to buy her steak dinners at the Ritz but, in the meantime, she often returned from her dates hungry enough that she had to go straight to the kitchen to make herself a sandwich. She tried to tell Isaac she didn't need fancy dinners, so long as they were happy, but over time, his promises just grew bigger. Now he said that he wanted to be able to buy them a car, a small house in Ventnor or Margate, some clout at the synagogue.

Sometimes Fannie wondered if it had been a bad idea for Isaac to go to work for her father. When Isaac began delivering bread for Adler's, she knew he viewed the job as temporary, as a place to catch his breath while he plotted his next move. But in 1928, two years after they were married and a year after Gussie was born, Joseph opened the plant on Mediterranean Avenue and stopped making bread in the back of the Atlantic Avenue store. Within a year, Adler's had increased its production tenfold, and Joseph invested in more trucks to deliver bread throughout southern New Jersey.

For the first time in Fannie's recollection, her parents seemed truly comfortable. And the expansion was good for Isaac and Fannie, too. Isaac got a promotion—overseeing all those delivery trucks, an office with a telephone, and a nice raise.

But the job made Isaac that much more beholden to Joseph, and Fannie thought it also gave Isaac too much insight into her father's financial affairs. Her parents' house on Atlantic Avenue, the checks they sent to Wellesley, and especially her father's support of Florence's Channel swim made Isaac resentful, in a way that felt unreasonable.

Isaac remained hell-bent on getting out from under Joseph's thumb, and he began putting aside all their extra money so that he might one day start a business of his own. Fannie thought the plan was shortsighted—why couldn't he see that her father would eventually retire from Adler's and that, if Isaac worked hard and was patient, the business would be his? At the very worst, he'd share the responsibility of running Adler's with whomever Florence married. On days when Isaac returned home from the plant in a good mood, Fannie tried to suggest that they use their savings for a down payment on a house instead.

When the stock market collapsed, in the fall of 1929, Isaac started staying away from the apartment for long stretches of time. When he was home, he went to bed early, barely acknowledging Fannie or Gussie. This behavior went on for weeks, until finally one night, Fannie shook him awake. "Enough. You have to tell me what's going on."

Isaac rubbed his eyes, disoriented. "I lost all the money."

Fannie felt relief wash over her. That was all?

"Isaac, it was what? Two hundred and fifty dollars?" said Fannie. "We can save it again."

"I used it to buy stocks on margin."

"What does that mean?"

"I put up our money, and the bank loaned me ten times that amount."

"I don't understand."

"The bank loans us the money, and when the market goes up, we pay the bank off."

"What happens when the market goes down?"

Isaac didn't say anything.

"Isaac?"

"The bank is calling in their margin. I've got two weeks to pay them in full."

It took several long seconds for Fannie to recover herself. She could scarcely imagine *ever* having twenty-five hundred dollars, let alone coming up with it in a fortnight.

"What will we do?" she finally asked.

Isaac didn't need to tell her that the only good option was to go to her father for help and hope that he wasn't in the same financial straits. Buying the Mediterranean Avenue property and building the plant had required capital, and she prayed her father's money was in the bricks and mortar of Adler's Bakery and not in the New York Stock Exchange. Fannie offered to talk to him but Isaac wouldn't hear of it. The financial markets and their repercussions were not a woman's concern.

It took Isaac several days to work up the courage to approach Joseph but, after he did, he felt relieved. Coming up with the cash Isaac needed wouldn't be easy, Joseph said, but he could do it. They agreed to a loan, at no interest, payable over ten years.

"How did he seem?" Fannie had asked Isaac after he explained the terms.

"What do you mean? He *seemed* like he was going to loan us the money."

"Was he surprised?" she asked, but what she really meant was disappointed.

After the banks fell, the tourists stayed home, and Fannie and Isaac watched as many of Atlantic City's steadiest businesses shuttered their doors. It was as if, almost overnight, Isaac stopped dreaming. He no longer came home from the plant with half-conceived business plans or sketched-out storefronts on the back of old receipts. He stopped talking about the house they'd buy, and he grew quieter, indifferent. He was less likely to laugh at Fannie's jokes, more likely to lose his temper with Gussie. Where he had once tried to please and even impress Fannie's parents, he avoided them instead, bowing out of Shabbat dinners and Sunday afternoons at the beach. But the most significant change, for Fannie, was Isaac's utter unwillingness to consider having a second child.

For two months after the crash, Isaac didn't touch Fannie. When he eventually returned to her, on a cold night in January, she nearly wept with relief. The wind off the ocean rattled their bedroom windows and the radiators, recently bled, creaked under the weight of their heavy responsibility. Fannie could feel the familiar pressure building inside her, as if she, too, had a valve that just needed to be turned a few degrees. She whispered, "Keep going," into Isaac's ear, but no sooner were the words out of her mouth than he withdrew himself entirely, spilling a warm pool onto the pale of her stomach.

"Why did you do that?" Fannie had asked, although she thought she knew.

"These aren't the circumstances in which I want to have another child."

Tears sprang to her eyes, but they remained concealed in the dark.

"What *are* the circumstances?"

"I don't know, Fannie," he said, sighing. "Not this."

Of all the men Fannie knew who had, in one way or another, been affected by the economic downturn, Isaac and his job at the plant seemed among the safest. In tight times, their friends and neighbors might give up new shoes and millinery but she couldn't imagine them dispensing with bread. She supposed things could always get worse but, in all but the most dire circumstances, Fannie felt sure her father would be able to protect Isaac. He'd pink-slip any number of bench hands, oven men, and bread wrappers before he put his own son-in-law out of a job. Isaac might not be striking out on his own, but they were never going to be destitute.

It was three years before Isaac stopped withdrawing when he climaxed. The first time, Fannie assumed he had merely made a mistake. But it happened again two nights after that, and then again the following week. She didn't say anything for fear he'd remember himself, but she began to feel hopeful, to look forward to those moments when she could sense her husband's muscles tighten, his breathing skip. Like she had in their early days, she locked her legs around him and arched her back, allowing her body to be pulled into his until she felt him shudder. In the dark, as Fannie waited for her husband's breathing to resume its normal patterns and to eventually lull her to sleep, she tried to convince herself that Isaac had turned a corner, that his acquiescence was actually an expression of certitude. But in her heart, she thought it more likely that Isaac had just given up.

~

"The only thing I can't figure out about this room," said Fannie to Isaac, "is where the radio is."

Isaac looked around the room, absentmindedly. "What makes you think you're meant to have one?"

"Some of the women down the hall have them. I can hear their programs at night."

Isaac pinched the skin at the bridge of his nose, as if he couldn't quite believe what he was hearing.

"Do you think I'm being selfish? Obviously, it's a very nice—"

"Knock, knock," came a voice from the hallway. Fannie sat up straighter when she saw it was Superintendent McLoughlin on her morning rounds.

"Oh, I see you have company," said the superintendent. She looked at her wristwatch.

"Mr. Feldman, you'll kindly recall that visiting hours begin at nine o'clock in the morning. It is only half-past seven."

"Is it that early?" he said with a sardonic grin, but McLoughlin did not appear to be amused.

Fannie wondered if she should ask about the radio, hoped that Isaac might do it so she didn't have to. McLoughlin intimidated her, had done ever since she'd met her last summer.

McLoughlin began to read through Fannie's chart, and Fannie took the opportunity to mouth the word *radio* to Isaac. He acted like he didn't understand what she was saying, and she rolled her eyes at him, exasperated.

"Your blood pressure looks good. It's still slightly elevated but nothing for us to be too concerned about. Has Dr. Rosenthal spoken with you about it?"

Fannie acknowledged he had.

"Good," said McLoughlin, closing the chart with a snap. Last summer, Fannie had assumed that somewhere in that chart, thick with notes, were answers. Why had she delivered so early? Was it her fault, Isaac's, God's? For a while, she had asked McLoughlin and Dr. Rosenthal every chance she got, but they never gave her any answers that satisfied her. Eventually, she'd stopped asking.

Isaac wasn't in favor of asking so many questions, then or now. She mouthed the word *radio* to him again, and he shrugged his shoulders, leaving her with no choice but to make her own inquiry. "We were just wondering, are the rooms equipped with radios?"

McLoughlin looked at Isaac. If Fannie didn't know better, she'd have said the superintendent scowled at him. "Not every room."

"Oh?" said Fannie.

"It's an extra charge."

"How much?" she asked.

"More than your father wanted to pay."

~

After McLoughlin left, Isaac and Fannie had very little to say to each other. Isaac sat on the edge of his chair, as if he might flee at any moment, and absentmindedly spun his hat around and around his forefinger. He had such long, elegant fingers.

Finally, Fannie couldn't take it anymore. "You'll ruin the brim," she said, and he stopped.

"Did you see Gussie yesterday?" she asked, trying to find a conversation that might suit them both.

"Hmm?"

"Gussie? Mother says she's doing well."

"Oh yes," he said hesitantly, "I . . . I did see her."

"I'm missing her something terrible," she said. "I guess I wasn't expecting it to be this bad. I mean, I was only in the hospital a week, maybe ten days, last summer."

"Mmmm."

Were all men such poor conversationalists when thrust into situations that made them uncomfortable? Or was it just her husband? "She seems all right? Happy?" Fannie asked.

At the word *happy*, Isaac looked up. His forehead wrinkled.

"Happy?" he asked, as if he hadn't understood the question.

"Happy."

"Yes, yes. Of course, she seems happy."

After several more conversations ended in this manner, Fannie set Isaac free. "You should get to work. Before McLoughlin has you forcibly removed for breaking hospital protocol."

She had been trying to be funny but Isaac didn't laugh. He was already on his feet, his hat on his head.

Isaac stooped to kiss her cheek, but she grabbed him by the tie and steered his lips toward hers. She needed to feel like the old Fannie for just a minute—the Fannie who had seen something remarkable in the way he looked at her. Isaac responded to the kiss, and for several long moments, they were back in their old hiding space, under the Boardwalk, at Sovereign Avenue. There was no Gussie, no loan, no Hyram. Their biggest worry was only whether Esther and Joseph would allow their eldest daughter to marry a man of no means.

When Fannie pulled away, Isaac's cheeks looked slightly flushed, and the makings of a smile had crept across his face. He touched her chin and kissed the tip of her nose before turning toward the door.

"Isaac," she called when he had nearly crossed the room's threshold. "I almost forgot."

She reached for the envelope, still without a stamp, on her bedside table and held it out to him.

"Will you be a dear and deliver this to Florence?"

Joseph

By the time Joseph arrived at Wischafter's Beach Concessions, on the morning after his daughter's burial, a beachboy of fourteen or fifteen years old was already unstacking chairs and unfurling oversized umbrellas.

"How much to rent a chair for the whole week?" asked Joseph, trying very hard to focus on the young boy's face and not the vast ocean behind him.

"Eight dollars," said the boy.

Joseph winced. He could buy one for less.

"There's also a three-dollar deposit."

Joseph reached for his wallet and began to count out the bills. He could never tell Esther he'd spent this much on something so frivolous. The boy removed a small pencil and a receipt book from his pocket.

"Name?" he asked.

"Joseph Adler."

The boy made idle chatter as he took down the rest of Joseph's information and signed the receipt.

"Hear about the drowning on Sunday?"

Joseph closed his eyes and saw his wife retching onto the floorboards of the hospital tent, after the beach surgeon had declared Florence dead.

"First one of the season," the boy continued.

Joseph forced himself to ask, "Are they saying who it was?"

"Some girl." The boy handed Joseph his receipt. "Bring this back at the end of the week—so you can get your deposit back."

Joseph could barely nod an acknowledgment. *Some girl.*

"That's yours," the boy said, pointing to a wooden chair with a blue-

and-white-striped canvas seat. A small "63" was stenciled on the frame with blue paint.

Joseph walked over to the chair, folded it, and tucked it neatly under his arm. With his free hand he touched his hat and started off in the direction of States Avenue. He hadn't gone more than two dozen paces, had barely made it off the sand, when the boy jogged up behind him.

"Sir, you can't take the chair off the beach. It's yours for the week but it stays in the sand."

Joseph put the beach chair down and reached for his wallet a second time. "I'll tell you what," he said. "Here's three more dollars. Let me take the chair, and when I return it, the deposit's yours to keep, too."

~

The bakery's administrative offices were on the third floor of the plant, well out of the way of the mixers, kneading machines, and dough dividers that cluttered the second floor and the ovens, cooling racks, bread-slicing machines, and bread-wrapping stations that filled the first.

When Joseph had designed the building six years ago, he had spent a great deal of time thinking about the best way to make a loaf of bread. So much of bread making had become mechanized—it was the only way to make any real money at it—that he had felt it necessary to reexamine every part of the process. He considered the ingredients he used—hundred-pound bags of flour, water, yeast, salt, the precise number of minutes it took for the dough to rise, the number of loaves of bread he could fit in an oven, how long the bread needed to cool before it could be removed from the tray, and now that the American public demanded sliced bread, how many slices he could get out of a loaf. Wherever there were efficiencies to be had, he found them. To that end, he had put the new machines on the first and second floors, and relegated himself, a secretary, Isaac, and a small fleet of driver-salesmen to the third. He had taken an office at the back of the building, where he could watch the delivery trucks load up each morning and putter into the lot, empty, at night.

Joseph's legs burned as he reached the top of the stairs and hurried toward his office. A few drivers were on the phones but Mrs. Simons was not at her desk, and for that, Joseph was exceptionally grateful. He propped the beach chair against his legs while he searched her desk for a sheet of stationery, which he found in the third drawer he tried. With a black pen, he wrote PLEASE DO NOT DISTURB in large block letters. Did that read too harshly? Perhaps it did. He added *Important Business* in cursive script underneath, hoping it softened the directive, and taped the crude sign to his door.

Once inside the office, Joseph closed the door behind him and locked it. Then he walked over to the window and rolled down the shade. He leaned the beach chair against the fireplace and went to his desk, where he rooted through his own drawers, looking for the stub of a candle. He used the matches in his pocket to warm the wax and secure the candle to the lid of an empty coffee can. Then he placed the makeshift candle holder on the mantel, lit the candle, and said a prayer. When he was sure that the flame would not go out, he unfolded the beach chair.

The Talmud described Job's suffering as he mourned the loss of his children, *Now they sat down with him to the ground for seven days and seven nights, but no one said a word to him because they perceived that the pain was very severe.* Job and his progeny had been dead for more than two thousand years, but Shiva chairs were still intentionally slung low to allow mourners to sit as close to the ground as possible.

Joseph sat down heavily in his makeshift Shiva chair, buried his head in his hands, and wept.

∼

There were good reasons to keep Florence's death from Fannie, but by the third day of his self-imposed mourning ritual, Joseph had come to the conclusion that a small list of people did indeed need to be told about his younger daughter's passing.

There was Clementine Dirkin, the swim coach at Wellesley. Joseph had never met her but Florence had always spoken fondly of her, and he assumed she could be counted on to tell the appropriate administrative staff and share the news with Florence's teammates. He imagined the girls gathering together, when they arrived back on campus in September, to console one another and decide how best to memorialize their lost friend. Would they dedicate a race to her memory? Lay trinkets of one kind or another in front of her locker? Install a plaque in the natatorium? Joseph wanted to believe that his daughter's death left a hole the girls would find impossible to fill.

Then there was the business of unwinding Florence's Channel swim, which Joseph wasn't entirely sure how to approach. Florence had made many of the arrangements herself, skirting Esther and going directly to Joseph to ask whether she might purchase a steamer ticket or book a month's stay at the Hôtel du Phare in Cape Gris-Nez. Joseph had balked at the figures Florence had presented but she convinced him not to look at the swim and its underlying costs as an expense but rather an investment. If she made it across the Channel, she'd earn back his money in sponsorships and speaking fees, and Adler's Bakery could boast that their rye bread had propelled the first Jewish woman across the English Channel. "I'll write the jingle," Florence had teased.

The most expensive part of Florence's plan had been engaging the coach who would steer her across the Channel. There were two men, in particular, Bill Burgess and Jabez Wolffe, who had successfully swum the English Channel themselves and now made their living helping other men—and a few women—do the same. They knew the Channel's tides and currents, could watch for the right weather and water conditions. It was the coach, Florence had explained to Joseph, who would make or break her swim. He would teach her how to navigate the currents, arrange for her meals, and engage the local pilot boat that would trail her the thirty miles to Dover. Most important, if she became overly fatigued or delirious, which could easily happen during the daylong swim, it was the coach who would make the decision to yank her from the water.

There had been a national uproar in 1925, when Wolffe had pulled Trudy Ederle out too soon. The rules were clear: if a swimmer was touched, for any reason, he or she was immediately disqualified. Ederle said she hadn't been ready to quit when Wolffe reached for her, and she complained loudly, to any journalist with a pen in hand, that he had tapped her out without cause. When she returned to France the following summer, engaging Burgess and not Wolffe to be her coach, she had also brought her father with her and given him strict instructions to watch Burgess's every move. Joseph thought the papers, at least, had made it look as if the father and daughter were a good team.

"If you want, you could come along," Florence had said to Joseph as he wrote a check, payable to Bill Burgess, for her deposit, "Be my right-hand man." The offer was tempting, but there was the bakery to consider, and also the cost of another steamship ticket and hotel room. Now, as he sat Shiva for his younger daughter, he wished he'd taken her up on it. Of course, they never would have made it to France, but Florence would have died knowing that her father's love for her was as wide as any channel she might ever try to conquer. Surely, she knew that anyway?

Joseph had no idea how to go about tracking down Bill Burgess. If he couldn't find Burgess's address in Florence's correspondence, he thought it likely that he'd find it in the notebook she had carried back and forth to Wellesley the last two years. For as long as Florence had been talking about swimming the English Channel, she'd been recording her training regimen, diet, and even her sleep in a small notebook with a pale blue cover. On it she'd written in bold lettering, FLORENCE ADLER SWIMS THE ENGLISH CHANNEL. As if it were already fact.

Joseph was impressed by her careful notes, neatly labeled diagrams, tables drawn with a ruler to keep the lines straight. On some pages, she'd glued newspaper articles about other swimmers, other long-distance attempts. He remembered feeling a little awestruck as he flipped through the notebook's pages, wondering if—hoping—his daughter applied the same exactitude to her schoolwork.

Yes, the notebook would surely deliver a clue as to Burgess's whereabouts. And, for Dirkin, perhaps a letter was the best course of action. Something she could pass along to the administration, to be filed away alongside Florence's partially completed transcript. Joseph heaved himself out of his beach chair and went to stand on the other side of his desk. He drummed the blotter as he considered his options. Finally, he called for his secretary, "Mrs. Simons, will you come in here for a moment?"

~

That evening, when Esther went to lie down, Joseph took the opportunity to tap lightly on the door of Fannie and Florence's old bedroom, which Florence had briefly shared with Anna.

"Come in," he heard Anna say from inside the room.

"Do you mind if I bother you for a minute? I'm looking for something."

Anna had been lying on her bed—Fannie's old bed—reading a book. But when he entered she sat up, kicked her feet over the edge of the mattress, and found her shoes. Joseph didn't mean to make her uncomfortable, wanted her to feel as if the space were hers, too.

"Don't get up," he said, but she was already standing. "Please, sit."

She did so tentatively. Her book remained closed, a finger sandwiched between the pages to hold her place. She watched him look around the room, as if he were inspecting it for the first time. Had he really never noticed how dark the room was at night?

"Is there a bulb out in that lamp?" he asked.

Anna peered under the shade and shook her head. "No, it's fine."

"It's dark in here. Hardly enough light to read by."

Anna looked at the lamp again, and then at the book in her hand. "It's all right."

Joseph made a mental note to look for a bigger lamp, with a stronger bulb.

The room was generously proportioned. Against one wall sat two brass beds, and between them was a Stickley bedside table that had belonged to Esther's mother. There were also two dressers, neither of which were particularly fine pieces of furniture. On the dressers were a few knickknacks—a kaleidoscope that Joseph had given Fannie when she was too old to get much enjoyment out of it and the Pageant Cup, which Florence hadn't bothered to remove when they'd moved out of the apartment last summer.

He began to open the drawers of Florence's dresser, then wondered if he owed Anna some kind of explanation. "I'm looking for Bill Burgess's address," he said.

She placed her book on the bedside table and walked over to the dresser, turned on another lamp, which cast even less light than the one beside her bed. "Bill Burgess is her coach?" she asked.

"In France, yes. Or maybe England."

"I haven't seen an address book."

"I wondered if it might be in her correspondence. Or maybe in that swimming notebook she kept. The one with the pale blue cover."

"That's here," she said, leading him over to the bedside table. She pulled open the drawer, letting the delicate brass handle clink against the drawer plate, then stepped aside, sat back down on her bed. "I haven't seen many letters. Is it possible she left them at school?"

Joseph nearly wept at the sight of the notebook. All of that energy, all of his daughter's hopes for herself, never to be realized. He picked the book up and sat down on Florence's bed, facing Anna. The inked words on the cover had run together since the last time he'd laid eyes on it. He ran his fingers along the words that were still legible: FLORENCE ADLER SWIMS.

He turned the first few pages slowly, reading every word. An entry from last July read, *Replaced my morning meal of toast with a banana. Felt like I could have swum forever*, and he had to stop. He wasn't going to be able to get through it, not in front of Anna. "Here," he said, handing the notebook to Anna. "Will you take a look? It's just an address I'm looking for. So I can write to him. Tell him she's—"

Anna nodded, opened the notebook, and began to turn its pages.

Joseph admired the girl's seriousness, her ability to focus on the task at hand. "You remind me a great deal of your mother," he said as he watched Anna study his daughter's neat handwriting. "Inez was the type of girl who couldn't be easily distracted."

Anna beamed. "She doesn't talk much about—her childhood."

"By that, do you mean, she doesn't talk much about me?"

The girl flushed.

"Why should she?" he said. "I am the past."

"Our pasts are important, no?"

Joseph shrugged an acknowledgment. He wondered how much Inez had told her, knew that, at the very least, she'd read the words he'd included in her affidavit of support. "It's funny what we remember."

Anna stopped turning the book's pages and looked at him, expectantly. He nodded his head at the notebook, urging her onward, then kept talking.

"Your mother had a bicycle and we used to ride it along the river. I pedaled, and she steered, and what I remember most of all is that her hair was always in my eyes and mouth."

"How old were you?"

He smiled to himself. "Maybe nine or ten years old. Just children."

Anna kept turning the pages of the notebook but her pace had slowed. "Did you ever think about staying?" she asked.

"I did." It was all he had thought about the autumn they were seventeen, after the steamship ticket had arrived in the mail from his brother. Inez had stared at the ticket when he'd presented it to her, as if she could will it away just by looking at it hard enough. "Marry me, then," she had said when she knew there was no keeping him in Lackenbach. "Take me with you."

Anna wanted a story, but Joseph wasn't sure she wanted this one. The hurried marriage proposal, the promise that he would send for Inez when he had saved enough money, the letters back and forth across the Atlantic, which came to a sudden halt when he met Esther—none of it made him look very good.

"How much has your mother told you?" he asked Anna.

"Not much," she said, looking up from the notebook once more. "Just that you were engaged and that it didn't work out."

Inez was a good woman, too decent to color her daughter's opinion of him with the truth.

"Anna," he said as she returned her attention to the task at hand, "I don't want you to worry about your mother. Your parents. If the affidavit doesn't work, there are other things we can try."

A tear slipped down Anna's cheek, and she wiped it away with the heel of her hand. "You don't think the consul will accept it?"

Securing a student visa for Anna had been one thing; securing visas for her parents was turning out to be quite another. Since Joseph wasn't a relative, he had to prove that Inez and Paul would not become public charges upon their arrival in the U.S.—that they could support themselves indefinitely, all without taking a job away from a deserving American. An impossible feat, considering the fact that their assets were frozen.

Joseph wondered how honest he should be with Anna. "I suspect we'll need more than my affidavit alone. But who can say?"

"You're kind to be considering this now, after—everything."

He had been willing to help Inez and Paul before Florence's death, so it seemed antithetical to turn his back on them now. He told himself that Florence would have wanted it this way but that wasn't all of it. Joseph appreciated staying busy and knew he got some relief from focusing on anything as straightforward as a visa application, for all its perils and pitfalls. If he followed the right practices and procedures, paid the proper fees, it might at least be possible to conjure Anna's parents out of thin air. The same could never be said for Florence. "It's nothing," he said as he watched Anna come to the last page.

"The address isn't here," she said as she closed the notebook. "Stuart will have it. Or be able to get it for you."

He reached for the little book, and she gave it to him with two hands, as if it were something fragile and dear.

~

Stuart was sitting in the beach chair, quite awkwardly, when Joseph arrived at the office on Friday morning. As Joseph entered the room, the boy stood, too fast, and the chair folded in on itself. The frame banged loudly against the floor, and Joseph flinched.

"Your secretary said you wanted to see me."

Joseph didn't say a word, just walked across the room to his desk, picked up the heavy oak swivel chair behind it, and carried it over to the fireplace.

"Sit here," Joseph said. "You'll be more comfortable."

Stuart started to argue, but Joseph held up his hand, refusing to hear a word, "You're doing an old man a favor, Stuart."

Beneath Stuart's healthy tan, he looked tired and gaunt. There were dark circles under his blue eyes, and Joseph wondered how much he'd slept in the five days that had elapsed since Florence's death.

"How's Fannie?" Stuart asked.

"You know, I'd like to tell you. But, you see, I'm not a very good father. I don't visit."

"The hospital?"

Joseph shook his head as he righted the beach chair. "I haven't been inside one since the war."

"I don't think that makes you a bad father."

Joseph frowned. "I could do better."

"Were you a medic? During the war?"

"An ambulance driver."

"You and Hemingway?"

"I suppose," said Joseph. "Except I was driving for the U.S. Army. And I'm not sure I made it look quite so glamorous."

He had to get to it, ask Stuart for what he needed, or he'd be telling war stories all morning. "Look, Stuart, I need some help tracking down Bill Burgess. To cancel the swim."

Stuart looked surprised, as if he had temporarily forgotten that Florence couldn't be both dead and a champion swimmer at the same time. He nodded slowly.

"I don't know where he lives, or if I can get the deposit back," Joseph said. "Florence handled it all."

"I have an address for him in Calais."

"Would you mind writing him? I'm not sure I feel up to it."

Stuart shook his head vigorously, the way people do, during a crisis, when they're grateful to have been given a task, no matter how small.

"I'll send a telegram. I can send one to the hotel, too. Just in case he's already left for Cape Gris-Nez."

"Thank you. Let me give you some money to cover the cost," said Joseph, reaching for his billfold, but it was Stuart's turn to hold up his hand.

"Please, no. This is the least I can do."

Joseph studied Stuart, who studied his own fingernails, bitten to the quick. "It's not your fault, you know?"

Stuart didn't say a thing, just nodded his head like a marionette.

Joseph tried to put himself in Stuart's place. What if he had lost Esther that first summer, when she was as much ephemera as she was an actual woman standing in front of him?

When Esther had checked into Chorney's, accompanied by her parents, in the summer of 1904, Joseph's command of the English language had been so poor that he had been afraid to talk to her. In lieu of words, he had offered her the best seat in the dining room, bestowed extra hard-boiled eggs on her at breakfast, and delivered her an unsolicited slice of Boston cream pie at dinner. Her parents had raised their eyebrows at his antics but had otherwise disregarded him, so sure were they that their nineteen-year-old daughter would not return the attentions of an Eastern European Jew so recently arrived from the old country. When he cleared their table one evening, and discovered the note Esther had left for him under her discarded napkin, he had thought his heart might stop beating in his chest.

My parents are going to the theater after dinner. If you can get away, would you care to go for a walk? I'll be in the lobby at half-past eight.

Esther

Joseph had never bused the dining room so quickly. At half-past eight, when the room was still not empty and the last of the dishes were still not clean, he traded an extra shift with another busboy for the chance to slip out early. Joseph stuffed his apron in an umbrella stand and rushed to the lobby, where he found Esther sitting on a small settee. She sat up straight and didn't appear to have been watching for him, which gave the impression, at least to Joseph, that she had been confident he would come.

Joseph offered Esther his arm, and they made their way out of the hotel and down Virginia Avenue to the Boardwalk, which was crowded with rolling carts full of mostly happy couples and a few dour ones. Without discussing it, they walked south, in the opposite direction of Nixon's Theater and Esther's parents. The piers buzzed with activity, and revelers streamed in and out of the grand lobbies of the big ocean-front hotels. Lights were strung from one side of the Boardwalk to the other, and the effect was dazzling—like a blanket of stars had been hung for their benefit. At the Chelsea Hotel the crowds began to thin, and they stopped to admire the city's bright lights, spread out behind them. "Don't you just love Atlantic City?" Esther said.

"Yes," said Joseph, watching her watch the skyline. In that moment he did love Atlantic City more than any other place he'd ever known. It was a city where a Jewish boy from Galicia could find work and live cheap and save his money and even have a little fun. But most of all, it was a city that had delivered this beautiful girl to him.

At Morris Avenue, they turned around. Esther stopped to pick up a small but perfect seashell, which someone had plucked from the sand only to abandon on the Boardwalk, and when she did, she let go of Joseph's arm. Eventually, she returned to him, seashell in hand, but then she did something unexpected. Instead of taking his arm, she moved her hand gently down his sleeve, over his shirt cuff, and into the warm center of his palm, where she laced her fingers between his.

"Is this all right?" she asked in a quiet tone, as if she were genuinely unsure what his answer might be.

In that moment, Joseph lost every English word he'd ever learned. All he could do was squeeze her hand in return. His face was close enough to hers that he wondered, briefly, what it might be like to kiss her but it was several more nights before he found out.

The kiss came on a moonlit night near Absecon Lighthouse, where the bright lights of the piers receded and the Boardwalk narrowed and veered toward the inlet. The beach was quiet and dark. Joseph was sure he had seen a humpback whale, its tail air-bound as it dove for krill, and he wanted Esther to see it, too.

Joseph moved closer to Esther, using her own hand to indicate the spot where the whale's silhouette had disappeared from view. She studied the horizon solemnly, and he became conscious of the fact that he was holding his breath.

"You are not seeing?" he whispered into her ear.

"I am not looking," she corrected him. The distinction was one of those subtleties of the English language that so often evaded Joseph in those early years in America. He understood it only later, after he had replayed the evening several dozen times in his head. Esther didn't let go of his hand but she did turn toward him, her breath warm against his cheek. When he brushed his lips against hers, very softly at first, the kiss was a question.

It was another week before Esther returned to Philadelphia with her parents and another year before she worked up the nerve to tell them she was marrying Joseph. If Joseph had lost her at any point after that first night she took his hand, he would have been haunted by her always.

Joseph allowed himself to linger in the memory of their early days together, then looked at Stuart. No, he didn't think he wanted to know the full extent of what Stuart and Florence had meant to each other, didn't think knowing that his daughter had been loved would make her loss any easier to bear.

"Do you remember the summer the Women's Swimming Association brought Charlotte Brown to Atlantic City?" Joseph asked.

Stuart's face momentarily brightened. "Out at the inlet? Sure."

"She was such a wee thing. Couldn't have been more than a year or two older than Florence at the time. Maybe five or six years old?

"When she dove into that water, Florence screamed for me to save her," Joseph said, chuckling at the memory. "She must have swum a half-dozen yards before I could convince Florence she wasn't in need of saving."

"I went with my father, too," said Stuart, and for a moment he looked very far away.

"Florence had seen the seventy-ton whale at Steel Pier, but there was something special about seeing a child her own size whip in and out of the water like a trout."

Stuart made a noise, something between a laugh and a long sigh.

"She could teach herself to do anything," said Joseph.

Florence liked to tell people that her father had taught her to swim. It made for a good story since Joseph didn't actually know how to swim himself. All he had really done was introduce her to the water, same as he'd done for Fannie.

He'd chosen a calm summer day and waited until the tide was low before telling Florence to get into her bathing costume. Then he'd led her down Metropolitan Avenue, across the Boardwalk, and past the bathing houses and chairs-for-rent to Heinz Pier. Over his shoulder, he carried a long cord of rope; he tied one end to a thick, wooden joist—far from the pier's pilings—and dropped the other over the side, watching it unravel in midair.

After they had retraced their steps and returned to the beach, Joseph waded through waist-deep water to retrieve the loose end of the rope, which he pulled to shore and carefully tied around Florence's small waist. He gave his homemade lifesaving contraption several hard tugs before pronouncing it sound.

"In the water, your arms and legs, they must always move," Joseph offered, his only instruction.

That afternoon Florence had learned to swim—nothing that resembled a real stroke but enough to keep her head above the water.

"The only thing Florence needed to know," Joseph said to Stuart, "was that I believed she could swim."

"You gave her a gift," Stuart said, meeting Joseph's eyes for the first time during his visit.

"Did I?"

Stuart frowned.

"I propose we make a deal," said Joseph. "From you, there will be no more talk of—"

A light knock on the office door interrupted Joseph's negotiations.

Mrs. Simons opened the door a crack. "I have Miss Epstein here to see you."

"Anna?" both men asked at the same time.

Isaac

When Isaac leaned back far enough in his desk chair, he could see Joseph's office door, which had been shut all week. He always kept one eye on the door since it benefited him to know his father-in-law's comings and goings, but this week, he had paid more attention to it than usual.

If Esther's instructions had been for both Joseph and Isaac to return to work and act as if everything were normal, Joseph was failing miserably at that task. Nothing about his shuttered blinds or that silly handwritten sign he'd posted on his office door looked normal. And on Thursday afternoon, when Mrs. Simons was summoned into Joseph's office and returned to her desk visibly shaken, Isaac was sure Joseph had told her the truth about Florence. The brittle woman—usually so stoic—dabbed at her eyes for several minutes before hurrying to the powder room, where Isaac could hear her sobs even over the exhaust fan.

On Friday morning there had been a revolving door of visitors to see Joseph. First Florence's friend Stuart, and then Anna. Stuart's visit made a certain amount of sense—the scrub had clearly been besotted by Florence. And everyone knew he was on the outs with his own father, so it wasn't a complete surprise to see him latching on to Joseph. But Anna's visit was less easily explained, and as a result, Isaac spent the better part of Friday wondering about it. To Isaac's knowledge, she hadn't come to the plant once in the more than three months she'd been staying with the Adlers. Today, she had remained inside Joseph's office for a quarter of an hour, maybe a little longer, and when she left, she had looked relieved. Since Isaac's office faced the street, he waited the thirty seconds he knew it would take Anna to make her way down the two flights of stairs and emerge from the building, then he stood up for a stretch and walked over to the window.

Interestingly, Stuart had waited for her. He sat out on the steps of the plant, hat in hand, face stretched toward the sun. When Anna pushed open the building's heavy front door, Stuart jumped to his feet. Though he had tried, Isaac wasn't able to make out what Stuart said to her, but he had watched the two of them walk off down Tennessee Avenue, before returning to his desk.

Anna was a hard one to figure out, partially because her accent was thick and partially because she had materialized out of thin air. The story was that Anna's mother, Inez, had grown up alongside Joseph but Isaac was sure there had to be more to it than that. It was one thing for Joseph to write an affidavit for Anna—everyone knew the affidavits were as meaningless as the pieces of paper they were written on. But putting her up in his spare room was something else altogether. Isaac didn't think it was the type of thing he'd do for just anybody.

There was little debate that things in Germany were getting bad. Since coming to power the year before, the Nazi Party had already removed Jews from the civil service, curtailed the rights of Jewish doc-tors, lawyers, and other professionals, forbidden performances by Jewish actors, and restricted the number of Jewish students allowed to attend German schools and universities. Joseph followed it all very closely and reported on the most notable offenses to Isaac as he came and went from their third-floor offices. In lieu of a greeting, Joseph would offer him a headline straight from the morning's paper, "They've revoked the licenses of Jewish accountants" or "No more medical school for Jews in Bavaria." According to Joseph, Roosevelt had his head in the sand, and if Americans waited for Congress to do something, they'd be waiting a long time. Like many of the Jewish businessmen in town, Joseph donated to the American Jewish Committee, and Isaac suspected his gifts were generous since his name was inscribed in the "golden book" and the president of the local chapter made a habit of calling on Joseph with some regularity.

It's not that Isaac didn't care about the plight of Germany's Jews. It's just that, in Russia, discrimination had been the least of people's worries. The stories he'd grown up listening to—about beatings and rapes and entire villages set ablaze—made it harder for Isaac to get worked up about the fact that Jewish merchants in Germany had to mark their shops with yellow Stars of David. He found it almost quaint that his father-in-law considered the persecution of Jews to be news at all.

Ostensibly, Anna was here because she hadn't been able to get into college in Berlin, or anywhere else in Germany for that matter. When her mother had written to Joseph, he'd apparently been all too happy to throw money at the problem. Maybe Isaac was old-fashioned but a girl not being able to go to college hardly seemed like an international crisis.

Isaac rolled a pencil back and forth between his fingers, then tapped it on his desk. He needed a plan. The weekend was nearly upon him, and if he wasn't careful, he would spend it in Esther and Joseph's living room, sitting a modified Shiva.

It wasn't that Isaac didn't mourn Florence's death or want to honor her life. In fact, he felt his sister-in-law's loss acutely. He could remember, on his early visits to the Adlers' apartment, twelve-year-old Florence interviewing him with the same ferocity as her parents but with much less tact. *Have you kissed her?* she asked once, looking him straight in the eye. Isaac, who had been the baby of his own family without ever managing to be babied at all, marveled at her confidence and got some satisfaction out of watching her grow into a woman who was every bit as loud and brash as the girl she'd once been.

Sitting Shiva for Florence would be painful. Excruciating without Fannie or any callers to offer up distractions. Isaac could try to disappear for a few hours on Saturday, tell Esther and Joseph he needed to visit Fannie. But he hated visiting the hospital almost as much as he hated visiting his in-laws' apartment. It wasn't just about Hyram. There was something about being on the maternity ward, surrounded by so many women, all of them concerned with the business of life and death, that left him feeling exposed. He could feel Fannie studying him, as if she could see him more clearly without the interference of the outside world.

Isaac remembered the letter Fannie had given him when he'd visited on Tuesday, and felt for it in his jacket pocket. It was still there,
folded in half, its corners beginning to curl. He removed it, smoothed it
at its crease, and studied his wife's handwriting. The loop of the *F*, the
generous *A*. What would Fannie do when she learned that Florence was
dead? Was Esther right? Would this news be too much for her to bear?

Isaac was not inclined to think so. But then again, he had been the
one who had urged Fannie to ride the Dodgem with him last spring.

It had been a pretty day, still two months before Fannie's due date,
and Esther had volunteered to watch Gussie for the afternoon. The
day had a carefree quality that reminded Isaac of that first summer,
before they were married. The two of them had eaten a hamburger at
Mammy's and then walked to Steeplechase Pier, which had recently
reopened. They picked their way through the crowd, admiring the loud
games and the brightly colored carousel at the center of the pier. Behind it sat a new ride with a big yellow sign that screamed DODGEM in
giant blue letters.

"Oh, I get it," said Fannie. "Dodge them."

Isaac watched as fifteen or twenty people, all in miniature metal cars
with thick rubber bumpers, whipped around a small rink.

"I suppose the point is to bump into each other?" he asked as they
watched a man, who looked oversized in his little car, plow into the car
of a small boy who must have been his son. Fannie didn't say anything,
just laughed when she saw the boy lurch forward in surprise.

Isaac pulled two quarters from his pocket, held them out to Fannie,
and said, "Shall we give it a spin? You've always wanted to learn to
drive."

Fannie shook her head no, inclined to stay on the sidelines, but Isaac
pushed.

"It'll be just like old times. Remember when we used to ride the
Roundabout?" he said, a twinkle in his eye.

"Do you think it's safe?" she asked, one hand resting protectively on
her stomach.

"Perfectly."

When Fannie started bleeding early the following morning, Isaac hadn't wanted to believe that the two incidents could be related. They had called Esther and Joseph immediately, told them that something was wrong and that they needed them to take Gussie right away. While they waited for Joseph to come with the car, Isaac had practically pleaded for absolution from Fannie, and if not that, then for Fannie to keep the correlative circumstances to herself.

"Fan, it was barely a bump. I mean, you didn't feel a thing, right?"

She didn't say anything, just looked at him with a terrified expression on her face.

"It was just fun, that's all," he said, a detectable note of fear creeping into his voice.

Hyram was born at six o'clock in the evening but it was a quarter past nine before Isaac learned of his son's arrival. A doctor, who introduced himself as Gabriel Rosenthal, came to find Isaac in the hospital lobby, and it was the way he said "Mr. Feldman" that made Isaac realize, with a kind of gross certainty, they would lose the child.

Fannie had suffered a placental abruption, Dr. Rosenthal explained. There had been nothing to do but allow her to labor.

"Is she—?" Isaac asked, not knowing how to finish the question.

"She's fine. We're watching her closely and it looks like the bleeding has stopped."

"And the baby?"

"He's very small," said the doctor. "It's unlikely he'll make it through the night."

"He?"

"Yes, a boy."

"A boy," Isaac repeated, numbly.

The doctor looked at him with apologetic eyes.

"May I see him?" Isaac asked.

"We don't recommend it."

"Yes, but I think I'd like to, if it's all the same."

The doctor led Isaac upstairs to the nursery, where a nurse gestured to a chair in the middle of the room. The room was lined with bassinets, but Isaac avoided looking inside them, terrified to catch a glimpse of his son before he had fully prepared himself for the encounter. The nurse walked over to a bassinet and reached for a bundle of blankets that didn't look much different from any of the others. She held the bundle close to her chest and hesitated as she neared Isaac.

When she handed the bundle over to Isaac, he was surprised at how heavy and warm it felt in his arms.

"He's hot?" he asked, alarmed.

"That's just the hot-water bottle," she explained. "We're trying to keep his temperature up."

He lifted a corner of the blanket to reveal the red, wizened face of a tiny, old man—all forehead, no hair, eyes closed tight. His head couldn't have been bigger than a billiard ball. Indeed, he was resting against a hot-water bottle, which had been wrapped in a towel.

The child was horrifying to look at, and somehow also vaguely beautiful. It was impossible, studying him, to pick out Fannie's sharp brown eyes or Isaac's hairline but it must have been the promise of those features, and others like them, eventually developing, that helped him see past his son's strangeness.

"I convinced Fannie to ride the Dodgem cars yesterday. At Steeplechase Pier," Isaac said as he stared down at his fragile son. He could feel his breath beginning to catch in his throat. A tear rolled down his cheek and landed on the baby's forehead. He wiped it away with his thumb, which seemed huge when held up against his son's miniature features. "Is this my fault?"

"I'm sorry. I'm not familiar with them," said Dr. Rosenthal.

"You just bump into each other. I hit her once, maybe twice. Hard, I think. I mean, not really. It's just an amusement." He knew he was talking too much and tried to make himself stop. "She was laughing."

"I wish we knew but sometimes these things aren't so easy to pinpoint," said the doctor in the same tepid tone in which he'd said everything else.

The nurse was kinder. "It's possible she had high blood pressure, or some other condition. Sometimes these things just happen."

It was hard for Isaac to comprehend that this child, who had to weigh less than two pounds, was the same baby Fannie had dreamed of for so many years. Why hadn't Isaac given him to her sooner?

Isaac's eyes settled on a card, which had been tucked into the baby's bassinet. It read, *Feldman, Baby Boy.*

"We're naming him Hyram," Isaac said.

The doctor gave the nurse a look, and she retrieved the card from the bassinet. She pulled a pen from her pocket and scratched through the words *Baby Boy.* Above the strike-through, she wrote *HYRAM* in big, block letters. Isaac liked the way the name looked when it was all spelled out.

"May I see Fannie?" Isaac asked.

"She needs to rest," the doctor warned. "Perhaps tomorrow."

Isaac knew what he wanted to say but it was hard to get the words out. "I think she might want to see him, before he—"

"That's not advisable."

"No?"

The doctor shook his head.

Sometimes Isaac wondered whether things would have been different if Hyram had in fact died that night, as the doctor warned he would. If Fannie had never seen him or held him or begun to hope that he might live. Surely, they both would have had an easier time coping with the loss, might have avoided retreating to the furthest corners of their marriage.

No, Isaac wasn't keen to spend the weekend at either the hospital or his in-laws' apartment. He placed the letter in the top drawer of his desk, and was about to push the drawer shut when Joseph knocked on the frame of his door, leaning against it for support.

"I'm going to head home a little early today," he said to Isaac.

"I was wondering if I might borrow your car on Saturday," Isaac asked.

Joseph looked confused. It was Shabbos, and he had no doubt assumed Isaac would spend Saturday at the apartment, squeezing a week's worth of mourning into a single day.

"My father took a fall."

"Oh—I'm sorry, Isaac."

"He'll be fine. But I thought I'd take Gussie to see him. Maybe stay in Alliance overnight."

Joseph didn't say anything. Isaac sensed that his daughter was acting as a salve in the apartment, and that at least for Esther, Gussie's presence—and the care she required—was providing a welcome distraction from grief.

"We'll be back early on Sunday. With enough time to end Shiva."

Joseph nodded his head slowly. "I'm sure it will be good for Gussie to get out of the house."

~

Isaac and Gussie could have taken the train from Atlantic City to Norma and walked the half mile between the railway station and Alliance. But arriving by car was much more fun.

Joseph's Oakland was a practical automobile, not at all flashy but also not without pep. Isaac followed Atlantic Avenue out of the city until, at Mays Landing, it became Highway 40 and he could pick up speed. He glanced over at Gussie to gauge her reaction. With the windows down, his daughter's hair whipped wildly across her face. Occasionally, she peeled a strand out of her mouth and tucked it behind her ear. He should have thought to tell her to bring a scarf. No matter. She seemed happy.

When he had arrived at Joseph and Esther's apartment at half-past nine that morning, Gussie had met him at the front door.

"She's been watching for you since a quarter past eight," Esther had told him, and Isaac wondered if she meant to insinuate that he was late, or that his daughter didn't see enough of him. Gussie wore a yellow-and-white gingham dress, which looked freshly pressed, and carried a rucksack and a bag from the bakery.

"I'm sending some rugelach to your father," Esther had said, "for his recovery. Will you give him our best?" and Isaac had immediately regretted his own duplicitousness.

Gussie didn't say much as the car sped down the four-lane road, and Isaac wondered if she'd gotten enough sleep.

"You all right?" he asked.

Gussie turned to look at him, seemed confused by the question. It was one, he realized, that no one ever asked her.

"You're sleeping okay?"

She nodded, returned her eyes to the road. Isaac wondered if it might be wise to address Florence's death directly, to let Gussie know that she could talk to him about it if she wanted. He considered what he might say to her. That death comes for us all? That Florence was with God? That they'd carry her memory with them, always? It all sounded ridiculous, so in the end, he kept his mouth shut. There was absolutely nothing to say to a seven-year-old about any of this sad business.

The little communities of Mizpah and Buena Vista rushed by, and it wasn't until Isaac coasted into Vineland that he was forced to slow down. The highway turned into a broad avenue, with rows of flowers and shrub trees bordering the houses that lined the street. While he was growing up in Alliance, Vineland had felt like a big city, though compared to Atlantic City, it was still a small town. Isaac's family had walked the half mile between Alliance and Vineland to purchase items they couldn't grow or make on the farm—things like winter jackets and shoes. As a boy, Isaac had assumed that Alliance would one day catch up with Vineland, that when his father and mother and their neighbors had worked hard enough, Alliance would also have a picture house and a pharmacy and a five-and-ten store.

On the other side of Vineland, the city lots gave way to countryside— big patches of fields between groves of birch trees. Isaac looked at his watch. It was a quarter past ten. He was sure he'd find his father at shul, particularly since he hadn't told him he was coming. Isaac turned onto Gershal Avenue and after a few more minutes pulled the car into the grass in front of Congregation Emanu-El. The Oakland was the only car on the property. Some of the men in the community, although certainly not Isaac's father, were doing well enough to own a car but no one would have dared to drive one on Shabbos. Isaac rather enjoyed the idea of the men saying their last Aleinu, closing their prayer books, and coming out onto the steps of the congregation to be confronted by Isaac and his automobile. He imagined them all returning to their farmhouses, telling their wives that Isaac Feldman looked like he was doing well for himself.

"Are we going in?" Gussie asked when Isaac threw on the parking brake but didn't cut the ignition.

"I think we'll wait for Grandpa out here."

Gussie asked if she could get out of the car to play, and Isaac agreed, watching as she skipped off in the direction of the tree line that bordered Saul Green's property. Twice she stopped to scavenge for sticks in the grass, finding first a twig and then a three-foot-long branch to wield. Gussie loved going to Alliance, though it was a fact that Isaac didn't bring her to visit nearly often enough. Just as Isaac had once thought Atlantic City exotic, his daughter now thought Alliance so.

"Hey, Gus-Gus!" he called, beckoning her back over to the car.

She ran toward him, cutting through the air with her stick. "I'm King Arthur!" she yelled.

"I think you mean Guinevere."

She came to a stop in front of the driver's-side door. "No, King Arthur. I have a sword. See?"

"Ah, I do. Look, Gus, I forgot to mention something."

She looked up at him, her eyebrows furrowed. Between her mother's absence and her aunt's death, the poor girl was probably waiting for another shoe to drop.

"Grandpa's a little sensitive about his fall. So, let's not bring it up in front of him."

"But Nana sent rugelach."

"Yes, yes. We'll still give that to him. We just won't tell him we hope he feels better. That way, we won't make him sad," said Isaac. "Do you understand?"

Gussie nodded slowly, and Isaac wondered, briefly, if his young daughter could see right through him. "Go have fun," he said, with an intentionally wide smile, and he watched as she ran off.

Isaac had read half of yesterday's newspaper before the doors of the synagogue opened. He watched as, one by one, Alliance's residents trickled out, the men removing their *taleisim* and pocketing their *yarmulkes* as they made their way down the steps and into the yard. All of the old men, Isaac's father among them, had built the clapboard temple together, milling the timber and framing the one-room structure when Alliance had no more than four hundred residents and less than a hundred homesteads. In many cases, men had prioritized the construction of the temple over their own homes, living in government-issued tents for an extra winter so that they could raise the roof in time for the High Holy Days.

Gussie met her grandfather at the foot of the synagogue's stairs and threw her arms around his thick waist before pointing toward the car. Isaac gave a small wave, then opened the door and got out. He met his father in the middle of the yard, Gussie bouncing back and forth between them like an excited fox terrier.

"Isaac," said his father, pronouncing his name *Itzhak.* "Dem iz a ongenem iberrashn."

"In English!" Gussie pleaded, "I won't be able to understand anything!"

"And that would be so bad?" said Isaac's father, grabbing at Gussie's nose and simultaneously slipping his thumb through his fingers. "Your nose, I have it." Gussie reached for her grandfather's hand, which he held just out of her reach.

"Can we give you a ride?" Isaac asked, knowing the answer would always be no on a Saturday.

"Your father, he is crazy," Isaac's father said, turning to Gussie. "Will you walk home with an old man?"

Gussie shouted an excited, "Yes!"

"We'll see you at home," Isaac's father said, over his shoulder, as he and Gussie began picking their way through the grass, making a path toward Gershal Avenue and the homestead that sat on the far side of the hamlet.

Isaac kicked at a tall weed, then walked back over to the car. Gussie was charmed by Isaac's father because she hadn't been raised by him. And his father could afford to be generous with his affection because he wasn't trying to convince his granddaughter to pull her weight on a failing farm. It had been a different story when Isaac was growing up.

His parents had arrived in Alliance in 1887 with nothing but a satchel of clothes and one small child—the eldest of Isaac's siblings. By all accounts, their early years as colonists had been bleak. Isaac wasn't entirely sure why this surprised anyone. His father had taught at the yeshiva in Volozhin and didn't know the first thing about farming. He had read the writings of Michael Bakal and Moshe Herder and believed in the Return to the Soil Movement, but that didn't mean he knew how to milk a cow or sow green beans. The Hebrew Immigrant Aid Society provided for some agricultural training but none of it could make up for the fact that Isaac's father was, at his heart, a philosopher and not a farmer.

Isaac turned the car around in the grass and pulled out onto Gershal Avenue. Within moments, he had overtaken his father and Gussie, who walked hand in hand on the road's narrow shoulder. When had his father's back become so stooped? He honked the car's horn as he passed and they both waved. At Almond Road, he took a right and wound his way toward his father's farm.

The farmhouse, like many others in Alliance, had begun to fall into disrepair. Each of the community's early settlers had been gifted forty acres of land but the Hebrew Immigrant Aid Society had written them mortgages to cover the other costs associated with getting their farms off the ground. Residents built their farmhouses and barns on credit, which required profitable harvests from the start. Almost none were profitable, and most people's mortgages quickly fell into arrears. To make ends meet, the men fell back on what they knew. At night, they traveled to Norma to work in the area's only garment factory, or they waited for the shipments of hand-sewing projects, which garment factories in Philadelphia and New York began shipping to Alliance and other Jewish agricultural outposts by the truckload.

Isaac was born thirteen years into his parents' failed agricultural experiment. The youngest of a dozen children, he was barely old enough to pull a sweet potato out of the ground when his older brothers and sisters began their exodus. The majority of them went to Philadelphia, thirty-five miles away. Two settled in New York and one went as far south as New Orleans. One died on a battlefield in France.

By the time Isaac was twenty, he, too, had begun plotting his departure. And not just because he couldn't envision a lifetime spent toiling in South Jersey's Downer soil. Alliance, and the Hebrew Immigrant Aid Society in particular, had crippled his once curious father, and what Isaac wanted was to go somewhere where he wasn't beholden to anyone.

The right thing to do would have been to sit down with his father, to tell him that he didn't want a farming life. But he couldn't bear to witness his father's disappointment. Instead he packed a few things in a bag, took forty dollars out of the old Campfire Marshmallows canister his father kept in the freezer, and set out in the dark to catch a southbound train from Norma at first light.

∼

Isaac had never left Salem County, much less New Jersey. From the train window, he watched in wonder as the flat farmland of New Jersey's coastal plain gave way to the rolling hills of Virginia's Piedmont region, North Carolina's pines turned into South Carolina's live oaks, and eventually Georgia's wetlands melted into Florida's swampland. By the time the train stopped in Jacksonville, it was packed with speculators headed south. Isaac had bought a ticket for Miami but all the talk in the car was of West Palm Beach, so when the train pulled into the station and half the passengers got off, Isaac did, too.

West Palm Beach sat across the Intracoastal Waterway from the resort island of Palm Beach and had initially been established as a service town—somewhere for the maids and cooks and bellmen who worked in the big Palm Beach hotels to live. But by the time Isaac arrived, it was already obvious that West Palm Beach was where the action was.

The trick to making it in West Palm Beach, said the other guys in the boardinghouse where Isaac had taken a room, was to land a job as a binder boy. Subdivisions in West Palm Beach were going in so fast and real estate agents were so busy closing deals, most negotiated entirely by mail with buyers up north, that none of them had the time to put an actual FOR SALE sign in the ground and sell to passersby—residents, snowbirds, and tin-can tourists who had driven down to Florida to see what all the fuss was about. Real estate agents sent binder boys out to these undeveloped subdivisions to get a binder, or down payment, out of anyone who so much as stopped to ask directions.

"How's your golf game?" one of the boys asked as he wrote down the name and address of an agent named Ted Blackwell on the back of an old receipt.

"Golf?"

"Blackwell likes to hire preppy college boys with a good swing. A decent tennis serve will work, too. You'll see." He handed Isaac the small piece of paper.

Isaac hadn't been to college and had never so much as picked up a golf club or tennis racket. But when he knocked on the door of Ted Blackwell & Associates the following morning, he had concocted a story so credible that he almost believed it himself. He'd gone to the University of Pennsylvania, where he'd studied Russian literature—an easy leap considering his lineage. When he wasn't reading Dostoyevsky, he played intramural tennis, and on the weekends, he visited his aunt and uncle on the Main Line, squeezing in a round of golf at his uncle's club every chance he got. He didn't like to brag, by any means, but he could hold his own.

Blackwell looked Isaac up and down as he listened to his pitch. Then he told him to follow him outside. "Get in the car," he said, nodding toward an Isotta Tourer that was parked on the street. Isaac knew it would do him no good to tell Blackwell that this was his first automobile ride, so he tried to be casual opening the door, climbing into the seat. Blackwell pulled the car out into traffic and drove across the causeway, through West Palm Beach, and then north for several miles, until the city fell away and they were surrounded by longleaf pines and rubber vines. Isaac hoped he looked comfortable in the passenger seat, like someone who was used to riding around in fine Italian cars.

"Ten years ago, no one thought this would ever be anything but swamp," said Blackwell as he waved at the greenery out the window.

Just when the landscape had grown so desolate that Isaac couldn't imagine selling it to a blind man, Blackwell began to slow the car. Ahead was a turnoff, marked by a pair of large and rather elaborately constructed brick columns. As the car approached the turn, Isaac saw that, hanging from the columns, there was a wrought-iron sign. He craned his neck, trying to read it, but Blackwell beat him to the punch: "Welcome to Orange Grove Estates."

Blackwell pulled between the columns and into Orange Grove Estates, or at least the entrance of what would one day be Orange Grove Estates. Fifty yards of road had been laid, the land on either side of it cleared, but the road ended abruptly in a thicket of palm fronds and brittle thatch. There was a small gatehouse, located just behind the sign, and a tennis court, tucked against the tree line, as if it had sprung from the earth like a shoot. Three cars were parked next to it.

"Was there an orange grove here?" Isaac asked.

"Not in my lifetime."

Blackwell pulled his car alongside the others and cut the engine. "Jim's busy right now, so we'll wait."

Jim was a boy, about Isaac's age, with a shock of blond hair and a noticeable swagger. Isaac watched from the car as he led two couples to the edge of the clearing, making sweeping gestures toward the thick underbrush that picked up where the road left off.

Blackwell looked at his watch. "Give him a quarter of an hour. He'll have both binders by noon."

Blackwell was right on the money. By five minutes till, Jim had the paperwork spread out over the hood of one car, each man so eager to sign that he would have killed his grandmother just to get ahold of her pen. Jim took their checks, folded them in half, and shoved them into his breast pocket. Then he handed each man a copy of the paperwork and shook his hand in turn. Isaac made note of the handshake—Jim used his left hand to squeeze each man's shoulder, as if they were old friends who had great affection for one another. He waved as the men got into their cars and drove away.

Once both cars were gone, Jim walked over to Blackwell's car and leaned into the open window.

"I brought you a new recruit," said Blackwell. "This is Isaac Feldman. UPenn grad. Train him up and then maybe I'll send him over to Sea Breeze."

Jim nodded toward the tennis court. "How's your game?"

"Fair, I'd say."

"I'll be the one to say," Jim said, the hint of a smile curling the corners of his mouth.

In the weeks that followed, Jim said plenty. He taught Isaac how to talk up Orange Grove Estates—mention how close it is to the beach, don't mention that it hasn't been plumbed. He told Isaac what to say when it looked like a buyer was waffling, something that was happening with less and less frequency these days, and how to handle the wives who thought they deserved some say over their husband's investment decisions.

The one thing that couldn't be talked around or through was Isaac's tennis game. "Show me your serve," Jim said, not a quarter of an hour after Blackwell drove off, leaving Isaac to catch a ride home with Jim.

Isaac did his best to hit the ball across the net and watched as it landed on the other side of the court with a satisfying thunk. *Not too bad*, he thought. Jim shook his head and tsked. "You've never hit a tennis ball before in your life."

Isaac worried Jim would out him to Blackwell, so he was pleasantly surprised when, instead, Jim offered to teach him how to play the game. He showed him where to stand and how to move, taught him how to serve and score.

"Why waste the money putting a tennis court in the middle of nowhere?" Isaac asked Jim one day, from the shade of a black mangrove on the property.

"It's a diversion, plain and simple," said Jim. "Palm Beach is years away from getting electricity and water all the way out here. A tennis court says we're building infrastructure, that we're here to stay."

"Are we?" Isaac asked.

"Sure, why not?"

Had Isaac known how quickly everything would end, he might have done things differently. He liked to think he would have spent less and saved more.

Jim, Isaac, and the rest of Blackwell's binder boys earned their commission when the binder checks cleared the bank, but even on a week when nothing cleared, it hardly mattered. Showing their binder receipts was enough to get them served in any of Palm Beach's restaurants and clubs. They'd flash their receipts at Bradley's Beach Club or John G's and drink until they couldn't remember their way home, only to have to return the following week to deliver half their earnings to the house manager. Isaac didn't mind. For the first time in his life, he had more money than he knew what to do with. The more he spent, the farther away his father's farm began to feel.

At the height of the boom, Blackwell was moving Isaac and Jim to a new subdivision every few days. He didn't even take the time to put in a fancy sign or a tennis court anymore. The people Isaac was selling binders to would have paid for swamp, so desperate were they to get in on a good thing. The prices were going up and up and up, and for a while, it seemed that the price of the property had no bearing on people's ability, or willingness, to pay. Somehow, somewhere, they always found the money.

Even Isaac, who knew that higher prices meant bigger commissions, wondered how high the market could really go. In early 1925, *Forbes* published a special report, warning that the price of real estate in Florida was based solely upon the expectation of finding a customer. In the months that followed, Isaac had to work to calm skittish buyers, and by that summer, he was losing more customers—people who still wanted a binder but couldn't afford the steep investment.

Construction costs skyrocketed, thanks to gridlock on the rails and a shortage of building supplies, and by the spring of 1926, the state's real estate market was in shambles. Blackwell's business was going belly-up, and he had little choice but to get rid of his binder boys.

Jim was determined to wait out the crisis in Florida, to see what other opportunities might arise, but Isaac had begun to wonder if it might be time to try his luck somewhere new. When Blackwell, who was enterprising to the end, scored Isaac a free seat on a Philadelphia-bound train, he took it. Isaac dreaded telling Jim, but his friend only laughed when he heard the news.

"You know Blackwell struck a deal with Applegate Funeral Home?"

Plenty of people liked to retire to Florida, Jim explained, but no one wanted to be buried in the swamp. Blackwell had guessed, correctly, that Marcus Applegate was buying round-trip tickets for his staff, every time they needed to accompany a casket north.

"Blackwell offered up his binder boys. Applegate only has to buy a one-way ticket, guys like you go back where you came from, and everyone's happy."

Isaac couldn't say he was happy but he raised his glass anyway, "To going back where we came from."

"But never forgetting the swamp."

After the casket was delivered, Isaac could have gone home. In fact, he did for a few days. But if Alliance had felt stifling before, it felt suffocating after five years in West Palm Beach. In the years Isaac had been gone, his mother had died and his father had grown slower, quieter, less sure of himself. The house had begun its gradual decline and so had his relationship with the man who could no more understand Isaac's meteoric success than the rapid waning of his fortunes.

Isaac was twenty-six and so poor that he walked the forty miles from Alliance to Atlantic City. It took him twelve hours. He would have walked to the ends of the earth to get away from that farm and the disappointed look on his father's face but, as it happened, he only needed to walk as far as Adler's Bakery.

~

Isaac sat out on the porch and watched his father and daughter's slow approach. Gussie ran ahead to open the gate, then held it open until Isaac's father entered the yard.

"Will you get your grandpa a drink of water?" Isaac's father asked her when they neared the porch, and she ran off, into the house, the screened door slapping at her heels.

"Gussie told me about Florence," he said, in Yiddish.

The use of Florence's name, so far from his in-laws' apartment, gave Isaac an odd jolt. Alliance and Atlantic City felt worlds away from each other.

"It came as a shock," said Isaac.

"Terrible."

"She was a good swimmer. A great swimmer, really."

"I remember. What do they think happened?"

"No one knows. Maybe a cramp. Or a rip current."

"And Gussie saw the whole thing?"

"Unfortunately, yes."

"Poor—" Isaac's father said, but stopped short when Gussie returned to the porch, walking ever so slowly so as not to spill the water, which she'd filled to the brim of a tall glass.

"Could I have a glass of water as well?" Isaac asked her. She sighed dramatically, as if she were always being put out with such requests, but then ran back inside the house.

"How is Fannie taking it?"

"We're not telling her," said Isaac, watching his father for some indication of his opinion on the matter. Surely other normal people thought Esther's plan preposterous?

Isaac's father gave nothing away, just asked, "Is the pregnancy so risky?"

"I've wondered the same thing. I don't know. Her blood pressure is a little high, and we don't know what happened"—Isaac paused—"last time."

In between the dozen Feldman children who had lived, there had been several others who had not. It had never occurred to Isaac to ask his parents about those children until after Hyram died, and by then his mother was gone and his father's memory was failing. There were logistical questions he had wanted to ask. Was it all right to plan a small burial for a dead baby? Should they sit Shiva? And then there were more personal questions. When would the pain in his chest go away? When would he stop seeing his son's face when he closed his eyes at night? In the end, he had asked his father nothing.

Gussie and Isaac sat with his father on the farmhouse's wide front porch into the early evening when the sun sank low in the sky. Isaac tried not to catalog the house's failings—the peeling paint, the wood rot, the tree that had grown too close to the porch.

When the mosquitoes came out, Isaac's father shuffled inside to take the *cholent* off the stove. He poured wine and unwrapped a loaf of rye bread, a few slices already cut away.

"No challah?" Isaac asked.

"No challah," said his father, "but this will do." Isaac wondered how often his father was getting into Vineland to shop and made a note to bring groceries the next time he visited.

Isaac knew that, if it weren't for this visit, his father would be back at the synagogue now, marking the end of Shabbos with the *Havdalah*. To his credit, he didn't try to get Isaac to go. Instead, he lit a candle and led a blessing, both tasks Isaac's mother would have done when she was alive. After he sang the *Shavua Tov*, Gussie joined in. *Eliyahu hanavi, Eliyahu hatishbi, Eliyahu hagiladi. Bimheirah b'yameinu, yavo eileinu, im Mashiach ben David.*

They made a modest dinner of the overcooked meat and potatoes, and Gussie fell asleep on the sofa in the front room because both men had forgotten that seven-year-old children still needed to be put to bed.

Isaac stacked their dirty plates on the drainboard and returned to the kitchen table with the bag of rugelach, a bottle of sherry, and two small glasses.

"How's business?" his father asked, reaching for the bag.

"Fine. Good." Isaac poured the sherry, allowing for an extra splash or two in his glass.

"Joseph is a lucky man to have you as his number two."

Isaac cringed. It was a loaded statement and his father, who would have given anything for Isaac to remain on the farm, knew it.

"Technically, I'm the head of sales. The bakery manager is number two."

His father dismissed Isaac's attempt at modesty with a wave of his hand and took a large bite of pastry.

"Joseph is sixty?"

"Closer to fifty."

"You'll be running the place in no time," he said, assuredly.

Would he? Isaac often wondered about that. Is that what he wanted? Was it what Joseph wanted? He'd never said as much. Isaac had spent his entire adult life trying to break out on his own, to be his own man. When he had married Fannie, he'd seen Adler's Bakery as nothing more than a soft place to land. He hadn't wanted to be trapped there any more than he'd wanted, growing up, to be trapped on the farm. But that was before Joseph expanded the business. Now Adler's was booming, and Isaac wondered if he could spend an entire career working in the back office, sustaining his father-in-law's dream. He knew lots of guys who would give their eyeteeth to have married into a family business like Adler's.

"I've got something new I'm working on—on the side," Isaac offered.

His father took another bite of rugelach.

"A land deal."

"In Atlantic County?"

"Florida."

His father furrowed his eyebrows, licked the cinnamon off his fingers. "I thought you were done with Florida."

"I thought I was, too," said Isaac. "But I got a call from an old friend last week. You remember Jim?" Why should his father remember Jim? Isaac could practically count the letters he'd written home from West Palm Beach on one hand.

His father shook the brown paper sack, eyeing the remaining pastries. He held the bag out to Isaac. "Take one."

Isaac did as he was told. They really were delicious. "Jim's working on a big deal. A developer went under and there's a lot of land that's coming on the market—cheap."

"How much land?"

"There's one package I'm looking at that's a little more than a hundred acres."

His father let out a low whistle. The farm was forty acres, and Isaac knew that, at harvesttime, it felt like it might as well be a hundred. "In Palm Beach?"

"The county, not the island," said Isaac. "Toward Lake Okeechobee. It's an old citrus farm."

"What would you do with it?" his father asked. Isaac had made it very clear he was no farmer.

"Sell it, when the time's right. Jim thinks he can get the price down to thirty dollars an acre. Land like that should be selling for at least two times that amount."

"That's still a lot of money to come up with." Isaac didn't ask but he could feel the question hanging in the air between them: *Do you have it?*

"I told him that the only way I can consider the opportunity is if I bring on some investors. Heck, it might even be something you want to get in on," Isaac said, surprised at his own audacity. He looked around the kitchen, then forced himself to finish the thought. "You invest a couple of hundred dollars. It doubles and then triples. Maybe does even better than that."

His father raised his eyebrows, humored Isaac with a soft chuckle.

"A thousand dollars could go a long way toward fixing up this house," Isaac pushed. "Maybe hire extra hands to help you with the harvest."

Isaac had hit on another sore point, so he got out in front of it, "Of course, if I were a better son, I'd come help you."

His father didn't say anything, just patted Isaac's hand.

∿

The following morning, Isaac's father made eggs for Gussie and black coffee for Isaac. When it was time to go, Isaac whistled for his daughter and carried her small bag out to the car. His father followed him outside. In his hand was the old Campfire Marshmallows canister.

"You said Jim thinks you can get them down to thirty dollars an acre?"

Isaac went mute as he watched his father pry the lid off the can and count out a small wad of bills.

"This should be enough for about ten acres?" he said, handing Isaac three hundred dollars. There was very little money left in the can.

Isaac had talked a good game the previous evening but now he wondered whether he'd pushed too far. If he took this money, combined it with his own, and bought the binder, he'd be on the hook for finding the rest of the money, for getting investors on board, for closing the deal.

It was a lot of pressure. But wasn't this what Isaac wanted? Not just the chance to make something of himself but the chance to show his father what he was capable of?

"You're sure about this?" Isaac asked.

Before his father could answer, Gussie came barreling out of the house and into her grandfather's arms.

"Come back to Atlantic City with us! Please!"

Isaac's father rubbed the top of her head and chuckled. "No cities for me, Augusta. But tell your father to bring you back soon."

"You can sleep in my room," said Gussie.

"Time to go, Gus," said Isaac as he held the car door open for her.

Isaac shook his father's hand and gave him a firm pat on the back. He couldn't bear to look him in the face, to catch his father studying him in the early morning light. "I'll let you know when the purchase has gone through," he told the patch of earth between them.

"Give my best to Fannie. And tell her parents I'm sorry."

Isaac nodded, got into the car, and started the ignition. He gave his father a small wave as he released the clutch and pulled out of the yard.

"Feel better!" Gussie shouted into the dust as the car sped down the farm's dirt drive.

As Isaac wound his way through Alliance and back toward Vineland, he could think of nothing but the money in his pocket. Between what Isaac had saved and what his father had just given him, he had enough for a binder. He'd call Jim first thing Monday and ask him to send the paperwork. Once Isaac signed, he'd have thirty days—maybe sixty—to get together the rest of the money to close the deal. Selling a few folks on an investment opportunity this good wouldn't be as easy as it had been in '25 but it wouldn't be hard either.

"Hey, Gus," Isaac said as they passed the synagogue and then the cemetery. "Grandpa said you told him about Florence."

"Sorry," she whispered from the seat next to him.

"It's okay. He's allowed to know."

"I thought he might be sad."

"Like you're sad?"

Out of the corner of his eye, Isaac could see her bob her head.

"I'm sad, too," he said.

"Mama will be the most sad," Gussie offered.

"That's true."

Isaac watched the road peel away in front of him for several minutes.

"Has your grandmother talked to you about how we're not going to tell Mother about Florence for a little while?"

His daughter nodded again. "Because of the baby."

"Right," said Isaac. "When you see her, it's going to be hard not to say anything."

Gussie was quiet for a few minutes.

"Why can't the baby know?"

Stuart

Florence had been dead a week, but Stuart continued to take the rescue boat out each morning at six o'clock, as if nothing had changed.

He had begun taking Florence out in the boat early the previous summer, when she had returned from Wellesley obsessed with the idea of swimming the English Channel. Since Ederle's swim in 1926, two other women had successfully made the crossing—one just three weeks after Ederle made headlines and another the following year. In the seven years that had elapsed since, no one else—woman or man—had made it across. *Why not me?* Florence had written to Stuart from school.

In her letters, Florence admitted to spending late nights at the library, reading through old newspapers, looking for clues as to how to best train for a Channel swim. She had so many questions, and her coach, who did all her swimming in the pool, could only answer some of them. Florence wanted to know how Ederle and the others had managed to stay warm, what they'd eaten, how they'd appropriately gauged the weather, and how they'd kept the salt water, which was a major irritant, from their eyes. Her list of questions had grown so long, she told Stuart, that she kept them in a small notebook, which she had bought expressly for that purpose.

When it came to open-water swimming, Stuart was Florence's best resource, and she wrote to him with increasing frequency as the winter months passed and her notebook grew fat with scribbling. Stuart didn't know the Channel but he knew the ocean—both what it could give a swimmer who was paying attention and what it could take away. As important, he knew Florence. He knew what each muscle in her body was capable of, where she had exposed weaknesses, where her confidence might be a gift and where it might get her into trouble. In one of her early letters, Florence had told Stuart that she wanted to attempt her crossing the following August, before she returned to Wellesley for her sophomore year, but Stuart persuaded her to give it one more year. *The English Channel*, he had written to her, *will still be there in 1934.*

Stuart suggested Florence spend the summer of 1933 training to swim the perimeter of Absecon Island. It was a twenty-two-mile swim, roughly the same distance as the swim from Cape Gris-Nez to Dover, albeit under much more pleasant conditions. The Channel's waters were rarely warmer than sixty degrees, and the air was just as cold. In the Straits of Dover, weather could change abruptly, so even if a swimmer left France under sunny skies, it was likely she'd encounter drenching rain, thick fog, and gale-force winds before she reached England.

Florence hadn't been keen to put off the Channel for another year but she did like the fact that Ederle had pulled off a similar stunt to great effect. Weeks before she swam the Channel, Ederle had swum from New York's Battery Park to Sandy Hook, New Jersey. Aside from the seventeen-mile swim being good practice, it had turned out to be excellent publicity. Stuart argued that, if Florence wanted the *Press* or one of Atlantic City's big businessmen to take her Channel swim seriously—and potentially sponsor it—she needed to make a name for herself in her own hometown, and she begrudgingly agreed.

Most mornings that first summer she was home from school, Florence had met Stuart on the beach in front of the Maryland Avenue beach tent. The sun wasn't yet up but, by the time he dragged a rescue boat across the sand and pushed it off its rollers and out into the open water, Florence seated at the bow, the horizon had turned pink. She didn't talk much as he rowed out past the breaking waves, but he liked having her in the boat anyway. On the nights when he stayed out too late at the Ritz's Merry-Go-Round bar or Garden Pier's ballroom, it might have been tempting to shut his alarm off and turn back over in bed. But instead, he nursed his coffee and gave Florence last-minute reminders to relax her shoulders or extend her pull a little farther. If she had questions she asked them but, more often than not, she simply nodded, stretched her arms above her head several times, pulled off her cover-up, and plunged into the water.

96   •   *Rachel Beanland*

While Florence swam, Stuart rowed behind her, careful to maintain a distance of several boat lengths, lest she stop suddenly and he plow into her. Sometimes he tried hollering at her, either to read from the stopwatch he kept in his pocket or to warn her she was veering off course, but between the cap she wore over her ears, the natural hum of the ocean's underworld, and the sound of her own arms churning the water around her head, it was difficult to get through to her. It didn't matter much anyway. She knew Atlantic City's landscape well enough to know that Central Pier was a half mile down the beach from Garden Pier, and that Million Dollar Pier was a half mile farther still.

Eventually, Stuart would shout to Florence that it was time to get back in the boat, and she'd acquiesce, allowing him to grab her under the arms and haul her over the side of the boat and into the bilge like a fresh catch. He knew there were many mornings she would have preferred to wave the boat away and to keep swimming, to return to the beach when it suited her, but Stuart, who made hundreds of saves each summer, wouldn't hear of it. "You're not invincible, you know," he often told her.

The row back to shore was always Stuart's favorite part of the morning. With her swim behind her and the sun in the sky, Florence was much more talkative. She'd wrap a towel around herself, swallow what was left of Stuart's coffee, and ask questions she already knew the answers to—did her frame look tighter and did he think she had a chance at the Pageant Cup again this year? That's one of the things he liked most about Florence. How sure she was of herself. He also liked her collarbones, which danced up and down when she laughed. Oh, and her eyes. He liked her eyes very much.

On days when Stuart didn't have to be up in the stand immediately, he took his time getting back to the beach. Florence frequently teased him, "My father has, at this point, already called the Coast Guard."

Now, without Florence in the boat, the vessel felt large and un- wieldy. The ocean was bigger, lonelier. The beach farther away. Stuart imagined rowing toward the horizon until he could no longer see the Boardwalk, or even the small spit of land on which Atlantic City was precariously perched. With no landmarks except the sun, could he find his way home? Would he want to?

~

Stuart was on his way to find breakfast when he came upon the Adlers, standing near the entrance of Steel Pier. At least it looked like the Adlers from so far away. He squinted, trying to get a better look, and counted heads. Joseph, Esther, Isaac, Anna, and little Gussie. Yes, it was definitely them. He raised an arm in the air and waved but no one seemed to notice.

"Mr. Adler. Mrs. Adler," he called, once he was within shouting distance. They looked up. Esther didn't look pleased to see him but she didn't look disappointed either. A good sign, he thought.

"Is everything all right?" she asked, an edge of concern in her voice, when they were close enough to hear one another properly.

He hesitated for a moment, unsure why she'd asked.

"Everything's fine. Or I mean, you know." Could he be a bigger dunce? Of course, things weren't fine. Florence was dead. Maybe Esther asked because she was worried he hadn't been able to put a lid on the lifeguards at the Virginia Avenue Hospital Tent? The poor woman had a lot on her mind. "I just saw you and wanted to say hello."

"Hello," said Isaac, in what felt like an intentionally flat tone. Was he mocking him?

"Out for a walk?" Stuart asked the group of them.

"Shiva's over," Gussie offered.

"Oh?"

"We go for a walk to mark the end of Shiva," said Joseph.

"Ah, I see," said Stuart, taking a step backward. "I didn't mean to intrude."

"Would you like to join us?" Esther asked, looking him straight in the eyes.

Stuart looked down at his weather-beaten leather moccasins and the sleeveless wool one-piece he'd worn out on the boat. He'd pulled his shorts overtop his uniform when he had left the beach but hadn't bothered to put on his shirt, which he held in one hand, the empty coffee thermos in the other. He could feel Esther, and maybe Anna, too, assessing his ensemble.

"I was on my way to get a bite before work," he said as he placed the thermos down for a moment and pulled the shirt over his head.

"We won't keep you," said Esther.

"No, no. I have time," he said quickly. "I was just trying to make excuses for being half-dressed. Is what I'm wearing all right?"

"You're absolutely fine," said Joseph.

Esther nodded, although it was hard to tell whether she was acknowledging that his attire looked passable or that she was simply ready for the family to set off again.

Stuart didn't know the etiquette for a situation such as this. Ordinarily, he'd have tried to make polite conversation, but if this walk was religious in nature, it would surely be more appropriate to say nothing. He walked in silence for several minutes, studying the back of Joseph's and Esther's heads as they made their way north. As they approached States Avenue, they slowed their pace and crossed the wide Boardwalk. Esther gripped the railing with both hands and looked out at the ocean.

It made sense that the family would come here, to the spot where they'd last seen Florence alive. It was early, not yet ten, and the beach was still quiet. In a little while, the lifeguards would arrive, drag their stands down to the water's edge, and give their whistles a long blast to signal that it was safe to swim.

Stuart knew the guards who had been assigned to the States Avenue stand this summer. Bing Johnson and Neil Farmer were both good guys but neither of them had half Stuart's experience. Stuart had gone looking for them last Sunday night, after he'd talked to Esther. When he found them, at a beloved bar not far from the Virginia Avenue Hospital Tent, he'd delivered her message—asked them not to say anything about who the victim was—but he'd also asked them to describe the save to him in detail. "She only struggled for a minute," said Bing, who was on what looked to be his fourth bourbon and water. "By the time we reached her, she was already unconscious."

Stuart had wanted answers but neither Bing nor Neil could provide anything concrete. If only Stuart had been at the States Avenue stand, like usual. He might have gotten to Florence faster. Or she might never have gone for a swim in the first place, content to spend her afternoon shouting wisecracks at him from the ground below.

Esther shook her head back and forth, as if she were shaking the image of her daughter's dead body from her mind. Joseph guided her away from the railing. Isaac and Gussie followed, and Anna and Stuart brought up the rear. Stuart intentionally slowed his pace, allowing a comfortable distance to grow between Isaac and him.

"I suppose you didn't have the chance to get to know her very well," said Stuart.

Anna didn't say anything.

"She was special. Different. Not like all the other girls around here."

Anna nodded, then wiped at her eyes.

"I'm sorry. I didn't mean to upset you."

"No, no. You're right to want to talk about her."

They passed a fortune-teller's booth that advertised two-dollar tarot card readings.

"It must be hard to be in the middle of all this. Especially when you hardly know the family."

"It's not so bad," she said. "For the first time in three months, I feel useful."

"I'm sure you've been a big help."

"Esther reminds me of my mother in many ways."

"You must miss her," said Stuart. "Your mother."

"Yes."

"Is it true that Mr. Adler and your mother were sweethearts back in Europe?"

Anna's eyes grew wide.

Stuart realized he'd overstepped. "Or maybe that's just what Florence thought."

Anna laughed out loud.

"What?" asked Stuart, grinning. "Is it funny to imagine them as sweethearts or funny to imagine Florence pondering the match?"

"Maybe both?"

"You were the subject of several letters home."

"I can't imagine what Florence must have thought," she said. "A strange girl arrives out of nowhere. She's not even a distant cousin, and suddenly she's living in her old bedroom."

"No one was complaining," he said, wishing he could catch her eye. He got the impression that she considered herself to be a nuisance.

At Virginia Avenue, the family passed the hospital tent but no one acknowledged it.

"So, you can neither confirm nor deny Florence's hunch?"

Anna smiled. "If I tell you something, you have to promise not to breathe a word."

He held up three fingers.

"They were engaged."

Stuart couldn't hide his surprise, didn't try. "Mr. Adler and your mother?"

Anna nodded her head. "My suspicion is that he broke it off when he met Esther."

"Fascinating."

"I know."

"Do you think he still loves her?"

"Who? My mother?"

"Sure."

"I would assume not," Anna said, as if she'd never considered the question, much less its answer. "Not that it really matters."

"Of course it matters."

Anna raised her eyebrows in amusement. She started to say something, and then stopped herself, pressed her lips together.

"What were you going to say?" Stuart asked.

"Nothing."

"Something."

"It's just that," said Anna, "sometimes, when he looks at me, I get the feeling he's rearranging my features, trying to recall my mother's face."

Stuart had nothing smart to say to that. He thought of the grainy photograph of Florence that had run in the *Press*, after she swam around the island last summer. It had captured her perfectly but he liked to think that, even in thirty years' time, he wouldn't need it to aid his recollection.

The procession came to a halt in front of the James Candy Company. A woman, whom Stuart didn't recognize, stopped Esther, and as he and Anna neared, he could hear her asking after the family.

"And how's your daughter?"

Esther's face crumpled.

"Still resting comfortably?"

"Oh, Fannie. Yes, still in the hospital. I think she's probably a little bored but so far, so good.

"Wonderful. And Florence? Still swimming every chance she gets?"

Stuart watched Esther visibly swallow.

Isaac, who hadn't even looked as if he were paying attention to the conversation, responded for her. "We couldn't get her out of the water if we tried."

Gussie looked confused and turned to her father, "Dad, but she can't—"

Before Gussie could get anything else out, Anna reached forward, grabbed her hand, gave the group an apologetic smile, and guided her inside the candy store. Stuart waited a few seconds to excuse himself, then followed them inside, where he found Anna and Gussie among several large bins of saltwater taffy. Anna was at eye level with Gussie, smoothing her hair as she spoke to the child in soft, soothing tones. Stuart had to get close before he could hear what she was saying.

". . . important not to tell."

Gussie looked like she was on the verge of tears. "But I thought we were just keeping the secret from Mother." Her lip started to quiver. "Because, because, because of the baby."

"Shhhh," whispered Anna. "It's confusing, I know."

Stuart approached the pair and crouched low. "I think your grandparents are worried that, if lots of people know Florence has died, someone will tell your mother. It makes it easier to keep the secret if only a small number of people know."

"We're like a special club," said Anna. "Have you ever been in a club?"

"Like a *secret* club?" Gussie asked.

"Yes, the most secret kind of club. The kind with handshakes and passwords and secret languages," said Anna.

"Some of the girls at school are in a secret club."

"Not you?" Anna asked.

She shook her head sadly. "In their club, they speak Pig Latin."

"But that's barely secret at all!" Stuart said, allowing a look of horror to fall over his face. "Everyone knows Pig Latin!"

"Our club is top secret," said Anna.

"And I'm a member?" Gussie asked.

"All of us are members," said Stuart, looking at Anna. "Everyone who knows what happened to Florence."

"Do we have a secret handshake?" asked Gussie.

"'Do we have a secret handshake?' Anna, can you even believe what this girl is asking? 'Do we have a secret handshake?' We've got a secret handshake *and* a secret language!"

He grabbed Gussie's small wrist and squeezed it twice before curling her pinkie into her palm and tugging at her thumb. "Is that secret enough for you?" he asked, grinning at her.

"And our secret language?"

"Anna, should we tell her the secret language? Do you think she's ready for something so top secret?"

Anna made a face, as if she were carefully assessing Gussie's secret-keeping attributes.

"I think she will do all right with such a big secret."

Stuart had to think fast to come up with something. "It's called ARP Talk, and it's *much* more sophisticated than Pig Latin. You have to say 'arp' before every vowel sound. So, your name is Garp-u-sarp-ie. And I'm Starp-u-arpart."

"What's Anna's name?"

"Arpann-arpa, of course."

Gussie practiced for a few minutes. She said the made-up words for beach and sand and home.

"You're quite good," said Anna.

"So, the club rules are pretty straightforward," said Stuart. "Don't share the secret handshake with anyone who's not a member, don't teach anyone who's not in the club the secret language, and—" He hesitated here. "Don't tell anyone that Florence is dead."

"Do I have to tell them she's alive?" Gussie asked.

Stuart looked at Anna, who shook her head no. "Nope, you can just change the subject. Or say nothing at all." Stuart eyed the bins of taffy. "Hold on one second."

He grabbed a large handful of individually wrapped pieces of taffy and put them in a small paper sack, which he took up to the counter to be weighed. When he returned, candy in hand, he distributed three pieces to each of them and instructed them to remove the waxed wrappers.

"This is a very solemn part of the initiation ceremony," he said, trying to make his face look serious. "I want you to put all three pieces of taffy in your mouth at once and repeat the following after me."

As Gussie unwrapped her candy, Anna whispered "thank you," to him over the top of Gussie's head.

He shrugged his shoulders, to indicate it was nothing. "You'd better unwrap yours, too."

When all three of them had worked the papers off their candies and placed the soft taffy in their mouths, Stuart said the only rhyme that came to mind, very fast: "One for sorrow, two for joy, three for a girl, four for a boy, five for silver, six for gold, seven for a secret, never to be told," and the girls repeated it, laughing at how ridiculous they all sounded.

They chewed in silence for several minutes, their mouths full of the sticky treat.

Gussie tried to ask Stuart something but it took her three tries before he could make out what she was saying.

"Should we initiate my father and grandparents?"

Stuart swallowed, then cleared his throat. "They're already full-fledged members of the club. If you want to, just to be nice, you can offer them a piece of candy."

"But we'll initiate my mother?"

Stuart tried to imagine a scenario in which Fannie had had her baby, been told about her sister's death, and recovered from both experiences sufficiently to sit with her daughter in James Candy Company, stuffing her mouth with taffy.

"Sure, after the baby's been born, and someone's had a chance to tell her about Florence," said Stuart, watching Gussie's face carefully to be sure she understood. He thought she did. Anna patted her head.

"Are we ready to go?" Stuart asked them both.

"Stop!" said Gussie just as he had begun moving toward the door. "What's our name?"

"Name?"

"Our club name," said Gussie. "All secret clubs have names."

"By Jove, you're right," said Stuart, smacking his forehead with the heel of his hand. "Anna, why didn't we tell her the club's name?" He was clearly stalling, a fact that Anna seemed to pick up on with little problem and that Gussie was willing to ignore.

"I don't know how we forgot," Anna said, offering up an apologetic smile but no name to go along with it.

His mind flashed through images: Florence tucking her hair under her red bathing cap, Florence plunging into the waves from the side of the rescue boat, Florence taking notes in the notebook with the pale blue cover. Quickly, it came to him.

"We call ourselves the Florence Adler Swims Forever Society."

∼

It was hard for Stuart to extricate his hand from Gussie's sweaty palm, but at a quarter to ten, he looked at his watch, made his apologies to Gussie and Anna and then Esther, promised to be in touch with Joseph as soon as he heard anything from Bill Burgess, and took off toward the Kentucky Avenue beach tent.

He'd made it half a block before he heard someone calling his name, and turned to find Anna running to catch up with him.

When she arrived in front of him, she was out of breath.

"I wanted to ask you something," she said when her breathing had returned to normal. "A favor."

"Sure."

She straightened, fidgeting with the clasp on a small handbag that had been tucked under her arm but that she now held in front of her like a shield.

"I can't swim," she said, her voice so quiet he wasn't sure he'd heard her correctly.

"Pardon?"

She cleared her throat. "I can't swim."

It wasn't surprising, really. Plenty of girls couldn't swim. In fact, most every girl he met couldn't—not really.

"You didn't swim in Berlin?"

She shook her head. "Never."

A seagull cawed overhead, and they both watched as it dove over the head of a sand artist, hard at work on a life-sized portrait of Neptune, and headed out to sea. Stuart imagined that Atlantic City would be a terrifying place to live if the ocean was nothing more than a threat.

"Do you want to learn?"

"I was hoping you might teach me," she said. "If it's not too much trouble."

"It's no trouble. I'll have you winning the Pageant Cup in no time."

She let out a short laugh. "No gold medals necessary. I'd just like to be able to save my own life."

~

"You're late," Robert said, as soon as Stuart staked his rescue can in the sand, tossed his things up to his partner, and hauled himself up and onto the lifeguard stand's wide wooden bench seat.

"I know," he said, pulling his whistle, which hung from a long string of lanyard, out of his pocket and putting it around his neck. "How are the waves?"

"They're all right. I'm watching that rip current over there. I've already warned a half-dozen folks to steer clear of it."

Stuart studied the break in the waves, counting the heads of the people who were swimming in its vicinity.

"Your father was looking for you."

"He came down to the beach?"

"No," Robert scoffed. They'd worked together for less than a month, but Robert already knew that was about as likely as fish flying. "He sent his lackey."

"Wilson?"

"That's the one."

"What'd he say?"

"To come by your dad's office, first break you get."

"Goddammit. It's bad enough he dragged me off the States Avenue stand. Now he thinks he can just summon me up to the hotel whenever he wants."

"I mean, I like having you and all, but I'm surprised Chief Bryant let him get away with it."

"I'm not," said Stuart indignantly. "My father underwrites this entire section of the beach. Always has. The hotel's also hosting the Lifeguards' Ball this summer—gratis."

"Still, you're one of Bryant's best guards, and he's gotta know he's making your life hell."

"Two o'clock," said Stuart. "You see what's happening?"

By the time Robert could say anything, Stuart had already given his whistle three short blasts and hopped down from the stand onto the hot sand. Robert scrambled to catch up as the two men ran to the rescue boat, grabbed hold of its sides, and heaved it into the waves.

"He's not struggling," yelled Stuart. "I think he's about to go under."

Beachgoers expected swimmers who were in distress to wave their arms and call for help but Stuart had learned that they rarely did either of those things. The signs that someone was drowning were often subtle and hard to see from several dozen yards away in a lifeguard stand. Distressed swimmers stopped using their arms and legs, stopped making forward or backward progress in the water. Under the surface, their bodies went vertical, as if they were climbing an invisible ladder, but in the briny Atlantic, that posture wasn't always easy to spot. Stuart had trained himself to watch for the way swimmers held their heads. A swimmer who was treading water could keep his chin above water but a struggling swimmer let his head sink so low that his mouth was barely above water level. With women and small children, their long hair often provided a clue: if their hair fell in front of their eyes, and they didn't immediately push it out of the way, it indicated that they probably didn't have the wherewithal to do so. But the biggest sign, which Stuart hadn't been able to get out of his mind since Florence's drowning, was that swimmers in distress almost always turned their bodies to face the shore.

In less than a minute, Robert and Stuart pulled alongside the man, whose head, save his mouth and nose, was entirely submerged. Stuart jumped into the water, his rescue can under his arm, and approached the man from behind, hooking his arms under the man's armpits. He kicked his legs as hard as he could to propel the man's head above the waterline and allow him to get one good breath of air. Then he pushed the man back under the water, and in one fluid move, pulled the rescue can under the waterline and in front of him. Once he had rolled the man onto the can, he watched as it buoyed him back to the surface. The man sputtered and gasped but he was breathing, which was all that mattered.

While Robert hoisted the man into the boat, Stuart treaded water and allowed himself to regain his own steady breathing patterns. He looked back at their lifeguard stand, which looked tiny in comparison to The Covington, rising out of the sand behind it. Did it even matter that the stand stood in the shadow of his father's hotel? That his father wanted to keep close tabs on him? In the course of just a few minutes, Stuart had saved a man's life and averted a family's suffering.

～

Stuart did not consider going to see his father until Robert and he had cleared the water and dragged the lifeguard stand and rescue boat back up onto high ground for the night. Together, they climbed onto the back of the stand and used their combined weight to tip it backward. On its side, it was protected from the overnight effects of high winds and drunken revelers.

Back at the beach tent, Stuart spent extra time wiping down his rescue can and straightening up the first-aid supplies. The guys who worked all the other stands on this section of the beach arrived at the tent in pairs, stowing their rescue cans, restocking their medical kits, and bragging about their biggest saves of the day. Stuart and Robert had made more than two dozen rescues over the course of eight hours, but two guys stationed at Michigan Avenue had plucked a young boy out of the water after they saw him fall out a window on Million Dollar Pier. Aside from the shock, he had been completely unharmed.

"It's a bear to pull a rescue boat up alongside those pilings," said Robert. "You win."

Stuart had worked the States Avenue stand for five summers, and he knew the guys who reported in to the Maryland Avenue beach tent like they were his own brothers. There was Charles Kelly, who spent every free minute combing the beach, trying to convince the prettiest girls to enter the Miss Beach Patrol Pageant. The contest only happened once a year—in July—but the joke was that Kelly recruited contestants year-round. James Parker lived for playing pranks on the lifeguards in the other Beach Patrol tents and would gladly hide a pair of oars or a couple of the rescue boats' drain plugs if it meant watching the guys in one of the other tents scramble to find them. And then there was Irish Dan, who was the best rower on the beach. When the waves got so big that they chased the crowds away, he challenged the other guards to sea battles, and when hurricane waves left even the ACBP's best guards beached, Irish Dan would take a boat out alone, bragging that he could see the jitney drivers making change on the Avenue. Captain Bryant often reminded him that he'd be spending a whole lot of change if a rescue boat broke in half while he was horsing around in it.

Stuart still went out with the Maryland Avenue guys at night but it was different now. He hadn't realized how much time they'd spent in the evenings simply unwinding their days. He still had stories to contribute—just yesterday he'd chased a purse snatcher halfway down the beach—but these were stories none of the guys had witnessed and therefore couldn't corroborate. Part of the fun came from retelling a story everyone already knew.

Florence's death had been the biggest story of the summer, by far, and it belonged to the guys at the Maryland Avenue beach tent. Ordinarily, a story like that would have lived forever, growing and changing with each retelling until it became a living thing. But the guys knew Stuart had been close to Florence, so when he asked them not to talk about it, they had honored the request.

"I'll kill anyone who breathes a word," said Irish Dan, giving Stuart a heavy slap on the back that pitched him so far forward he nearly fell face first into the sand. Stuart believed him.

Stuart understood that it would take time and effort to get to know these new guys at Kentucky Avenue, so when someone suggested that they all get a beer at the Jerome, he decided his father could wait until the following day.

~

At a quarter to nine in the morning, Stuart allowed one of The Covington's doormen to usher him off the Boardwalk and into the hotel's lobby.

"Morning, Mr. Williams."

"Morning, Henry."

The Covington wasn't the largest hotel on the Boardwalk but it was large enough that Stuart didn't enjoy telling people his father owned it. He could see their expressions go blank, as they calculated his father's net worth and determined that Stuart was not just well off, but rich. Stuart was neither of those things—not really. His father's money came with too many strings attached, and the money he made lifeguarding and coaching was just enough to cover his bar tabs and the rent he paid for a room in Mrs. Tate's Northside boardinghouse.

It's not that Stuart wanted to disassociate himself from the hotel entirely. The Covington had been a good place to grow up, although

Stuart had liked it better when the place was still called Covington Cottage and felt like a ramshackle retreat. Back then, there was always wicker furniture on the veranda, which overlooked the ocean, and there was never enough staff to keep up with the sand that got tracked across the lobby's Oriental rugs and stuck in the cracks of the wide wooden floorboards.

Stuart's great-grandfather had built the cottage in 1873—just three years after the Boardwalk went in. Philadelphians had discovered the allure of the shore, and the United States Hotel, with its six hundred rooms, couldn't keep up with demand. Stuart's great-grandfather could see that Atlantic City needed more hoteliers and, with the backing of his own father, purchased a tract of beachfront property where he could build a relatively simple wood-framed structure. Covington Cottage boasted eighty rooms, a half-dozen beachside changing tents—where attendants made extra money selling buckets of seawater with which to rinse off—and easy access to the railroad station. When Applegate's Pier went in, near the already busy hotel, business boomed.

In the 1890s, Stuart's grandfather expanded the hotel's footprint, adding two wide wings to the cottage, which remained the beating heart of the establishment. That iteration of the hotel was the one Stuart knew the best. There was a restaurant where, in the mornings, a colored woman named Mama K served up stacks of golden pancakes, a library with lots of soft furniture, and plenty of good hiding places, but the hotel wasn't yet so big that Stuart could get lost in it. His father had begun doing the payroll and much of the ordering, but the day-to-day management of the hotel remained the domain of his grandparents. His grandfather oversaw the front of the house, his grandmother planned the menus and arranged the lobby's fresh flowers, and there were always odd jobs for a young boy who needed constant occupation. In the summer months, when Stuart wasn't reordering the room keys that hung on pegs behind the front desk or running newspapers up to the rooms, he spent long hours in the swimming pool, practicing his trudgeon.

Stuart was ten years old when his grandfather died, and within just a few short years, it was as if Stuart's father had erased him entirely. He hired a New York architectural firm to design a massive new addition for the hotel, and the plan they came back with called for knocking down Covington Cottage completely, save the façade of the original structure, to make way for two twenty-three-floor towers that would be the tallest in Atlantic City, if not New Jersey. The surviving veranda would become an arcade of shops and the swimming pool would be demolished to make room for a larger one. As construction got under way, Stuart's father hired a New York advertising agency, too, and the ads they created, which referred exclusively to a place called "The Covington," beckoned tourists to stay at Atlantic City's "Skyscraper by the Sea" and exalted the hotel's ocean views, private bathrooms—complete with faucets that pumped healing salt water directly from the ocean—and other modern amenities such as radios, telephones, and baby cages. Mama K was given an early retirement, and in her place, Stuart's father hired a chef, also from New York, who had been trained at Paris's Cordon Bleu and could turn out a menu that was both appealing to an American palate and written entirely in French.

Stuart nodded at a young man behind the reception desk whom he recognized but couldn't name. The thing about being the boss's son was that, whether Stuart wanted the attention or not, every single member of the staff knew exactly who he was—and who he wasn't. When he had been coming along, everyone from the front desk attendants to the waiters to the gardeners had been kind to him, no doubt imagining that one day he'd be signing their paychecks. But as he grew older, and it became clear that he wasn't interested in going to work for his father, he thought he had noticed the staff's patience with him withering.

Stuart got into the elevator alongside the bellman, Cy, and a middle-aged couple who might as well have been holding placards that read FROM PHILADELPHIA'S MAIN LINE. Cy pressed the button for the second floor, where the hotel's administrative offices were located, without waiting for Stuart to ask.

There had always been a type of guest The Covington attracted—monied, white, and Protestant—but never more so than after Covington Cottage reopened as The Covington. Stuart had noticed that, over time, much of his resentment toward the hotel itself had been redirected toward the people who frequented it. And, of course, toward his father, who maintained his grandfather's belief that Jews—and most definitely Negros—had no business staying at a hotel as grand as The Covington.

Florence had been the one to point out The Covington's discriminatory practices to Stuart, back when she was swimming for the Ambassador Club, and he remembered feeling embarrassed that he hadn't even noticed there were no Jewish names in the hotel's guestbook. "That's why my parents don't like you," Florence had said, as simply as if she were explaining why she was late to swim practice. Stuart had initially felt stunned, so unfamiliar was he with the sensation of being disliked by anyone, but then he'd begun to pay attention. When he looked around The Covington's dining rooms, bars, and ballrooms, he saw the East Coast's most privileged elites, all eager to spend their holiday pretending they lived in a world that didn't actually exist.

Cy let Stuart off on the second floor, and Stuart tipped his head to his companions. He could feel his chest tighten and his breathing grow shallower as he arrived at the administrative suite. Since it wasn't yet nine o'clock, the desk of his father's secretary sat empty. He grabbed a peppermint out of a glass jar she kept beside her typewriter, then rapped on the door that led to his father's office.

"Who is it?"

Stuart didn't feel the need to announce himself, given the fact that his father had summoned him. Instead, he just turned the doorknob and went inside.

"You made it, I see," said his father, looking at his wristwatch.

"I did."

"Twenty-three hours later."

Stuart refused to be riled. "I'm here," he said as he sat down, uninvited, in one of two leather club chairs that faced his father's desk, an expensive Bauhaus contraption of mahogany and tubular steel that he'd paid to have shipped from Germany. Stuart unwrapped the pep-permint as slowly and loudly as possible and popped the candy into his mouth.

His father just looked at him.

"Yes?" Stuart asked, when he could stand his father's quiet surveillance no longer.

"I heard about Florence Adler."

Stuart didn't like the sound of her lovely name on his father's tongue, didn't like the way he referenced her by her first and last name, as if Stuart wouldn't have understood whom he was talking about, otherwise.

"How did you hear?" asked Stuart.

"It doesn't matter."

"It does, actually."

"Chaz told me."

"The chief?" Stuart would have liked to hide the look of consternation on his face but he had a poor poker face. Was Chief Bryant so deep in his father's pocket that he'd come running right over to The Covington as soon as he'd gotten word that Florence had drowned?

"He was worried about you."

"He could have told *me* that."

In response, his father lit a cigarette.

"You can't keep interfering like this," said Stuart.

"Since when did extending sympathy to one's son become interfering?"

"I must have missed that part."

"What part?"

"The part where you offered your sympathy," said Stuart, pocketing the candy wrapper and reaching for a glass paperweight that sat on the corner of the desk.

"I'm very sorry, Stuart. I am."

"Perhaps you should have led with that."

"Stuart, really. You're being ridiculous."

"I'm being ridiculous? *I'm* being ridiculous? I'm not the one who's so intent on keeping tabs on my twenty-four-year-old son that I paid off his boss to get him reassigned to my beach."

"So that's what this is really about?"

"You had no right to get me reassigned to the Kentucky Avenue stand. And you have no right to pretend to care about how Florence's death is affecting me. You had no use for her when she was alive."

"She was a perfectly fine girl. I just thought you would have been better off lavishing your limited attention elsewhere."

"What's that supposed to mean?" Stuart realized he was squeezing the paperweight so tightly that his hand had begun to sweat.

His father didn't say anything, just tapped the end of his cigarette against an ashtray that was very much in need of being emptied.

"What you meant to say," said Stuart, "was that I would have been better off lavishing my attention on someone who wasn't Jewish."

"I didn't say that."

"Yes, well, you might as well have."

"Do you know what I think?" his father asked.

Stuart didn't answer, just replaced the paperweight on the desk and stood to go.

"I think it suits your purposes to think of me as a villain. As long as you do, you feel justified spending your days in the sun and your nights at the club."

"What would you know about my purposes?"

"I know one thing," said his father as Stuart walked toward the door. "There may be plenty of men around here who make a career out of serving on the Atlantic City Beach Patrol but you're not one of them."

Stuart opened the door of his father's office and walked through it as his father barked, "It's high time you got off the beach."

Anna

When Anna arrived at the Knife and Fork Inn, the restaurant was already crowded with businessmen sipping cocktails and dining on thick, red lobster tails. She'd been surprised when she arrived at the intersection of Atlantic and Pacific avenues, having carefully followed the directions Joseph had given her that morning, to find a building that looked as if it belonged in Belgium or the Netherlands, with its stepped gables and terra-cotta roof. The stucco exterior was dotted with little knives and forks, and she had stood for a moment, admiring the detail before reaching for the handle of the big brass door. The restaurant was dark, with thick, leaded windows that sparkled in the sunlight but let in very little light. The windows had been cracked open but there was no breeze, and the heat from the kitchen made the summer feel inescapable.

The maître d' led Anna upstairs, to a larger room, lined with leather-tufted banquets. Linen-covered tables dotted the center of the room, and at one of them, Joseph and Mr. Hirsch, of the Atlantic City chapter of the American Jewish Committee, had already taken their seats. Joseph gestured toward her and said something to Mr. Hirsch and both men stood as she approached.

"Anna, Eli Hirsch," said Joseph, pulling out a chair for Anna before the maître d' could do so.

"I'm so pleased to meet you, Mr. Hirsch."

"Likewise. Joseph's told me nothing but good things."

"He's very kind to me," she said as she took a good look at Joseph. Anna had worried all morning about whether this lunch meeting would be too much for him.

A waiter filled Anna's water glass and asked if she'd like a cocktail. She hesitated, tempted to order one but unsure what to ask for.

"She'll have an old-fashioned," said Joseph, raising his own glass, and Anna gratefully agreed. The Adlers had told her that, until just a few years ago, alcohol consumption was prohibited here and everywhere in the U.S. Looking around Atlantic City, and certainly this dining room, it was hard to believe such a thing could be true.

Mr. Hirsch touched the rim of his already empty glass, indicating to the waiter that he'd like another.

"So, Joseph tells me you arrived in March?"

"Yes."

"On a student visa?"

Anna nodded her head affirmatively.

"You're a lucky girl to have had your paperwork sail through the consulate so quickly. Every Jew in Germany wants to get out, and U.S. officials are worried they're going to be overrun."

"I applied last fall, after I was admitted to New Jersey State Teachers College."

"That's a funny school for you to have found all the way from Berlin."

"I may have had something to do with it," said Joseph. "Sherm Leeman sits on the board of governors."

"Is this guy telling me you couldn't have gotten in on your own?"

"Oh, I don't—"

Joseph interrupted. "She's a very smart girl. Her parents just asked me to do what I could."

"You wouldn't have thought I was so smart if you'd seen me in Berlin. I was denied admission to every single university I applied to."

"I have to assume it had nothing to do with your grades," said Mr. Hirsch.

Anna could feel her face go crimson.

"The university admissions committees are controlled by the Nazis. You didn't consider going to school in France? Or Belgium?"

"I don't speak French. Just German, Hungarian, English, and a little Yiddish." She looked over at Joseph. "My father studied English literature at the University of Vienna, and my mother knew Mr. Adler, so—"

The waiter returned, placing an amber-colored cocktail, garnished with a bright red cherry, in front of Anna. She took a small sip and tried not to wince as the whiskey hit the back of her throat.

"And your parents' visa application was denied?"

"Yes," said Anna. "Recently."

"And the reason they cited?"

Anna glanced at Joseph, unsure how much of the talking he wanted her to do. He seemed far away, and she wondered, yet again, if it'd been a good idea to let him make the lunch date. After all, Florence had been dead less than three weeks.

"That Mr. Adler wasn't an immediate relative," she finally said.

"I assume your affidavit said that you'd provide them with an income?" Mr. Hirsch said, speaking to Joseph directly.

"Forty dollars a week."

"But you didn't promise a job?"

"Aaron Wexler told me that can make things worse."

"He's right," said Mr. Hirsch, taking a swallow from his glass. "It's a mess. The consul doesn't want to let anyone in who might become a drain on society, but God forbid you tell them you plan on working. They don't want to see Americans forfeit a single precious job."

"It's hard to prove you won't be a drain on society if you're not meant to work," Joseph agreed.

Mr. Hirsch ordered the lobster salad, and Anna told the waiter she'd have the same thing. She had never had the sweet meat and had to refrain from scraping her plate clean. The drink, combined with the food, left her feeling bolder.

"We were hoping you'd be able to advise us on our next steps," she said to Mr. Hirsch as she put down her fork.

"The way I see it, you've got a few options," he said, wiping his mouth with his napkin. "You can submit more reference letters, or even try to find a second sponsor who will provide an affidavit of his own— anything to try to make up for the fact that Joseph is not a relative. Or you might try to establish a bank account in your parents' name and deposit enough money into it to prove they won't become public charges."

Anna thought about the fifty precious dollars she kept hidden inside her copy of Thomas Mann's *The Magic Mountain*, which she'd brought from home. Her parents had warned her that the money needed to last, that they didn't know when or if they'd be able to send more.

"How much money is enough?" said Joseph. He'd barely touched the trout on his plate.

"That, my friend, is the riddle. A thousand? Maybe more? Does it need to be enough to help them land on their feet or live indefinitely? No one is getting a straight answer."

Anna made a quick grab for her drink and held it up to her lips only to realize it was empty. She had the same nervous feeling, listening to these two men discuss her parents' future, that she'd had when she got off the SS *New York* at Ellis Island. She was young and healthy and had all the right paperwork but she couldn't help feeling as if the immigrant inspectors and medical officers were looking for reasons to turn people away. That if she dragged or coughed or said the wrong thing, she'd dash her parents' dreams and ruin her only chance at an education.

"Should we do both?" Joseph asked. "Send more reference letters and establish a bank account?"

"It certainly couldn't hurt but perhaps try the letters first. If their application is denied, you'll just lose a few months."

Anna's heart sank. It had already been three months since she'd seen her mother.

"I'm more than happy for the committee to write a letter," said Mr. Hirsch. "With the amount of money we've raised in the past year, one would hope the consul general is beginning to take us seriously."

"I appreciate it," said Joseph, glancing at Anna.

"And I think we could swing a letter from Congressman Bacharach, attesting to your ability to support the Epsteins. Two more letters ought to be enough to get them through. Particularly if one's from a congressman." Mr. Hirsch beckoned to the waiter, indicating that he'd take the check.

"I know Ike Bacharach but I'm not particularly close with him," said Joseph. "You think he'd really be willing to write a letter?"

"He owes me a favor. I'll arrange it if you send me the particulars."

"It's the first thing I'll do when I'm back at the office."

Anna thought of Joseph's office, of the forlorn beach chair she'd seen in front of the fireplace on her last visit. It was hard for her to tell if he considered Mr. Hirsch's request a welcome distraction from his grief or an unwanted interference. Maybe it was both.

The waiter brought the check, and Mr. Hirsch reached for his wallet.

"Let me get this," said Joseph. "You've been a big help."

"Nonsense," said Mr. Hirsch, counting out six one-dollar bills and putting them on the table.

The maître d' brought him his hat, and he stood to go.

"Miss Epstein, there is one other solution to your parents' predicament."

"What's that?" Anna asked, sitting up at attention. She watched him put on his hat.

"Marry yourself an American," he said as he straightened the brim.

Anna let out a little laugh.

"Oh, don't look at me like that, Joseph," Mr. Hirsch said with a wink. "It's still the quickest way I know to get a visa."

~

The drink, combined with the afternoon heat and Mr. Hirsch's promises, had left Anna feeling light-headed. At the door of the Adlers' apartment, she dug in her purse for a handkerchief and her compact, blotted the perspiration from her neck and the skin around her hairline, and assessed her overall appearance in the small mirror. She made a face at herself and probably would have made several more had the door not opened to reveal Gussie.

"I thought I heard you out here!"

Gussie extended her hand to offer the secret handshake, and Anna shut her compact with a snap, slipped it back into her purse alongside the handkerchief. Then she reached for the little girl's wrist.

"Wharp-ere warp-ere yarp-ou?" Gussie asked

"Let's speak in English for now, okay?"

For a moment Gussie looked crestfallen but then her face brightened. "I have a letter for you!"

"Oh?" Anna had received a letter from her mother, just a few days ago, but perhaps her father had written. In place of long letters, he usually sent articles or a short story he'd torn from the pages of the magazine *Kladderadatsch*. Maybe it was all the years he'd spent studying and teaching English, but he seemed to understand that reading German, for Anna now, had become a kind of treat.

Gussie led her into the kitchen, where the table was covered in old newspapers, cut to bits.

"What are you working on?"

"Nana says Mother likes the Dionne quintlets."

"Quintuplets."

"That's what I said." Anna had clearly irritated the girl. She raised her eyebrows at Gussie, who was rooting through the paper scraps, looking for something. Hopefully Anna's letter hadn't been cut to shreds, too.

"So, you're cutting out pictures of the babies?"

"Yes, see?" Gussie held up a piece of blue construction paper onto which she'd glued a half-dozen versions of the same photo Anna had seen plastered on every periodical at every newsstand in Atlantic City. In it, the quintuplets' doctor loomed over a bassinet, in which all five babies, each in her own bunting, were packed like sardines. It was hard to make out their faces.

It seemed a little tactless to present a pregnant woman at risk for miscarrying with a collage of baby pictures, but Anna had to assume Esther had sanctioned the activity.

"Where's your grandmother?"

"In her bedroom, lying down."

"Ah."

"Here it is!" Gussie said, removing a folded piece of paper from underneath a three-day-old section of the *Atlantic City Press*.

Anna's heart sank. The note wasn't in the light blue aerogram envelope she'd become accustomed to looking for on the dresser in the Adlers' entryway. In fact, the note wasn't in an envelope at all.

"Have you read it?"

Gussie nodded earnestly and handed the note over. Before Anna could unfold the piece of paper, Gussie blurted out, "It's from Stuart!" and scurried around the table to read the note, once more, over Anna's shoulder.

Anna,

Now is as good a time as any to learn to swim. Your first lesson is tomorrow evening at six. Meet me at the Kentucky Avenue beach tent?

Stuart

"How did you get this?" Anna asked Gussie.

"He dropped it off."

Anna sucked in her breath, wondering how Esther would feel about a would-be suitor of Florence's dropping off notes for Anna.

"Did your grandmother see it?"

Gussie shook her head. "She was in her room."

Anna thought for a minute. "Maybe we don't tell her? In case it makes her sad."

Gussie didn't acknowledge Anna's request. She just walked back around the table, picked up the pair of scissors, and began to cut out a baby in a Gerber's advertisement. The baby was jolly and round, old enough to sit up and smile. Behind the child's head read the words *For Babies Only*. Anna assumed Gussie knew that this baby wasn't one of the Dionne babies, none of whom could have been easily confused with a bouncing six-month-old. Gussie put a careful dot of glue on the backside of the baby's picture and pressed it onto her collage.

"So, you're including other babies?" Anna asked, unable to help herself.

"Mother likes them," said Gussie, defensively, as she began cutting away at the next clipping. Anna couldn't be sure but, from across the table, the baby looked like Charles Lindbergh Jr. She stood and peered over Gussie's work, trying to read the photo's caption. After his transatlantic flight, Charles Lindbergh had become extremely popular across Europe. His son's kidnapping had made headlines on both sides of the Atlantic, and Anna imagined that the German people had followed the case almost as closely as their American counterparts. After the child's body was discovered, the coverage had slowed but, now that the trial was under way, the beautiful boy's picture was back in all the papers.

"Gussie, don't use that picture."

"Why?"

"Because."

"Because why?"

"Because"—Anna hesitated—"that baby is dead."

Gussie put her scissors down. "Like Hyram?"

Anna nodded.

Gussie placed the clipping back down on the table and smoothed its edges. Was she hurt? Anna couldn't tell.

"Do you have a bathing suit to wear?" Gussie asked, and Anna wondered if this was the child's own small attempt to get back at her. She didn't have a bathing suit. She'd worn a cotton dress to the beach on the day Florence had died, and Gussie knew it.

"I don't," Anna admitted, watching Gussie for a response.

"You could wear one of Florence's."

"I think that might be unkind."

Gussie shrugged her shoulders. "She can't wear them anymore."

～

Anna waited until the apartment grew quiet, Gussie tucked into bed on the sun porch, Esther and Joseph retired to their bedroom down the hall. Then she rose from her own bed, went to Florence's dresser, and switched on the lamp. She thought she remembered Florence keeping her bathing suits in the top left drawer, but when she slid it open, as quietly as she could, she was confronted with a jumble of slips and stockings. So, she eased the drawer closed and tried another one.

Florence's drawers were a mess, which came as no surprise to Anna. She was the type of person who left wet bathing suits hanging on bedposts and her shoes in exactly the spot where she kicked them off at night. Magazines and books were left open to the page where she'd stopped reading, a testament to her assumption that she'd return to them before too long.

Anna, who was grateful the Adlers had found room in the apartment for her at all, had been in no position to demand that Florence make her bed or push in her drawers. For the brief time the two girls had shared the room, Anna had just tidied up after her—folding down the pages of Florence's books and magazines so that they might be stacked on the dresser and lining up her shoes, toes in, under the window, where Anna kept her own. Anna would have liked to think that Florence appreciated her efforts, but she wasn't sure she even noticed. Florence struck Anna as the type of girl who was used to being looked after, used to getting her own way. She blew in and out of the room with the confidence of a person who had been the family's baby for two decades, who believed everyone was always glad to see her and that she could achieve her wildest ambitions if for no other reason than that no one had ever told her she couldn't.

In the third drawer she tried, Anna found what she had been looking for. Among Florence's underwear and brassieres were a handful of bathing suits. Anything Anna had seen Florence wear in the days before she died was immediately discarded—a Jantzen molded-fit in a burnt-red color and a teal Zephyr with a black belt that cinched at the waist. She shuddered when she realized that the suit Florence had worn to the beach two Sundays ago was, like its wearer, undoubtedly gone forever.

At the back of the drawer was a plain black bathing suit that Anna didn't recognize. She held it up to get a better look at it. The wool was stretched, the cut not nearly so modern as the suits Florence had worn this summer. Would Stuart recognize it as belonging to Florence? Anna sincerely hoped not. She placed the suit on the dresser top and pulled her nightgown over her head. For a moment, she stood in front of the bureau's mirror, not moving, just studying her naked body.

She was not nearly so curvy as she'd been in high school. In the last year, there had been the worry over whether she would go to school, then the worry over whether she'd get a visa. Once her visa application had been approved and she knew she was really leaving Berlin and her family behind, it had been hard to eat much of anything, and during the six-day crossing from Hamburg, she'd been unable to hold down so much as a cracker. Even when she'd arrived safely in Atlantic City and Esther had begun spooning generous servings of noodle kugel onto her plate, Anna found it difficult to eat much. Now she blamed homesickness, and perhaps Florence's death, for the fact that she could count her own ribs. She reached for the suit, pulling the scratchy fabric up and over her hips and then her breasts until it snapped taut against her shoulders. When it was on, she stepped back to examine herself, trying to see as much of her body as the small mirror allowed. The suit cut into her thighs in an unbecoming way, but otherwise, Anna was pleased with the result. She moved her arms through the air in big circles, the way she'd seen Florence do before entering the water.

Somewhere in the apartment, Anna heard a small crash and then the creak of floorboards as Joseph or Esther moved to retrieve what Anna could imagine was a fallen book or a dropped shoe. Terrified that Esther would discover her wearing Florence's suit, Anna scooped her nightgown up off the floor, switched off the lamp, and dove for her bed. Under the cover of darkness and a thin bedsheet, she wriggled out of the suit and back into her nightgown. What would Anna say if Esther discovered the suit was missing? The poor woman hadn't set foot in the girls' room since Florence had died. Surely, she hadn't kept track of the bathing suits her younger daughter had carted back and forth between the house on Atlantic Avenue, the apartment, and Wellesley?

~

Anna was all nerves by the time she left for the Kentucky Avenue beach tent on Tuesday evening. She was nervous to get in the water, where she knew she'd have no control of her own body, but she was more nervous to approach a tent full of lifeguards she didn't know and ask for Stuart. What if the lifeguards couldn't understand her accent? Or worse, thought she was one of those silly girls who Florence had liked to make fun of—the ones who chased lifeguards up and down the beach. What if Stuart wasn't there? It was possible he'd changed his mind about the whole thing. She worried she'd been too forward asking for the lessons in the first place. Ever since Florence had drowned, she'd just felt so overwhelmed. Somehow, her inability to swim felt like an indicator that she was ill fit to be here at all. If, at any point, the ocean might swallow her up, what would the rest of this big and disorderly country do to her?

The beach was beginning to clear, and while the beach tent was full of guards hustling back and forth, it was easy to spot Stuart, who had to be half a head taller than most of the men on the Patrol and was definitely the most handsome.

"I've been keeping an eye out for you," he said as he stacked a bunch of oars against one of the walls of the tent.

"Am I late?"

"No, not at all."

He threw a final oar on the pile and shouted to someone inside the tent, "Bernie, I'm out of here."

Anna was surprised when Stuart started toward the Boardwalk and not the ocean. She hesitated to follow him, wondering if perhaps he was just retrieving something, but he called over his shoulder to her, "You coming?" so she hurried to catch up.

"Where are we going?" Anna asked as Stuart stopped at the base of the steps that led up to the Boardwalk to brush the sand from his feet.

"You can learn to swim in the ocean but it's easier to learn in a pool."

"Pool?"

"Sure," he said, gliding his feet, still sticky with sand, into a pair of old moccasins. "You'll save yourself being clobbered by waves, and I'll be able to see your stroke."

He stood then and took the stairs two at a time. Anna's sandals were full of sand but she felt self-conscious around Stuart and didn't want to keep him waiting while she removed them to shake the sand out.

As she walked up the stairs and across the Boardwalk, the sand sprayed from the toes of her sandals like confetti from a parade float.

Stuart led them to the doors of The Covington, almost directly across the Boardwalk from the beach tent, where a man in a purple jacket with gold buttons held the door open for them. "Evening, Mr. Williams," he said to Stuart.

"Evening, Henry."

"Do you come here often?" Anna asked, when they were through the door and making their way across the lobby, which was very grand.

Stuart gave her a funny look and let out a small laugh, "Not if I can help it."

Florence had said something about Stuart's father owning a hotel, but Anna had naively assumed she meant one of the little kosher hotels that lined Atlantic City's side streets. Well, maybe not kosher, but at least small. She had pictured a narrow, three-story building with perhaps a dozen rooms and an elderly hotel proprietor who spent his days pointing tourists toward the beach. Surely, this couldn't be the hotel Florence meant?

"They let you use the pool?"

"Sort of," said Stuart as he grabbed her arm and steered her toward the elevator.

"Second floor, Cy," he said to the bellhop, when the elevator doors opened and they stepped inside. This had to be his father's hotel, Anna decided. How else would Stuart know the name of the bellhop?

When the elevator doors opened on the second floor, Stuart gestured for Anna to get out. "Cy," he said as they stepped off the elevator, "I'm not here."

"Didn't see you," said the bellhop.

Anna saw a small sign that read ADMINISTRATIVE OFFICES but Stuart led her in the opposite direction, down a long, carpeted corridor, dotted with club chairs and cocktail tables. Long, heavy curtains hung in the windows, which was too bad because they obscured the view of the beach, on one side of the hotel, and a large Italianate terrace on the other. Halfway down the corridor, they came to several sets of French doors, each of which led out to the terrace. "After you," said Stuart, holding one of them open for her.

The terrace was lovely, nestled between the hotel's two tall towers like a precious gem. At its center was a large swimming pool, and surrounding the pool was a little cabana and an abundance of lounge chairs, potted plants, and statuary. On the far side of the pool, stairs led from the terrace down to a lawn of perfectly manicured grass, completely enclosed by a tall ironwork fence.

"It's hard to believe I'm still in Atlantic City," said Anna.

"It's a whole different world, all right."

Scattered around the terrace were the last of the day's bathers and a handful of people, already in their evening wear but committed to having a poolside cocktail before dinner.

"Are we allowed to be here?" Anna asked Stuart as they put their things down on a lounge chair in a quiet corner of the terrace.

"Is the pope Catholic?" said Stuart, which Anna tried her best to interpret before giving up. Sometimes American expressions made no sense at all.

Stuart slipped off his shoes, walked over to the swimming pool, and dove in. Anna worried he'd hit his head on the bottom of the pool, but he popped up smiling a moment later. "Come on in," he called to her.

Anna's hands shook as she went to unbutton her dress. Why ever had she thought swimming lessons would be a good idea? She was uncomfortable at the thought of standing before Stuart in nothing but a borrowed bathing suit, and she was terrified to get in the water. Surely it would have been less painful to avoid the ocean for the rest of her life. Anna pulled the dress down around her knees and stepped out of it, her back to Stuart. Then she took more care than necessary to fold the garment. When the dress was neatly put away and she'd shoved her hair into a cap, there was nothing left to do but turn around and make her way toward the pool. She kept her eyes on the pavement, not daring to make eye contact with Stuart.

"Are you nervous?" Stuart asked, forcing her to look up.

Anna let out an uncomfortable laugh. "Yes, quite."

At the edge of the pool, she crouched down and tried, as gracefully as she could, to sit. Her legs dangled in the water, which was colder than she'd imagined.

"It's only about three feet deep here. You can stand," he said, extending his hand to help her into the pool.

She had no choice but to grab it and slide off the pool's edge and into the cold water. "Oh!" she said, without meaning to. She shuddered as the water hit her skin.

"It's not bad, right?"

Once she got used to the temperature, the water actually did feel kind of nice. It was an odd sensation, to be standing in several feet of water, much different than soaking in the tub at the apartment.

"I'm only going to teach you one thing today."

"Oh?"

"Don't sound so disappointed," Stuart said, smiling at her. "You're going to learn to float. If you can float, you can swim."

Before Anna could say anything, Stuart fell backward and began to demonstrate. "See how my arms are extended and my chin's up. I keep my chest out, too."

Arms, chin, chest. It didn't look that hard.

"The trick with floating," said Stuart, righting himself, "is that you've got to relax. If you're not relaxed, you'll sink like—"

A rock? Florence? Anna could understand why he had abandoned the metaphor.

She grabbed hold of the pool's edge and attempted to dip her head and shoulders into the water.

"Not that way. Come out here," said Stuart. "I'll hold you up."

Anna moved toward Stuart, as if she were walking in slow motion. When she reached him, he placed his hand, gently, on the small of her back and coaxed her to lean backward until she was staring up at The Covington's roof line and the dusky sky that peeked out between the hotel's looming towers. She shot her arms out to the side and puffed up her chest but could do nothing about her clenched stomach muscles. The very idea that Anna might relax in this setting was laughable.

It was such a strange sensation, to feel the weight of her body resting in the palm of Stuart's open hand, like she was a small bird instead of a girl, already grown.

"Tilt your head back more," said Stuart, his voice garbled and far away. "Tilt your head until you can see nothing but sky."

Was it even possible to do so? Anna lifted her chin until the hotel's edifice disappeared from her peripheral vision and all she could see were clouds, turned pink by the sun as it sank beyond the Thorofare.

Anna didn't feel Stuart's hand against her back. Had he let go?

"Now breathe," she heard him call to her.

Only then did Anna realize she'd been holding her breath. She let the air out of her chest but as she did so, she could feel herself begin to sink. The sinking feeling made her panic, and her head slipped beneath the surface as she tried to feel for the floor of the pool with her feet. Almost immediately, Stuart grabbed her under an arm and pulled her up.

"Embarrassing," she sputtered when she'd wiped the water from her eyes.

"Why embarrassing?" Stuart asked with a grin. "No one's born knowing how to swim."

"I'm an adult, not a small child."

"Children have it easy. Adults always have a much harder time learning."

"Why is that?"

"Children believe they can swim, so they do," said Stuart. He reached out and grazed her wool-clad stomach with the tips of his fingers. "Adults carry around all of their fears right here." He touched her chin, briefly. "And here."

Anna blinked. She wanted to remind him that there were good reasons to be afraid but she worried she'd ruin the evening. Instead, she told him she'd try again.

They spent the next hour floating around The Covington's pool as it slowly emptied of people. As Anna grew more confident, Stuart removed his hand from her back, and eventually he started floating beside her, their outstretched arms and legs occasionally bumping into each other as they drifted from one side of the pool to the other. Anna liked knowing that Stuart was next to her without feeling compelled to speak to him. With the water in her ears muffling the sounds of the outside world, she could almost pretend she was back in Germany, and that the boy floating next to her would whisper, *Komm schon. Lass uns gehen*, when it was time to go.

By the time Stuart deemed Anna highly proficient at floating, it had gotten dark and the tips of her fingers had turned to prunes. A waiter, who was clearing away empty cocktail glasses and straightening wayward chaise lounges, warned them that the pool would be closing in a few minutes. Anna could tell Stuart was about to say something to him, when a middle-aged man in a three-piece suit walked out onto the terrace and straight toward them.

"Stuart, if you'd told me you were coming, I would have had something sent out." Anna thought she detected Stuart's shoulder muscles tighten.

"Anna, this is my father, John Williams. Father, this is Anna Epstein."

She made a move to get out of the pool—it felt improper to meet Stuart's father, or anyone for that matter, wearing nothing but a bathing suit—but Stuart grabbed her wrist and muttered, quietly, "Please stay."

She looked at her wrist and then at Stuart. "I'm pleased to meet you, Mr. Williams," she said.

"Ah, an accent. Germany, I presume?"

"Ja ich bin Deutscher," she said, trying her best to be charming.

"What brings you to Atlantic City?" Mr. Williams asked.

Anna was about to answer when Stuart spoke for her, offering up the curtest of explanations: "College."

Mr. Williams gave Stuart a warning look, so Anna added, "I start in the fall."

"No good schools in Germany?"

Again, Stuart jumped in. "Not if you're Jewish." Anna thought she detected a challenge, of sorts, in the tone of Stuart's voice. As if he was daring his father to say something. But Mr. Williams seemed perfectly reasonable and said only, "That's too bad."

By the time Stuart's father took his leave, a few minutes later, the evening's mood had changed. Stuart seemed quieter and less confident, and Anna had begun to shiver with cold.

"Let's get you dried off," said Stuart as he hoisted himself out of the pool and walked over to the little cabana, water streaming from his bathing suit, to grab two towels. Anna shimmied along the pool's edge to the ladder, hopeful that she could display more grace getting out of the pool than she'd exhibited getting into it.

"You seem angry with your father," she said as Stuart handed her a towel.

"I don't know if *angry* is the right word," Stuart said, towel-drying his hair. "Maybe frustrated."

Anna unfurled the towel and wrapped it around her torso.

"He's been wanting me to come work for him for years. Ever since I finished high school."

"In college even?"

"Didn't go."

Anna pulled her towel tighter and arched her eyebrows at him.

"You're surprised?"

Anna could feel the color rising in her face. "A little."

"At some point, I decided that if he wanted me to do something, it had to be the wrong thing."

"But *you* didn't want to go?"

Stuart shrugged.

"So why—"

"I got into Temple but it wasn't an Ivy, so he had a hard time hiding his disappointment."

Anna wasn't familiar with the term *Ivy*, and she hated to interrupt to ask.

"That was the same summer I started lifeguarding. I was making my own money and began to envision a life in which I wasn't beholden to a guy I could never please."

"He's really so unhappy?"

Stuart nodded his head at the hotel. "He wasn't content to own a hotel that my great-grandfather and grandfather had built. He had to tear it down and build the biggest hotel in Atlantic City."

"It's the biggest?"

"Not anymore," Stuart said, with a hint of amusement on his face. "The Traymore did a big addition the year after he reopened. Now we're the third biggest, soon to be the fourth."

"Maybe it's not so terrible," said Anna, who was trying to reconcile Stuart's stories with her own, albeit brief, impressions of his father. "That he wants the best for himself. And you."

"Maybe. If it didn't extend to all areas of his life." Stuart lifted his eyes to the sky, gesturing toward the top of The Covington's south tower. "There's a penthouse apartment up there, where he's installed a prettier, younger version of my mother."

Anna didn't know what to say. She could scarcely believe she was having this conversation at all. "Does your mother know?"

"Everyone does. My mother hasn't set foot inside the hotel in five years, maybe more. Can you imagine the two of them running into each other in the lobby? We've got a house in Ventnor but as soon as the weather warms up, Mother heads off to our summer cottage in Cape May."

"I'm sorry."

"Oh, don't be," said Stuart. "Every family has its issues. I offer my family's up to you only as explanation for why I'm such a pain in the ass."

～

Anna's least favorite part of learning to swim was sneaking back into the Adlers' apartment after Stuart dropped her off each evening. What she was doing wasn't wrong but she also knew that there was something tactless about taking up the same pastime as a beloved daughter, so recently drowned. She tried to imagine explaining her motivations to Esther and cringed at the thought.

"Where did you get off to?" a voice called from the kitchen as Anna tiptoed down the apartment's long hallway. Anna stopped in her tracks, squeezed her eyes shut for a long second, then allowed herself to move in the direction of Esther's voice. She found her polishing silver at the kitchen table.

There was no getting around the fact that Anna's hair was still wet. She tucked a loose strand behind her ear. "I was down at the beach for a little while." Not a complete lie.

"You went swimming?" said Esther, not looking up from the tarnished serving spoon she worked between her hands with a rag.

"Just got my hair wet."

Esther let out an audible humph and Anna wondered how much she suspected. By now, Anna had had four swimming lessons. Stuart had taught her how to breathe, inhaling big mouthfuls of air that she slowly exhaled, through her mouth, underwater. He'd insisted that she practice her breathing technique for an embarrassingly long time, first by dipping her face in the water and then by bobbing along the side of the pool. Anna cringed, imagining what the hotel's paying guests must think of her—a grown woman who could spend a half hour bouncing in and out of the water like a metal spring. Eventually Stuart had taught her to push off from the side of the pool and glide along the top of the water with her arms positioned above her head, and most recently, he'd added a scissor kick to the enterprise. Anna was meant to push off the wall, glide until her body lost its momentum, and then continue to kick until she had to come up for air. She grew mildly annoyed when Stuart kept telling her the same thing—that she needed to kick her legs harder if she wanted to keep them anywhere near the surface of the water. But she forgave him because he also promised her that, with time and practice, she'd continue to improve.

"Do you need help?" Anna asked, with a nod toward the neat stacks of silverware Esther hadn't yet gotten to. She prayed the answer was no, could think of nothing worse than having to pull out a chair, sit, and make polite conversation as Florence's wet bathing suit soaked through her dress.

Esther shook her head, stared at the spoon in her hands forlornly, as if the reflection the shallow bowl of the spoon offered her were one she didn't recognize. Anna felt an urge to rest a hand on Esther's shoulder, to tell her the silver could wait, that maybe she was pushing herself too hard. But instead she said a quiet good night and slunk off to her bedroom, where she wasted no time removing her dress, peeling off the wet bathing suit underneath, and hanging it from the bleed valve on the backside of the radiator, where Esther was unlikely to find it if she went looking.

~

Just as Anna did not feel she had the right to be homesick, when her parents and Joseph had sacrificed so much for her to come to America, she also did not feel she had the right to mourn Florence's death. She could help with Gussie, taking her on outings to Steel Pier or the Inlet. She could make simple meals on the afternoons when Esther looked too far away to slice a tomato, much less make sandwiches. She could run books and magazines over to the hospital for Fannie. In doing those things, she liked to believe that she was acknowledging that Florence's death had meant something to her.

The truth was that Florence's death had meant a great deal to Anna. More than anyone else in the Adler family, Florence had seemed attuned to Anna's deep unhappiness. Immediately, she'd begun suggesting outings to Anna. The outings were never presented as options—more like commands. "Come with me to White Tower. I'm dying for a hamburger," she'd said on the afternoon of her arrival, after she'd greeted her parents and put her things away. It was Florence who had given Anna her first proper tour of Absecon Island. She'd pointed out all of her favorite spots—Absecon Lighthouse, which sat at the northern tip of the island, and the Italianate mansion with the funny address—One Atlantic Ocean—that perched at the end of Million Dollar Pier. Both, Florence said, served as guideposts when she was out on the open water. Anna learned where to get the best fried oysters and the tastiest egg sandwich, and since she enjoyed being told these things, she didn't dare admit that she'd never dream of spending so much as a nickel on a sandwich she could just as easily make at home.

Florence's attentions went a long way toward pulling Anna out of her melancholy but they didn't cure her, by any means. She still missed her parents fiercely and worried about them constantly. The night before Florence died, the two girls had returned home from the pictures to find a letter from Anna's mother on the dresser in the apartment's entryway. Anna had grabbed it, torn it open, and begun reading it on the spot, while Florence summarized the plot of *Little Miss Marker* to Joseph, who sat in the living room reading.

"Anything interesting?" Joseph had asked, over the hum of his daughter's monologue.

"Didn't you think the little girl in the film was brilliant?" said Florence. "Mark my words, she's going to be a big star."

Anna ignored her and read a small excerpt of the letter aloud, translating as she went, "A new statute has just come out of the Reichsregierung. The Nazis are levying a special tax on Jewish émigrés, equal to twenty-five percent of our capital." Florence stopped talking.

"She goes on," said Anna. "'Considering the other seventy-five percent of our money is already earmarked for the Sperrkonto, this is very bad news indeed.'"

"What's the Sperrkonto?" asked Florence.

"A crime is what it is," said Joseph. "The Nazis are telling Jews that, if they want to emigrate, they can only take two hundred Reichsmarks with them. Everything else, minus the taxes, goes into a special state-owned bank account, which they can tap if and only if they return to Germany."

"They can't do that!" Florence said, indignant.

"Unfortunately," said Joseph, "very few people are telling Hitler 'no' these days."

"So, they'll have to start over here? With nothing?" Florence had barely gotten the question out before she spit out a solution. "You'll help, won't you, Father?"

"Of course I'll help. But it's not so straightforward. They need that capital to prove they won't be a drain on the U.S. economy. It's a requirement for getting a visa."

"It's a paradox," said Florence.

"Exactly."

Anna didn't know what the word for *paradox* was in German and wondered if she should interrupt to ask. The letter shook in her hands. "You're sweet. Both of you. But I think I'm going to go to bed."

"Of course," said Joseph. "We can talk more tomorrow. Remember, Anna—this isn't a setback. Not yet."

"I know." She could feel her voice beginning to break. "It's just a lot. To take in."

"Get some sleep."

She folded the letter and made her way out of the room.

"Anna," Joseph called, when she had already disappeared around the corner and down the hall. She stopped, retraced her steps, hovered in the living room's doorway. "Your parents are not so old they can't start again. None of us ever are."

Anna dared not cry in front of Joseph. So, when she felt her chin begin to tremble, she pressed her lips together—tight—and tried her best to nod her head believingly.

In the bedroom, she kept the lights off, crawled into bed with her clothes on, and wept. After several minutes, the door creaked open and shut and the springs of the bed next to hers groaned.

"Anna?" Florence asked. "You all right?"

She tried to say yes but her words dissolved on her lips. It was as though this setback had released a torrent in her, and now she was crying for all sorts of reasons that had both nothing and everything to do with the content of her mother's letter. She cried because Esther had barely spoken two words to her since her arrival and because she wasn't in a university lecture hall in Berlin and because she was unlikely to see her school friends for years, if ever again. She cried because she missed the way her mother twisted her hair out of her face and the way the tobacco in her father's cigarettes smelled when he rolled them at their kitchen table. And she cried for Germany. How was it possible to both pine for and resent a place so much at the same time?

"Do you think it's so unlikely the visa application will be approved? Even with everything Pop's working on?" Florence asked.

Anna shook her head, a signal she wasn't sure Florence would be able to interpret with one side of her face buried in her pillow.

The springs under her own mattress rasped, the mattress bending to absorb the weight of a second person. Florence had moved to the edge of Anna's bed and begun repeating a soft "shhhhh." She stroked Anna's hair, and Anna let out a whimper. The gesture reminded Anna of all the times her mother had tucked her into bed and soothed her to sleep. When Anna's shoulders continued to heave, Florence lay down beside her in the dark, took hold of her hand, and waited.

Anna could feel Florence studying her in the dark, and eventually, that sensation—of being carefully considered—did calm her. Her convulsions became shudders and her sobs hiccups. She opened one eye and then the other, and was able to make out Florence's features, so close that she couldn't focus on them. Even the sharp line of her nose and the arch of her eyebrow blurred. Anna pulled back several inches so that she could view Florence properly.

Florence moved to brush a tear from Anna's cheek, running her thumb along her cheekbone. Was it possible that, in only three months of living among strangers, Anna had forgotten what it felt like to be touched? Florence lifted her head off the pillow and stared at her as if she were awaiting the response to a question Anna hadn't heard her ask. She leaned forward and kissed the spot on Anna's cheek where the tear, fat with anticipation, had sat so recently. Anna held her breath as Florence scattered several small kisses across her cheek, like tiny seeds that might take root and grow into something sturdy. Florence brushed her lips against the corner of Anna's mouth and pulled back slightly, as if watching for some signal. Did Anna want this? It was hard to know anymore. Without giving herself any more time to think, Anna lifted her head, ever so slightly, from the pillow and let Florence's mouth, warm and inquisitive, absorb her heartache.

July 1934

Gussie

When Gussie pressed her ear to the bathroom door, she thought she could hear her grandmother crying. The noise sounded a bit like the call of a baby fox, or at least what Gussie imagined a baby fox might sound like. For a moment, Gussie allowed herself to imagine a small woodland creature, skating across the hexagonal tile floor and making its home among her grandmother's bath salts and her grandfather's foot powder. Both the existence of a baby fox in the bathroom and the idea that her grandmother might be crying seemed equally preposterous.

Gussie turned the glass doorknob and slowly pushed open the door. The bathroom had filled with steam, and it took Gussie a moment to locate her grandmother, who was lying in the big claw-foot tub. When Esther saw Gussie, she sniffed and wiped her eyes with the heels of her hands.

"Are you sad about Florence?" Gussie asked in a small voice.

Esther contorted her mouth into something that resembled a smile but didn't make her eyes squint. "Yes, very."

It was difficult not to stare at her grandmother's breasts, which bobbed along the surface of the water, big and floppy with nipples the size and color of gingersnap cookies. Gussie wondered if her own chest would ever develop to such a degree. The thought of carrying something so large around with her, everywhere she went, was a terrifying prospect. When Esther noticed Gussie studying her chest, she shifted in the tub and submerged the buoys beneath the cloudy bathwater.

"Grab the stool over there," Esther said. "You can keep me company while I finish up."

Next to the commode was a small three-legged stool that Esther sat on when she gave Gussie baths. Gussie picked it up and positioned it close to the tub. She liked it when her grandmother took baths because it was easy to get and keep her full attention. Now, more than usual, she had questions she needed answered.

"What happens to people when they die?" Gussie asked when she was a few minutes into her vigil.

Her grandmother seemed startled by the question. After several seconds passed, she whispered, "Oh, darling. I wish I knew."

"Do we go to heaven?"

Her grandmother cleared her throat. "It's a good question, but Jews believe it's not the most important question."

"What is the most important question?"

"Whether you've been a good person. Done good things for other people."

"Florence used to take me for pickles on Heinz Pier, which was a very good thing."

Her grandmother's eyes grew wet again. "Yes," was all she said before she slipped farther down into the tub, allowing her ears to sink below the waterline. Her grandmother's hair looked darker when it was wet, and Gussie liked the way it moved in the water.

"Nana," said Gussie, trying to be heard through the water. "Nana."

"Hmm?"

"What about Hyram? He didn't have a chance to do good things." At the mention of Hyram's name, her grandmother surfaced, tilting her head to clear her ears. Gussie repeated her question.

"Babies are always doing good things. Hyram made your parents happy and you happy. That's enough."

Had Hyram made Gussie happy? She wasn't so sure.

"Can I shampoo your hair?" Gussie asked.

"I've already shampooed it but I'll take a little crème rinse."

Gussie's heart fluttered. Nothing thrilled her more than getting the chance to do things she wasn't normally allowed to do, and washing her grandmother's hair fell squarely in that category. Esther sat up in the tub, water streaming from her head and shoulders, and Gussie grabbed the glass bottle of Breck from the little shelf that sat nearby.

She untwisted the cap and concentrated on pouring a modest dollop of the concoction into her hand. The crème felt cool in her palm and smelled of coconut. She rubbed it between her hands before working it through her grandmother's hair, which was surprisingly long when wet.

"My mother doesn't use crème rinse."

"Your mother has such lovely hair, she probably doesn't need to."

Gussie pulled her fingers through her grandmother's hair, working quietly for several minutes. She was particularly careful when she got to the tangled pieces, which Gussie knew, from personal experience, could make a person yelp.

"Would you like me to take you to see your mother?" Esther asked.

It had been weeks since Gussie had been to the hospital. Her grandmother said it was because children weren't often allowed on the maternity ward, and her father said it was because they'd all been so busy, but Gussie knew the real reason was because no one trusted her to keep a secret.

This frustrated Gussie. Even before her induction into the Florence Adler Swims Forever Society, she had been extremely good at keeping secrets. She never told anyone when her parents argued in their bedroom at night or when her father muttered not-nice things about her grandparents under his breath. On the days when her mother was too sad to get off the sofa, Gussie never let on to her grandmother. She hadn't breathed a word about Anna borrowing Florence's bathing suit, even after Gussie went looking for it and found it damp and draped behind the radiator. And, most important of all, Gussie had never told a living soul about her own plan to marry Stuart.

"Remember, if we went, you wouldn't be able to say a word about Florence," warned Esther as she stepped out of the tub and toweled herself off.

Gussie trailed Esther into her bedroom, uttering promises as she went. The way her grandmother had talked, she assumed they'd go to the hospital as soon as Esther had put on a fresh dress; however, after Gussie watched her remove a girdle from a drawer, consider it briefly, then put it back in its place, she began to second-guess herself. When

Esther slipped on a housedress, Gussie knew her grandmother had no intention of leaving the apartment.

"What about the hospital?"

"Please don't whine."

Gussie rephrased the question and asked it in a falsetto: "Nana, are we going to go to the hospital now?"

"I told you I'd take you, but not today."

"When?"

"Soon."

~

Gussie banged around the apartment loudly for the next hour. During that time, she managed to knock over the hatstand in the front hall and spill half her grandmother's lavender oil down the bathroom sink. Both accidents, of course. Then she refused to eat lunch, despite the fact that her grandmother was serving tuna fish sandwiches, which were a particular favorite of Gussie's. When Esther had had enough, she sent Gussie to her room and told her to stay there until she could figure out how to be more pleasant. Gussie didn't dare bellow as she stomped off to the sun porch but she did make sure she slammed the door with plenty of umph.

It was hard to be pleasant when so much was going wrong. Gussie swiped some of the treasures on her windowsill to the floor but she was careful to avoid upsetting the tiny ceramic animals that had come in the Cracker Jack boxes her grandfather kept leaving on her bed. There was an otter and a pig and a seal that balanced a ball on his nose. When she was satisfied with the mess, she threw herself onto the bed, grabbed hold of her Raggedy Ann doll, and studied the tiny wormholes in the beadboard ceiling.

After a half hour or so, there was a light knock on the door.

"Let's go for a walk," Anna said, peeking her head around the door.

Gussie was annoyed. People were always deciding what she should be doing.

"I don't want to go for a walk. I want to go to the hospital."

"Well, your grandmother wants you to go for a walk. She gave me some money and said we should go to the Pier to see the parakeets." Anna jingled the coins in her hand, as evidence. When Gussie didn't make a move, Anna said, "You probably don't care for them. Or hot dogs?"

Gussie didn't say anything, just went back to staring at the ceiling. For a dime, the parakeets at Steel Pier would hop up onto a stick, grab a fortune out of a fancy bird-sized castle, and saunter down a miniature boardwalk to deliver it. The offer was tempting but not nearly so tempting if she had to go with Anna.

Anna patted the edge of the door and made like she was about to close it. "I'll go tell her you're not interested."

Gussie sat up in bed. "Wait!"

～

It was National Children's Week in Atlantic City and everywhere hotels, restaurants, and stores had posted signs, welcoming children to the resort and advertising specials to their parents. There was a children's parade and a sing-along on the beach and, yesterday, there had been a big fireworks spectacular for the Fourth of July. At the end of the week, one lucky kid was going to be named mayor of Atlantic City for a day. Gussie had begged her grandmother to let her register, particularly after she had spotted the spiffy badges all the children wore on their collars, but Esther explained that the program was only for children from out of town whose parents were staying in cooperating hotels.

Even without a badge, Gussie had to admit—only to herself, definitely not to Anna—that the day had turned around. She and Anna caught the second half of the sing-along, and when they stopped at a hot dog stand on the Boardwalk, the cashier gave Gussie a special Children's Week button with their change. She didn't and wouldn't have asked Anna to help her pin the button to her lapel but Anna did it anyway.

"Let's go in there," Gussie said to Anna, her mouth stuffed with hot dog, as they walked past Couney's Premature Baby Exhibit, across from Million Dollar Pier.

Anna looked at the hand-lettered sign on the window and at the tiny baby asleep in a little glass box in the window display. A poster, affixed to the door, claimed ONCE SEEN, NEVER FORGOTTEN."

"You have to pay a fee to go in," said Anna, counting the change in her hand. "You won't have enough money to see the parakeets, too."

"I know," said Gussie, already pulling open the exhibit's heavy glass door. "I've seen the parakeets a hundred times. Besides, they always tell girls the same thing."

"What's that?"

"You will have a large family."

"What do they tell the boys?"

"Oh, you know. All the normal things. That they'll be successful and earn tons of money and go on lots of adventures."

Anna let out a small noise and helped her with the door, and as Gussie walked through it, she felt an odd surge of satisfaction, as if she had won something big and important.

Inside was a long room with a worn wooden floor, whitewashed walls, and a ceiling stenciled with green vines. A line of seven incubators, small glass boxes that sat on tall metal stands, lined one wall, and between each one sat a potted palm tree, as if the nurses, who walked back and forth in fitted white dresses and funny hats, were trying to convince the babies that they were living on a tropical island instead of in a Boardwalk amusement.

"The next lecture begins at three o'clock," said an attendant, who exchanged the coins Anna handed her for a receipt and a leaflet.

A metal handrail prevented visitors from getting too close to the babies, which was unfortunate, as far as Gussie was concerned. She grabbed hold of the railing and hoisted herself into the air, leaning her body as far over the railing as she dared. From that vantage point, it was easier to read the little signs that sat propped above each incubator.

"Gussie, get down."

"I'm reading the incubator charts."

"You can read them with your feet on the ground."

That was not true. And moreover, Gussie did not like it when Anna told her what to do. She thought about reminding Anna that she was not her mother but she had a feeling that Anna would march her home if she did. Instead she let out a loud sigh, loud enough, she hoped, to let Anna know she was annoyed, before slowly lowering her feet to the floor.

The signs provided visitors with the babies' names and birth dates, along with some numbers and symbols that Gussie didn't bother trying to interpret. She loved reading the baby's names, some of which were so silly that they had to have been made up. Who named a child, even one who was likely to die, Marigold? Perhaps Marigold's family had been too nervous to name her themselves? Or was it possible that Marigold wasn't the baby's real name and that her actual name was Mary or Margaret?

"Hyram was in that one, over there," Gussie said, pointing to an incubator in the corner. "I think."

"I didn't know Hyram was here. I wouldn't have—"

"Let me come?"

Anna looked uncomfortable. "You visited him here?"

Gussie nodded, cautious about giving too much away.

"With your parents?"

Gussie didn't say a word. She just trailed over to the corner unit where a baby no bigger than a squash lay sleeping, bundled in white blankets. Sometimes Anna was quite daft. Of course, Gussie's parents wouldn't have brought her here. It had been Florence who had asked if she wanted to go, Florence who had understood how frustrating it was to be told she had a baby brother she could not see.

He had been so tiny, smaller than many of the other incubator babies. His head had looked large, in proportion to the rest of him, and his body was covered in downy white hair that Florence had promised would disappear as he grew. His arms and legs were long and thin, nothing like the chubby appendages Gussie saw on the babies in the Easter Parade. Mostly, she was surprised by how red he was.

"He looks like a boiled shrimp," she had told her aunt, who twisted her mouth into a small frown.

On that visit, Florence had encouraged her to slip beneath the railing to get a better look at her baby brother. She'd stood close to the incubator, her fingers on the glass.

"He can hear you," Florence said. "Tell him anything you want him to know."

Gussie thought for a minute. What *did* she want Hyram to know?

While she stood there, trying to think of something to say, a pair of tourists walked up beside Florence. It was easy to see they were from out of town. People from offshore always carried more bags than necessary and had a habit of wearing their beach shoes into the shops.

"This one can't have a prayer of making it," the man remarked to his wife.

Gussie turned around to get a better look at him, taking in his bulging shirt buttons and the camera that hung around his neck. What did it mean to have a prayer?

"Hey, mister," said Florence, tapping the man on the arm. "This little girl is his sister, and your comments aren't very helpful—or kind."

The man just blinked at Florence, too surprised to speak, while his wife apologized profusely and ushered him quickly toward the door. Once it swung shut behind them, Florence urged Gussie to continue.

She bit her bottom lip, thinking hard, before she finally said, "Hi, Hyram, it's Gussie—your sister. It's nice to meet you."

Had Florence known Hyram would die when she took Gussie to see him? Was that, perhaps, why she'd taken her? Gussie couldn't be sure.

Anna touched Gussie's shoulder, and Gussie reminded herself that the baby in the incubator in front of her was not Hyram. He was some other baby—the placard said his name was George. It was possible that George had his own big sister, who anxiously wondered if she'd ever meet him.

Anna began to play with Gussie's hair, and Gussie pulled away from her instinctively. Anna was not allowed to pretend to be Florence. Not now and not ever.

"Let's go, Gus," said Anna. "I'm afraid this might not have been a good idea."

Florence had been so good at knowing what Gussie needed, even when the thing she needed was as big and scary as visiting her baby brother at Couney's. But Anna wasn't like that. She was afraid of everything and everyone. Of course, she'd be afraid of this place and what Esther would think if she discovered they had come.

~

Gussie's father rarely left the plant during the day, which is why, as she and Anna walked back to the apartment, it was such a surprise to see him sitting in the window of Kornblau's, eating a corned beef sandwich as if it were a Saturday afternoon.

Gussie tapped on the glass and waved, then did a little dance and rushed toward the restaurant's entrance. Anna called for her to wait but Gussie ignored her. She hadn't seen her father in days.

The entrance of Kornblau's was crowded with parties waiting for tables. Gussie had to weave through a sea of people, offering apologies as she ducked under elbows to get to her father's table, which was positioned in the far corner of the dining room, near the window.

Gussie loved surprises. When she had tapped on the glass, her father had looked so surprised to see her. His eyebrows had moved up on his face, and he'd put his sandwich down before motioning her inside. Had he motioned her inside? It didn't matter. Either way, he was very, very surprised.

"Father!" she said, when she'd finally arrived in front of his table. She went to give him a hug but he was seated at a booth, and it was tricky to maneuver around the table, which was bolted to the floor. She banged her hip bone on the lip of the table, and the pain made her squeeze her eyes shut.

"Hey, Gus-Gus," he said into her hair. "What are you doing here?"

She opened her eyes and realized he was sitting across from a man she didn't know.

"Vic, this is my daughter, Gussie. Gussie, this is Mr. Barnes."

"Nice to meet you, Gussie."

Gussie didn't know what to say. She just nodded her head and looked around for Anna, who was slowly making her way through the crowded restaurant. It would be better when she arrived and could help fill the strange silence.

"Isaac," Anna said, when she finally caught up with Gussie.

"Anna, this is Vic Barnes. Anna is a friend of the family's."

Anna extended her hand and Mr. Barnes took it. "Pleased to meet you." Then she turned back to Isaac. "We're sorry to have interrupted."

Gussie inched closer to her father, sure that Anna was going to suggest they leave. She could smell his shaving cream and the tonic he put in his hair. His visits to the apartment had grown less and less frequent, and she knew it might be several more days before she saw him again.

"You're not interrupting," said Mr. Barnes, who hadn't yet managed to let go of Anna's hand. Mr. Barnes reminded Gussie of a badger, or maybe an otter. He had a long neck and a skinny face, with a mustache that obscured his lips entirely. Gussie didn't like the way he leered at Anna and was relieved when Anna pulled her hand free and used it to smooth her skirt.

"Gussie, we should be getting back," Anna said in a singsong voice that was much cheerier than the one she normally used.

"Isaac, you mentioned the land in Florida but you failed to mention this lovely asset."

What was Mr. Barnes talking about? Gussie hated it when adults spoke in code. Gussie's father cleared his throat, and Anna, quick as a sand crab, grabbed Gussie by the hand and yanked her out of the booth and to her feet.

"Owww—"

Before Gussie had time to issue any more exclamations, Anna said, "We'll let you get back to your conversation. Gussie just wanted to say hello. Nice to meet you, Mr. Barnes. Isaac, give my regards to Fannie."

"When are you coming over?" Gussie thought to shout at her father as Anna began dragging her back the way they had come.

Gussie didn't know why but by the time Anna had pulled her all the way out of the restaurant and onto Pacific Avenue, she was crying. It wasn't nice of Anna to force her to leave so abruptly. And it wasn't like her father not to give her a big hug hello. Ever since Florence had died, no—ever since her mother had gone into the hospital, no—ever since Anna had come to stay with her grandparents, everyone had been acting so strangely.

"I want my mother," she whispered as tears welled in her eyes and rolled down her cheeks. Anna offered her a handkerchief and waited patiently for her to make use of it. The handkerchief had pale pink flowers at the corners and a scalloped edge, and in one corner, it was initialed *AE*. Gussie wondered if Anna's mother had made it for her, and then asked as much. Anna nodded her head, yes.

"May I keep it?" Gussie asked, peering up at Anna, who looked far less sure of herself, considering the request, than she'd looked just a few minutes earlier, storming out of Kornblau's. Gussie didn't know why she wanted the handkerchief so much. She just knew that if her own mother had stitched her anything half as pretty, Gussie would have carried it around in her pocket like a kiss.

Esther

Esther had grown to hate the mornings, particularly those first few moments of consciousness, when she did not yet recall that her younger daughter was gone. For several seconds upon waking, her eyes remained shut tight, the images from her dreams still etched upon the back of her eyelids. When she opened them, she found the familiar artifacts of her bedroom—the white iron bedframe, the cherry dresser, the rocking chair by the window—all unchanged. Sometimes, for Esther to recall that Florence was dead, she had to first remember that tucked away in a dresser drawer were the trinkets Fannie and Florence had made for her in school—everything held together with paste—or that Joseph had purchased the rocking chair so that she could nurse her babies. The remembering was the worst part of her day, and she wondered how many days would have to pass before she felt Florence's death in her bones, the way she knew her own name or the contours of her husband's face, and could no longer be surprised by it.

It was always a little later—after she'd pushed the sheets off her sticky skin but before her bare feet touched the floor—that Esther remembered she was keeping the truth from Fannie. She lay in bed, listening to the quiet whir of the oscillating fan on her dresser and making mental lists of (1) people who knew Florence was dead and (2) people who were at risk of finding out.

On the first list there was herself and Joseph, Isaac, Gussie, Anna, Stuart, the lifeguards and bystanders who'd been on the beach that day, Abe Roth and his staff, Rabbi Levy, the members of the Chevra Kadisha, Samuel Brody, Superintendent McLoughlin, Dr. Rosenthal, and the nurses whom he'd pulled into his confidence. Esther didn't like how many people were on the list but she took some comfort in knowing that, with the exception of the lifeguards and bystanders on the beach, she could identify most of them by name.

It was the second list that caused her the most anxiety. Esther was certain Joseph hadn't told anyone, but she couldn't be sure about anyone else. How many people had Samuel had to talk to in order to keep Florence's name out of the paper? Who had been sitting around the dinner tables of the women of the Chevra Kadisha when they had returned home to cold suppers? It was possible that Isaac had told acquaintances and even perfect strangers about Florence's death. She pictured him doing it not out of sorrow but out of spite. And then there was Gussie, whom she had kept very tight tabs on but who was impossible to truly control.

Whether Esther liked it or not, she was going to have to allow Gussie to visit Fannie in the hospital. There was no more getting around it. Gussie asked for her mother daily, and Fannie for Gussie. Esther had lied to Fannie about Gussie's whereabouts on so many different visits that she'd begun making notes for herself on a small slip of paper she kept tucked in the interior pocket of her handbag. She found that if she reviewed the notes before her visits, it was easier to keep her story straight. After her visits—usually in the lobby of the hospital—she retrieved the slip of paper and a pen from her handbag and made any necessary additions.

Initially, Esther had said Gussie had caught a summer cold and that she didn't want Fannie, or any of the babies on the ward, to catch it. When Isaac had taken Gussie to see his father, she'd extended that trip, with Isaac's blessing, by several days. She felt guilty telling Fannie that Gussie was busy playing with friends from school, considering that Esther had actually forbidden such activity on account of the risk it posed, but she had used the excuse anyway—on several occasions now. And the other day, she had felt particularly desperate and explained Gussie's absence by saying that she'd recently enrolled in baton-twirling lessons. The ease with which such an outrageous lie slipped off Esther's tongue frightened her. When this was all behind her, Esther wondered if she'd even remember what was real.

The problem, which Esther could have foreseen if she'd considered the situation more carefully, was that she now had to prepare Gussie to answer questions on a wide range of topics instead of just one. Fannie might ask Gussie about Florence, but she might also ask about her health, her recent trip to Alliance, her friends, or—heaven forbid—her newfound talent for twirling.

Through the bedroom door, Esther could hear the scraping sound of a chair being dragged across the kitchen floor. She pictured Gussie, still in her nightgown, reaching for the plates Esther kept in the drainboard above the sink. A moment later, she heard the lid of the bread bin bang open. Gussie was such a capable girl, always had been. Esther listened for the sound of the Hoosier drawer opening, the clang of silverware. Could Gussie be coached? What choice did Esther have other than to believe that she could?

Esther swung her feet to the floor and reached for her dressing gown. Maybe she'd make oatmeal for the two of them, and Anna, if she was up. Gussie liked hers garnished with a big pat of butter and plenty of brown sugar but Esther could do better than that. She'd slice the fat, ripe peaches she had bought at Wagenheim's two days ago. This morning called for something extra sweet.

∼

Gussie skipped up the steps of the hospital's Ohio Avenue entrance and would have skidded across the lobby's floor, on her way to the stairs, had Esther not grabbed her by the collar of her sundress and pointed at a chair.

"Sit," Esther said.

"Nana, I know."

"None of that. Sit."

Gussie rolled her eyes, a habit that was new and also completely infuriating.

"Let's go over everything one more time."

"Give mother a kiss, tell her I've missed her. Don't say anything else."

"You may, of course, speak to your mother. But if she asks you about Florence—"

"Don't tell her she's dead."

Esther stared at her granddaughter. Children could be so mean. She remembered thinking so when she was raising her own girls. They were often too honest, the words they chose too blunt. Their worlds were big and bold and colorful but they were not yet able to distinguish that colors had values, that words had nuance. They described the people around them as old or young, ugly or beautiful, fat or thin, never recognizing that there were kinder, gentler, more forgiving words that lay in between. Sometimes, when Gussie talked about Florence's death, so matter-of-factly, Esther couldn't help but feel like she'd been cut open, left exposed.

"Right, don't tell her she's—gone. If she asks, we'll say she's very busy getting ready for her trip to France. She's swimming a lot. Busy shopping."

"We can say she swam to New York!"

"No, certainly not. Don't make up anything."

"But it's all made up."

"Don't be smart," warned Esther, already second-guessing her decision to bring Gussie along. "It's best if you don't say anything about Florence. If your mother asks about her, just let me answer."

Was she really going to let Gussie into that hospital room? Fannie's due date was still more than a month away. If the baby was born now, there could be no guarantees. Not that there ever were with these matters.

"And remember," said Esther, wagging a finger at Gussie, "if I tell you to go wait in the hallway, you go with no—"

"Mrs. Adler?"

Esther whipped her head around to find Fannie's doctor standing no more than five feet behind her.

"Dr. Rosenthal," she said, standing up straight. The man was too attractive to be single but she hadn't heard the first thing about a wife. It was a wonder any of the nurses on the maternity ward got anything done.

"I thought that was you."

It was almost ten o'clock in the morning. By now, he must have completed his rounds. "How's Fannie today?"

"May I speak to you privately?"

Esther's breath caught in her chest. She nodded, held out a hand to indicate that Gussie should stay where she was, and followed the doctor toward the far corner of the lobby, out of her granddaughter's earshot. "Is everything all right?"

"Fannie's blood pressure is a little higher than we'd like it to be."

"Higher than normal?"

"Not so much that we're panicking. It's quite common for it to creep up in the late stages of pregnancy. But we're watching it carefully."

"And if it doesn't change?"

"It could be an indicator of more serious problems."

"Meaning?"

"The baby would need to come out," he said, quietly.

Esther studied the floor tiles, trying to make sense of what he'd just said.

"I wondered—she still hasn't been told about her sister, correct?"

"Correct."

"I didn't think so, and I obviously wasn't going to ask her. But I did wonder if the two things might be related."

Esther needed to sit down. She looked around for a chair but they were all out of arm's reach. Was Dr. Rosenthal suggesting that Fannie might have learned of her sister's death but kept the news to herself? In all of Esther's plotting, she had never considered that possibility. She had always imagined that, if Fannie inadvertently learned of Florence's drowning, the first phone call she'd place would be to her mother. That Esther would get the chance to explain.

"Do *you* think she knows?" Esther asked.

"I don't have any indication that she does," said Dr. Rosenthal. "I spoke with the superintendent and several of the nurses on the ward, and no one's noticed anything out of the ordinary. They said a few friends of Fannie's popped by yesterday afternoon, but everyone seemed to be in high spirits."

"Which friends?" Esther asked, but Dr. Rosenthal gave her a look that indicated he wasn't the keeper of Fannie's social calendar. "I'm sorry."

"You're fine."

"So, you still think there's a chance someone told her?"

"I think maybe I was just hopeful that there was an explanation for the high readings."

"Have you spoken with Isaac about any of this?"

Dr. Rosenthal shook his head. "We haven't seen him in several days."

Esther cocked her head to one side. What could be keeping Isaac from the hospital? Really, it was absurd. With no child to look after and a job that, by Joseph's account, he performed only adequately, what else did he have to do besides visit his bedridden wife?

"You must be just missing him," she said. "I think he visits directly after work."

"He must," said Dr. Rosenthal, who looked far from convinced.

Out of the corner of her eye, Esther noticed that Gussie was out of her chair and hopscotching her way across the hospital's lobby.

"Can we go up, Nana?" she asked, her voice very close to a whine. Esther abhorred whining.

"Going to see your mother now, are you?" Dr. Rosenthal asked, tussling Gussie's hair. She ducked out of his reach and hid behind Esther's skirt.

Dr. Rosenthal gave Esther a kind, if not slightly regretful, smile and began to move toward the stairs. When he was several feet away, he turned back.

"You know, Mrs. Adler, when Superintendent McLoughlin first presented this plan, I thought it all rather peculiar. Perhaps even cruel."

Esther narrowed her eyes at him. Hiding Florence's death from Fannie might be unconventional, but she'd never once thought of it as cruel.

"But Fannie's almost a month further along now, further than she made it with the last baby. So, who's to say?"

～

On the ward, several of the nurses greeted Esther by name.

"Good morning, Mrs. Adler."

"Morning, Mrs. Adler."

Dorothy, whom Esther had unfortunately come to know quite well, had taken it upon herself to establish more casual terms: "Morning, Mrs. A."

In Esther's opinion, Dorothy spent far too much time standing around and gossiping. Even when she was being useful—changing the sheets or giving Fannie a sponge bath—she was always so terribly slow that Esther fought the urge to yank the bedsheet or basin from her hand and do the task herself.

Esther nodded grimly at each of the nurses as she passed and tightened her grip on Gussie's hand. As they approached Fannie's room, she leaned down and hissed in Gussie's ear, "Remember. Not a word about Florence."

At the door, which was ajar, Esther paused, forced herself to rework her facial muscles into a more pleasant composition. She practiced a smile. Those were always difficult. Grins were more manageable. She might have stood in the corridor all day, putting off the inevitable, had Gussie not broken free and zipped into the room ahead of her. By the time Esther rounded the corner, the girl was already in her mother's embrace.

Fannie peppered Gussie with kisses, exclaiming how much she'd missed her between each breath.

"I've missed you, I've missed you, I've missed you, I've missed you!"

Esther stiffened. Mothers today were so much more demonstrative than those of Esther's generation had been. She wasn't sure what it got them, other than whining children.

She watched as Fannie made room for Gussie in the bed, patting the spot beside her. She folded her tall and lanky daughter under her arm like she was no bigger than a kitten.

"Where have you been, my sweet girl?" Fannie cooed. "Having all sorts of adventures without your mother?"

Gussie merely smiled and burrowed her head into Fannie's chest.

Fannie's stomach had grown rounder, her breasts larger, in the four weeks since Gussie had last seen her mother. Esther wondered what the girl made of it all. Did she remember that Fannie had looked like this once before? It was hard to know what Gussie recalled from her mother's last pregnancy.

"I brought you something," said Gussie as she unfolded a piece of blue construction paper she'd tucked away in a pocket. Esther had never seen it before, and her chest tightened as she watched her daughter purr over its unveiling.

"Oh my!" remarked Fannie, in an unusually high voice. Esther walked around the bed to get a look at her granddaughter's work.

Gussie had made a collage of babies, each one cut out from a magazine or newspaper. There were pictures of the Dionne quintuplets, a few babies that had been clipped from newspaper advertisements, and smack-dab in the middle of the collage was a photograph of the Lindbergh baby.

"Oh, Gussie," said Esther, unable to hide her disappointment. How had she missed this? Had she been paying so little attention to the girl?

"I *love* it," said Fannie. "How did you know I would?" She kissed the top of Gussie's head and handed Esther the collage. "Mother, will you put this on the dresser? Somewhere I can see it?"

Esther tucked Gussie's handiwork into the frame of the dresser's mirror, then nudged a table lamp a few inches to the left so that poor Little Lindy was partially obscured by the shade.

She turned back to the bed and tried to appreciate the scene in front of her—mother and child reunited—but found she couldn't concentrate. Her hands trembled, so she busied them tidying up Fannie's bedside table. The nurses never did a very good job keeping up with it.

"Was Isaac by yesterday?" Esther asked, as casually as she could, while she hung Fannie's robe, discarded in a nearby chair, in the wardrobe.

Even with her back to Fannie, she could feel her daughter's hesitation. "He popped by for lunch yesterday."

Fannie was lying, of course. Anna and Gussie had seen him eating at Kornblau's. Esther turned around and eyed Gussie, curious if she'd caught the discrepancy. If she had, she gave nothing away.

"And has your father been by to see you lots?" Fannie asked Gussie. It broke Esther's heart that she had to ask.

Gussie looked at Esther and shrugged her shoulders. The child was clearly terrified of saying the wrong thing.

"Oh certainly, Gussie always enjoys seeing him around the apartment," said Esther. Technically, that was not a lie.

"And how's our Channel swimmer?" Fannie lobbed.

"Very busy right now," said Esther. "Between practices and packing, we rarely see her." She didn't dare glance at Gussie.

"And she's still set to leave on the tenth?"

"Yes, the tenth."

"And does she plan on visiting me before she departs? Or has she washed her hands of her troublesome older sister entirely?"

"Fannie—"

"Mother—she hasn't been by in close to a month. It's outrageous."

Esther's confidence bloomed. Dr. Rosenthal was no doubt right about Fannie's high blood pressure, but he was wrong to suspect that Fannie knew about Florence's death. Never would she have been able to get those last words out if she knew the truth.

"Your father hasn't visited either," said Esther, grasping for a reasonable defense—and distraction. "You're not outraged with him?"

"We both know he'd sooner eat his own hat than visit a hospital."

It was true. Joseph wasn't the type to go anywhere near a hospital, and Fannie knew it as well as Esther did. How did men manage to get away with that? What if Esther hadn't been the type to make dinner in the evenings? They would all have starved.

"Your sister sends her love."

"Bullocks. She didn't even respond to the letter I sent her."

"Letter?"

"I wrote to her—almost a month ago."

"And sent it to the apartment?"

"Isaac delivered it."

"Maybe he misplaced it?" Esther suggested, as gently as she could.

She had always hated refereeing the girls' arguments but never more so than now, with one precious girl unable to defend herself and the other frightfully unaware of her own advantage. What Esther wouldn't have given for her daughters to have been close. When they were young, they had done all right together, despite the seven years that separated them. But something changed as they grew older. By the summer Fannie met and married Isaac, the girls might as well have been two planets orbiting different suns.

It was the same summer Gertrude Ederle traveled to Calais to swim the English Channel. The coverage was extensive, even with so little to report in the days leading up to the big swim. Both Florence and Esther had scrambled to read Joseph's paper when he was through with it; the two might as well have been reading about Greta Garbo or John Gilbert. Trying to predict the Channel's tides proved to be every bit as exciting as trying to figure out which movie stars were in town for premieres at the Warner Theatre, where they were staying, and whether someone from their party might pop in for a sweet bun at Adler's. Esther would tsk over Ederle's photographs as if she were the girl's matchmaker: "She really is a rather homely girl. How will she marry?" Florence, only twelve but already old enough to enjoy goading her mother, said slyly, "Maybe she doesn't want to."

Fannie rarely stuck her head into the living room, much less the newspaper Esther and Florence clutched between them. She had begun seeing Isaac, whom she'd met while working behind the counter at Adler's, and in recent weeks, Isaac had made enough trips to the bakery for challah bread that it would have been safe to assume he was saying the HaMotzi every night of the week and not just on Shabbos. Isaac had called at the apartment a handful of times, awkwardly sitting in the living room until Joseph—out of discomfort more than anything else—granted the couple permission to stroll the Boardwalk without a chaperone, provided Fannie was home by nine o'clock sharp.

Nearly six weeks to the day after their courtship began, Fannie arrived home from one such walk and announced that Isaac had asked her to marry him. Esther had long anticipated the engagement of her daughters and expected such news to leave her feeling euphoric. But instead, she found that Fannie's announcement discomfited her.

Isaac was six years older than Fannie but not so old for their age difference to matter. He was a quiet sort but Esther knew many good and quiet men. Isaac was poor but Esther reminded herself that Joseph had been poor when she had married him. They had built Adler's together, which had been half the adventure. No, there was something else—something more unsettling than Isaac's age or income or even his loquacity. She heard it in the tone of his voice. A belief that he was owed something. Esther did not think it unusual for a man to be dissatisfied with the circumstances into which he'd been born but she had no patience for a man who did not believe in the transformative powers of his own hard work.

There had been no good way for Esther to convey her concerns to Fannie without pushing her away. So, when Fannie had stood before Esther and Joseph in the living room, waiting anxiously to hear what her parents thought of the match, they had stuck to practical questions of common concern. Esther asked when the couple intended to marry, and Joseph wanted to know if Fannie planned to complete the second year of her secretarial degree. Florence took the opportunity to ask whether she should begin to call Isaac *brother*. "Isaac should suffice," said Esther, without taking her eyes off her older daughter. It was much later that night, after the girls had gone to bed, that Esther realized she'd failed to give Fannie her congratulations.

By the time Ederle was ready to enter the Channel waters, Fannie's wedding preparations were well under way. Joseph insisted they hold the ceremony, which would be a small affair, at Beth Kehillah. There was some conversation about a luncheon at The Breakers, but Esther decided a hotel reception would be ostentatious and potentially uncomfortable for Isaac since his family was not of means. She insisted that there was nothing the matter with holding the luncheon at home and that the gefilte fish they'd buy at Casel's was every bit as good as what they'd find on The Breakers' menu. Esther could tell Fannie was disappointed but she cheered considerably when Esther suggested that they take the train to Philadelphia to purchase Fannie's wedding dress at Wanamaker's.

Ederle landed on a small beach a few miles north of Dover, England, at approximately half-past nine on the night of August 6, and the wires lit up as scores of American journalists transmitted news of the accomplishment back to a country that had been collectively holding its breath. Florence had been glued to the radio all day, yelling updates from the living room as they came in. Eventually Esther stopped pretending to attend to her daily chores, found some socks that needed darning—usually a task she saved for the evenings—and joined her.

Europeans, asleep in their beds, had to wait until morning to learn that the Channel had been conquered by a woman but, in Atlantic City and elsewhere in the United States, Ederle's accomplishment made the evening radio programs.

When the news broke, Joseph was home but Fannie was out running errands. She arrived back at the apartment to find the family exuberant but gave them only the briefest of greetings before hurrying back to her bedroom to get ready for an evening out with Isaac. Esther watched Florence thump down the hallway after her: "Fannie! Trudy did it! She made it!" From where Esther sat on the sofa, she could hear her elder daughter reply with a brief, "Yes, I heard." Something about the emptiness of that response made Esther's chest begin to hurt.

Within two weeks, Fannie was married and had moved into Isaac's apartment. Esther told herself it couldn't be helped—the slow dissolution of the girls' relationship. Fannie was busy learning to make a home, and after she had Gussie, learning to be a good mother. Florence was years away from any of that. She was still young enough to love being at home with her parents, to ask for penny candy after dinner, and to treat the Ambassador Club swim tryouts like they were preliminaries for the Olympic Games. Esther had told herself that one day, when the girls were older, their age difference would matter less. Florence would get married and have children, and Fannie would be there to offer advice on the best way to burp a baby or remove a stain from a shirt collar.

Maybe, eventually, they would rediscover each other. She pictured two old women, walking the Boardwalk arm in arm. That they would never get the chance to come back to each other, to start again, was inconceivable to Esther, even now.

Gussie and this new baby would also be seven years apart in age. Was it an unlucky number? As Esther stood in a hospital room, watching her elder daughter seethe with resentment toward a sister who could neither make amends nor fight back, she prayed that Fannie would be able to knit her children's lives together more neatly than Esther had managed to.

"Have you been to the beach much?" Fannie asked Gussie, obviously trying to change the subject.

Gussie looked at Esther.

"Not much," Esther said. "It's so crowded this time of year."

"Anna goes," Gussie offered.

"To the beach?" Fannie asked.

"I suspect the girl's trying to teach herself to swim," said Esther. "She won't confirm it. Just lurks about."

"That's not true," said Gussie.

"What's not?" said Fannie.

"She doesn't lurk. And she's not teaching herself to swim."

"Then what's she doing?" asked Esther.

"*Stuart* is teaching her to swim."

Esther started to say something, then realized she didn't know what to say. Stuart? Really?

"Why wouldn't she just ask Florence to teach her?" Fannie asked Esther. "Are Stuart and she an item? Doesn't Stuart have a thing for Florence?"

Esther flushed. She could feel herself losing control of the conversation, of Gussie, of the secret.

"I couldn't say," said Esther, trying her best to look not only uninformed but uninterested. She stood up and grabbed for her handbag. "What I can say is that I need to get your daughter home to her lunch. Gussie, give your mother a kiss good-bye."

"It's so unfair," Fannie whispered into her daughter's hair. "I didn't even get to see you twirl your baton. Bring it the next time you come?"

"My baton?"

Enough was enough. Esther grabbed Gussie's hand and yanked her from the bed.

"Don't keep her away so long next time," Fannie shouted after them as Esther herded Gussie out of the room and into the corridor.

Esther waved a hand in the air, threw a "See you tomorrow" over her shoulder, and shut the door behind her with a louder bang than she'd intended.

It wasn't until she and Gussie were down the stairs, through the lobby, and out the hospital's front doors that her breathing returned to normal. Still, her legs shook. They walked over to Pacific Avenue, and Esther hailed a jitney to take them the rest of the way home. The driver pulled the string that opened the car door, and Esther waited while Gussie climbed in and scrambled to the far side of the car.

"So, Stuart's really teaching Anna to swim?" she asked once she was inside the jitney, the door shut behind her.

"Should I not have said that?" Gussie asked. "I didn't know that was a secret."

"No, no. It's fine. You did fine."

Something wasn't sitting right with Esther, and she didn't know what it was. She wasn't thrilled about Anna spending time with Stuart, and most certainly didn't like the idea that he might be so quickly redirecting any affection he'd once had for Florence. But she reminded herself that Stuart was as unsuitable a match for Anna as he'd been for her daughter. She didn't know Anna's parents but she could only imagine that Anna would be on the next boat back to Germany if she announced she was going out with a goy, even a very wealthy one.

No, there was something else.

The jitney rolled past Agron's Furs and Elfman's Shoes and the Block Bathing Suit Co. In the window of Block's a large sign read JANT-ZEN BATHING COSTUMES. ON SALE NOW!

That was it, thought Esther. Anna didn't own a bathing suit.

~

Esther felt hot with rage as she entered the apartment. Her hands trembled as she removed a few dollars from her wallet, rolled them up tight, and handed them to Gussie.

"Anna!" she called into the quiet apartment. "Will you go by Lischin Bros. and pick up some veal cutlets? Take Gussie with you."

When the girls were gone, Esther locked the front door of the apartment and walked directly back to the bedroom Anna had shared with Florence. She hesitated, briefly, in the doorway. It had been almost a month since she'd seen any of Florence's things. A shudder ran through her body but she shook it off, pushed back her shoulders, and forced herself forward.

Florence's bed was made, her dresser a little neater than she'd left it. It was tempting to turn over each of the objects on the dresser top, to feel the heft of the books and earrings and Pageant Cup, to picture the last time her daughter had held each item. But Esther did not allow herself that pleasure. She walked straight over to Fannie's old dresser, now occupied by Anna, and began opening drawers.

It didn't matter that Florence had owned several fine bathing suits and that Anna had none, that Florence was dead and could wear none of them and that Anna was alive and slim enough to stretch any one of the suits across her limber frame. In another time, Esther might have been generous. *Why don't you borrow a bathing costume of Florence's?* she pictured herself saying to Anna if Florence was still away at college or already in France. But not now. She sifted through one drawer and then another, looking for the evidence that Anna was usurping her daughter's life.

In the bottom drawer of Anna's dresser, she found no clothes at all, just a stack of neatly bundled papers. Esther picked the packet up and began to thumb through it. It was all of Anna's immigration paperwork, paper-clipped according to some system Esther could not interpret. There were medical records, school transcripts, a police clearance, and a copy of Anna's acceptance letter from New Jersey State Teachers

College. So much paperwork for one person. One piece of paper came loose and fluttered to the floor, and Esther stooped to pick it up.

It was a copy of Joseph's affidavit of support, neatly typed and notarized by the Atlantic City commissioner of deeds. Joseph had completed the section, for naturalized citizens, at the top of the form, and had then gone on to list his age and occupation, his weekly earnings, and his assets. He'd outlined the balance of his bank account and the value of his insurance policies and real estate holdings. Esther sucked in her breath when she got to the section of the form where Joseph had been asked to list the names and ages of his dependents. The words *Florence Adler (19)* jumped out at her from the middle of the page.

Farther down the page still, Joseph had listed Anna's information—her full name, her sex, her birth date, and the country of her birth. Under *occupation*, he indicated that Anna was a student, and under *relationship to the deponent*, he had typed *Please see addendum.*

Esther forgot the bathing suit completely and began to dig through the papers in earnest, looking for the addendum. Joseph had submitted several supplements to the affidavit—everything from bank statements to copies of his personal income tax returns—so it took some time to locate the document she wanted. Finally, she found it near the bottom of the stack. It was a typed letter on Joseph's stationery that began, *To Whom It May Concern.*

He wrote, *I understand that this affidavit of support would be looked upon more favorably if I were a close relative of the applicant.* Esther scanned the next several sentences, in which Joseph did his best to document the childhood Inez and he had shared in Lackenbach. She assumed he was making enhancements here and there, anything to demonstrate the durability of the relationship. Esther would likely have done the same.

At seventeen, the applicant's mother and I became engaged to be married. Esther went back and read the sentence again. Engaged? Joseph? *The engagement lasted for a period of three years after I immigrated to the United States, and while we did not ultimately marry, I remain committed to the welfare of both her and her family.*

Esther felt like a fool. How had she not realized it all along? Of course, Joseph had been promised to someone. It explained the three years he'd spent with his head down, working day and night, first at Kligerman's in Philadelphia and then at Chorney's. He had been saving to bring Inez over. Now Esther understood why it had been she who had asked Joseph to go on that first walk, why he had looked so startled when, later, she had reached for his hand. He had been spoken for. At what point, she wondered, had he written to Inez and called off the engagement? Assuming, in fact, that he had been the one to call it off at all.

Esther read the rest of the letter but she couldn't take anything else in. The fact that this letter existed at all, much less in the bottom drawer of Anna's dresser, meant that Anna also knew the specifics of Joseph and Inez's relationship. How had the girl managed to sit on information so compelling? Maybe she assumed Esther knew the truth, had always known it.

What did Esther really know about her own marriage? What did anyone ever know about a relationship that could look as transparent as a Coke bottle one moment and as milky as sea glass the next?

In the early days, Joseph had been besotted by Esther. She had felt it in his glance, his touch, even the way he breathed—a little more deeply when she was near him. She had felt similarly, had been willing to disregard her parents' wishes and marry him, move to Atlantic City, and start a life from scratch.

As they aged, the longing they had felt for each other was transmuted into a calm and constant love Esther could see all around her. It was in the bakery and the house but—most importantly—in the two beautiful girls they raised together.

In thirty years, Esther had never looked back. She'd never had reason to.

Fannie

Now that Fannie's blood pressure readings were higher than normal, Bette and Dorothy and Mary and the rest of the nurses on the ward were in and out of her room with much more regularity.

Twice a day one of them popped in, the sleek, metal case of the Baumanometer tucked under an arm, a stethoscope stuffed in a pocket. Each time the nurse wrapped the cuff around her arm and pumped it tight, Fannie tried to clear her mind, to concentrate on breathing normally. It helped to find a spot on the wall in front of her, some smudge or imperfection that she could focus on as she breathed. If it was true that her own ill feelings could contribute to high blood pressure, she didn't want an errant thought about her husband or her sister to send her into the operating theater.

Outside of mealtimes and these twice-a-day readings, the nurses had started making up reasons to check in on Fannie. They plumped her pillow and adjusted the light—turning lamps on and off and opening and closing the curtains as the sun shifted in the sky. Now they were always rearranging her bedsheets, too. They pretended to be tightening the corners but Fannie assumed that, when they lifted the sheets, they were actually inspecting her ankles. "Are they big as boats yet?" she'd ask, to which the reply was always no.

On slow days, Bette would pop her head around the doorway and ask if Fannie wanted company. Even when Fannie was feeling tired or out of sorts, she never said no. Who knew when she'd get another visitor? Her mother came by most days but on the days no one visited, the quiet of the room was deafening.

"I brought you these," Bette said as she handed Fannie two newspaper clippings about the Dionne quintuplets. While Fannie scanned the articles, Bette interrupted. "Only one of them has any information."

It was clear that, while the public demanded a daily accounting of the babies' welfare, there was less and less genuine news to report.

"Stop the presses, Bette," said Fannie. "'Mrs. Dionne Leaves Bed.'" When she read it aloud, the headline sounded even more ridiculous. The babies were thirty-eight days old. Why shouldn't their mother be out of bed?

"You've got a week after you deliver, and then we're giving you the boot."

Fannie couldn't imagine spending six more weeks in bed after the baby was born. She hoped Bette was right—that she'd be up and around within a week. Secretly she hoped that, within six weeks, she'd have her waist back.

She reached for the copy of Sara Teasdale's poems her mother had brought her, and opened the book to "Truce," where she'd taken to stowing all of her quintuplet clippings. She slipped the newest clippings alongside the older ones. By now there was a thick wedge of them that made the book's spine bulge.

"Are those any good?" Bette asked.

"What?"

"The poems."

"Oh," said Fannie, thumbing through the pages that were not stuffed with clippings. They felt stiff beneath her fingers. "I have to admit, I haven't read them all."

"With all this time on your hands?"

"You sound like my mother."

"My sincerest apologies," said Bette, teasingly, as she held out her hand for the book. Fannie gave it to her, and she flipped to a page near the end and began to read aloud, "'Laid in a quiet corner of the world, there will be left no more of me some night.' Good God, these are depressing."

"Bette, should I be worried?"

Bette closed the book with a sharp clap, as if she'd suddenly remembered herself. "There's no need," she said briskly as she walked around the bed and replaced the book on Fannie's bedside table. She met Fannie's eyes and offered a sweet smile, but when she straightened her cap, which didn't need adjustment as far as Fannie could tell, Fannie knew she was lying.

~

One person who did not appear to be at all worried by Fannie's mounting blood pressure was Isaac. He came and went from the hospital as if it were F. W. Woolworth's and he was ticking his obligations off an imaginary list: knock lightly, kiss wife on head, sit but not too comfortably lest wife believe you might stay for a while, explain why you haven't visited in several days, indicate you have a very important meeting for which you mustn't be late, look at watch several times, stand and stretch, remark on how the time has flown, kiss wife once more. Most of the time, he was in and out of the room within half an hour.

Fannie could put up with the long absences but she worried about what they were doing to Gussie. Between her mother's silence on the subject, the strange way Gussie had acted on her last visit, and the little information she managed to drag out of Isaac, Fannie felt sure he wasn't visiting their daughter. At least not frequently enough for her liking. Fannie knew she was biased but she *actually* thought Gussie was good company. She was funny and quick and kind, and behind her eyes, which were as big as oceans, there was a light of understanding that Fannie recognized as both familiar and extraordinary. What must it be doing to her to feel so pitifully ignored by her own father?

Lately, Fannie had begun to wonder if there might be something wrong with Isaac. He'd spent the whole of his last visit talking about a trip to Florida he wanted to take with Fannie and Gussie after the baby was born.

"We can take the train down," he had said from the edge of his seat. "See the Everglades. Jim says you can pay a guide to take you through the wetlands by boat."

"The Everglades?" Fannie repeated, slowly.

"Sure. In Florida."

"I know where they are."

"There are alligators and sea turtles and all sorts of birds. Gussie would love it."

"You want to take a newborn baby to the tropics in the heat of summer? Are you mad?"

"It'd just be for a few weeks. Long enough to take a look around. Put my eyes on some land that's up for sale in Palm Beach County."

"Land?"

"Jim gave me a tip on a parcel of land. Near Lake Okeechobee. About a hundred acres off Conners Highway."

"You want to buy land in Florida?"

"Prices are low."

"Didn't Florida go bust?"

"That's why it's such a good investment."

"Isaac," she said slowly, trying to get his full attention, "we can't even pay for this room."

"Yes, well—"

"And what about a house? Or paying back my father?"

"This deal is what's going to get us there. I'll hold on to the land for a few years and when we go to sell, I'll make a good profit."

"Please tell me you haven't already signed."

"All I've bought is the binder."

"Is it refundable?"

Isaac looked at her like she didn't have a clue in her head. "A binder is a deposit."

"That you can or can't get back?"

"I've got forty-five days to get together the rest of the money."

"You're not answering my question," Fannie persisted. "If you don't raise the rest of the money or if your wife loses her mind, can you get it back?"

"No."

Fannie suddenly felt short of breath.

"But, Fan, I'll raise the money."

She grabbed hold of her stomach with both hands and tried to concentrate on taking deep, slow breaths, like the kind she took when Bette or one of the other nurses took her blood pressure. Had sheer irritation ever sent a woman into early labor?

"Fan?"

She was reluctant to meet Isaac's gaze, scared that if she did, she might say something she'd later regret. Eventually, she let out a long sigh and turned to face her husband. "I can't talk about this now."

Her head pounded. Dr. Rosenthal had warned her to pay attention to her body's signals. Headaches, stomach pains, and swelling in the legs could all be signs that something was wrong. Of course, those symptoms could also be signs that she was eight months pregnant and feeling extremely anxious and put out. She leaned back against her pillows, permanently propped upright, and closed her eyes. When she did so, did the pressure subside? She thought it did.

"I want to—" Isaac started to say, but Fannie held up a hand to stop him. She was so tired of his big ideas, of never having a cent to their name. With her eyes shut tight, she could pretend he wasn't in the room, wasn't in the process of throwing over their life.

Fannie breathed slowly, in and out.

Eventually she fell asleep but, when she did, she dreamed she was in the Florida wetlands. The baby, so newly born, was missing, and Fannie waded through brackish water, calling its name at the top of her lungs. The mud along the bank was thick, and her feet couldn't get good purchase. Eventually she was forced to swim but the weight of her wet nightgown slowed her progress, as did the alligators that nipped at the hem. After what felt like hours of swimming but was probably only minutes, Fannie discovered the baby, afloat atop a giant lily pad. The baby was motionless and pale and shimmered in the hot sun, as if it had been submerged in the water for several hours first. Three vultures circled overhead. Fannie screamed, trying to ward off the birds, but now she couldn't recall the baby's name. In her confusion, she screamed, "Florence!"

All day, Fannie had waited for her sister to walk through the door of her hospital room, and all day, she'd been disappointed when one nurse or another bustled in instead. If Florence's ship was leaving from Chelsea Piers on the tenth, it was likely she'd take the train up to New York on the ninth and stay overnight, somewhere close to the port. If that was indeed the plan, then today was Florence's last day in Atlantic City, and by extension, the last day she might reasonably pay her sister a visit. Fannie looked at the small clock that sat on her bedside table. It was nearly seven o'clock in the evening.

"Selfish, selfish, selfish," Fannie muttered under her breath as she heaved herself out of bed. Her feet were beginning to feel heavy, a sensation she thought she remembered from her first pregnancy.

There was only one thing to do. She'd borrow the telephone in the nurses' lounge and call the apartment. Ask to speak to Florence directly. It was dinnertime. Everyone was sure to be at home. In fact, it was likely her mother had cooked a big meal, a special send-off for the Channel swimmer. She imagined the table laid with her mother's Adams Ironstone Calyx Ware and silver-plated cutlery. Sometimes, on special occasions, her mother filled a vase with fresh-cut cornflowers. Were they in bloom now? Fannie couldn't remember.

She steadied herself. She had gotten so little practice lugging this new body around. Even her trips to the bathroom, which had begun to feel like outings, had been curtailed. Most of the nurses, with the exception of Dorothy, who was lazy, now urged her to use a bedpan instead.

Fannie barely managed to tie her robe around her midsection. She had no hope of getting her feet into her slippers—it was as if they'd shrunk two sizes—so she kicked them under the bed and padded, barefoot, out of the room and down the hall.

Dorothy was in the lounge eating a tuna sandwich when Fannie rounded the corner. "Hey! What are you doing out of bed?" she asked, wiping her mouth with the back of her hand. The smell of the tuna invaded Fannie's nostrils and nearly turned her stomach.

"I was hoping to use the telephone."

"You're not supposed to use this one."

"I don't have one in my room."

"Yes, well . . ." said Dorothy. Her voice trailed off.

Dorothy had been behaving oddly for several weeks now, and Fannie began to worry she'd overheard her poking fun at her, to Esther or one of the other nurses. Fannie had also complained about Dorothy to Superintendent McLoughlin on at least two occasions, and she suspected her mother had as well.

"I have to call my sister." Fannie didn't wait for Dorothy to grant her permission. Rather, she made her way toward the small table where the telephone sat, figuring that if Dorothy didn't like what she was doing, she'd stop her.

"Your sister?" Dorothy asked.

"That's right," said Fannie, the handset already in hand. She dialed the operator and waited until she heard the familiar, "Number, please."

"Yes, can I have 4452, please?"

While Fannie waited for the line to connect, she strummed her fingers against her stomach. What was the right tone to take with Florence? She was angry, sure, but also disappointed. She had learned that sometimes, with Isaac, disappointed worked better.

Her father answered the phone.

"Hi, Pop."

"Fannie?"

It had been almost six weeks since Fannie had seen or heard from her father, and it felt good to hear his voice—always quiet and calm—in her ear.

"How is everything?" she asked.

A few seconds slipped by before her father said anything. "Oh, you know how it is."

She didn't, so she tried a different tack.

"How's the bakery?"

"We just hired a few new drivers. I think we've almost got enough manpower to start distributing in Philadelphia."

"Wow. Philly?" she repeated, astonished. Isaac hadn't breathed a word of this to her. Did he think she wouldn't find it interesting? "How easy is it to increase production?"

"Your mother's eager to . . . say hello."

Fannie ignored him. Now that she had him on the phone, she didn't want to be passed off to her mother. "How's Gussie?" she asked.

"She's fine. Eating a giant serving of rice pudding as I speak."

"I miss her like crazy."

She could hear her mother whispering to him in the background.

"And how's Florence?" asked Fannie. She could feel the hair on her arms stand up. "That's really the reason I called. I assume she leaves for New York tomorrow."

"Here's your mother—"

Fannie sighed. Sometimes there was no moving beyond the roles each of them played. Her father, a quiet supporter. Her mother, an assured arbiter. What was Fannie's role? Did she even have one anymore? Had she ever had one?

"Fannie?" Esther said, too loudly, into the telephone.

"Hello, Mother."

"You're not meant to be out of bed. Where are you?"

"The nurses' lounge," said Fannie, eyeing Dorothy. Dorothy had stopped eating her sandwich and was watching Fannie intently. "One of the nurses was sweet enough to let me use the phone." She flashed Dorothy a smile.

"I don't think that's a good idea, walking all the way to the lounge in your condition."

"Well, it's too late now," said Fannie, unable to stop herself from rolling her eyes. "I actually called to speak to Florence. Can you put her on?"

The phone line went quiet, and for a moment, Fannie wondered if they'd lost their connection. "Mother?"

"What?"

"Can I speak to Florence?"

"Yes, oh, you know what? I think she just stepped out."

"I thought you were in the middle of dinner? Pop said Gussie's eating rice pudding."

"She had some errands that couldn't wait," her mother said, then paused, as if she were reading Fannie's mind. "I think she said she was going to stop by the hospital, too. To say good-bye."

"Well, she doesn't have much time. Visitors' hours end at nine."

"Right."

Was Florence really so angry with Fannie that she'd ignored her apology letter? Then put off a visit until the last hour of the last day she was in Atlantic City? She and Florence had fought—surely—but they'd gotten in terrible arguments before and had always managed to patch things up quickly enough.

"You know how she is," her mother said, with what sounded like forced enthusiasm. "Just leaves things to the last minute. I'm sure she'll be by soon."

Fannie glanced over at Dorothy, who was looking more uncomfortable by the second. She had thrown the crusts of her sandwich away and was wiping down the tabletop with her unused napkin.

"Which train is she catching tomorrow?"

Now it was her mother's turn to sigh. "I can't recall."

"You can't recall?" Fannie's mother had never failed to recall anything in her entire life. She could recall the moment Fannie had lost her first tooth, the number of matzo balls she'd made for last year's Seder, and the name of every flower she'd ever planted in the beds at the Atlantic Avenue house. But she could also recall more practical things—the telephone extensions of every member of Beth Kehillah's women's committee and the names of anyone who had ever been late paying on an account at Adler's, at least in the years before she stopped working behind the counter.

"It's either the Pennsylvania Railroad or the Central of New Jersey, the two twenty-five p.m. or the four thirty-five p.m.," said Fannie. "Which is it?"

Fannie was so distracted by the conversation that she failed to notice Mary enter the room. When she tapped her on the shoulder, Fannie nearly dropped the handset.

"I need you to finish up this call," she said, before turning her attention to Dorothy. "Who's she talking to?"

Esther was saying something about the train schedule but Fannie had stopped listening. Was Mary angry at her or Dorothy? It was hard to tell. "Mother," she said. "I think I have to go. Tell Florence I'm counting on her to come by. Really."

She replaced the handset on the receiver. Her back ached and her feet felt like bricks. Maybe her mother was right and she shouldn't have gotten out of bed.

"Sorry," she said to Mary. "I just needed to speak with my sister."

"This phone's not for patient use," Mary said, shooting Dorothy a withering look. There was still a small dab of mayonnaise on the nurse's top lip. "Dorothy, will you get her back to bed?"

No one on the hospital's staff had ever spoken to Fannie in such a stern voice, and for a brief moment, she felt almost guilty for implicating Dorothy.

Dorothy got to her feet slowly, as if she'd rather be doing anything else, and gave Mary a wide berth as she guided Fannie out of the lounge. As they walked down the hall, she muttered to herself. Fannie thought she heard her say, "I can't believe we're doing this," but that hardly made any sense. Doing what? And who was the "we"—surely not Dorothy and Fannie?

"What did you say?" Fannie finally asked, when they'd reached her room.

"Huh?"

"You said something."

Dorothy was either hard of hearing or had chosen to ignore Fannie's question.

"Listen, Dorothy, I really am sorry if I got you in trouble."

Dorothy ignored her. All she said, as she turned the bed down was, "In you go."

~

Fannie awoke to the fluttering kicks of the baby inside her. The sensation of being prodded from the interior of her own body had never grown old. She pushed down her bedsheet and lifted her nightgown to reveal her bare stomach, hard and round. Sometimes, on mornings like this, when the baby was active, she could actually see her stomach tremor, the muscles subtly bending to accommodate the jut of a tiny fist or the heel of a foot. She imagined this baby vaulting off her pelvis, swinging from her ribs.

Fannie reached for her water glass on the bedside table, and saw a folded piece of paper leaning against the glass. Across the flap, her name was written in pretty script. Confused, Fannie picked up the note.

Now she remembered—she had stayed up later than usual, waiting for Florence. First, she had worried that her sister wouldn't make it to the hospital before visiting hours ended, and then, as nine o'clock came and went, that she wouldn't come at all. Fannie had tried not to doze but it had been impossible not to; she was always so tired now. At one point, she'd stirred and could have sworn she overheard Mc-Loughlin reprimanding Dorothy but now she realized she must have been dreaming.

The handwriting on the note wasn't Florence's—it was neater and more controlled. When Fannie unfolded it, she saw that the message, which was short, had been written on a piece of hospital stationery.

Fannie,

Florence stopped by tonight but you were already asleep. You looked so peaceful that she hated to wake you. She asked me to tell you that she loves you, and that she'll be thinking of you and the baby constantly over these next few weeks.

Bette

Fannie let the note slip from her fingers. It fell closed and settled on her lap. Was this really it? Florence was going to leave for France with no real good-bye? The thudding pain in Fannie's temples had returned. She picked up the note again and reread Bette's words. *She asked me to tell you.* Why would Florence have passed along a message through Bette when she could simply have woken her? Or asked Bette for a piece of stationery and a pen and written the note herself? Surely, Florence could have spared the two minutes it would have taken to toss off these few lines. Did she care so little about Fannie? Fannie's breathing started to quicken. She crumbled the note into as tight a ball as she could manage and, letting out a low growl, threw it across the room and out into the hall.

Fannie pulled her nightgown back down over her stomach. Her hands had gone numb, and she could barely feel the cloth of the gown beneath her fingertips. A wave of nausea washed over her and then she was hot, so incredibly hot, that she kicked her sheets all the way to the bottom of the bed.

Dr. Rosenthal and a nurse Fannie didn't recognize walked past her room on morning rounds. The doctor stooped to pick up the wad of paper, then glanced into Fannie's room, as if he were trying to calculate its trajectory.

"Fannie?" he said, hurrying into the room.

Fannie's breath was coming in short bursts now. She had tried to put her head between her knees but found she couldn't, not with the bulge of her stomach in the way. All she could do was lock her arms around her knees and rock back and forth, trying to get a gulp of air. It wasn't working. What was wrong with everyone? Florence, Isaac, her mother, even Gussie? It was as if no one cared what happened to her.

"Fannie, can you hear me?" Dr. Rosenthal said. His voice sounded very far away and also like he was shouting. Why was he shouting?

She wanted to nod her head but it took so much effort.

"Helen, get the curtains. Make the room as dark as you can."

Fannie heard the heavy whoosh of the curtains closing out the sun.

Dr. Rosenthal put a hand on her back and steadied her. "You have to breathe, Fannie. You understand?" he said.

She couldn't.

"Did you get bad news?"

She nodded her head, tried to speak. "My sister—"

He moved his hand to her shoulder, squeezed it tight, and whispered, "I know."

"She, she, she left for France without saying good-bye."

Dr. Rosenthal removed his hand from Fannie's shoulder. "Right," he said as he busied himself monitoring her pulse and taking her blood pressure. Finally he sat down on the bed beside her. "Fannie, your numbers are very high. I'm tempted to induce your labor right now."

The threat shocked Fannie back into her own consciousness. "It's too soon."

"Well, then, listen to me. I don't give a damn whether your sister is swimming around the horn of Africa, and, from this point forward, neither do you. Your only concern is this baby and carrying it safely to term. Do you understand?"

Fannie couldn't make so much as a word in response.

"Do you understand?" repeated Dr. Rosenthal.

She nodded vigorously.

He removed the extra pillows from behind her back, told her to lie down, and then, perhaps thinking better of his directness, added "please." As she did so, he scribbled something on a small piece of paper and handed it to the nurse. "Will you get this?" he asked, quietly. "A hundred milligrams."

When Fannie was flat on her back, staring at the dark ceiling, he spoke again. "Here are my new rules: No daylight, no getting out of bed. Helen is going to give you something that will help you relax, and we're going to see if you can get your blood pressure down on your own."

"And if I can't?"

"I think you can."

The nurse hurried back into the room, carrying a small tray. She set it on the table beside the bed and asked Fannie if she could roll over onto her side.

Fannie did as she was told and a moment later, she felt the pinch of a needle in the soft flesh of her backside. As the nurse pushed the syringe down, Fannie imagined its contents spilling throughout her body, enveloping the baby, touching all the neglected parts of her. The baby kicked. *I'm here with you,* Fannie thought, though she had never felt so alone.

Joseph

On the day his younger daughter would have sailed to France, Joseph found he was too distracted to get much of anything done.

"Mrs. Simons, is that pair of binoculars still around here somewhere?" he called from his office as he searched his desk for his keys.

Joseph pulled the car around the front of the building and was about to turn onto Mediterranean Avenue when he noticed a man, dressed in a seersucker suit, walking toward him. The man was almost directly in front of the car when Joseph realized he was Stuart. He rolled down his window and called to him.

Stuart looked relieved to see him and doubled back to talk to him through the open window. "Good to see you, Mr. Adler."

"No bathing suit?"

"Day off," he said. "Since I was paying you a visit, I thought I'd put on real clothes."

Joseph liked the boy's sense of humor, always had. "Did you hear from the coach?" Joseph asked.

"I did," he said, reaching into his pocket for an envelope. "That's why I was coming to see you. Burgess enclosed a check for the entire deposit."

Stuart handed Joseph the airmail envelope, and he took it, studying the return address, the French stamps, the Calais postmark.

"He said he was very sorry to hear the news."

"That's kind of him."

"He's known for being tough to deal with, so I was a little surprised he parted with the money so easily."

"What are you doing this morning?" Joseph asked.

"Coming to see you."

"Do you want to take a drive? I can have you back in Atlantic City by midafternoon."

A look of surprise came over Stuart's face. "Sure," he said.

Joseph patted the exterior of the car's door. "Get in, then."

Stuart hurried around the front of the car and climbed into the passenger's seat. "Where are we headed?" he asked, when the door was closed behind him.

"Highlands."

Stuart nodded his head, as if he understood perfectly. When a few long seconds had passed, he asked, "Why Highlands?"

"You'll see."

Joseph crossed the Thorofare and eventually the marsh, then traced the coast. "Have you ever been to Highlands?" he asked Stuart when they were on Highway 4 North, the car beginning to pick up speed.

"Once, to Highlands Beach, for a lifeguard competition."

Joseph wondered if Florence had tagged along. Last summer, when she'd returned home from school, she'd scarcely ever been at the apartment. It had been difficult to keep up with her whereabouts—she'd spent so much time training for the Absecon Island swim. "Did Florence go?" he asked.

Stuart shook his head no. "It was three summers ago."

Joseph didn't have anything to say to that, could hardly remember what any of them had been doing three years ago.

The two men fell quiet, listening to the steady rush of air that whipped around their heads and beat against their eardrums. Out their windows, New Jersey's coastal plains passed by. Joseph hadn't laid eyes on the ocean until, at seventeen, he had boarded the SS *Frankfurt* in Bremen. Now he couldn't imagine living somewhere where he couldn't see the sea.

"Did you know Trudy Ederle was from Atlantic Highlands?" said Stuart. "Or at least she spent her summers there."

Joseph did remember that. Half the news stories had claimed she was a resident of Manhattan, where her father owned a butcher shop, but the other half had claimed she hailed from Highlands, where her parents had a summer cottage. Highlands Beach was where she and her sisters had learned to swim. Joseph was sure that, if he wanted to discover the Ederles' cottage—maybe even knock on the front door, all it would take would be a quiet inquiry at a local establishment or two. "She probably doesn't get back much these days."

"Probably not," Stuart agreed, letting the car go quiet again before he asked, "So, assuming we're not dropping in on the Ederles, what's in Highlands?" He gestured at the binoculars that Joseph had tucked into the seat. "Bird-watching?"

Joseph glanced at the binoculars, then at Stuart. Would it be kinder to let him in on the plan now or later? He wasn't quite so quick-thinking or clearheaded as Esther, wasn't ever certain that he knew what was in anyone else's best interest. No, he'd tell him later, Joseph finally decided. He was enjoying the ride—and Stuart's company—too much to sap all the pleasure from the day.

Joseph had been to Highlands several times before but the craggy landscape always took him aback, so different was it from the rest of the Jersey shore. A yellow ribbon of sand stretched from Cape May to Atlantic City and all the way to Sea Bright, but when it reached the Atlantic Highlands, a headland rose more than two hundred feet above sea level. A long and narrow sandbar stretched into New York Harbor, protecting Highlands from the worst of the northeast's winds, and it was that sandbar, the Navesink Highlands in the background, that Joseph had first laid eyes on when he had come to America. He had stood on the deck of the *Frankfurt*, among hundreds of other hopeful immigrants—Austrians, Poles, Russians. A murmur went through the crowd. "New Jersey," someone said to the person next to him. "New Jersey?" the next person asked. Everyone knew about New York but nobody knew about New Jersey. "America," someone translated. A tiny American flag waved at them from the Twin Lights but only the young, whose eyes were still good, could see it. Joseph let out a whoop and jumped in the air, causing some of the older women who stood nearby to eye him with suspicion. It would be another half hour before the Statue of Liberty and the docks of Ellis Island came into view, before the tugboats came to meet the ship and lead it into the harbor but, as far as Joseph was concerned, he had already arrived.

Joseph turned the car onto Light House Road. After a few minutes, the road started to rise up toward the light station and he downshifted. The car chugged up the steep incline, and at the tree line, the base of the Twin Lights came into view. Stuart let out a low whistle.

"Not bad, eh?" Joseph said.

The Twin Lights of Highlands looked more like a military fortress than a lighthouse. The entire structure—keeper's quarters, storage facilities, and two towers—was made of brownstone. Joseph pulled the car off the road and parked it under a tree. "Grab the binoculars, will you?"

The pair walked out onto the brow of the hill where the Twin Lights sat. Joseph walked the length of the station several times, wading through the tall summer grass, as he eyed Sandy Hook Bay and the harbor beyond the sandbar. Finally, when they were standing in front of the south tower, he said, "This should do" and made a nest for himself in the grass. Stuart handed the binoculars to Joseph, removed his jacket, and joined him.

"Mr. Adler?"

"Joseph."

"Joseph," said Stuart. "Are we watching for birds or large steamships?"

Joseph didn't answer him, just studied the coastal highway below them, the bay and sandbar and harbor beyond. In the distance, he could make out Brooklyn's skyline. Around a bend he could not see, he knew Chelsea Piers was busy, people pouring from the terminal onto the decks of ocean liners that would transport them to Southampton and Plymouth, Vigo and Le Havre.

The *Lafayette* was small in comparison to most of the liners that crossed the Atlantic. Florence and he had settled on it because it didn't stop in Southampton, and because it could make the transatlantic crossing in a quick six days. The ship's manifest was also small—the ship could accommodate just one hundred and fifty people—which had made Florence hopeful that she would have the tiny, indoor swimming pool to herself. Joseph had tried to remind his daughter that the pool was probably no bigger than a matchbox but she hadn't wanted to hear it.

When Joseph tried to imagine what Florence's sea voyage might have been like, swimming miniature laps in a miniature pool, all he could see was Florence at barely five years old, swimming her first laps in the Hygeia Baths. At the end of the summer season, when the ocean had turned cold and the tourists had gone home, Joseph had walked Florence north along the Boardwalk, as far as Heinz Pier, where a large electric sign advertising the baths directed people into a stuffy Georgian building with a limestone façade and an iodized copper roof. Even such a big sign couldn't have prepared Florence for what she saw when Joseph paid the admission fee and led her inside on that brisk, autumn afternoon.

In the center of a three-story room sat a gigantic swimming pool, full to its brim with seawater that had been pumped from the ocean a hundred yards away. The sounds of frolicking bathers ricocheted off the underside of the building's metal roof.

"I can swim here?" Florence had asked, disbelievingly.

"You can," Joseph said as she stood on the brick deck, still bundled in her coat and hat. Had Joseph not clapped his hands and motioned Florence toward the changing rooms, she might have stood there all afternoon, watching one man after another dive from a tall metal platform that was positioned along the far side of the pool.

"Where are all the girls?" Florence asked her father when she returned to the pool deck in her bathing costume. Joseph scanned the room. Everywhere he looked, he saw nothing but men and, in some cases, adolescent boys. He nodded toward several long rows of chairs, tucked underneath the second-floor balcony and shrouded by potted ferns, where a number of women and small children perched like goldfinches.

"Why are they sitting over there?" Florence asked.

"They can't swim."

"Should you teach them?" she had asked, and he had been so touched by her question that he wondered if she didn't have a point.

A steamship blared its horn as it entered New York Harbor from the Hudson River and headed out to sea. Joseph picked up the binoculars and studied the ship, looking for the name on its bow.

"That's not it," said Stuart. "It's too big."

Joseph replaced the binoculars in his lap.

"Mr. Adler, may I ask you something?"

"Joseph."

"Right, sorry," said Stuart, who was very obviously never going to feel comfortable calling Joseph by his first name.

"Go on."

"Do you ever regret keeping Florence's death a secret?"

Joseph let out a long breath and moved the binoculars from one hand to the other, absentmindedly adjusting the diopter as he did so.

"If you don't want to talk about it—"

"I don't mind talking about it. Don't mind talking about her. In fact, I like hearing people like you say her name."

What could Joseph say? Keeping the secret had never been a choice. Not a real one. He thought carefully about where to begin. "When I was growing up in Hungary—what's now Austria's Burgenland—we never had anything. My parents pinched and saved for my brother's steamship ticket, and when he was settled in Philadelphia and finally making some money, he paid for mine. My mother cried when the ticket arrived in the mail. She knew she couldn't follow me, knew, in fact, that she might never see me again."

Stuart didn't say anything but he didn't need to. Joseph knew he was listening.

"In my first years in America—in Philadelphia and then Atlantic City—I used to wonder at my parents' decision. Had they been right to send my brother and then me? Would it have been better to use the ticket for my father, who might have immediately made a better income? If he had done well enough, he could have sent for the whole family." Joseph plucked at a blade of grass. "But then I became a parent, and I had my answer. You give your children every possible chance.

"My daughter is gone. Nothing I do will return her to me. I try to tell myself that I am not hurting Florence or her memory by keeping her death a secret. What I am taking from the people who knew her—the chance to mourn her death and memorialize her life—can be returned to them.

"I don't know if Esther's right—if this news would prove too much for Fannie to bear. What I do know," said Joseph, raising his head, "is that this baby, this new life, is the most important thing."

Joseph looked over at Stuart. "I wish—"

Just then, they heard the long blast of a horn and looked up to see a small steamship making its way through the watery gap between Staten Island and Brooklyn. Was it the *Lafayette*? Joseph jumped to his feet, binoculars still in hand, but when he put the instrument to his eyes, he couldn't get it to focus.

"You look," he said, handing the binoculars to Stuart, who had also stood at the sound of the horn.

Stuart held the binoculars to his eyes, adjusted the diopter, and spent a long moment studying the ship through the lenses. "It's her," he finally said.

Joseph stared at the *Lafayette*, watching as it made its way toward the mouth of New York Bay. He hadn't thought further ahead than putting his eyes on the French steamship. Now, as he watched it round Seagate and head out past Long Beach, growing smaller and smaller until it eventually become a black dot on the horizon, he tried to recall why this errand had seemed so necessary.

Florence was not on that boat, would never arrive in France. He would not find her on the shores of the English Channel or at the Hygeia or even on the beaches of Atlantic City. He looked over at Stuart, who was openly weeping as he watched the boat disappear from view. Maybe Joseph's daughter was to be found in the people who loved her the most.

~

Joseph offered to drive Stuart as far as the corner of South Carolina and Atlantic avenues, where the Boardwalk National Bank was located on the ground floor of Schlitz's Hotel. He parked the car and stared out through the windshield at the bank's window bars, painted green, and the pair of paneled doors that led inside. Was he really going to do this?

"You bank here?" Stuart asked as he swung the car's passenger door open wide.

"Since the day I arrived in Atlantic City."

Joseph's knees cracked as he climbed out of the car. He didn't like the fact that his body had begun to feel the effects of a long drive or too much time spent in any one position. He patted his jacket pocket, making sure Bill Burgess's check was still tucked inside.

On the sidewalk, Joseph considered putting an arm around Stuart but, in the end, he settled on a firm handshake. "Thank you, Stuart."

"For what?"

"For Burgess. For today."

Stuart didn't say anything, just squeezed his hand in response.

Once they had parted ways, Joseph hurried into the bank. When the receptionist asked how she could help him, he retrieved the envelope from his pocket. "I'd like to speak with someone about opening a new account."

~

Joseph was back in the office by a little after three o'clock in the afternoon. He walked through the plant, checking on the assembly line, before making his way to the third floor, where Mrs. Simons sat at her desk, typing away at her Underwood. When she saw him come up the stairs, she hit the return, pushed her chair back, and stood to greet him.

"I was starting to worry," she said as she handed him a stack of checks to sign.

He took the stack, opened the door of his office, and deposited the checks and his binoculars on his desk. Mrs. Simons followed close behind, the most important pieces of the day's mail in hand.

"The Baker Perkins rep is going to be by on Thursday to talk to you about the dough dividers. I put him down for eleven o'clock. And Katz

& Hanstein says they're no longer manufacturing the eighteen-ounce bread bags. Do we want to go with the next size up or look for a new supplier? They're promising we won't even notice a difference."

Mrs. Simons had been good to Joseph during the past month. Privately, he knew she mourned Florence's death but, at the office, she had committed herself to making Joseph's life easier, his days shorter. She no longer waited for Joseph to dictate correspondence; instead, she just left the letters, already drafted, on his desk for review. She was such a talented writer and a thorough editor that Joseph rarely, if ever, changed anything. She knew all of Adler's suppliers by name, and whereas before she might have just stamped their invoices as received and cut their checks, now she got on the telephone and haggled with them over their prices.

"Let's order enough bags to get through August," said Joseph. "In the meanwhile, you can start shopping the order around."

Mrs. Simons made a note on the steno pad she had carried in with the mail.

"There's something else," he said. "Will you call Anna right away and help her send a telegram to her parents? We'll pay for it. Have her tell them that they should hold off submitting the new affidavits until they receive a bank statement from me."

"Bank statement?" Mrs. Simons asked, looking up from her pad.

Joseph handed her a thin piece of paper. At the top were the names Paul and Inez Epstein and at the bottom was the account balance— twelve hundred dollars. The money from Florence's Channel swim plus a little more besides. "Then will you take this down to the post office and send it to them via airmail? Anna can give you the address."

Mrs. Simons took the account statement and pretended not to study it as she turned to go.

"Oh, there's one more thing," she said from the doorway. "Eli Hirsch wants to know if you'll consider cochairing the fall campaign."

Joseph had known it was only a matter of time before Hirsch asked him for something. A request for a big donation, Joseph had been expecting. Cochairing the campaign was something else altogether.

"Shall I tell him it's a bad time?" Mrs. Simons asked.

Joseph thought of the two reference letters—the American Jewish Committee's and Ike Bacharach's—which Hirsch had executed in record time. "No, you'd better not."

Mrs. Simons raised her eyebrows before making another notation on the pad.

It was all well and good for the members of Beth Kehillah and Rodef Shalom to give their spare change to the American Jewish Committee, but lately, and particularly today, Joseph felt weary of all the altruism. Hirsch's organization had raised nearly a million dollars in the past year, ostensibly to help people just like Inez and her husband, but Hirsch hadn't offered up a dime of it when Joseph and Anna had explained the couple's predicament over lunch. Where was all the money going?

Joseph's real worry was that no amount of money would cut through the bureaucratic red tape, much of which had been imposed by the American government and not the Nazis. He thought it very telling that, when push came to shove, Inez had not placed her faith in the Hebrew Immigrant Aid Society or the German Relief Fund or the American Jewish Committee but in a man she hadn't seen in more than thirty years.

~

Joseph tapped lightly on the door of Isaac's office.

"Yes?"

"I'm going home for dinner. Why don't you come?"

"There's so much to do here," said Isaac. "I might stay for a while."

There was perhaps nothing that annoyed Joseph more than his son-in-law pretending to be busy. Isaac was supposed to be running the sales team but everyone—including the driver-salesmen—knew that Mrs. Simons was really in charge. In the mornings, the drivers went over their orders and tweaked their routes, reporting any discrepancies to Mrs. Simons before they got on the road. And in the late afternoons, when they returned to the office to work the phones and follow up on the next day's orders, it was Mrs. Simons who got peppered with questions about inventory and pricing. If a big order came through or a new customer came on board, the drivers celebrated with Mrs. Simons, not Isaac, who spent most of his day just trying to keep up. When she eventually retired, Joseph had no idea what he and Isaac would do.

"The work will be here tomorrow," Joseph said to Isaac. "Come."

Isaac stood, nodded a few times, as if he were trying to collect his thoughts, and began shuffling the papers on his desk, in search of something. Eventually he located a thin manila folder and put it in his satchel.

"Did you see Fannie yesterday?" Joseph asked when they were on the street.

"Unfortunately, I didn't get over there."

"Esther says Dr. Rosenthal has Fannie on a new regimen. To get her blood pressure down."

"That's good."

Joseph wondered at his son-in-law. Did he not want to know what the regimen was? He seemed completely distracted.

"Did I see Stuart this morning, in front of the plant?" Isaac asked. If he was asking, then of course he had. When Joseph had invited Stuart to get in the car, Isaac had undoubtedly seen the whole thing from his office window.

"I took a drive up to Highlands. Asked him to go. Stuart was too polite to turn an old man down."

"You're not old."

"No?"

"I would have been happy to drive you."

"Next time?"

They crossed Atlantic Avenue and made their way north.

"You seem distracted, Isaac," said Joseph. "Is it Fannie or something else?"

"Hmm?"

"I said that you seem distracted."

Isaac shifted his satchel to his other shoulder. "I guess I am."

"Want to talk about it?"

Isaac hesitated for a moment, then released a torrent. "There's a good opportunity for me in Florida. A guy I know is selling a parcel of land, outside of Lake Okeechobee, for thirty dollars an acre. If I can get together three thousand dollars, it's mine."

"That's a lot of money."

"I've been shopping it around to investors. All I need is a few more people to buy in, and then it's a win for everyone."

"A lot of men in this town lost their shirts on Florida land deals in '26."

"Sure, I know," said Isaac. "It's part of the reason I'm getting this parcel so cheap. Playing the long game."

They passed City Hall. "Did you hear the Commodore is sick?" Joseph asked, eager for a distraction. The city commissioner, Louis Kuehnle, was an Atlantic City legend.

Isaac couldn't be deterred. "I thought it might be a good opportunity for *you*. A chance to diversify your investments. If you agreed to buy fifty acres, I'd have enough commitments to close the deal."

"Have you talked to Fannie about any of this?"

"A little."

"What did she say?"

"You know how women are. They've got no head for business."

How could Joseph tell Isaac that his plan was not just stupid but irresponsible? That investing in real estate he'd never seen was akin to buying the air he breathed. Sure, it was there but could he touch it?

"It's a bad time for me," said Joseph, thinking about the bank statement he'd just given Mrs. Simons. Directly in front of them sat the old bakery, the apartment above it.

"I still owe Abe for the burial, and I'm trying to help Anna's parents get over here, if I can." Joseph was also paying for Fannie's hospital room—Isaac hadn't even attempted to pay the bill since Esther had upgraded her to a private room—but he let that go unsaid.

"Anna's parents?"

"Right."

"Can't they pay their own way over?"

Joseph couldn't believe his son-in-law's gall. What concern was it of his? In another few steps they'd arrive at the apartment, and if Joseph was going to speak his mind, he needed to do so quickly, before Gussie caught sight of them and careened into her father's arms. "I don't like to bring this up, but do I need to remind you about your loan?"

"Which I pay on every month."

"I would argue that, if you've got enough money to invest in land deals, you might consider paying me in full. Or, at the very least, paying a portion of your wife's hospital bills."

They were nearly at the door that led up the stairs to the apartment. Joseph felt for his keys in his pocket. Had he gone too far? He tried to remember a time when he had been this honest with Isaac and couldn't. It felt surprisingly good.

"I'm sorry if that sounded harsh," he said, his back to Isaac as he put the key in the lock and turned it. "I didn't mean for it to but I'm just tapped." Joseph opened the door and held it for his son-in-law but when he turned around to look for him, Isaac was gone.

~

Esther had been unreachable ever since Florence died, but in the past week, her demeanor had turned icy. No one had ever described her as warm but, for Joseph, the seriousness with which she approached their lives had always been part of her appeal. She could be dismissive with customers and stoic with her own children but, in front of Joseph, she revealed herself. If he caught her with her guard down, her shoulders relaxed and her eyes bright, if she laughed at something he said or if she reached for his waist, intent on pulling him close, he felt sure he had earned the most coveted prize on earth.

There was little chance that Esther would pull him close this evening. When he entered the apartment, still puzzling over his conversation with Isaac, he followed the smell of schnitzel back to the kitchen, where he found his wife muttering over the stove. Joseph moved to kiss her hello but she swatted him away.

"Where are Gussie and Anna?" he asked.

"Gussie's in the back, cutting up more magazines, and Anna's out."

"Out where?"

"How should I know where? I'm not her mother."

There was an accusation in her retort, and Joseph felt it with all the blunt force Esther had intended. Ever since Florence had died, Joseph had wondered whether he was asking too much of Esther. Was it cruel to allow a girl almost precisely Florence's age to share their home? And not just any girl—Inez's daughter?

He wanted to tell her about the drive up to Highlands and the *Lafayette* sighting, about Bill Burgess's refund and the account he'd opened for Inez and Paul. But he didn't dare say any of it, not until her mood lifted.

Joseph tried a safer topic. "Dinner smells good."

Esther was not going to be distracted by a simple compliment. "If I had to guess where Anna was, I'd tell you that she's on the beach, getting a private swim lesson from Stuart."

"Our Stuart?"

Esther narrowed her eyes at him. "I didn't realize Stuart was ours."

"You know what I mean."

"He most certainly wasn't Florence's."

"You don't know that."

"Here's what I know," said Esther, straightening her back and drawing in all her breath. "I want Anna out."

Isaac

Isaac's instinct, after he had turned on his heel and left Joseph fumbling for his keys on the sidewalk in front of the Adlers' apartment, had been to go directly to the hospital, find Fannie, and tell her everything. He'd start with Florence's death and the manic lies Joseph and Esther had told in the subsequent month but then he thought he might go further. It would feel good to tell her that her parents hated him, that they were turning Gussie against him, that he was sure her father was in love with Anna's mother, and that he was never going to run Adler's if Joseph had anything to do with it.

He imagined going further still. What if he could admit to Fannie that he was a disappointment to his own father, that he was a terrible father to Gussie, that he suspected that it was his fault Hyram was dead? Did she already know all those things? Maybe she did and there was nothing to tell.

When Joseph had thrown the loan in his face, Isaac had been flabbergasted. In the five years since the two men had entered into the agreement, Joseph had never once brought it up. Isaac fulfilled his end of the deal, paying the loan's installments by check, which he deposited directly into an account Joseph had established at the Boardwalk National Bank for that purpose. And in return, Joseph acted as if the loan didn't exist at all.

His father-in-law's discretion was appreciated but didn't help Isaac feel any less indebted to him. The loan was always there between them, the same way his own father had been permanently shackled to the Hebrew Immigrant Aid Society. Isaac hated feeling beholden to anyone, and these days, he felt beholden to everyone—even Dr. Rosenthal, who had accepted Isaac's confession the night of Hyram's birth and, miraculously, done nothing with the information.

An elderly couple pushed open the hospital's heavy door, and Isaac held it for them as they moved outside. The man gripped the woman's hand, and Isaac watched as he helped her down the steps, one at a time. While the door was still open, two young women in jewel-toned dresses skipped up the stairs and past him. One of them carried a yellow balloon that read IT'S A GIRL! in fancy script, and the other called out a quick thanks to him over her shoulder. Isaac, mesmerized by the swishing of their skirts, followed them across the lobby and up the stairs to the maternity ward, where he watched as they swooped into a room a few doors down from Fannie's.

Isaac forced himself to slow down, to consider what he would do when he arrived at his wife's room. He had pictured telling Fannie this secret ever since the night Esther had called him with the news. He imagined sitting beside her hospital bed, holding both of her hands in his, and saying what? That was always the part that got him—how to say it. *Fannie, your sister drowned.* No. *Fannie, your sister drowned in early June.* No, no, no. While Isaac didn't necessarily believe that the news would send Fannie into an early labor, he had come to think that a healthy baby, already safely delivered into her arms, might make the telling easier.

On his walk over to the hospital, Isaac had tried to catalog the possible repercussions of telling Fannie the truth. All matters of health and well-being aside, what was on the line? It was possible that Joseph might demand repayment of the loan, even fire him, although both moves would be hard, if not impossible, for his father-in-law to pull off without penalizing Fannie in the process. If Isaac told Fannie that Florence was dead, Esther would never forgive him, certainly. But it was not as if she liked him now. Slightly smaller servings of brisket, delivered acerbically onto his plate at Shabbos dinners, seemed like something he could live with. The reality was that Esther and Joseph would have to be careful with him, or risk alienating their only surviving daughter, their only grandchildren. If either of them made Isaac's life uncomfortable, he'd be tempted to give up Atlantic City altogether, to move his family somewhere where they could start fresh. He pictured Fannie setting up house in a tract home in West Palm Beach. On Saturday nights, maybe they'd go out with Jim and his new wife.

Isaac had almost convinced himself that divulging the secret was the right thing to do when he rounded the corner into Fannie's room and nearly walked straight into the wardrobe. The room was dark.

"Fannie, you in here?" he called quietly.

"I'm here." Her voice sounded far away, but it couldn't be farther away than the bed where he knew she was lying.

Isaac stood still, one hand on the wardrobe, waiting for his eyes to adjust to the dark.

"Should I cut on the light?"

"No, no. The doctor wants it like this."

"Pitch-black?" It wasn't pitch-black, not really. The window shade had been pulled down but there was a generous crack of light between the bottom of the shade and the windowsill. Within a few seconds, he could make out the shape of the wardrobe, the outline of Fannie's bed, even the magazine on her bedside table. Isaac shut the door, held his hands out in front of him, and moved carefully around the bed to the chair by the window. When he had the chairback in his grip, he moved it closer to the edge of the bed and sat down, heavily. He heard the sheets rustle, Fannie move in the bed, and eventually, when his eyes were fully adjusted, he saw her face, turned toward his.

"It's like this all day?" Isaac asked. Joseph had told him something about a new treatment regimen but he had been so deep in his own thoughts that he hadn't even asked about it.

"All day."

"Why?"

"Dr. Rosenthal thinks it will help bring my blood pressure down."

"The dark?"

"A few things."

"Is it really that high?"

"I don't know. Yes?"

Had their conversations always been so circular? Fannie had been in the hospital for close to two months, and it was as if, in that time, he had forgotten how to talk to her. Had he ever been any good at it? He wasn't sure.

Isaac's conversational skills couldn't have been much better when he had wandered into Adler's Bakery eight years ago.

"Can I help you?" Fannie had asked, with curiosity, as she leaned into the counter.

Isaac ordered a loaf of challah, hoping it would keep him for a meal or two, then reached into his pocket and counted out the last of his loose change. He'd been in Atlantic City for nearly a week, and if he didn't land a job soon, he'd be walking the forty miles back to Alliance with his tail between his legs.

"This is your first time here?" she said as she bagged the bread.

"I'm new to town."

"From where?"

Isaac hated claiming Alliance as his hometown. It told people too much about him. "West Palm Beach."

Fannie raised her eyebrows as she handed him the bag. "Exotic."

"Sometimes," he said, wanting badly to come off as a guy who got around.

Isaac handed Fannie the change. She was an attractive girl, not beautiful like some of the girls he'd gone out with in West Palm Beach, but definitely pretty.

Isaac bought three more loaves of challah, on three subsequent visits, before he saw Fannie again. The following Friday, to save himself from buying a fourth loaf unnecessarily, he walked past the store twice, just to be sure she was working behind the counter.

"I came in yesterday but you weren't here," he said, once he had made it to the front of the line.

"I'm at secretarial school on Thursdays."

"Ah. And Wednesdays?"

"You came in on Wednesday as well?" Fannie asked, a large smile spreading across her face.

Isaac tried to think of what he used to say to prospective buyers at Orange Grove Estates—people who had no business buying property but who wanted it very badly all the same. Sometimes, the right approach was to play along, to treat them like Rockefellers while ignoring the holes in their shoes. But other times, it paid to be honest, to acknowledge that the payments might make things tight at first but that, if they hung in there, they'd be rewarded.

He couldn't offer Fannie dinner, or even a cocktail. The people behind him in line stirred, and he tried to think of something fast. "I'll take another loaf," he said. "And maybe later we could walk over to the harbor and feed some to the ducks."

She laughed then. "We won't tell my father what you think of his bread."

"Actually, I think this loaf is very fine," Isaac said. "It's the other two loaves, back at my room, that have gone a little dry."

One look at her and he knew she was sold. If he'd been selling binders, he could have asked her to sign one on the spot.

"Hey, Fan," Isaac said, into the dark void of the hospital room. "Do you remember that first day we met? In the bakery?"

"Ummm-hmmm," she said.

"What did you think of me?"

The room was quiet for a minute.

Isaac stood up and moved over to the bed, feeling for the edge of the mattress and the thin sheet that covered his wife. He touched her shoulder. "Move over?"

She turned away from him, inched toward the far side of the bed to give him enough space to crawl in beside her. When they were settled, his arm around her bulging middle, her backside nestled against his groin, the sheet pulled over them both, she spoke. "Back then, I thought that if I didn't touch you, I might die."

He smiled into the nape of Fannie's neck, could feel himself becoming aroused. Their courtship had consisted of little more than a series of long walks, each an excuse to discover the quietest parts of Atlantic City, the places where they could explore each other in private. Between New Hampshire and Maine avenues, the crowds thinned considerably but the Boardwalk remained elevated. In the evenings, after the sun set, Isaac would lead Fannie down the stairs to the beach and under the Boardwalk, where he could kiss her mouth, her neck, her collarbones, and as they grew more comfortable together, even the pink flesh of her breasts, her nipples hard as cherry pits in his mouth. The footsteps of the occasional passerby overhead mingled with the crash of the waves to drown out Fannie's soft moans. Several times Fannie had begged for all of him, but Isaac practiced enough restraint for them both, waiting until her parents had agreed to the marriage, until he had started work at Adler's, until their wedding date was within sight. On the day that Trudy Ederle swam the English Channel, while the rest of Atlantic City's residents sat with their ears close to their radios, Isaac had secreted Fannie up to the room he'd rented on Lexington Avenue, and devoured her. "First American Woman Finishes," Fannie had proclaimed into his bare chest, and he had rolled her over onto her back and begun again.

"Did you worry?" he asked now.

She shifted slightly to make room for his erection between them. "Worry?"

"That I wouldn't be enough?"

She hesitated, or at least he imagined she might have if they hadn't been interrupted by a subtle tremor that emanated from the spot beneath his hand.

"Do you feel that?" Fannie whispered.

"That's him?"

"Or her."

"Right. Or her."

Isaac couldn't tell Fannie that Florence was dead. Not today. He liked her like this—warm and supple, forthright and forgiving. He moved his hand across her stomach and along her hip bone, fingering the waist of her underwear. He tugged at the garment slowly, pulling it down over her exposed hip.

"Isaac, the baby," Fannie warned, which might have convinced him to stop had she not, at the same time, shifted her weight to accommodate him as he worked the underwear down around her knees.

It had been two months, maybe longer, since he'd felt his way into the warm, wet spot between her thighs. "I'll be gentle, Fan. I promise."

He needn't have promised much. He was barely inside her before his body started to buzz and then to pulse. On this front, he could hold nothing back.

~

Isaac's tryst with his wife was enough to buoy him for the remainder of the week. The following morning, he was at his desk earlier than normal, prepared to make the necessary concessions to his father-in-law. Joseph, of course, would hear none of it and accepted all of the blame for their dispute. After all, Isaac was fulfilling the terms of their loan agreement, and he presumed the hospital fee would be worked out. How his son-in-law spent the rest of his income was entirely his own affair. The following evening, Isaac was in good enough spirits to accept a dinner invitation from Esther and Joseph, and would have, if forced, described the walk from the plant to his in-laws' apartment with Joseph as pleasant. After the meal was finished, he even made the time to take Gussie out for a custard at Kohr's. He saw Fannie twice more that week, although on neither occasion did they dare shut themselves in the room as they had on Tuesday evening.

Isaac's good humor might have lasted him into the weekend were it not for a note he got from Vic Barnes, asking if they could meet for a drink at The Covington the following Monday night. Isaac felt sure that, if Vic wanted to buy in to the Florida deal, he would have come and found Isaac directly. Why waste three days' time, particularly when he knew Isaac was working under a deadline?

Isaac hated meeting anyone—for business or pleasure—at The Covington. If the hotel's management made a point of saying Jews weren't allowed to stay in the guest rooms, it stood to reason they also didn't want them sipping vermouth and gin out of their martini glasses. No waiter was going to be so bold as to check Isaac's ID at the bar, see the last name Feldman, and ask him to leave, but the idea made him uncomfortable nonetheless. He wondered if Vic hadn't suggested the place for that reason.

He scanned the room, saw Vic seated at a small table near the back of the bar. Vic might not have been Jewish, but even he looked out of place at The Covington.

"Vic," said Isaac as he approached the table.

"Isaac." Vic didn't stand up, which wasn't a good sign.

Isaac pulled a chair out and sat down. "What are you drinking?"

"A gin rickey."

He hailed the waiter, pointed to Vic's drink, and thrust two fingers in the air.

Vic launched into a long-winded story about a crackdown on liquor licenses, but Isaac had no patience for it; he had kept him in suspense for long enough. At the first pause in conversation, after their drinks had arrived, Isaac interrupted him. "So you've had some time to think?"

Vic cleared his throat, sat up straighter. "I've talked to some of my guys. No one thinks Florida is coming back."

"It's been eight years."

"Yeah, and the prices have remained flat."

"Which means they're ripe for a rebound."

"Maybe," said Vic. "Or maybe all of those nice parcels of cleared land are going to slowly sink into the swamp."

Isaac cringed, thinking about Orange Grove Estates and the plots he and Jim had sold for Blackwell—not a single one of them cleared. He imagined the knotweed and saw grass eventually wrapping its way around the tennis court, until the netting all but disappeared.

"This guy, Jim, who's arranging the purchase, he knows Florida. Has worked in the business for fifteen years now, first in sales but now as an appraiser. If he says this property's undervalued, then mark my words—it's a good buy."

"If you say so. But the way I see it, there's plenty to invest in, right here in Atlantic City."

Isaac drained his glass, willing the meeting to be over. "In Atlantic

City, thirty dollars won't buy you a big enough lot to put a shack on. You buy forty or fifty acres in Florida, that's a lot of land."

"Yeah, but Atlantic City isn't going anywhere."

Isaac signaled for the check.

When Jim had offered Isaac this deal, he had known Florida wouldn't be an easy sell. Not like it was in '23 or '24. Plenty of people had lost money on land deals in Florida, and those who hadn't had lost their shirts when the stock market crashed three years later. The country was still recovering, and Atlantic City, for all its playful pretense, wasn't any different. Vic had been a good prospect, partly because Isaac knew that neither the Florida boom nor the crash of '29 had touched him. At that time, all Vic's money had been tied up in bootleg liquor.

"I think you're making a mistake," said Isaac.

"Maybe." Vic didn't look convinced.

"If you change your mind, you'll need to act fast. I'm talking to several interested parties right now but held off on taking anyone else's money until I knew what you were doing." This was, of course, a lie. Isaac had talked to everyone he knew, and only a handful of them could be termed *interested*. Three other people, besides his father, had put up money, and Isaac wouldn't have dreamed of telling any one of them to wait on Vic Barnes.

Isaac had less than three weeks to get the rest of the money together. If the binder expired before he could close on the property, he'd lose his deposit, and there would be little, if anything, Jim could do to help him. It was one thing to lose his own savings but he'd put his father's money toward the deposit, too. The idea of watching the money from that Campfire Marshmallows can disappear made Isaac's stomach roil.

Vic stood to go, gestured toward their glasses—Isaac's empty, Vic's second glass untouched. "You've got these?"

Isaac nodded, begrudgingly, as Vic patted him on the shoulder. "See you around," Vic said.

Isaac watched Vic walk out of the bar and across The Covington's lobby. He reached for his wallet, paid the bill, then decided there was no reason to let Vic's drink get poured out, so he picked up the glass, sweaty in his hand, and took several large sips. Condensation spilled onto the table in big, fat drops.

As Isaac held the glass up to his mouth, he saw a familiar-looking girl cross the lobby. Anna? Her hair was wet and hung down her back— he'd never seen it like that—but it had to be her. He watched her walk toward the bank of doors that led out to the Boardwalk. She was with a man, but Isaac couldn't make out who he was. From the back, he almost looked like Stuart. Esther would be fit to be tied.

Isaac drained the glass, put it down on the table, and hurried to catch up with the pair. Why hadn't he thought about Stuart before? The ne'er-do-well son of one of Atlantic City's richest hoteliers would be the perfect investor. All the money in the world and no practical experience doing anything besides sitting on a beach. Stuart was holding a door for Anna when Isaac called to them both from the far side of the lobby.

Anna stopped, turned. Stuart studied the lobby's expanse, looking for the source of the sound. When they saw that it was him, Anna looked discomfited but Stuart seemed relieved.

"Isaac, good to see you," said Stuart, extending his hand. Isaac shook it, then ushered them both through the door and out into the night air of the Boardwalk.

"Been swimming?" Isaac asked Anna, with a nod toward her wet head. What he really wondered was whether they'd just come from a hotel room.

Anna didn't answer him, so Stuart did. "I've been teaching her the basics." He grinned at her, then added, "She's a quick study."

"That's great," said Isaac, trying hard to come off sounding like an affectionate older brother, a difficult feat considering he had barely spoken to Anna in the four months she'd been living with his in-laws. When Isaac went over for dinner, Esther was always there, ready and able to carry the conversation.

"And you?" Anna asked.

"Met someone here for a drink."

Anna and Stuart offered empty acknowledgments, then looked at each other.

It was at least a fifteen-block walk back to the Adlers' apartment, and Isaac's apartment was four blocks past that. If Isaac accompanied them, he'd ruin everyone's evening—that much was clear. He needed to get Stuart alone, but not here. If only Isaac had been a little kinder to him all along. It wouldn't be so awkward now.

"You still rowing in the mornings?" Isaac asked Stuart.

"I try to."

"I'd love to come out with you one of these days. See Atlantic City from a new perspective." Isaac didn't see how the view could be much different from what he saw from the end of Steel Pier, but he hoped the excuse sounded plausible. Anna didn't look as though she bought Isaac's enthusiasm but Stuart was more generous. If he was suspicious of Isaac's motives, he didn't let on.

"Anytime. You never know—I might turn you into a rower."

"You going out tomorrow?" Isaac asked.

Even Stuart looked baffled now. "Sure am."

"Maybe I'll come."

"I'll be out on the beach at six." Stuart gestured toward the stretch of sand directly in front of The Covington. "Right over there."

Isaac raised his fingers to his forehead in a mock salute. "Aye aye, Captain." Then he looked up and down the Boardwalk, desperate for an excuse to take his leave. "I'd love to walk back with you both but I promised Fannie I'd pick her up some macaroons from Segal's."

Anna and Stuart weren't even capable of feigning disappointment. "Of course," both of them said at the same time. As everyone said their good-byes, Isaac studied Stuart carefully. The trick to being a good sales-man was being able to correctly identify people's desires. If Isaac was to have any hope of selling Stuart on Florida, he had to figure out what Stuart cared about. He didn't know much about him, but there was something about the way Stuart looked at Anna, as they turned to go, that gave Isaac a decent place to start.

~

Isaac had had two drinks—downed in quick succession—when he suggested tagging along on Stuart's predawn row. Now, in the sober light of the early morning, he wondered why he had thought the excursion seemed like such a good idea.

He waved at Stuart as he neared the rescue boat, and once he was within shouting distance, called out a buoyant "Ahoy!" It was important, he thought, to convey as much joviality as the early morning hour allowed.

Stuart put two sets of oars and a rescue can into the boat. "Do you prefer the bow or the stern?"

Isaac hadn't considered the fact that Stuart might expect him to row. Once or twice, last summer, he'd seen Stuart and Florence taking the boat out, and Florence had always sat motionless at the front. Was that the bow? Growing up forty miles inland, Isaac had never needed to learn the parts of a boat. "I don't have a preference," he said to Stuart.

"Let's get her out in the water and then you can take the bow." Stuart tapped the front of the boat.

Getting the boat in the water was no easy feat. It looked simple enough when the lifeguards pushed it off its wooden rollers and into the ocean but, in actual fact, the boat was a heavy beast. "You take this thing out on your own? I'm impressed."

"I do, but when you're by yourself, there's no room for error."

The same was true for swimming, Isaac supposed. Look at poor Florence. Isaac didn't like to think about Florence much, had tried, in the six weeks since her death, to push her from his thoughts. She had driven Fannie mad at times, but he'd always thought her perfectly fine. A little brash. And maybe too excitable. But she was a good daughter and a doting aunt. He realized, now that she was gone, that she'd also acted as a useful buffer, drawing some of Joseph and Esther's attention away from Isaac's own small family.

"The key to keeping water out of the bilge is to heave the boat out onto the crest of a wave, as fast as you can," said Stuart as he watched the water. "Push it into the curl of a wave and you'll damage the boat."

Isaac gripped the edge of the boat and waited for Stuart to give a command.

It came a few seconds later. "Go!"

Stuart leaned into the other side of the boat and Isaac could feel the boat's inertia begin to shift. Isaac dug his heels into the sand and pushed hard until the boat began to move, slowly at first and then faster. His ankles were wet and now his knees. He worried he'd soon be in over his head. "When do we get in the boat?" he yelled across the beam.

"Now!" Stuart heaved himself over the edge and into the stern of the boat, then reached down, gripped Isaac's hand, and pulled him up and over the side. Isaac grabbed for the forward thwart but could make no attempt to sit down until they'd made it through the breaking waves closest to the shore and out into calmer water. When they had both found their seats, Stuart handed him a pair of oars.

"I didn't think to ask but do you swim, Isaac?"

Isaac was clinging so tightly to the frame that he was sure he'd left permanent marks where his fingernails had pressed into the soft wood. He made a conscious effort to loosen his grip and fold his hands more casually in his lap.

"I'm all right," said Isaac, which didn't exactly answer the question. Stuart eyed him cautiously.

"What you're going to want to do is slip the oars into the oarlocks."

To think that he had to add rowing to this mix. It seemed unlikely that, between trying not to fall out of the boat and trying to propel it forward, Isaac was going to have any time or energy to talk about the Florida deal.

"You want the paddles to enter the water like knives. Pull hard when they're at ninety degrees, and then give yourself time to glide."

Eventually Isaac got the hang of it, and his confidence grew. It wasn't so bad being out here. In fact, it was nice. All the familiar noises of the shore—the dings of the Boardwalk amusements, the blasts of the lifeguards' whistles, the organs that played on the piers—fell away, leaving only the sound of lapping water against the boat.

"It's so quiet," said Isaac. "I can see why you like it."

Stuart didn't say anything, just kept rowing. He seemed content to let silence sit between the two of them, which wasn't going to do Isaac any good. He tried a different tack.

"So, Anna's doing well with the swimming?"

"I think so. Considering she'd never swum until a few weeks ago."

"She's a pretty girl."

"Yes," said Stuart tentatively, as if he wondered where Isaac was going with the comment. Isaac wished he knew. He just knew he had to bring the conversation around to Stuart's hopes and dreams and— eventually—Florida.

"It's a shame about her parents."

"Shame?"

"How they can't get out of Germany."

"Oh?"

"Their visa application keeps getting denied. Or at least that's my understanding."

"What's the issue?"

"Aside from the fact that the American consulate probably has it out for Jews?" Isaac could see Stuart wince, so he tried to temper his remarks. "I don't know the specifics." If Isaac wasn't careful, he was going to inadvertently sell Stuart on investing in the American Jewish Committee.

For the next half hour, Isaac concentrated on rowing the boat in a straight line. He didn't make another attempt to steer the conversation until they passed Absecon Lighthouse and Stuart gave the signal that they were going to turn around. The Covington was a tiny dot on the beach, barely distinguishable from the Traymore Hotel next door.

"All of these beautiful beachfront properties," he said. "They're really something, aren't they?"

Stuart nodded, appreciatively.

"I give a lot of credit to men like your grandfather. They arrived on a barren beach—nothing more than a railroad station next to a pile of sand—and imagined what Atlantic City might become. They were geniuses, all of them."

"It was actually my great-grandfather."

Isaac didn't skip a beat. "Even more impressive." A seagull cawed overhead. "That's the way it was in Florida, when I lived down in West Palm Beach."

"You were down there for how long?"

"Five years. Worked for a great guy—selling real estate."

"What brought you back up here?"

"When the bottom fell out of the market in '26, there was no more work."

"You liked West Palm Beach?"

"I would have stayed forever if there'd been a job for me. The area's beautiful. It's what I imagine Atlantic City was like fifty or sixty years ago. Still rife with opportunity."

"Not since the crash, I suppose," said Stuart. It was the perfect opening for Isaac's pitch.

"You'd be surprised. A lot of investors foreclosed in the fallout, and the banks are finally trying to off-load all those properties. Or you've got investors who've been sitting on land for the past eight years, watching the prices plummet, and are ready to sell even if it means taking a loss. My friend tells me that buyers are getting big parcels of land for a song. Everything's so undervalued."

Stuart raised his eyebrows and bobbed his head, as if he were taking it all in.

"I'm actually thinking about buying some property myself. West of West Palm Beach. A big citrus farm near Lake Okeechobee. It was bought by a developer who went under. My friend's got me a deal, paying thirty dollars an acre. You can get a lot of acreage at that price."

"Would you move down there? Build on it?"

Isaac shook his head. "I don't think I'll ever get Fannie out of Atlantic City. Not after—"

Florence. Definitely not the best topic to bring up right now. Stuart looked at Isaac, then out at the horizon. "Right."

"The beauty is, you don't need to move down there to make money. The prices are going to go up."

Stuart reminded Isaac to adjust his oars. The sea was getting rough.

"I've actually got a few friends going in on it with me. It's a big enough parcel of land—a hundred acres—that it makes sense to buy in together." Isaac swallowed and then went for it. "It might even be something you'd be interested in."

The Covington was coming into clearer focus, and Isaac watched Stuart look for it among the other grande dames that lined the beach.

"If you're anything like me," said Isaac, "you want something that's yours. This might be—"

Before Isaac could get the rest of the sentence out, a big wave crashed over the side of the boat and sent him flying into the ocean. The water swirled around him and he panicked, unable to tell up from down. He flapped his arms and kicked his legs, desperately trying to appropriate a swim stroke but he couldn't breathe, couldn't orient himself. Is this what Florence had felt like, frightened and alone in a dark cocoon of briny water?

Isaac felt something bump against his back. Was it the boat? A piece of driftwood? He tried to grasp it, couldn't. But then he felt someone grab him from behind and realized Stuart had found him—miraculously—in the nubilous water. Stuart pulled Isaac to the surface, where he grabbed a large mouthful of air before being pushed under the water again and rolled onto Stuart's rescue can. The can buoyed him back up to the surface and he held it tight while Stuart pulled him over to the boat, which had drifted a dozen or more yards away.

"Hold on," Stuart yelled as he hauled himself into the boat, then quickly reached down into the water and grabbed Isaac under the armpits. "I'm lifting on three. One, two, three." Isaac felt his weight shift, his belt catch on the lip of the boat, but he was too exhausted to help Stuart in any way.

The boat had taken in at least six inches of water, which lapped against Isaac's leather loafers—now ruined. Stuart didn't say a word as he rowed the rest of the way back to the Kentucky Avenue stand. Isaac's oars remained still—perched in the oarlocks—while Isaac stared at the sky and tried to collect himself. He would have liked to break the silence, once he recovered himself, but he wasn't sure where to begin. After Stuart drove the boat onto the beach, Isaac stood, carefully, and tried a simple "thank you."

"Sure," said Stuart as he popped the cork plug on the bottom of the boat to let the water drain.

Isaac began to panic. He couldn't let one badly timed wave kill his chances with Stuart. He reached for his wallet, forgetting that his cards would be useless, also soaked through.

"You can find me at the plant," he said, after he'd shoved the wet wallet deep down into his pocket, "if you'd like to learn more about that opportunity in Florida. I'd love to—"

"You're something," Stuart said, interrupting him. "You nearly drowned out there." He positioned the rollers in front of the boat and instructed Isaac to lift.

"I know. And I appreciate what you did, saving me."

"Here's what I'd appreciate," Stuart said, when the boat was up and they'd begun pushing it back to the stand. "I'd appreciate you remembering that, while I may be a nice guy, I'm not a complete idiot."

Isaac stopped pushing. "I never said you were."

"We've known each other for almost a decade, and you've never spoken more than two words to me. On the day you decide to take up rowing, you also have a cockamamie real estate deal you want me to—what—invest in? Pitch to my father? You know I don't actually have access to any cash?"

Isaac didn't know what to say to that. If Stuart didn't have access to his father's checkbook, he was as unlikely an investor as Gussie was. And Isaac's plan to raise the rest of the money was as worthless as any he'd ever concocted. Isaac shuddered at the idea of admitting to Fannie that he'd squandered more of their savings but what he really couldn't stomach was the thought of going back to his father empty-handed, of admitting that the old man's hard-earned money was gone.

"I was just making conversation, Stuart. No need to get upset."

"Well, next time you want to make conversation, why don't you do it on dry land?"

Stuart's words stung. Who was he to order Isaac around? Isaac felt the urge to hit him or, at the very least, to shove him—hard—onto the packed sand. He clenched his fists, then unclenched them and wrung the water out of his shirttails instead. There had to be a better way to get what he wanted. There almost always was.

Stuart

Stuart watched as a storm took shape on the horizon. At the height of a busy Atlantic City summer, an overcast day came as a welcome relief to the members of the Beach Patrol. Absecon Island's permanent residents stayed away from the beach, opting to be more productive at home or at the office, and the summer residents hunkered down in their vacation rentals, reading magazines and playing Parcheesi. Only the day-trippers, with no place to go, tried to make the best of things. They spent as much time at the beach as they could bear before giving up and seeking shelter at the arcades and amusements of the piers.

By midafternoon, there were so few people in the water that Robert took the rescue boat out, just to break up the tedium. "Whistle if you need me to come back," he said as Stuart waved him off.

Stuart's biggest concern wasn't that he'd have to make a save while he was down a boat, but that the impending storm would interfere with Anna's lesson, which was still a couple of hours away. On lesson nights, Anna arrived at the beach tent at six o'clock on the nose. If Stuart wasn't yet finished putting away his gear, she waited patiently, and then they made their way across the Boardwalk to The Covington, where he had finally managed to convince her to stop asking him if they were really allowed to use the pool.

In the distance, Stuart could see lines of rain, like gray thread, fastening the clouds above to the ocean below. He couldn't cancel Anna's lesson if he wanted to; he was stuck in this chair until six o'clock. It occurred to him that Anna might not come, might decide on her own that the weather looked too bad to warrant leaving the Adlers' apartment. A sinking feeling came over him. If she wasn't at the beach tent, waiting for him, he knew he would be disappointed.

A hundred yards off the coast, beyond Robert and his rescue boat, a group of porpoises moved south. Occasionally, one of the beautiful creatures would throw itself into the air, landing back in the great, green lake with a flick of its tail, but more often, they skimmed the water's surface, showing off no more than a nose here and a fin there. Stuart could have watched them all day but they never stayed that long.

"Do you see that?" a small voice said from the sand below. Stuart looked down from his chair to find Gussie staring up at him.

"Hey you," he said. "What are you doing here?"

"I came to see you."

Stuart scanned the beach. If Gussie was here, Anna had to be close by. Maybe she intended to cancel the lesson and had brought Gussie along for company. He hoped like hell Isaac hadn't brought her. It had been a week since Stuart had seen him, and he liked it that way. "Who are you here with?"

"Nobody."

"Nobody?"

She shrugged her shoulders. "Can I come up?"

She actually couldn't come up. It was one of the rules. No one but an Atlantic City Beach Patrol employee was allowed in the stand.

Stuart looked up and down the beach, one eye out for the chief. He was probably at home playing Parcheesi, too.

"Come on up but be quick."

Gussie was an agile child but she still had a hard time heaving herself onto the platform. After a few failed attempts, Stuart reached down, grabbed her hands, and hoisted her up.

"Here," he said, handing her his sweater and an ACBP cap. "Put these on." He was kidding himself to think that Chief Bryant would spy a sixty-pound child in his stand but discount her because she was wearing the proper uniform.

"Does your grandmother know you're here?"

"No."

"She's going to panic when she realizes you're missing. You can't stay long."

Stuart wondered if he should call Robert back. The beach was quiet enough that he could walk Gussie home. Maybe it'd give him a chance to see Anna, to make alternate plans.

"Oh, there they are again!" Gussie shouted, the ACBP cap falling down over her eyes. She pushed it back up on her head and looked at Stuart. "Dolphins."

"They're not dolphins. They're porpoises."

"How can you tell?"

"The fins. Dolphins have curved fins, and porpoises' fins look like little triangles."

"I like dolphins," said Gussie. "They have their own special language."

Stuart gave his best dolphin impression.

"What were you saying?"

"I said, 'Your grandmother is going to skin your hide.' "

"It's like how we have ARP talk."

"True." It was hard for Stuart to comprehend how this child could be Isaac's. She was so thoughtful and earnest.

Stuart and Gussie watched the last of the porpoises swim beyond Million Dollar Pier and out of sight. The wind was picking up and the rescue boat was getting smaller with each passing minute. If the waves got much bigger, Robert would have to turn around.

"Stuart," Gussie said, tucking a piece of hair that had escaped the cap behind her ear, "if Florence hadn't died, would you have married her?"

The question felt like a kick between the shoulder blades. Stuart pictured the brunt force of her remark knocking him off the stand and into the hard-packed sand three feet below.

"That's a big question for so small a girl."

"I'll be eight soon."

"I guess that's true." How could he explain his relationship with Florence in terms a little girl—even one as precocious as Gussie—might understand? That there had been days when his wanting had felt like an open wound that needed to be tended to immediately, and other days it had felt like a bone he could bury in the backyard, something to come back to when Florence was ready, if she would ever be ready.

"Did you love her?" Gussie asked.

"I did but it wasn't that simple."

"Why not?"

It was a good question. Why hadn't it been that simple?

"Well, for one thing, I'm not Jewish."

"Does that matter?"

Stuart turned to look at her. "It shouldn't but it does."

"What are you?"

"Nothing. Maybe Protestant? I don't really know anymore."

"So Jews can't marry Protestants?"

"I think Jews prefer to marry Jews."

Gussie squeezed her lips together and her chin began to quiver. Worried she might cry, Stuart scurried to fix what he'd said. "I don't know that that was it, though. I was also her coach."

Another poor excuse. He wasn't nearly as noble as all that. If Florence had given Stuart even a small sign, during one of those early morning practices, he would have been tempted to make love to her, right there in the bilge of the boat. But she had never given him the slightest indication she was interested.

"Are coaches not allowed to get married?"

Stuart laughed. "No, they are." When Florence returned from France, he had imagined that he might tell her how he felt and see if she felt the same way. If the revelation changed the dynamic of their friendship, then that would have been something he had to live with.

"I made you something," Gussie said, reaching into the pocket of her sundress.

She withdrew a small rock and handed it to him.

Stuart turned it over. On one side she had painted two miniature sea horses.

"How lovely, Gus. Thank you."

"I wanted to ask"—her voice suddenly a whisper—"if you might marry me?"

❦

By six o'clock that evening, when Robert and Stuart lowered their life-guard stand into the sand, secured their boat, and headed toward the beach tent, the sky had not yet opened up but the storm clouds had settled squarely over the Boardwalk. As they approached the tent, Stu-art convinced himself that Anna likely wouldn't be there. Who could blame her? Any minute, it was going to pour.

Stuart put away his rescue can and the pair of oars he and Robert had taken that morning.

"Can I help with anything?"

He whipped around to find Anna standing a few feet behind him, the shoulder strap of her bathing suit peeking out from the neckline of her cotton dress. A pale pink cardigan hung from her shoulders.

"Good! You came. I was worried the storm would keep you away."

"There's no storm yet."

No sooner were the words out of her mouth than a raindrop landed on Stuart's cheek. Anna turned her face up toward the sky, and Stuart took the opportunity to grab her hand. "Come on, let's hurry."

They ran up the stairs and across the Boardwalk, through the lobby of The Covington, and up the hotel's back stairs to the second floor. By the time they tumbled out the door and onto the pool deck, Anna was out of breath and Stuart had begun an impersonation of his father that had them both cackling. "Shhh, whisper," he said in the loudest whisper imaginable, which only caused her to laugh harder. The deck was empty. In preparation for the coming storm, all the chairs had been stacked against the walls, the umbrellas removed. Someone had taken all the towels and seat cushions inside.

Anna took off her cardigan and placed it aside. The first time Stuart had brought her to The Covington, she had been shy about getting undressed in front of him. He remembered her turning away from him to unbutton the front of her dress. Now, as the rain began to pick up, she reached for the material that cinched around her waist and pulled the dress up and over her head in one fluid movement. Anna wore Florence's old Ambassador Club suit, a uniform that Stuart would have recognized anywhere. He didn't have the heart to mention it, knew she had to be wearing it because she didn't own a suit of her own. She had surely picked it because it was the plainest of Florence's suits, the least likely to attract attention. On Florence the suit had seemed like a second skin. But on Anna, Stuart realized he was conscious of the fact that it was an article of clothing, and that, under the right set of circumstances, it could be removed.

Stuart shook the image from his head, pulled his shirt over his head, kicked off his shorts, and took a running leap at the pool. At the last minute, he grabbed Anna's hand and pulled her into the water with him. She let out a yelp, submerged, and then surfaced. The rain was falling harder now. Big droplets bounced off the surface of the water, hitting the undersides of their chins. The pool water was so cloudy Stuart couldn't see the bottom.

Anna had gotten much better at the crawl, and she swam three or four lengths before stopping to ask Stuart a question about her breathing technique. He took the opportunity to distract her. "I assume Gussie made it back in one piece?"

"She did. Thankfully, Esther didn't realize she was gone until about thirty seconds before she walked in the door."

"Did Gussie say where she'd been?"

"Are you trying to figure out how much trouble you're in?" she asked, moving closer to him.

"Something like that."

"She told Esther she wanted to give you something."

"That's true."

"What was it?"

"A rock."

"That's all?"

"It came with a very sweet marriage proposal," Stuart said, unable to wipe the grin from his face.

Anna raised her eyebrows and splashed water at him, but not so hard that any got in his face. "Be serious."

He laughed. "I am."

"What did you tell her?"

"That if she reached the age of twenty, and decided she wanted to marry an old man, she was welcome. But if, in the meantime, she fell in love with someone younger and more handsome, she should feel free to ask to be let out of the arrangement."

"Poor Gussie."

"Am I such a terrible prospect?"

"I think you are likely to break her heart," said Anna, in a serious enough tone of voice that Stuart began to wonder if they were still talking about Gussie.

"Anna, I want you to know something. Florence and I were never a—"

"I know," she said, quickly, as if she were embarrassed that he had felt the need to explain.

"You do?" he asked.

"She"—Anna's voice faltered, then returned to her—"told me a little."

Stuart was struck by an overwhelming urge to wrap his arms around her, to protect her from the storm that was brewing above their heads.

"I loved her," he said, not quite believing that he was saying the words aloud for the second time that afternoon. For some reason, it felt important to be honest with Anna. "But I never said anything. And I don't think she felt the same way."

Anna wrapped her arms around her chest, and Stuart worried he shouldn't have said anything. Not two minutes ago, he would have sworn she wanted him to kiss her. "Are you cold?" he asked. "Do you want to get out?"

She shook her head no. "What was it you loved about her?"

Stuart dipped his head back in the water and looked at the sky, let the rain leak into his mouth, run down his nose. He raised his head, forced himself to look Anna in the eyes. "I suppose I loved how brave she was. And capable. There was almost nothing she wouldn't or couldn't do."

"Like the Channel?" she asked, holding his gaze.

"She would have made it across, definitely. But it was more than just that one swim, or even swimming at all. You felt lucky if you got the chance to watch her make a sandwich."

Anna wiped at her eyes. Was she crying? With all the rain, it was impossible to tell.

"Do you want to get out?"

She nodded and he pulled himself out of the pool and onto the deck, looking around for anything dry they might use in place of a towel. Anna's dress and his shorts were both soaked. A chaise lounge was covered in a piece of oatmeal-colored canvas, embroidered with the words *The Covington*, and Stuart figured the underside had to still be dry. He whisked it off and carried the armful of canvas over to Anna, who had just emerged at the top of the ladder.

"It's not particularly soft but it'll do the trick," he said, wrapping the canvas, which was as big as a tent, around her shoulders.

"Thank you."

"Come over here where it's dry," Stuart said, leading her toward the rear of the pool deck where the roofline of the hotel created a small overhang—no more than a foot or two in depth. Anna offered him a portion of the canvas, which he draped around his own shoulders. The pair leaned together, pulling the canvas around themselves, and watched the rain come down.

"How are things going with your parents?" said Stuart. "Isaac says not so good."

Anna scrunched up her nose. "Isaac?"

"He's probably not a very reliable source?" Stuart said with a laugh.

She shook her head, pulled the canvas a little closer. "Actually, their prospects seem better."

"Oh?"

"We've got two extra letters now, besides Joseph's. And Joseph was very generous and started an account at the Boardwalk National Bank for them, so I think that will help."

So that's what Joseph had done with the check on the afternoon they'd returned from Atlantic Highlands. Put the money in an account in Anna's parents' name. He was a good man. "That's great news, Anna."

She looked up at Stuart then, her face as open and effervescent as he'd ever seen it. He liked the idea that Florence's death, her failure to do the one thing she'd ever wanted, was making it possible for Anna's family to be reunited. He thought Florence would have liked it, too.

They stood in silence for several long and quiet minutes. Finally, Stuart broke the spell. "I guess we could go inside. I might be able to find us some robes."

"This is nice," was all Anna said but it was enough to make him stay right where he was.

~

Stuart could hear Mrs. Tate's heavy footfalls on the stairs that led up to his room. His landlady was a large woman, with fat feet and swollen ankles, and it was rare for her to take the stairs at all, let alone all the way to the boardinghouse's third floor. The wood risers groaned under her weight, and—as if in response—Mrs. Tate did as well.

The sound caused Stuart to sit up in bed, rub his eyes, and look around for a shirt. He had begun to dig through a pile of dirty clothes when he heard the knock at his door.

"Mr. Williams?" On the other side of the door, Mrs. Tate was doing her best to catch her breath.

"One minute." Stuart spied a sweater and pulled it over his head.

"You have a package."

Odd, Stuart thought. Mrs. Tate usually left all mail—packages included—on the table under the stairs. In the three years he'd lived here, how many times had he overheard her telling a tenant that she wasn't the Pony Express? A dozen times? More?

"You didn't have to come all the way up," he said as he opened the door but, when he saw the package in her hand, he knew why she had made the trip.

It was one of The Covington's gift boxes—the kind that they used in the shop on the first floor, purple with gold lettering foil stamped on the lid—and she had to be curious as to its contents, not to mention the lineage of her third-floor tenant. She handed it to him.

"This didn't come via post?" Stuart asked, already knowing it hadn't.

"A nice man in a fancy jacket dropped it off for you."

Wilson, probably. "Was the man bald, with a dark mustache?"

"No," she said. "Sandy-colored hair, a clean-shaven face. He was a very sharp dresser."

The description matched that of his father but that couldn't be right. Stuart's father was most definitely not in the business of delivering his own packages.

"Well, thanks," said Stuart, moving to close the door.

"You're not going to open it?" she asked, letting her curiosity get the better of her.

Stuart felt bad for Mrs. Tate, bad for anyone who lived vicariously through people she barely knew. "It's probably just a shirt."

Mrs. Tate didn't move an inch. Stuart had no idea what was in the box, but it seemed he would have no choice but to open it with Mrs. Tate as witness. He tucked the box against his body so that he might use a free hand to wiggle the lid up and off. When he had freed it, he looked behind him for a place to put it but Mrs. Tate was quicker than that. "I'll hold it for you," she said, her hand already extended.

Whatever it was was wrapped in a layer of The Covington's custom-printed tissue paper—white with small interlocking Cs. A notecard, snug in its envelope, sat on top of the paper, and Stuart held it aside.

"What's the occasion?" Mrs. Tate asked as Stuart pulled aside the paper but he didn't answer. He'd seen enough.

"No occasion—just something being returned to me," he said, grabbing the lid back from his landlady before she could argue. "Thanks so much for delivering it."

Mrs. Tate looked crestfallen, though how much was related to the fact that she would never know the contents of the box and how much was related to the fact that she now had two flights of stairs to travel to get back to her apartment, Stuart didn't know.

Stuart waited for her to turn toward the stairs before softly closing the door behind her. Alone in his room, he tossed the box onto his bed and tore open the note, which was written on his father's stationery— *John F. Williams* engraved across the top.

Stuart,

Your friend left this behind yesterday evening. I thought she might want it back.

As ever,

Your Father

P.S. Next time, I'd urge you to keep the covers on the chaise lounges. The frames are made of Teak, which doesn't hold up well in the rain.

Inside the box was Anna's pink cardigan, professionally laundered, pressed, and folded. Stuart would have liked to have thrown the box against the bedroom's far wall but he hated to return a wrinkled garment to her, so he contented himself with ripping his father's note in half and then in quarters.

The rain had never relented. Eventually, it had started to grow dark and Anna had had to get home, so Stuart darted out from the overhang and across the pool deck to retrieve her dress and his shirt and shorts. He must have missed the cardigan entirely. When he returned to Anna, their clothing in hand, she had already folded the canvas chair cover and placed it aside. The dress was soaked through, so Stuart had wrung it out for her, but even then, it was impossible for her to get into it on her own. The fabric stuck to her skin like seaweed. "Let me help you," he offered, and she had held up her arms as he pulled the wet fabric over her head, across her breasts—her nipples hard against the bodice of her bathing suit—and down around her hips. Stuart didn't know what irritated him more—that he hadn't kissed her then or that his father had likely been watching the scene unfold.

Anna

It was obvious that Anna had done something to upset Esther, although Anna couldn't be sure what that something was. In the last several weeks, Esther had turned quiet, except when she was ordering Anna around. This evening, after an early supper, she had handed a copy of F. Scott Fitzgerald's new book to Anna and instructed her to go to the hospital and read to Fannie. Anna had tried her best to get out of it. "She hardly knows me," said Anna. "Wouldn't she prefer you?"

"Probably," said Esther, putting a hand on her back, "but I just can't bear it today."

Anna wondered how she could bear it any day. On Sunday, Florence would have been dead two months. Anna tried to imagine what it would be like to lose a child and then to trudge over to the hospital each day, sit with Fannie, and pretend everything was fine. It had to be exhausting.

Then there was the issue of Fannie's room, which was so dark and depressing it would make anyone want to avoid visiting. When Anna arrived, she dragged the chair close to the window and pulled the blinds up six inches so she'd have enough late afternoon sun to read the book's fine print.

Fannie looked as if she were dozing but the moment Anna raised the blinds, she heard a quiet voice from the bed say, "You're going to get us in trouble."

"Am I?" Anna asked. "Should I lower them?"

"God no. It's nice to get a little light."

"What does your mother do when she reads to you?"

"She doesn't."

Anna looked at the book in her hand. The way Esther had talked, Anna assumed Fannie couldn't go a single day without being read to.

"Well, I'm just here to keep you company, so I'm happy to do either."

"What did you bring?"

"Tender Is the Night."

"I haven't read it."

"Neither have I."

The book might as well have been set in Atlantic City, Anna realized as she began to read, "'On the pleasant shore of the French Riviera, about half way between Marseilles and the Italian border, stands a large, proud, rose-colored hotel. Deferential palms cool its flushed façade, and before it stretches a short dazzling beach. Lately it has become a summer resort of notable and fashionable people—'"

Anna read until the sun sank in the sky, until Rosemary Hoyt had been drawn into the Divers' circle of friends and Dick Diver had acknowledged the girl's attraction to him. Rosemary wasn't just attracted to Dick Diver—she was completely infatuated with him. And Anna found herself wondering if the feeling was so different from the buzzy sensation she got when she looked at Stuart.

Once, when she thought Fannie had fallen asleep, she folded down the page and placed the book on her bedside table. "Don't stop, please," Fannie had whispered, so Anna picked up the book and continued, squinting her eyes to make out the words in the evening's fading light.

"Isn't it interesting that Rosemary's mother wouldn't be a proponent of marriage?" said Fannie, at one point, when Anna paused to pour herself a glass of water.

"I guess marriage didn't work for her. Remember, she's got two dead husbands."

Fannie leaned on her elbows in bed. "But I don't think Rosemary's mother is referencing her own experiences. It's bigger than that."

"Lie down." Anna went back and skimmed the pages she'd just read. "I suppose Mrs. Speers believes Rosemary is special, deserving of the chance to earn a living and stand on her own two feet."

"Do you think that's a better kind of life?" asked Fannie. "Not being beholden to anyone?"

Anna thought of Joseph and the money he'd deposited in the bank account at the Boardwalk National Bank. "We're all beholden to someone."

"You know what I mean," said Fannie. "A husband. Someone you'll never please."

Anna tilted her head and looked at Fannie. Was Fannie's marriage so imperfect? She couldn't stop herself from asking, "Is Isaac hard to please?"

Fannie just nodded and stared at the ceiling. Suddenly, she seemed very far away. Anna didn't know what to say to her, found it hard to defend a man whose company she did not enjoy. Eventually, Fannie was the one to speak: "Sometimes I feel as though I've spent the last eight years holding my breath."

Anna understood the sentiment—what it felt like to lose control of one's own destiny. "I think most women make some sacrifices for their own security, or the security of the people they love." She looked at Fannie's round belly.

"Not Rosemary Hoyt," said Fannie with a short laugh.

Anna flipped the book over and studied the photograph of Fitzgerald on the dust jacket. He was a handsome man, with features that weren't unlike Stuart's. "I think it's possible that Mr. Fitzgerald wrote a woman who doesn't exist."

~

Anna arrived home from the hospital to find a familiar airmail envelope waiting for her on the dresser in the Adlers' front hall. The front was littered with stamps, most of which had Hitler's face on them.

The contents of the letter, written in her mother's native Hungarian, were brief.

Dearest Anna (and Joseph),

We provided the bank deposit slip, along with the letter indicating that the account had been established in our name and that we had permission to draw a hundred dollars monthly in the first year. The consul-general laughed and asked what we'd do in the

*second year. He is demanding that some amount of money be put
in an irrevocable trust in our name and wants us to show evidence
that we have permission to draw from its earnings. We tried to ask
how much money would be enough—to which he replied, "I'll tell
you when it's enough." Not very helpful. We know people who have
gotten visas with nothing more than an affidavit from a distant
cousin, so this new development is particularly disheartening.*

*Joseph, I know there's not much more you can do. You have
your own family to consider. I remain grateful that Anna is safely
in the United States and look forward to learning how she is
settling in at school.*

*As for us, there's a rumor that the American consulate in Vienna
is friendlier to Jews. Leaving Germany and waiting for a visa in
Austria might be a prudent decision, particularly since we are now
considered stateless in the eyes of the German Reich. My worry is
that if we go and the consul there needs us to present additional
documents, they will be more difficult to obtain from outside the
country. The U.S. consulate here keeps urging Jews to wait it out in
Germany. Apparently, the Americans think Hitler's government will
soon be toppled. I wish I could believe this but everything we see, in
the streets and in the newspapers, seems to indicate otherwise.*

My love to you, Anna. And my sincere thanks to you, Joseph.

Inez

Anna pictured her mother, a coat tightly cinched around her waist, a
folio of papers clutched to her chest, standing before the consul general,
making a case for herself. She could picture the little room where the
interviews were conducted, the way the people waiting in the lobby—
almost all German Jews seeking visas—refused to so much as whisper to one another, lest they say or do anything that might ruin their
chances of being granted a visa. The officials who had conducted Anna's
interview had sneered at her documents—more than fifty in total—and

asked a series of questions that in any other circumstance would have been considered impertinent. When had Paul met her mother? When had they married? Was Anna illegitimate? At every turn, Inez had produced the right document—Anna's father's military records, his death certificate, her mother and Paul's marriage certificate. By the time Anna received her student visa, she or her parents had passed through the doors of more than twenty-five government agencies.

Anna would show the letter to Joseph but she suspected her mother was right and that there was not much more he could do. It had been one thing to plead for his help when what she needed was an affidavit, even several of them. Everyone knew that affidavits were of no real consequence; no American who signed one for Jewish relatives, friends, or even acquaintances actually expected to have to provide financial support to them forever. But this was different.

Anna folded the letter and carefully placed it back in the envelope. She hurried to her bedroom, grabbed her handbag, and tucked the envelope inside it. Then she shouted down the hallway, toward the kitchen, "Esther?"

Esther was at the sink, scouring a pan. She didn't look up.

"Where does Eli Hirsch work? Is his position with the American Jewish Committee full-time?"

Esther looked surprised to have been asked about Mr. Hirsch, and also slightly curious. But asking Anna why she wanted to know would have meant engaging her in a real conversation—something Esther hadn't done in weeks. So instead she answered Anna's question in as few syllables as possible: "The office is on Vermont Avenue. Near the lighthouse."

"Thanks."

"If you're heading out, could you take Gussie with you?"

Anna had already turned to go, so she merely waved a hand over her shoulder and called behind her, "Sorry, not now. I can't." It was, she realized, the first time she'd ever told Esther no.

∼

At least some of the money Eli Hirsch raised for the American Jewish Committee had to have been poured into its offices, which were large and

lavishly appointed. A secretary greeted Anna, asked if she had an appointment, and when Anna admitted she didn't, took her name and hurried
down the hall, no doubt planning to tell Mr. Hirsch about his unan-
nounced visitor in person so she couldn't be overheard speaking into the
telephone. When the secretary returned a few moments later, she looked
vaguely disappointed to tell Anna that Mr. Hirsch would, in fact, see her.

"Anna," Mr. Hirsch said, standing, when the secretary led her into his
office at the end of the hall. "What a pleasure."

"Thank you for seeing me."

"Of course," he said, leading her away from his desk and over to an
arrangement of furniture by the window—a small sofa and two club
chairs, all expertly upholstered. "What can I do for you?"

"It's my parents," said Anna, pulling her mother's letter out of her
purse. If Mr. Hirsch had been able to read Hungarian, she'd have handed
it to him and saved them both the trouble but, instead, she summarized
the letter's contents.

As Anna spoke, he pressed the pads of his fingers together and closed
his eyes. Was he listening? It was hard to tell. When she finished, she
didn't give him time to say a word. "What she doesn't tell me—ever—is
how bad things must be getting. My father's been out of work for over a
year, and I read enough in the papers to know Jews aren't just being let
go from their jobs. Before I left, that tourist couple was beaten nearly
to death, and Kalterborn's son, too."

Mr. Hirsch had opened his eyes and was now staring at Anna intently. "Parents will always try, I've found, to protect their children."

"Yes, well, I'd like to be in a position to protect my parents," Anna said.
"At lunch last month, you made a joke, or at least I thought it was a joke—
about marriage being the surest way to get my parents out of Germany."

Mr. Hirsch threaded his fingers together and gave her a sad smile
that didn't touch his eyes. "Things would be much easier if you were
an American citizen."

"What would change?"

"Your parents would qualify for a preference visa. Spouses of U.S.
citizens get first preference, and parents get second preference."

"So, they'd skip to the front of the line?"

"Not exactly. The consul might still give them the runaround. But candidates for preference visas don't have to worry about proving that they won't be a public charge."

"What about converting a student visa to a permanent visa? Applying for citizenship through the regular channels?"

"It's all such a mess right now. It might take years. Or never happen at all. My understanding is that you'd have to leave the U.S. and wait out the application process somewhere else—maybe Canada, or Cuba."

"And if I married?"

"It's relatively simple. You wouldn't have to worry about the visas, just apply for citizenship. You—or rather, your husband—would file a petition with the commissioner general of immigration at the Department of Labor, requesting that your parents' visa application be classified as nonquota, or preference. They'd look at your marriage license, maybe do a little additional digging, and then inform the State Department of your request. The result would be that the consul would move your parents' visa application from the quota pile to the nonquota pile, and as you know, the nonquota pile moves much faster."

Anna thought of Stuart. In the pool the other night, and later when he helped her pull her wet dress over her head, she could have sworn he wanted to kiss her. She had wanted it, too, in a different way than she'd wanted Florence's kiss, the night she received the letter. With Stuart, she had felt a quiet thumping in her chest that made it difficult to focus on anything he said. It was as if a gong had been struck somewhere in her center, the sound and its accompanying vibrations reverberating outward, toward her face, her hands, her feet.

"Do you have children, Mr. Hirsch?"

"Yes, four daughters and a son."

"And if one of your daughters did what you're proposing—turned down college to marry instead—would you be angry?"

"If her husband could support her and she thought he would make her happy, no."

"What if he was a gentile?"

Mr. Hirsch squeezed his lips together. The room was so quiet Anna could hear the ticking of the clock that sat across the room, on the corner of his desk.

"We live in trying times, Miss Epstein."

"So, you might forgive her?"

"I might."

~

Anna returned to the apartment for just long enough to retrieve her copy of *The Magic Mountain* and remove a five-dollar bill from its pages. She tucked the money in her purse and took it to the Block Bathing Suit Co. on the corner of Pacific Avenue and St. James Place, where she placed it on the counter.

One of the saleswomen, a girl who couldn't have been much older than Anna, asked if she could help her, and Anna tried not to think of how she'd explain such frivolity to her mother, when she said, "I want to buy the most beautiful bathing suit you've got."

It was as if the girl understood Anna's urgency, could sense that something important was on the line. Immediately, she began plucking suits of every shape and color out of the drawers behind the counter. "Do you know your size?" she asked as she eyed Anna's bust.

"I don't. I'm sorry."

"It doesn't matter," said the salesgirl as she led Anna toward a dressing room in the back of the store. "Get undressed."

For a half an hour, the girl handed Anna one bathing suit after another. "That one you're wearing was featured in the *Atlantic City Press* last weekend. Did you catch the piece Alicia Hart wrote?"

"What was it about?" Anna asked through the curtain as she yanked the legs of a black-and-white suit down around her thighs. It wasn't flattering.

"Checking up on your weight before you buy a new swimsuit."

Anna made a face in the mirror. "I guess I don't have time for that."

"Try this one," said the girl as she dangled an emerald-green bathing suit around the edge of the curtain.

Anna seized it at once. "It's a beautiful color."

"I think it will look nice with your hair."

Anna was in it in a flash. "Oh, wow," she said as she looked at herself in the mirror. She didn't think she'd ever seen a suit so pretty. It was made of nylon, not wool, and tied around her neck, leaving her back exposed. The suit pushed and pulled in all the right places—accentuating her small waistline and breasts—but it was the color that made the biggest impression. In the suit, Anna's ordinarily pale skin glowed.

The salesgirl peeked her head into the dressing room, and when she saw that Anna was dressed, pushed back the curtain so she could see her properly. "You look lovely."

Anna stared at her reflection, from all angles, trying to see herself as she imagined Stuart might.

"If you don't buy that suit right now, I'm going to call my manager."

"How much is it?"

"Three dollars."

Anna felt a stab of guilt, thinking about the money. But it *was* a beautiful suit, dazzling even. "I'll take it."

At the counter, the salesgirl folded the suit carefully, wrapped it in tissue paper, and tucked it away in a brown box, which she tied tight with a piece of twine. Anna took the box and thanked her, then ran back to the apartment, so eager was she to lay eyes on the suit once more.

Back at the Adlers', Anna went straight to her bedroom. She tossed her purse on Florence's bed and sank onto her own, where she wasted no time tearing open the box's neat packaging. The bathing suit was as beautiful as it had been in the store, and most important of all, it had never belonged to Florence.

Anna went to the radiator and retrieved Florence's suit from its hiding place. She walked with it over to Florence's dresser, rubbing the nubby material between her fingers. After she had brought it to her lips for a brief moment, she folded it carefully and tucked it away in the same drawer where she'd found it.

～

When Anna arrived at the beach tent the following evening for her regularly scheduled lesson, Stuart surprised her. "I thought we'd graduate you to the ocean. See how you do in the waves."

"No pool?"

"No pool," he said, cuffing her lightly in the arm.

Anna liked The Covington's pool, liked the quiet seclusion of their little bowl of water. There had to be a hundred or more hotel rooms with views of the pool deck but when she was in the water with Stuart, dusk wrapping itself around their wet shoulders, she felt protected, safe.

"But first," said Stuart, "can I drag you out for a drink with a bunch of the guys from my old beach tent? Everyone's meeting at Bert's."

"Is tonight a bad night?" Anna asked, thinking of the emerald-green bathing suit she wore under her dress. "We don't have to—"

"No, I want you to come."

It had been more than a month since Stuart had given Anna her first swimming lesson, and in that time, they'd never gone anywhere but The Covington's pool. He walked her home each night, all the way to the sidewalk in front of the apartment. There had been several nights when they had walked past a crowded diner and she had been tempted to ask if he wanted to stop. But asking had always felt too forward, as if she were extending the relationship beyond its natural bounds and possibly even trying to usurp Florence's role in his life. Florence was the one, she imagined, who squeezed into diner booths with Stuart, sipping coffee and sharing slices of pie.

Bert's was located on the Boardwalk, close to the Maryland Avenue beach tent, and by the time Stuart and Anna arrived, a bunch of guys and a handful of girls had already pushed several small cocktail tables together and ordered a round of drinks. Stuart procured two chairs from an empty table nearby, and Anna watched as everyone at one end of the seating arrangement moved their own chairs to make room for him.

Anna felt sure people had been happily making room for Stuart his whole life.

Stuart pulled out Anna's chair, and she sat down in it. "Anna, this is Charles Kelly," Stuart said, introducing the man to his left. Charles was accompanied by a pretty girl Stuart didn't know.

"I'm Lillian," said the girl, reaching her hand across the table.

Anna extended hers. "Pleased to meet you."

Stuart continued around the table, introducing her to a half-dozen members of the ACBP. When he got all the way around the table, he clapped the shoulders of the man who sat on Anna's other side and said, "And this is Irish Dan, the craziest son of a gun you'll ever meet." Irish Dan removed an imaginary hat from the top of his head and tipped it toward her.

Anna bent her head low, pretending to curtsy. "No surname for you?"

"Doyle," he said and stuck out his hand. "Nice to meet you."

"What makes you so crazy?" she asked, idly, as Stuart took a seat and ordered two beers.

"I have a habit of reacting first, and thinking things through later."

"That doesn't sound so crazy."

"Stuart," Irish Dan said, raising his voice so as to be heard over the other conversations, "I like this girl."

Stuart smiled, winked at Anna, and said, "Me too."

The chairs were pushed close, and Anna was acutely aware of the number of inches that separated Stuart from her. If she moved her knee, even slightly, it might knock against his. Did he think about these sorts of things, too?

Their beers arrived and Stuart handed Anna hers, icy cold in the bottle. "Cheers," he said as they clinked the bottlenecks. She took a short sip.

"You two going to the Lifeguard Ball?" Lillian asked. Anna was fairly certain Charles kicked his date under the table because a moment later, Lillian looked at him apologetically and said, "I was just *asking.*"

Anna didn't know what the Lifeguard Ball was and certainly didn't know how to answer the question, so she was relieved when Stuart didn't miss a beat. "I haven't asked her yet but I'm hoping so." Anna turned in her chair to look at him. "It's at the end of the summer. Will you come?" he asked quietly.

She didn't know what to say, especially in front of so many people she didn't know, so she just said, "Yes."

Stuart's face broke into a broad smile then, and he reached into Anna's lap to give the hand closest to him a celebratory squeeze. The touch of Stuart's skin against hers sent a jolt through her body, and Anna wondered immediately if he'd felt it, too.

When, instead of removing his hand, Stuart weaved his fingers through hers, Anna stopped listening to a word that was being said around her. All she could concentrate on was the way Stuart traced her knuckles with his thumb.

They might have sat like that all night, blindly learning the contours of each other's hands, had Lillian not declared her seat no good. "It's dull as doornails over here. Stuart, switch seats with me," Lillian said, already standing. "I'd much rather talk to Anna than Charles."

Was Stuart obligated to play Lillian's game of musical chairs? Anna didn't think so but she also knew he was too polite to say no.

"Charles, I thought you said this one liked you," Stuart teased. He let go of Anna's hand, and she watched, crestfallen, as he stood, grabbed his beer, and moved across the table from her. When he looked at her, from the seat Lillian had so recently abandoned, she thought he turned up the corners of his mouth, apologetically, but it was hard to tell because Anna was too embarrassed to study his face for long. Her hand burned in her lap.

Anna had always thought Stuart handsome and had always known him to be kind but she wondered if she was giving those feelings more credence than they deserved, now that Eli Hirsch had so plainly spelled out her options. She looked around the table. Every one of Stuart's friends on the Atlantic City Beach Patrol was a gentile. She knew for a fact that his father's hotel didn't rent rooms to Jews. Surely, he didn't want a Jewish wife? Except, Anna reminded herself, he had confessed to loving Florence.

Lillian plunked herself down in Stuart's empty chair. "I like the view from here much better," she said, winking at Charles. Anna was inclined to hate her, not just for banishing Stuart to the far side of the table but for the easy way she captured the group's attention. She was so casual, so frank, so painfully American.

"You're German?"

Anna nodded and took a sip of beer. It wasn't worth explaining that she had been born in Hungary.

"When did you meet Stuart?"

"A few months ago."

Lillian very clearly wanted more explanation but what was there for Anna to tell? *We were introduced by a girl who's now dead.*

"And you've been seeing each other since then?"

Anna glanced across the table at Stuart, wondering if he'd heard Lillian's question. Charles was in the middle of a story of his own, but there was something about the way Stuart sat, upright, one ear toward Lillian and Anna's conversation, that made Anna wonder if he was try-ing hard to listen in.

"Stuart's been teaching me to swim."

"Oh, so you're not seeing each other?" Lillian persisted.

The phrase *seeing each other* seemed like such a strange euphemism for dating. Anna stared at her hand—still in her lap. What could she say other than no? She shook her head.

"In that case," said Lillian, "half the girls in Atlantic City will sleep easier tonight."

"Oh?"

"It's true. Charles says they *all* fall for Stuart. A handsome member of the Beach Patrol who also happens to be the heir to a hotel fortune. What could be better, right?"

Anna took a long swallow of beer. Lillian was unbearable.

"There was some girl he was hung up on for a while. But I think that's all in the past now."

Who was she talking about? Florence? Anna had to get away from Lillian. She drained her beer, put the bottle down on the table, mum-bled something about having to use the lavatory, and disappeared into the back of the bar, where a waiter pointed her toward the water closet. After she had found the little room, she closed the door behind her with a grateful thud, threw the lock, and leaned heavily against the door's louvered slats.

Lillian sounded incredibly crass, the way she talked about Stuart. But was Anna any better? Wasn't she just another girl who was trying to convince Stuart to fall in love with her? The girls Lillian knew wanted Stuart for his father's money, and Anna wanted him for his citizenship. He probably deserved a girl who wanted neither.

There was a light knocking on the door of the water closet. Anna felt the vibrations in her shoulder blades. "I'll be out in a minute," she called.

"It's me," said Stuart. "What do you think about getting out of here?"

~

Outside Bert's, the sun had begun to set and the sky looked almost lavender. Stuart suggested they walk along the beach, instead of the Boardwalk, so they both kicked off their shoes and carried them in their hands as they made their way south along the edge of the sand.

"When we get closer to the apartment," Stuart said, "we can decide whether we still want to swim." Anna could tell he was being gentle with her. Usually, when it came to her lessons, there was no getting out of them. But he seemed to sense that the outing had gone poorly, or at least not well.

"I'm sorry I moved seats," he said.

Anna let out a little laugh.

"What?" he asked, smiling. "I didn't know she'd be so bad."

"She's terrible."

Stuart scrunched up his nose. "I feel rather bad for Charles."

"Charles! What about me?"

"You're right, you're completely right," said Stuart, nudging her shoulder affectionately with his. "For the record, I can't get *any* girl in Atlantic City."

"Oh?"

"Kitty Carlisle performed at the Nixon Theatre last month, and she wouldn't even return my calls."

Anna grinned. He'd obviously heard every word Lillian had said. "You must have been despondent."

"I was," he said with a grin. "Want to swim here?"

They'd come to a spot of beach not far from Steel Pier. By the time Anna could respond, Stuart had already dropped his shoes in the sand and pulled his shirt over his head. Tentatively, she began to undress.

"Is this okay?" Stuart asked, sensing her trepidation. "If you hate swimming in the ocean, we'll go back to the pool tomorrow."

"It's fine," she said as she worked the buttons on her dress. She didn't feel fine, she felt like a complete fraud. Her dress slipped off one shoulder, exposing the bright green suit underneath.

"Anna Epstein, do I detect a new bathing suit?"

She could feel her face flush but she made a point of giving him what she hoped was a coquettish smile.

"Let me see it. All of it."

Anna skipped the rest of the buttons and pulled the dress over her head instead. "Ta-da," she said, hoping she came off like a girl who was always buying new bathing suits and parading them around the beach.

Stuart seemed to sense she needed reassurance. "You look beautiful." He grabbed her hand, briefly, and said, "The suit's nice, too."

Suddenly Anna wished for the dingy black bathing suit at the back of Florence's drawer, an article of clothing that allowed her to hide in plain sight.

"Anna, is there something else the matter?" Stuart asked.

How much should she tell him? It was hard to know. If she shared too much, she ran the risk of him seeing right through her, of recognizing that her affection was muddied with other desires. If she didn't share anything, how would he ever know what she needed?

"I heard from my mother yesterday. Things aren't looking very good for my parents."

"What are they saying?"

"That there's not enough in the bank account Joseph opened." She held her balled-up dress in front of her chest.

"What about the affidavit?" asked Stuart. "You said there were more letters now."

"The consul wants them to come from close relatives."

"And your parents have no relatives in the U.S.?"

Anna shook her head. "Just me."

"Right, of course," Stuart said, acknowledging his slip with a small laugh. "You couldn't sponsor them, I suppose?"

"I'm on a student visa." She used her free hand to tuck a piece of hair behind her ear.

"There's nothing else Joseph can do?" Stuart asked.

"He's done so much already."

"How much was in the account?"

"Twelve hundred dollars," she said, and watched Stuart's eyebrows jump.

"And the consul is saying it's not enough? That's crazy."

"They told my parents they'd want to see 'some amount' of money in an irrevocable trust."

"How much?"

"They didn't say. But if the expectation is for them to live off the interest, without touching the principal, we're probably talking about close to five thousand dollars."

Stuart let out a low whistle.

"I know."

"What does Joseph say?"

"Nothing definitive. But I'd be surprised if he can part with that much money."

"Few people can."

They stood there in silence for several minutes. If only Anna knew what to say or do to turn the evening around. It was possible that, at this point, it was already too far gone.

"Do you know Eli Hirsch?" Anna finally asked.

"Vaguely."

"I went to see him yesterday." A sand crab scurried past their feet, and they both watched it disappear into a hole in the sand. "He thinks my best option is to forget school and try to get American citizenship. Then my parents would qualify for a preference visa, which is far easier to get."

"Wouldn't your parents be crushed?"

"My father hasn't worked in over a year."

"How easy is it to get American citizenship?"

"If I applied for permanent residency, not very easy." Anna inhaled and forced herself to look at Stuart. "But if I married an American, it's fairly straightforward."

Had she really repeated Eli Hirsch's suggestion aloud? Anna wasn't drunk, by any means, but the beer had left her feeling bold.

"Is that what you want?" Stuart asked, his brow furrowed. "To marry?"

Anna couldn't bear to meet his eyes for a moment longer. Instead she looked away, studied the way the sand stuck to her toes. All she wanted this very instant was to put her dress back on. "I don't know."

"Do you have your eye on one American in particular, or will any American do?" Stuart's voice had a hard edge to it. Anna had never seen him angry, didn't know it was even possible to elicit such a response from him.

"Stuart, please." She reached for his hand again, the same hand that had felt like it was another part of her under the table at Bert's, but he shook it away. "Let's just swim, okay?"

"It'll be dark soon," he said, looking up at the sky and then back at her. "I think we've lost our window."

Anna bit her lower lip. How had she made such a disaster of this?

"Can you make it the rest of the way home?" he asked. "I told some of the guys I might try to meet back up with them when we were through."

Through? She nodded vigorously, wanting badly for him to know she was fine, although it didn't look like he was waiting for an answer. He had already scooped up his shirt and shoes and begun walking back down the beach. Anna watched him get smaller and smaller, wondering if at any point he might glance over his shoulder to find her still standing in the same spot. But he never did.

August 1934

Gussie

By the time Anna and Gussie arrived at the beach, on Saturday morning, to watch Atlantic City's annual pageant swim, a hundred or more swimmers had been corralled behind the start line.

A few ACBP lifeguards had cleared a wide path to the water's edge. Now they patrolled either side with their arms outstretched. "Move back!" someone called, so Gussie and Anna and several hundred other spectators took a half-dozen large steps backward.

More lifeguards were stationed in rescue boats along the course, ready to disqualify swimmers who cut corners or dive for the ones who had overestimated their own abilities. It'd be easy to do so, as the course was challenging. Swimmers entered the water in a mad dash at States Avenue and, presuming they didn't get a fist or a foot in the face, swam out into open water, where the waves could be especially unforgiving. The rule was that the swimmers had to make a sharp turn at the orange buoy and swim 220 yards north to Garden Pier. Only after they'd rounded the second buoy, past the pier, could they return to shore.

Gussie scanned the course, looking for Stuart. He wasn't at the start line but it was hard to tell if he was in one of the rescue boats. A few guards dangled from Garden Pier, where they had a bird's-eye view of the race and could holler at the swimmers below, but Gussie couldn't make out their faces from this far away.

At precisely ten o'clock, a man with a megaphone stepped up to the start line and welcomed the swimmers and spectators to the event. The crowd cheered, and Gussie clapped her hands excitedly. She looked over at Anna, whose arms were folded across her chest. She had never looked so miserable.

At breakfast, Gussie had pleaded for someone to take her to the pageant swim but no one had been inclined to do so. "Not this year," her grandmother said, resignedly, as she passed Gussie the lox.

"But we always go," Gussie complained, and the grown-ups just looked at each other.

Finally, her father, who was making a rare appearance at the apartment, broke the silence, "Gus-Gus, we always go because Florence always swims it."

"So?" said Gussie, "I like it no matter what."

Gussie *had* always liked attending the pageant swim but it was particularly thrilling last year when Florence had won the whole thing. Gussie and her parents and grandparents had gone down to the beach to witness the spectacle, and everyone had screamed and carried on as Florence made her way out to sea. Gussie could no more pick out her aunt, among the dozens of swimmers, than she could the beak of a bird in the sky but she had continued to yell, "Go Florence!" as the family hurried down the Boardwalk to watch the finish. When Florence emerged from the water, she offered the crowd a thousand-watt smile then ripped off her cap, waving it above her head triumphantly. She'd beaten all the girls, including the girls she'd swum with for the Ambassador Club and the WSA girls who had come down from New York. Mayor Bader gave huge silver trophies to the six best swimmers, three men and three women, and Gussie loved hearing her aunt's name called last.

"I'm not going to be able to see," Gussie said to Anna after a tall man in a straw hat moved in front of her.

"You'll be fine."

Gussie darted in front of the man just as a gun went off and the swimmers—both men and women—stampeded past her, a flurry of arms and legs flying over the sand.

Last year, Florence had been near the back of the pack but it hadn't mattered one bit. By the time the first women arrived at the buoy, she was already in the lead.

"Were there this many people here last year?" Anna asked when the last of the swimmers had thrown themselves into the waves and the crowd had quieted slightly.

"More," Gussie said. The answer didn't sound right but she liked the idea of the race being better—in every possible way—when Florence had been in the water and her family had been on the sidelines. If Anna didn't believe her, she didn't let on.

Gussie could tell Anna liked the race because, as they walked toward the pier, she kept asking questions about it. She wanted to know why the race was called a pageant and what the prize was and how this year's crop of swimmers compared to previous years'. Gussie answered what she could. When she didn't know the answer, she just made something up. Anna couldn't expect her to know *everything*.

Gussie dragged Anna toward Garden Pier. The pier was lined with shops on either side of its central promenade but the main attraction was the pier's flower beds, which were crowded with exotic plants and dotted with gazebos and even a small pond. At the end of the pier sat a large exhibition hall that blocked Anna and Gussie's view of the ocean.

"Shouldn't we just wait on the beach?" asked Anna. "That way we'll be sure to see everyone exit the water."

"There's a bit of pier around back," said Gussie as she navigated the crowded promenade. What she didn't tell Anna was that she thought it likely Stuart would be at the end of the pier. It's where he had stationed himself last year, after he'd seen Florence off at the start.

When they had made their way behind the exhibition hall, Gussie scanned the crowd, looking for Stuart's head of blond hair. It took several minutes before she spotted him, standing amid a big group of lifeguards who were whooping and hollering over the railing.

Gussie raised her hand in the air and called to Stuart, and she thought she saw him turn his head but then Anna tugged at her hand to let a group of children pass, and by the time she had a view of the railing again, Stuart had disappeared. Where could he have gone? Surely, he'd seen her?

A terrible thought occurred to Gussie. Could Stuart be avoiding her? Her stomach grew queasy. It had taken her the better part of a week to work up the nerve to ask him to marry her, and she had spent an entire afternoon painting the pair of sea horses, which she had forgotten to explain, when she gave the rock to him, were *actually* Stuart and Gussie. If she had explained, he might have asked why she'd painted sea horses instead of people, and she didn't want to get into *that*. Everyone knew it was extremely difficult to paint people who looked like people. Sea horses were much easier. How often did anyone see a real sea horse up close? Not very often.

Sea horses or no sea horses, Gussie had been pleased with Stuart's response to her proposal. She hadn't expected them to marry immediately, so she wasn't put off by waiting until she was grown-up. But maybe all his talk about marrying her when she was older was just his way of saying no. Like how, when she asked her mother if she could buy penny candy at Fralinger's, the answer was always "Later." Could it be that he didn't really want to marry her at all?

When Anna eventually let go of Gussie's hand, Gussie circled back around the exhibition hall, toward the promenade, to see if she could catch Stuart. It seemed unlikely that he'd pop into one of the shops on the arcade but maybe he had gotten stuck talking to someone on his way back to the beach. She checked the amphitheater and each of the little gazebos near the pier's entrance before she realized that she'd forgotten about Anna, who would be furious with her for wandering off. Gussie turned around and hurried back toward the rear of the pier but had only made it as far as the front of the exhibition hall when she heard her name being called repeatedly. She turned to see Anna running frantically along the promenade.

"I'm here!" Gussie called.

Anna stopped in her tracks and looked around the pier wildly. Gussie could tell it was taking her a moment to locate her voice, amid all the commotion, so she called to her again. "Over here!"

When Anna laid eyes on Gussie, her face flooded with relief but then it was as if a curtain came down over her features. Her eyes narrowed and her mouth pinched shut. She walked straight over to Gussie and without saying a single word, slapped her across the cheek.

No one had ever slapped Gussie. She was so surprised by what Anna had done that she didn't even think to cry out.

"I thought you had fallen off the pier and drowned."

"I was just looking for—"

"I'm not finished."

Gussie rubbed her cheek.

"I am sorry you are having a rotten summer. A rotten year, really. Hyram, Florence, your mother's hospital stay, your father. You don't deserve any of it."

"I was just—"

"I said I wasn't finished. You have every reason to be angry and your grandparents have every reason to want to coddle you. But when you are with me, you will never disappear like that again. Do you hear me?"

Gussie was too embarrassed to say anything, so she just nodded. Was it possible that everyone on the pier had heard Anna's rebuke? How many of them had witnessed the slap? Gussie felt her face grow warm and suspected her cheeks were flushed. Anna looked at her for what felt like ages and then did something unexpected. She grabbed Gussie by the shoulders and pulled her close.

Anna's body was warm and damp with perspiration but being locked in her arms wasn't an entirely unpleasant feeling. Her embrace wasn't so different from that of Gussie's mother. Or even Florence. Their hugs had always felt sturdy and sure. Gussie rested her head against Anna's shoulder and allowed the pounding in her chest to slow.

"What's wrong with my father?" she finally asked.

"Oh, forget I said anything," said Anna as she pulled back to get a better look at Gussie. "If we hurry, do you think we'll still make the finish?"

The fastest swimmers had already arrived on the beach by the time Anna and Gussie exited the pier and made their way back onto the sand. The swimmers stood with their hands on their knees, catching their breath, and enjoying the occasional pat on the back from an excited spectator. "Well done!" Gussie shouted in the direction of three girls in Ambassador Club swimsuits.

"Is that their uniform?" Anna asked, nodding her head toward the bathing suits all three girls were wearing.

"Yes," said Gussie, giving Anna a curious look. It was an odd question, and Anna seemed struck by the answer.

There was still time to cheer on the finishers in the middle of the pack, and most definitely the stragglers, so Gussie and Anna spent the next quarter of an hour screaming at the breaking waves and the people who rode into shore on them.

As Gussie cheered, she thought she could hear Stuart's voice, strong and deep, over the collective shouts of the crowd but she didn't dare turn around to find him. Partly, she worried she'd upset the peace—so newly established—between Anna and her. And partly, she didn't like the idea of looking at a person who didn't want to look at her.

When the last of the swimmers had reached the shore, the race's dignitaries began testing the megaphone and clearing their throats. A man in a three-piece suit stepped gingerly onto the podium, which was just a large wooden box decorated with flowers and bunting. "Who's that?" Gussie whispered to Anna as the crowd surged forward but she simply shrugged.

Now it was harder to ignore Stuart, who stood directly in Gussie's sight line. She caught his eye, and he gave her a small wave and a half smile. Her heart swelled. Maybe he had liked the marriage proposal just fine and she had worried for nothing.

Gussie looked over at the podium where last year's winners—three men and two women—had gathered. Were they going to be asked to announce the awards? Distribute the medals? Gussie felt Florence's absence sorely then and reached for Anna's hand, expecting a gentle squeeze of acknowledgment.

But Anna wasn't paying any attention to Gussie, and her hand hung limp by her side. Anna was looking at Stuart, and when Gussie turned back to him, she realized that his eyes, which looked sad and maybe slightly confused, were locked on Anna's.

Surely Stuart didn't love Anna? In Gussie's opinion, Anna wasn't always even all that likable. Stuart had told Gussie on the beach that day that she was free to marry someone her own age but he hadn't said anything about himself. She hadn't even considered the fact that Stuart might fall in love first, before Gussie had a chance to grow up. Her heart started to beat hard in her chest and she crouched down in the sand so she could think more clearly.

Gussie was so distracted that she might have ignored all the speeches entirely but for the mention of her aunt's name. Florence Adler. She looked up at the podium. What had the man with the megaphone said? Now he was asking people to bow their heads, to observe a moment of silence.

"What did he just say?" Gussie whispered, rising to her feet.

"He said the committee wanted to honor Florence's memory."

"What does that mean?" she asked, rubbing her cheek, which still stung.

Anna was already pulling her in the direction of the apartment. "It means everybody knows."

Esther

After Anna and Gussie had left for the pageant swim and Isaac had made his own hasty escape, Esther washed and dried the breakfast dishes and put them away.

In a fortnight, the renters would be gone, back to Philadelphia, and she and Joseph could move back into the house on Atlantic Avenue. For several years, Joseph had advocated keeping a set of pots and pans, some dishes and flatware, even some sheets and towels at the apartment. But each summer, when it came time to close up the apartment, Esther packed everything up anyway. She preferred to believe that, by the following year, they might be able to say no to the rental income and see what the summer breezes felt like on their own front porch.

Esther knew she would never move past Florence's death—not really—but if she could distance herself from the apartment, where her daughter had most recently lived, she thought she might be able to think more clearly. By Labor Day, she'd have returned Gussie to her parents and Anna would also be gone. Esther craved an empty house and, more than anything, the chance to be alone with her grief.

"Joseph," Esther called down the hallway to the living room, where she knew her husband had to be hiding behind a newspaper. "Would you mind going downstairs and getting me a few of the packing crates?"

She listened for a response but didn't hear so much as the rustle of a page.

"I thought I might pack up some of Florence's things."

He still didn't answer her—she was sure her request had surprised him—but a moment later she heard the click of the latch on the front door and his footsteps on the stairs. She moved into the bedroom her girls had once shared and tried to ignore the evidence that Anna was now the room's only occupant.

Esther took a deep breath and began opening the drawers of her daughter's dresser. She scooped up the clothes and undergarments and swimsuits and moved them, in big armloads, over to the bed, where she could get a better look at everything. In the jumble, she spotted Florence's old Ambassador Club suit—so well-worn the black wool looked gray. She held the suit to her face as she considered the pile of clothes in front of her. What would she do with all these things? Keep them? She doubted Fannie would fit into any of them, not after a second baby. She stopped herself. *Third* baby. Anna had a slim waist and could probably wear almost everything but giving Florence's clothes to her was out of the question.

Joseph appeared in the doorway, carrying a stack of three empty crates. He set them down on the floor beside Florence's bed. "Do you want help?"

Esther placed the swimsuit on top of the dresser and looked around the room. What she wanted was her daughter back. She thought about telling him that but instead she just said, "I'm fine."

She moved one crate onto the bed, reached for a camisole, refolded it, then placed it at the bottom of the crate. Did Joseph plan to hover in the doorway all afternoon? She wished he would leave her alone but, to her disappointment, he wandered over to the dresser, opened a drawer, and removed a pair of motorcycle goggles Florence had retrofitted for her swim around the island.

"It was a smart idea," he said. "Dipping the goggles in paraffin." The wax had begun to flake off in large chunks, and he picked at a piece that hadn't yet pulled away from the leather.

Esther let out a short sigh. "A lot of good it did her."

"She made it around Absecon Island."

"And that should please me?"

"It pleased her."

Esther held on to the crate in front of her with both hands.

"You'd do it all again?" she asked, tentatively. "Teach her to swim, encourage the practicing and the competitions? Knowing how this all ends?"

"Of course not." He moved around to the other side of the bed, picked up a pair of stockings, and began to fold them. Her heart sank. He clearly intended to stay.

"Not like that," she said, reaching for another pair of stockings just like the ones between his fingers. "Fold them in half first. Then roll them."

Joseph looked at her, his eyes so full of pity it made her want to scream, but did as he was told.

He bungled three pairs before he spoke again. "There wasn't any part of you that enjoyed watching what she could do in the water?"

Esther unfurled the hosiery Joseph had folded and refolded it to her liking. *Had* Esther gotten something out of Florence's swims? She had certainly never enjoyed the helpless feeling she got when her daughter was out in the open water. But, in small ways, Esther supposed she had enjoyed Florence's triumphs. She had liked complaining to the grocer that her daughter was eating her out of house and home. He would weigh a big bunch of bananas or a bag of glossy oranges and cluck agreeably. She liked the way the mothers of the younger girls in the Ambassador Club always made a point of asking, whenever they bumped into Esther, how Florence was doing at Wellesley. Esther would recite as many lines from Florence's letters as she could remember, fully aware that the news would be reported back to the girls on the team. She wondered whether, if she ran into those women now, she would tell them to keep their precious daughters out of the water. She could picture Florence rolling her eyes at that.

"I am allowed to miss her, too," Joseph said quietly.

Esther could feel a quiet rage building inside her. How dare Joseph try to twist this moment inside out until it was about something else altogether. The words were out of her mouth before she could consider what she was saying: "At least you have Anna."

Joseph looked confused. "What does that mean?"

"How did you phrase it again?" She tossed the rolled-up stockings into the crate and moved over to Anna's dresser, where she yanked open the bottom drawer and grabbed at the thick stack of papers.

"Esther, those aren't yours."

She flipped through the pages frantically, looking for the copy of Joseph's affidavit. "It's here somewhere."

"Those documents are important. You should put them back."

"Here," she said, waving the affidavit in the air. She scanned the addendum, looking for the line that had made the hair stand up on the back of her neck. "'At seventeen, the applicant's mother and I became engaged to be married.'"

She read the rest of the paragraph aloud, including the part where he claimed Anna was *like a daughter to him*, before thrusting the affidavit at him.

"You wrote this. And, what, three months later your daughter is dead? *Kena horah.*"

Joseph closed his eyes and leaned against the bedpost. "You think the evil eye killed our daughter?"

"What should I think?"

He opened his eyes and looked at her before he said anything. "That she got a cramp. Or got caught in an undertow." His voice cracked on the word *caught.*

"She was a good swimmer," she said as she began to sob.

"Esther." He tried to move toward her, stockings in hand, but she held the stack of papers in front of her like a shield.

"Don't touch me."

"I'm sorry I didn't tell you about Inez."

"I feel like an idiot. That first summer we met, how much of it was real?"

"All of it," said Joseph as he pried the papers from her hands and pulled her toward him.

"When did you end it with her?"

"Do you remember the night you took my hand? In front of the Chelsea?"

Esther nodded her head.

"I wrote to Inez that night."

"What did you tell her?"

"That I wanted to be the kind of man who followed through on his promises but that I had met a woman whom I knew I'd never be able to let go of."

"Why didn't you tell me about her?"

"I don't know. Fear, probably."

What bothered Esther the most, when she really thought about it, was not that Joseph had loved someone else but that he hadn't trusted her with the information. Had he thought her so fragile? Their relationship so flimsy?

"All this time, you've been working with Anna to get Inez and Paul to the U.S, and I've been left to wonder why she matters. Instead of sitting around like a dingbat, I would have appreciated being given the chance to rise to the occasion."

Joseph sat down on Anna's bed, placed his hands on his knees. It took him several long seconds to find his voice.

"I've always regretted the way I treated Inez."

"You wish you'd married her?"

Joseph looked at her as if she were deranged. "No, I just wish I'd been honest with her."

"You were."

"I think I knew, long before I met you, that I wouldn't marry her. I should have told her sooner."

"You were young."

"It's no excuse."

"So, this is your penance?" Esther waved her arms at Anna's dresser, her bed. "Bringing her daughter to the United States?"

"I should have done it a long time ago."

"Brought her to the U.S.?"

"Both of them. After the war. It would have been easier then."

"Why didn't you?"

"I didn't want to hurt you."

Esther let out a short laugh that sounded angrier than she'd intended. She was so tired. Had that little blue letter really arrived a year ago? She put the stack of papers back in the drawer and moved her hands to her face, rubbing her eye sockets with the tips of her fingers. Inez could have asked for anything from Joseph, and he would have said yes because he was a decent man. Of that, Esther was sure.

"There's something else, Esther."

She watched her husband run his hands up and down the length of his thighs. "What?"

"We got another denial letter from the U.S. consulate."

"The affidavit is no good?"

"It's more than that. The consul wants to see hard-and-fast proof that Inez and Paul will be able to support themselves when they arrive in the U.S."

"If they can't get their money out of Germany, how can the consul expect them to prove anything?"

"I've provided my own bank statements, auditors' statements, deeds. Have promised to offer my support until Paul can get on his feet. But none of it is enough."

Esther felt a twinge of pity. For Anna, yes, but also for Inez and Paul.

"So, there's nothing more to do?"

"Maybe. Now the consul's suggesting sponsors open U.S.-based bank accounts in the applicants' names."

"Which you have not done."

Joseph didn't say anything, just looked away.

"You're telling me you established a bank account in Inez's name?"

He glanced at her briefly, then down at her feet.

"What did you fund it with?"

He didn't answer.

"Joseph, what did you fund it with?"

"The money from Florence's Channel swim, and some more besides."

Esther felt sick. "How much?"

"Twelve hundred dollars."

She grabbed the brass footboard of Florence's bed and steadied herself. "You put twelve hundred dollars in an account in her name?"

Joseph just nodded.

"What happens to the money if they never get out of Germany? Can you get it back?"

"A beneficiary can inherit it upon their death."

"And the beneficiary—"

Joseph looked her straight in the eyes.

"Anna," said Esther, softly. It all came back to Anna. Anna might as well have usurped Florence's life completely.

"It felt like the right thing to do. If they don't make it out, Anna will have no safety net. Assuming she stays."

"Safety net? What about Fannie? Is she entitled to a safety net? How about Gussie? Did you think of them at all?"

"I think about them all the time."

"If you had asked me, I might have suggested that we use the money to pay Isaac's portion of the hospital bill or forgive that damned loan you made him. Give our daughter a clean slate."

"You think money is all it's going to take to give Fannie a clean slate?"

They didn't speak of it often, their mutual dislike of their son-in-law. What was there to say? That they should have been more vocal, should have demanded more for their elder daughter? That they'd let Isaac's Jewish faith obscure his other—less desirable—traits?

This, she realized, was what it felt like to grow old. Eventually people felt so weighed down by the yoke of their own bad decisions that they could scarcely move.

"When the renters are out of the house," Esther started, "I wonder if I shouldn't move back into it on my own."

Joseph didn't say anything, just nodded his head in a motion so repetitive that Esther felt the urge to cross the space between them and grab his face between her hands to steady it.

"Neither of us likes the idea of this apartment sitting empty," she said.

Joseph neither scoffed nor pleaded. All he said, when he finally managed to look at her, was her name.

～

"Esther," said Anna, from the other side of the cracked bedroom door. "Are you in here?"

Esther dabbed at her eyes, and Joseph straightened his collar. "You're back?" she said as Anna pushed open the door.

"I'm sorry if I'm interrupting." Anna looked from Esther to Joseph to the tangle of clothes on top of the bedspread.

"We're just going through some of Florence's things," Esther explained. The bottom drawer of Anna's dresser was still open, and Esther worried Anna would see she had rifled through her paperwork. "Where's Gussie?"

"In her room."

"And how was the pageant?"

"Good." Anna glanced at the open drawer and then at Joseph, who looked lost in thought. "I need to tell you both something."

Joseph looked up from the stockings he held in his hands.

"At the awards ceremony, after the swim, they held a moment of silence in Florence's memory."

Esther blinked, twice, trying to comprehend what Anna had just said. "A moment of silence?"

Anna nodded.

"Did you hear that, Joseph?" Esther asked her husband, but he didn't respond, just began to run his thumb and forefinger along his eyebrows, which were knitted with worry. Now wasn't the time to push him on Anna or on Inez and Paul's immigration papers or on who would go where at the end of the season. "Joseph," she repeated, "what do we do?"

Fannie

Fannie sat bolt upright in bed. She held her stomach with one hand, grabbed hold of the mattress with the other.

"Nurse!" she yelled into the dark of her hospital room. "Nurse!"

This feeling was nothing like the small pinches of pain she'd felt periodically over the last several weeks. "If you shift your weight and the contraction goes away," Dr. Rosenthal had told her recently, "it's a Braxton-Hicks—nothing to worry about."

"Isn't it typical that a woman's health condition should be named for a man?" she had said through gritted teeth as she shifted onto her other side.

Now the pain was so consuming she could scarcely recall her own name, much less anyone else's. It was as if an iron anvil had been placed on top of her pelvis. All she could do was try to breathe.

Fannie didn't remember much about her previous labors. Gussie had been born such a long time ago now, and Fannie had been so young then, and also so naive. She had assumed her body would do what it was supposed to do when it was supposed to do it, and it had. Then Hyram had come early enough that there had been no false labor, only the real thing, with all the ensuing pain and heartache.

The cramping eased, and Fannie relaxed her grip on the mattress. She thought to check the time but couldn't see the clock.

From the nurses' lounge, she could hear the hum of a radio. "Nurse!" she tried again, louder this time.

By the time Dorothy appeared in her doorway, Fannie had been seized by another contraction. The pain shot from her back through to her abdomen. "I think it's begun," she tried to say, but had difficulty getting the whole sentence out.

"Looks that way. How regular are they coming?"

"I don't know. I've only had a few."

Dorothy put her head back out into the hall. "Hey, Helen! Call Dr. Rosenthal, will you? Fannie looks ready to go."

For a brief moment, Helen's face appeared beyond Dorothy's. Then it disappeared. "Would you please have her call my husband, too?" Fannie asked, between deep breaths.

"You hear that?" Dorothy said, over her shoulder. She turned back to Fannie. "While we wait on Dr. Rosenthal, let's see if we can try to get you comfortable."

Dorothy rearranged Fannie's pillows and urged her to relax against them. Of course, Fannie couldn't relax but she could and *did* take notice of Dorothy's conduct. In this particular set of circumstances, the nurse came off as extremely competent.

"My guess," said Dorothy, "is we'll move you to the labor room soon."

With Hyram, Fannie had been put on such a heavy dose of morphine she could barely recall the labor room at all. She had drifted in and out of consciousness, numb not only to her contractions but to the moments between each contraction, too.

The delivery room was harder to forget. The bright white light, the long white leggings that, once on, acted like straps, securing Fannie to the table. She had felt like a chained animal, had been sure she would die with her hands and feet in the stirrups and an ether mask clamped onto her face. The idea of being back in that same room, alone, trapped in a twilight sleep from which she couldn't wake, made her feel dizzy with fear.

Within a few minutes, Helen returned with word that Dr. Rosenthal was on his way. "I couldn't reach your husband," she said, "but I called your parents."

"Is my mother coming?"

"It sounds like it."

Fannie felt a wild urge to send word to her sister in France but reminded herself it would be best to wait until she was holding a healthy baby in her arms. While she waited for the doctor, she composed the telegram in her head. BABY ARRIVED TODAY STOP NO COMPLI-

CATIONS STOP WISH YOU WERE HERE STOP. Was the "wish you were here" part too much? It was true.

Dr. Rosenthal arrived and examined Fannie promptly. He turned to Dorothy. "How long since the last contraction?"

She looked at her watch. "Ten minutes."

"She's not dilated."

"What does that mean?" Fannie asked them both.

"It means," said Dr. Rosenthal, "that this baby might be willing to wait a little longer."

"Is that something we want?" asked Fannie.

"You're not due for two more weeks. So, probably. As long as your blood pressure remains in check."

Fannie didn't know whether to feel relieved or disappointed. She wanted to give the child every advantage but she thought she might go crazy if she spent another hour, let alone another fortnight, in her hospital bed.

Dr. Rosenthal promised he'd be back to check on her in half an hour and instructed Dorothy to stay with Fannie until he returned. Dorothy looked disappointed but didn't argue. She made a big show of plumping Fannie's pillows and refreshing her water but after Dr. Rosenthal was gone, she let out a large yawn and sank into the chair beside the window.

"What time is it?" Fannie asked her.

She looked at her watch. "Nearly two."

"What were you listening to? In the lounge."

"Oh, just reruns of *Palmolive Beauty Box Theater*. There's nothing on at this time of night."

"Is it dreadful working nights? I don't know how I'd stay awake."

"It's all right. It's quieter and there's usually less to do."

Fannie pulled the bedsheet over her stomach.

"Did you work before you got married?" Dorothy asked.

"If you don't count helping my parents behind the counter at the bakery, no. I got married at nineteen, so there wasn't much time for any of that."

"I want to get married."

"Do you have a boyfriend?"

"No," said Dorothy, flatly.

Fannie cocked her head to get a better look at Dorothy. She really was a very peculiar person.

"Well, try not to get too bothered by it. That's Florence's strategy. She doesn't pay any attention to the boys, and the result is that they all love her."

Dorothy gave her such a funny look that Fannie immediately wondered if she'd said something offensive. Was it wrong to compare Dorothy to Florence? They had been in the same class, after all, and Dorothy was always rattling on about Florence, or at least she had, earlier in the summer.

"What?" said Fannie.

"Nothing."

"No, what?"

"It's not my place to say anything."

"But?"

"Were you two close? Are you close?"

"Florence and me? I suppose. Maybe. I mean, yes," said Fannie.

"So, think about it for a second. Isn't it strange that you haven't heard a word from her?"

Why was Dorothy needling her? Fannie wondered if she was still upset about the phone call. "Well, she's in France now, you see."

"Knock, knock," came a voice from the hallway. Fannie would have recognized the warm timbre of her father's voice anywhere.

"Pop?" Fannie said.

"I'm told we might soon have reason to celebrate."

Fannie's heart felt big in her chest. Her father hadn't set foot in a hospital in close to twenty years but here he was, standing in front of her. He looked smaller, perhaps a tad frailer than he had in the spring. "Have you been ill?" she asked. God, she sounded just like her mother.

Joseph made a show of looking himself over, inspecting his arms and legs, the backs of his hands and the toes of his shoes. "Fit as a fiddle."

Had it been so long that she'd forgotten what he looked like? Surely, he hadn't shrunk. He walked over to the bed and kissed Fannie on the forehead, pressing his lips against her skin for several long seconds, as if he were trying to make up for his absence.

"Where's Mother?" she asked when he had finally pulled away and taken a seat on the edge of the mattress. She wondered at Dorothy for not moving out of the way, allowing her father the chair. He wasn't an old man but he wasn't a young one either.

"She'll be here shortly."

Yesterday, Fannie had been surprised when Esther stayed late at the hospital, remaining at Fannie's bedside until well past the dinner hour. Then, today, she'd barely left her alone. When Bette had brought Fannie her dinner tray this evening, Fannie had practically had to beg her mother to go home.

So, where was she now? Suddenly, it occurred to Fannie. "She's looking for Isaac, isn't she?"

Joseph pressed his lips together, as if he were trying to refrain from saying the thing he most wanted to say. "The nurse who called said she tried him first. He must not have heard the phone ring."

"Must not have," she said, unable to meet her father's eyes. The ring of the telephone in their apartment was so shrill that, for years, she had unplugged the receiver whenever Gussie napped. Where could Isaac be?

"I may have woken you for nothing," she said, glancing at Dorothy, who seemed utterly bored by their reunion. "A quarter hour ago I felt certain I was about to be wheeled off to the labor room but now I'm not so sure."

"I'm glad for the excuse to come. I should have done this months ago."

"If it makes you feel any better," said Dorothy, from her chair, "men are never any good at this."

"Dorothy," Fannie said, desperate to get the girl out of her room, at least for a few minutes. "Would you give us a little time? I promise he'll come get you if anything changes." Dorothy looked unsure of herself, torn between wanting very much to be back in the lounge, listening to her radio program, and not wanting to upset Dr. Rosenthal. Finally, she got up and left.

When Dorothy had rounded the corner, Joseph shook his head and chuckled, "That must be the one your mother's always complaining about."

"She's a pip."

"I don't know how you've stood it," said Joseph as he moved around the bed and took a seat in Dorothy's vacant chair. "A whole summer in this bed."

"I'd have much preferred to be anywhere else," said Fannie. "I'm so jealous of Florence, I could scream."

Her father looked away from her, and Fannie immediately regretted the remark. She sounded catty, when what she wanted was to come off as generous, patient, and kind. So, she tried again.

"Honestly, the hardest part's been being away from Gussie."

Joseph didn't say anything, just nodded appreciatively. Then they both allowed several quiet moments to pass.

"Your mother says you've been following the Dionne quints quite closely," he said, finally. "Have you heard the littlest one is getting a radium treatment for a tumor on her leg?"

Fannie felt a great tenderness for her father, who she knew did not approve of the reportage of sensational stories and who certainly did not believe it necessary for newspaper editors to devote multiple column inches to the daily activity of five infants—quintuplets or not. Of course, Fannie already knew about the radium treatment. Bette continued to bring her clippings, although they were hard to read in the dark of her room. "Dr. Rosenthal says radium can cure anything."

"Is that so?"

"Well, not anything. But lots of things. Not me. And not Hy—" Fannie stopped herself. Why had she done that? Bringing up Hyram when she was so close to going right back into that same delivery room. She kept one hand on her stomach, feeling for the slightest indication that another contraction was imminent.

"Fannie, I've been thinking about it a lot this summer. I think we did the wrong thing with Hyram."

"The incubator?"

"No, the burial. We should have buried him at Egg Harbor."

Halakhah was clear. There were no burial rites or mourning traditions for babies who died before their thirty-first day of life. Despite Fannie's pleadings, her child had been buried in an unmarked grave.

Fannie felt her face grow hot, her eyes well with tears. "I thought you said Rabbi Levy wouldn't allow it."

"I should have pushed harder," said Joseph. "Insisted."

"You quoted Maimonides to me."

"Maimonides lived seven hundred years ago. What does he know? He didn't see the way you loved that baby."

On the day Hyram had slipped away, the nurses at the incubator exhibit had called Fannie at home and told her to hurry down to the Boardwalk. By the time she arrived, they had transferred her baby to an incubator in the back, out of view of the mobs of summer tourists that snaked around the perimeter of the exhibition hall. She had hoped to catch her son's last breaths, to feel the grip of his tiny finger as he touched the edges of the next world, but he was already gone when she arrived.

"Mother said it was frivolous to name him."

"What did either of us know about losing a child?" said Joseph. "We should have said *Kaddish*, observed Yahrzeit."

Fannie had known, sitting in front of that incubator, that there would be no funeral, that they would not sit Shiva. In lieu of a funeral prayer, she issued an apology to her tiny son. "I'm sorry for not taking better care of you," she whispered.

That memory, which was usually so vivid, grew blurry as the baby inside Fannie tugged hard at her insides. She squeezed her eyes shut tight and dug her fingers into the hospital mattress. As the pain subsided, Fannie reminded herself that this baby did not care that the one before it had not lived.

"Should I get the nurse?" her father asked, already halfway across the room.

"What time is it?"

"Nearly a quarter after two."

A half hour had elapsed since her last contraction. She didn't need Dorothy Geller to tell her that she had a long way to go.

"Let's wait a little longer."

Joseph returned to his chair and slowly lowered himself back into it.

"Thank you," said Fannie. "For what you said about Hyram."

"Sometimes I worry, Fan. That I got so caught up with turning Florence into a champion swimmer, I forgot to ask what you wanted out of life."

"Oh, Pop. I'm fine."

"Are you?"

"I think so. I hope so."

"Being a wife is obviously very important," said Joseph slowly, "but I don't think it's the only thing."

"What else is there?" She had meant to pose the question sarcastically but it hadn't come off that way.

"I see Mrs. Simons, at the plant. She has a husband but is also a skilled secretary and an extremely competent logistician. She seems happy. Or maybe *fulfilled* is a better word."

Had Fannie ever felt fulfilled? Perhaps that first day she had held Gussie in her arms. Most days she hardly felt anything at all. It had gone on like this for so long, even before Hyram's death, that she had forgotten there was any other way to feel.

"Once this baby is a little older," said Joseph, "I wonder if you might want to come work for me."

"At the store?"

"No. In the office. At the plant."

It was a thrilling idea in theory but in practice it might be a great deal more discouraging. "Alongside Isaac?" she asked, trying to imagine how she'd navigate her marriage if there were no natural boundaries, no quiet places to seek refuge. She pictured packing two lunch pails each morning. At midday, when they took their break, Isaac would eat his pickle and hers, too.

"Perhaps."

"I wonder if Isaac would like that?"

"Does it matter?" her father asked quietly.

Fannie didn't have a quick answer to that. Nothing witty or sharp. She certainly couldn't act taken aback, not when they both knew that Esther was turning over every stone in Atlantic City, looking for her husband. She wished her mother had come to the hospital first. Fannie might have given her some places to look. Or told her not to bother.

"You're a smart girl. Always have been," said Joseph.

Truth be told, Fannie didn't even really know what people did in offices. In secretarial school, she had learned how to write memorandums and business letters and how to answer a phone but she had quit before they'd gotten to anything very tricky.

"I don't know anything about business."

"You'll learn."

Joseph

When Dr. Rosenthal returned to check on Fannie at a quarter to three, Joseph stood and excused himself. "I'll wait in the corridor," he said, although he wasn't sure either of them heard him.

He worried he wasn't doing a very good impression of Esther, who would—were she here—know what questions to ask Dr. Rosenthal and what to say to reassure Fannie. Both his girls had been born in the apartment over the store, and on each occasion, he'd done nothing more than pace the living room and say a prayer when the midwife brought word of a healthy daughter, and more importantly, a healthy wife. *Shehecheyanu.*

He heard his wife's footsteps in the stairwell before she appeared in the corridor. From where he stood, outside Fannie's room, he could fully appreciate her approach—the sure clip of her heels, the hard-set chin, the way her eyes were, perhaps for the first time in two months, open wide. Only her mouth, pinched at both sides, gave her away. She was afraid.

"Did you find him?" he asked when she was close enough that he could use a loud whisper.

"I gave up and left a note on the door of their apartment."

"Where the hell could he be?"

"They haven't moved her?"

"Not yet. I think soon." He studied his wife's anxious face.

They stood in silence for several minutes, still unsure of what to say to each other in the aftermath of their argument. When Joseph could stand it no longer, he spoke. "Bub, Mrs. Simons came to see me this afternoon."

A look of concern flashed across Esther's face. He knew she liked Mrs. Simons, always had.

"She's fine," said Joseph. "It's Isaac."

"What now?"

"She thinks he's been stealing money from the company."

Esther didn't look surprised. Just tired. "How?"

"He brought on a few new accounts this month. In Northfield. Opened lines of credit for each of them. But Mrs. Simons says they've actually been paying for their orders in cash."

"And she thinks Isaac's been pocketing their payments?"

"She's certain of it."

She closed her eyes, kneaded the bridge of her nose with her fingers. "Have you talked to him?"

"Not yet."

"What will you—"

The door opened and Dr. Rosenthal stepped into the hallway.

Esther looked up. "How is she?" she asked him.

"I want to give her a few more hours, see if she progresses on her own," he said. "If she does, then we'll move her."

"May I see her?" Esther asked.

"Yes, but be quick. She needs to rest. You two should probably get some sleep as well."

"Isaac may be on his way over," said Esther, and Dr. Rosenthal cocked a disbelieving eyebrow.

"I'll wait for him downstairs," offered Joseph. He reached for his wife's hand and squeezed it, nodded at the door of Fannie's room. "Go."

Esther didn't squeeze his hand back, didn't turn to look at him. As he watched her disappear into the room, he was struck, for the first time, by the full weight of their decision to keep Florence's death from Fannie. It was exhausting to sit with Fannie, to so carefully consider every word, every facial expression. He had agreed to his wife's plan but had not helped her see it through. It was no wonder she was angry all the time.

The lobby was empty. Joseph took a seat close to the door so he would be sure to see Isaac coming. What was his son-in-law doing out at three o'clock in the morning? He knew Esther had had good intentions when she insisted that Gussie come to stay with them for the summer but now Joseph wondered whether it might have been better to require Isaac to look after his own child. Esther could have watched Gussie during the day, while Isaac was at the office, but if their granddaughter had gone home with her father in the evenings, it was likely Isaac would have spent considerably less time putzing around Atlantic City, doing God knows what.

Isaac arrived at the hospital a few minutes later. When he yanked at the big front door, he let in the smell of the ocean breeze, which whipped across Absecon Island at night. Joseph watched Isaac scan the lobby. He raised a hand, then waited for his son-in-law to cover the distance between them.

"What's happening?" Isaac said, in lieu of a greeting.

Joseph was not inclined to give him the information he wanted, certainly not yet. "Where were you?"

"I must not have heard the phone ring."

"Or your mother-in-law pounding on your front door?"

Isaac didn't even blink. "Right."

"So, I am to believe that, in the middle of the night, you woke up and thought, 'I'd better check the front door to see if anyone's left me a note.'"

Isaac reached into the pocket of his trousers and pulled out a wrinkled piece of paper, which he balled up and tossed onto Joseph's lap. "Right. Now what's going on?"

Joseph grabbed up the piece of paper and unfolded it, smoothing it against his knee. Sure enough, it was Esther's note, short and to the point. In big letters she had written, *The hospital tried to call you. Fannie is in labor. Where ARE you?*

This behavior of Isaac's was new, and it made Joseph nervous. Isaac might have always disliked Joseph and Esther but, until now, he had acted deferentially toward them.

"Are you drunk?" Joseph asked quietly.

"Where's Fannie?"

"In her room but you can't go up there right now."

Isaac turned toward the stairs.

"Stop," said Joseph. "The doctor said no more visitors."

Isaac ignored him and kept walking in the direction of the stairs. Joseph was out of his chair in a split second, at Isaac's side before he could fully consider his next move. He grabbed Isaac by the shoulder and yelled "Sit down!" in a voice far larger and louder than he'd ever used with his son-in-law, with anyone for that matter. Joseph watched Isaac wind back his arm, then watched it dawn on him that he was about to clock his father-in-law. "Please, sit down," Joseph repeated, in a quieter voice than before.

Isaac unclenched his fist and returned it to his side. He looked around, found the nearest chair, and sank into it. Joseph followed, sitting in the chair next to him.

"Their plan is to try to let her get a little rest, and then take her to the labor room in a few hours."

Isaac nodded vacantly. Did he even care?

"What's going on, Isaac?" He didn't smell like alcohol, just sweat.

Isaac didn't answer.

"Is this about the Florida deal? I'm sorry I didn't buy in."

"It's too late for any of that."

"Investing or apologizing?"

Isaac let out a short laugh. "The first one. Or maybe both."

"How much did you lose?"

"About five hundred. Plus everything my father had."

Joseph turned his head to get a better look at his son-in-law. Was he hearing him correctly? "Does that include the money you took from Adler's?"

It was Isaac's turn to look surprised.

"Mrs. Simons figured it out," said Joseph, "the new Northfield accounts."

Isaac made no denials, didn't even bother searching for an excuse.

How could a man who had so much always manage to believe he had so little? It was as if, looking at Isaac, Joseph could see straight through to the end of Fannie's life. She might live a half century beyond her sister but she was always going to be burdened by a husband who was dissatisfied with his own existence, with hers as well. If Joseph did nothing, Fannie would drown, too, just much more slowly.

He did some quick calculations. Isaac had been repaying the loan for almost five years, which meant that more than a thousand dollars had accumulated in the account Joseph had established at the Boardwalk National Bank. In all the years Isaac had been making the payments, Joseph had never once considered forgiving his son-in-law's debt. He thought of the money in the account as Fannie's and imagined returning it to her eventually in the form of an inheritance or something more tangible that he could watch her enjoy. He had contemplated using it to help the couple buy a house or send Gussie to college. The trick, he had always known, would be to find the thing that Isaac's greed couldn't spoil, the thing he couldn't beg, barter, or steal out from under Fannie's nose. The thing that would most directly improve his daughter's life. What if that thing was ridding her of Isaac?

"There's a thousand dollars in the account at the Boardwalk National Bank," Joseph said.

Isaac shot a glance at Joseph. "You'd let me have that?"

"With some stipulations."

Isaac didn't say anything, just sat up straighter in his chair. Joseph knew he had his attention. Was he really going to propose this?

"Leave town."

"You want us to move?"

"Just you," said Joseph. Then he held his breath.

It was possible that Isaac would let out a loud laugh and relay this offer to Fannie the first chance he got. Tonight? Tomorrow? After the baby's safe arrival? In any of those scenarios, Joseph was sure to lose his remaining daughter. And Gussie, too. What would Fannie think of him if she learned he had tried, unsuccessfully, to buy off her husband? Other parents might be accused of meddling but this was something else altogether.

"For good?"

Joseph didn't hear the question, so worried was he that he had just made the largest mistake of his life. "Hmm?"

"You want me gone for good?"

Maybe it was best not to answer that question so directly. "Isaac, when I look at you, I see a man who wants a different kind of life."

"What man doesn't wake up some days wanting a different life?"

"Me."

"Even now?" Isaac asked, waving his hands around at the hospital's surrounds. "After this summer? There aren't things you'd change?"

"Of course there are," said Joseph. "But even on the day I buried Florence, I was glad for every one of the days that had preceded it."

"And you think I'm built so differently?"

"I think there are men who are not well suited for family life." Joseph didn't want to insult Isaac, if anything he wanted to flatter him. So, he added, "Particularly men who have seen something of the world, who have a keen interest in business."

"Fannie might disagree with you."

"She might," said Joseph. "Which is why I'm hoping this conversation can remain between us."

Isaac looked at him again. Both of them knew Joseph had just handed Isaac a sizable bargaining chip.

"Where would I go?"

"I don't know. Back to Florida maybe?"

"I may not be cut out for real estate."

"I'll give you a good reference," said Joseph. "Do something else."

"A grand won't last long if I can't find work."

Joseph began to feel hopeful. Isaac hadn't spit in his face, hadn't stormed off to find Fannie. If he was doing any amount of math, it meant he was considering the offer. "I could throw in some more."

"How much?"

What a son of a bitch. Isaac was going to take the offer, Joseph realized. Maybe not in its current form, maybe not tonight. But eventually they would strike on the right number and he would go. Fannie, Hyram, Gussie, this new baby. Isaac would shake them all off like brambles stuck to the leg of his trousers after a long walk in the woods. Was this the right thing for Joseph to do? It didn't feel good but neither had watching his elder daughter disappear into an unhappy marriage.

"A few thousand." Now Joseph was dipping into his own savings, into money he might have used for Inez and Paul. He had wanted to tell Anna that she could count on him for more help but Esther's words rang in his ears. *What about Fannie? Is she entitled to a safety net?*

"How would this work?" Isaac said.

"I'll give you a lump sum to get you started. Withdraw it from the bank and hand it to you." Joseph had to think fast. How was he going to ensure Isaac didn't walk back into Fannie's life five years from now? "Then I'll send you monthly payments for the rest of my life."

"And if you should die?"

"I'll outline the agreement in my will. Make sure you're taken care of."

Isaac rubbed his eyes and looked at Joseph. "When do you envision all of this happening?"

Joseph looked at his watch. "The bank doesn't open for another five hours or so. Go home, sleep on it, and if it's what you want to do, meet me there at ten."

"The baby?"

"Wait if you want. But I think it will make it harder."

"Make what harder?" Esther asked, and both men jumped.

"We didn't hear you," said Joseph as he pulled himself to his feet.

"You must be more tired than you realize," she said, never taking her eyes off Isaac, who remained in his chair. "You made it, I see."

"I did."

Esther's contempt for her son-in-law simmered so close beneath the surface of her skin that it was all Joseph could see. He would have liked to take her aside, to tell her his plan, but he couldn't risk it. Fannie would be fragile after the baby was born, particularly after she was told about Florence. Esther might very well advocate waiting until Fannie was on her feet. Or, in the plain light of day, leaving well enough alone.

"Still no progress?" Joseph asked.

Esther shook her head. "The doctor is insisting we go home." To Isaac, she said, "It looks like I ruined your night for nothing."

"Oh, it's fine," said Isaac.

Esther tilted her head and narrowed her eyes at him. "I wasn't apologizing."

Dear God. His wife was going to undo all the progress he had just made. Joseph reached for Isaac's shoulder and gave it an affectionate squeeze. "Tomorrow?"

Isaac looked very far away. He blinked hard, twice. "Hmm?"

"Tomorrow. We said ten."

"What's happening at ten?" said Esther.

Joseph didn't answer her, just looked at Isaac with a steady gaze.

"I'll come by the apartment at ten," said Isaac. "I'd like to see Gussie."

The mention of his granddaughter's name made Joseph's legs go numb.

"There's a good chance we'll be back over here," said Esther.

Joseph studied his son-in-law's face, trying to discern his intentions. Had he underestimated Isaac? There was only one way to know. "I'll wait."

Isaac

Isaac was surprised to find that, even after eight years of marriage, he could still fit everything he owned in one suitcase. In the breaking light of the early morning, he had packed his clothes and his good pair of shoes, his pomade and his shaving brush. Now he walked from one room of the apartment to another, examining the contents of cupboards, closets, and drawers, looking for items that were his and his alone.

In a chest in the bedroom, he found the *tallis* he'd worn to services when he was growing up, the *tzitzis* at each of the four corners tied by his mother's hand. He packed it away in his suitcase. In a drawer in the kitchen, he found the old can opener that he'd bought at a five-and-dime in Florida. Technically, it was his and not theirs. He picked it up, felt the heft of it in his palm, and placed it back in the drawer. What if Fannie needed to open a can of dried milk or processed peas for the baby and couldn't find it?

In the dining room, Isaac removed an old shoe box from the sideboard. In it, he and Fannie had stored important papers, photographs, letters that one or both of them wanted to keep. He took out his birth certificate and set it aside, then considered a recent bank statement. There was no point in bothering with it; nothing was in the account anyway. Near the bottom of the box, there was a small stack of letters that his father had sent him during the years he lived in West Palm Beach. One of them, written out of anger shortly after Isaac left Alliance, told him not to bother coming home. Another delivered the news that his mother had died. Isaac couldn't bear to think of his father now, so he left the letters as they were—sandwiched between Gussie's immunization card and a bill of sale for the Monitor Top refrigerator.

Once he was settled, he'd write to his father, enclose a check to cover what was missing from the Campfire Marshmallows can. It would be a relief to square up with the old man, even if the accompanying letter was hard to compose.

At the very bottom of the box was a portrait of Fannie, Gussie, and Isaac. Fannie had had it taken at Perskie's when Gussie was two or three years old. The child had been tired and refused to sit still, and the image had suffered as a result. Fannie looked miserable, and Gussie was a blur, her likeness closer to that of an aura than a little girl. The photographer had offered to retake the photograph, and so this failed version had been relegated to the shoe box—too dear to be thrown out but too imperfect to be framed. Isaac held the photograph close to his face and studied his own expression, which was not as dour as Fannie's but every bit as distant. He tried to remember the particulars of that day. Had they eaten breakfast together? Gone for a long walk? Had he been happy? He moved to put the photograph back in the box but decided to keep it aside instead.

There was one document Isaac knew he wouldn't find in the shoe box. He tried to remember what he'd done with it. He had carried it in his jacket pocket for several weeks this summer but, at some point, he had surely put it away. In a box? A drawer? Where? He could picture the envelope, its corners tattered, his wife's handwriting scrawled across the front. He walked back to the bedroom, checked the pockets of his suit coat, and came up with nothing. It was possible that he had left it at the office. He looked out the bedroom window, which faced Atlantic Avenue. A paper boy whizzed by on his bicycle. Two blocks east, the sun was rising over the Atlantic. Isaac checked his watch. He had three hours before he was due to meet Joseph. There was still time.

~

Joseph seemed very relieved to find Isaac at his front door at a few minutes after ten. If Joseph had gotten any sleep the night before, Isaac couldn't tell. But then again, Isaac hadn't slept at all.

"Come in."

"Where's Gussie?"

"In her room," said Joseph, taking a step backward to allow Isaac to maneuver past him and down the narrow hallway.

Isaac began to make his way toward the sun porch and could hear Joseph following a few steps behind. "Where's Esther?"

"She went back over to the hospital."

"Any word?"

"No, none."

"I thought I might take Gussie for a walk."

"I don't know that that's a good idea."

"Sure, it is."

Isaac found Gussie playing jacks on the floor of her room. Her back was to him and her hair shone in the bright light of the morning sun. He watched her count off several attempts before he interrupted.

"Threesies, huh?"

She whipped her head around to find him leaning in the open door-way. "Father!" she said as she jumped up, sending the little red ball and several jacks skittering across the hardwood floor.

Isaac's throat grew tight as he felt her arms reach around his waist. Eventually, he found his words: "Get your shoes on, Gus-Gus."

"I'll come," said Joseph.

Isaac stifled a laugh. "You will not."

"Why can't Papa come?" Gussie asked as she rooted around under the bed for her sandals.

"Because Papa is very busy," said Isaac, reaching for one sandal, which he had spotted under her bedside table. He tossed it onto the floor, beside her. "Isn't that right, Papa?"

Gussie scooted back out from under the bed, holding the second sandal up in the air, triumphant.

"I'm not," said Joseph. "In fact, I'd prefer to come."

Isaac found it impossible to make eye contact with Joseph, so he simply turned and began walking toward the front of the apartment. He passed Esther and Joseph's room and then Anna's. "If you must send someone to mind us, send Anna."

Isaac called to Gussie over his shoulder and kept walking, out the door and down the stairs to the waiting sidewalk. Gussie followed a few steps behind.

"Should we wait for Anna?" Gussie asked when she was outside. She bent down to finish buckling her sandals.

Isaac looked over his shoulder at the bakery and the little door that led to the building's upstairs apartment. "She won't be long."

"Where are we going?"

"A walk?"

Isaac had thought about where he wanted to take Gussie, about how he wanted to remember her and she him. He pictured her on the Boardwalk, the wind ruffling her hair, but couldn't think much further ahead than that.

He took Gussie's small, sweaty hand in his and headed down Virginia Avenue, toward the ocean. By the time they passed the Islesworth Hotel, Anna had caught up with them, although she seemed to instinctively know to keep her distance. He wondered how much Joseph had told her.

"Want a frozen custard?" he asked Gussie as they approached the Boardwalk.

"It's ten in the morning."

"Right." Isaac had grown so unfamiliar with reading his daughter's cues that he could no longer tell discordance from disinterest. "Shall we get one anyway?"

Gussie shrugged her shoulders, and Isaac led her several more blocks to Kohr Bros., where he exchanged two nickels for a pair of cake cones, piled high with an orange-and-vanilla swirl.

"You forgot Anna," said Gussie as he handed one to her.

"I don't think she's hungry," he said, glancing over his shoulder at Anna, who was pretending to be well occupied with a rack of souvenir postcards, which sat outside the shop next door.

"How do you know? Hey, Anna—"

Isaac poked Gussie's arm and said, "Knock it off."

Gussie stared at her feet and the cone in her hand leaned perilously to one side. He hadn't meant to upset her and certainly didn't want his reprimand to become a lasting memory. Isaac reached out, righted the cone, touched Gussie's chin.

"Sorry, Gus." To Anna, he shouted, "Do you want a cone?"

She shook her head no.

"See, she doesn't want one." Gussie seemed satisfied, so he asked, "Do you want to get a chair? Sit for a while?"

Gussie made slow progress as she followed Isaac onto the sand and toward a row of canvas-clad beach chairs. The custard was melting fast in the hot sun, and she stopped every few feet to lick the cone and her own hand clean. Isaac had rented two chairs and pulled them close together by the time Gussie caught up with him.

"Sit," he said, reaching for his handkerchief. He wondered if he should wait until she was finished before allowing her to mop herself up with it. If he had been more gracious to Anna, she probably would have managed the cleanup. He looked behind them. Anna had remained on the Boardwalk, where she stood leaning against the railing, as watchful and rigid as an egret in the marsh grass of the Thorofare.

There was no good way to tell her, Isaac decided. Whatever he said was sure to break her heart. "Gus-Gus, I'm going to go away soon."

Gussie stopped working on her cone and looked over at him. "Where?"

"Florida, probably."

"Florida," she repeated—the word almost a question but not quite.

"You've never been there but it's very pretty. And hot."

"How long will you be gone?"

"Awhile."

"How long?" she asked again. Isaac stared at his daughter. She could scarcely wait for the first day of school, her birthday, or the Easter Parade. Time moved slowly for a girl of seven. Weeks felt like months, months like years. Could she even comprehend real years? That enough of them, when strung together, made up a lifetime?

"Maybe a year, or a little longer." He added, "It could be a very long time, in fact."

"What about the baby?"

What could he say? That he wouldn't meet the baby? She'd never understand. "I think you'll be a very good big sister. You're such a big help and so very kind."

Gussie didn't answer, didn't arch her back into the compliment, the way she often did when adults said something nice about her. In fact, Isaac might have wondered if she'd heard him at all but for the fact that she had stopped licking the custard. She leaned forward in her chair, holding the cone away from her body, and for several minutes, both of them watched in a kind of quiet torpor as the treat dripped down her hand and onto the sand. Isaac held his handkerchief at the ready but didn't hand it to her, not until the mess had congealed into a thick pool between them.

~

When they arrived back at the apartment, Joseph asked Anna to look after Gussie and led Isaac into the kitchen, where he'd spread out several pieces of paper, neatly typed.

"What's this?"

"Everything we discussed last night."

Isaac whistled. "You had a longer night than I did."

"Aaron Wexler drew it up this morning."

Isaac sat down in a kitchen chair, picked up one of the documents, and began to scan it. "You don't trust me to stay gone?"

"I think, with something this sensitive, it's better if we spell out the terms."

Isaac tried to focus on the small type.

"The terms are the same," said Joseph. "Aaron recommended we add something about divorce."

"Divorce?" It hadn't occurred to Isaac that he and Fannie would divorce.

"It just says that if Fannie ever wants one, you'll grant it to her."

"And if I want one?"

"Do you?"

"Not particularly. But for the sake of argument, let's say I did."

Joseph looked uncomfortable. Aaron must not have accounted for that in the contract. "If you asked for one and Fannie didn't want to grant it, we'd all be in a rather awkward situation."

"Because you'd have to show her this contract."

"Well, yes," said Joseph. "And because she hasn't actually agreed to anything."

"Relax, old man," said Isaac, thumping Joseph on the shoulder. "I don't want a divorce."

Isaac read the document twice. The money added up, and his inheritance would be generous. He wasn't to contact Fannie but he could write to Gussie twice a year. "It says here that you're supplying my train ticket?"

"I got you a seat on the four o'clock. You can go all the way to Miami, or get off sooner."

"Don't even trust me to get out of town on my own?"

"I just thought it'd be easier."

Isaac let out a sharp breath. "Nothing about this is easy."

Joseph looked at Isaac, then at his hands. "I know."

"Where's a pen?" said Isaac. There were already two on the table but Joseph was so flustered, he handed Isaac a third one, from his breast pocket.

"Wait," said Joseph.

"What for?"

"We need a witness," he said, and called for Anna, who entered the room so quietly that she might as well have been a light fixture or a potted plant.

"So, I suppose Joseph has filled you in?" Isaac said when she sat down across from them at the kitchen table.

Anna looked embarrassed to be in the room. Joseph handed her a pen and she took it without looking either man in the eye. Isaac assumed that this deal of Joseph's negated any assistance he might otherwise have offered her parents.

Isaac held the nib of his pen over the signature line and hesitated, briefly. Was this what he wanted? To leave and not come back? If he stayed, could he change? Become a better husband? A better father? A better son?

Joseph leaned forward, ever so slightly, in his chair. How badly his father-in-law wanted him gone. Isaac stared at the contract hard, until the words began to blur together. He suspected Fannie would be fine without him. Gussie, too. It was an awful lot of money. Isaac pushed every pure and decent thought he'd ever had from his head and signed.

~

Joseph instructed Isaac to wait outside the bank while he went in to make the withdrawal. The idea miffed Isaac initially. It wasn't as if what they were doing was illegal. But what did Isaac really care? He set down the suitcase he'd carried from the apartment and removed his hat. When Joseph emerged, several minutes later, with a fat deposit envelope, he handed it to Isaac.

Isaac peeked inside at the stiff bills. "It's all there," said Joseph. "Just write when you've got an address where I can start sending the checks."

Isaac slid the envelope into the interior pocket of his jacket and felt for the other envelope, unyielding against his rib cage. He pulled it out and handed it to Joseph. "This is for you. To give to Fannie."

"You didn't go see her?"

"I did. Last night, after you left the hospital."

"I wondered."

"I didn't tell her I was leaving."

"So, this letter—"

"Isn't from me."

Joseph looked confused.

"Open it if you'd like."

Joseph slid his finger under the flap, which Isaac had intentionally left unsealed. He pulled out a single sheet of paper, unfolded it, and began to read.

"It's from Florence?" Joseph asked, clearly startled.

"Fannie will think so."

Joseph kept reading.

"Fannie and Florence fought. Just before Florence died," said Isaac. "And Fannie's spent the whole summer stewing about it. She wrote Florence an apology and asked me to deliver it but, of course, there was no one to give it to."

"So, you forged a reply?"

"Of sorts. If you don't give it to her, she'll think Florence died angry with her."

"Did she?"

"Maybe," said Isaac. "Does it matter?"

Joseph returned to the letter and read it all the way to the end. At Florence's signature, which Isaac had gotten just right, Joseph let out a soft moan.

"If you tell Fannie you found this letter in Florence's things, I don't think she'll figure out Florence couldn't have written it."

"It's very good. Where'd you learn to do this?"

"There are probably some good reasons the Florida real estate market collapsed."

Joseph shook his head and refolded the letter, which he slid into the pocket of his own jacket.

"So, you'll give it to her?"

"At some point, all this lying has to end."

"Please."

"Maybe," said Joseph.

"It might be the only worthwhile thing I've ever contributed to this family," said Isaac. "If you don't count Gussie."

Joseph let out a choked laugh. "Lucky for you, I do."

Without any more discussion, the two men began walking in the direction of the train station. Isaac thought about telling Joseph that he didn't need accompaniment, that he was capable of catching the train just fine on his own. But it wasn't all bad having someone see him off, to leave Atlantic City under the pretense that there were people who would think fondly of him when he was gone.

Stuart

In the elevator, on Tuesday morning, Stuart silently rehearsed what he'd say to his father.

He had been running through the conversation in his head all morning, really ever since Saturday when he'd seen Anna at the pageant swim. Throughout the race, she had been careful to avoid looking in his direction—even when she and Gussie had walked out onto the pier. But back on the beach, during the awards presentation, she had had no choice but to see him, and he her.

Stuart tried to put his finger on what had bothered him about all Anna's marriage talk. It wasn't that he couldn't see himself as her husband, or she his wife. In fact, he could see their life together quite clearly. And it seemed nice. Better than nice. Damned near perfect. No, what bothered Stuart was that all Anna's figuring had made him question what was real. Had she been as oblivious to his family's wealth and position as she'd initially let on? Had she really wanted to learn to swim? Had she truly felt the weight of Florence's loss? Until that night on the beach, it would never have occurred to him to ask these questions, though if he had, he would have answered each one with a resounding *yes*. Now, he couldn't be sure.

Stuart was embarrassed to admit to himself that there was at least some small part of him that didn't give two shakes about Anna's motivations. If she married him for his citizenship but he got the thrill of kissing her warm lips and the pale skin that was left exposed when the strap of her bathing suit fell off her shoulder, weren't they both winning?

In the end he decided that she was right to have been straightforward with him. Would he have rather she said nothing and simply allowed him to fall further and further in love with her, never recognizing what she needed? The way he figured it, everyone needed something.

It had occurred to Stuart, as he walked back to his boardinghouse after the pageant swim, that Anna might both need something from him and also want him for her own unselfish reasons. The trick was figuring out how to separate the two.

It wasn't a trick that was wholly unfamiliar to Stuart. These last several years, the Atlantic City Beach Patrol, the dingy Northside room, and even cantankerous Mrs. Tate had allowed him to keep his father at arm's length. As long as Stuart remained financially self-sufficient, he had assumed he could make any life he chose for himself.

When Stuart realized what he had to do, his impulse had been to hurry to The Covington and get the whole idea out to his father in one giant breath. But he had decided to wait. It was too important a request to rush, so he had spent two long days watching the surf and practicing his pitch. Now here he stood in the elevator, still completely unsure of what to say.

The elevator arrived on the second floor, and Stuart nodded to Cy before making his way to the administrative suite, where his father's secretary, Louise, sat at her desk, guarding the door to his office with nothing more menacing than a stare.

"Is my father available?" he asked.

"He will be soon," said Louise, glancing at the telephone on her desk. "He's wrapping up a call."

Stuart took a seat in one of the chairs that lined the far wall. He was tempted to take a peppermint from the glass dish on Louise's desk but didn't want to risk walking into his father's office with his mouth full. After several minutes of jiggling his knee, the light on Louise's phone switched off and she said, "You can go in now."

Stuart stood, smoothed his pants, and made his way into his father's office.

"Morning," he said, closing the door quietly behind him.

"To what do I owe this pleasure?" his father asked, looking up from a stack of papers.

The lead-in was the part Stuart was least sure of. Should he make polite conversation about the Phillies' double header or get right to the point? He considered walking over to the bar in the corner of the office and pouring his father a scotch. Anything to ease his way into the conversation. But all of it—the baseball stats and the booze—seemed disingenuous. Stuart wanted to be the type of man who said what he meant.

"I want to talk to you about something," he finally said, then thought to add, "It's important."

Stuart watched his father shift in his chair.

"I was thinking I might hang up my whistle at the end of this summer. Start learning the business."

Stuart's father put down his pen and blinked at him, hard, as if he were trying to process what he'd just heard. "This business?"

"Yes, the hotel business. The Covington." Stuart couldn't believe he was saying it. Long ago, he had convinced himself that going to work for his father would feel a little like dying. "I realize I have a lot to learn."

"Are you in some kind of trouble?"

"None," said Stuart.

His father leaned back in his chair, appraising his son. "Then why?"

"Well, the business has been in our family for—"

"No, I mean, 'Why now?'"

This was a question Stuart had counted on. Did he dare admit that he loved Anna? That if his father brought him on, there was some chance he'd be bringing Anna on, too? Stuart cleared his throat, working hard to get the next part out. "There are things I want, that I need."

His father remained quiet, patted the desk once and then twice, then stood and walked over to one of the office's floor-to-ceiling windows, which overlooked the Boardwalk and the ocean beyond. A pair of heavy drapes obscured the view, and he pushed them out of the way to get a better look at something. "This isn't a bad life," he said.

"It's not that I thought it was," said Stuart. "It's just—" He hesitated.

"Just what?"

"That it didn't feel like mine."

"Do you think it ever will?"

"I hope so."

His father's attention was elsewhere. Stuart got out of his chair and went to join him by the window. Outside, a kite bobbed in the air. The string of the kite led across the Boardwalk to the beach, where a small boy and his father yanked and pulled at the spool.

"There's something else," Stuart said, a few minutes later, when they'd both watched the kite plummet into the sand.

Stuart's father turned his head to look at him.

"I need some money."

"Is she in trouble?" his father asked.

"Who?"

"The Jewish girl. In the pool."

Stuart marveled at his father's disregard for basic social conventions. "Her name's Anna. And we haven't—" He stopped himself. What business was it of his father's?

"How much?" his father said, with a slow shake of his head.

"Five thousand," Stuart said, trying hard not to wince as he said the number aloud. His great-grandfather had spent less building the original hotel.

"*Thousand?*"

"I know it's a lot."

"Christ, son. What's the money for, if not for Anna?"

"I can't say." The three little words were like a dagger, and he could tell he'd wounded his father with them.

"What are you mixed up in, Stu?"

"Nothing."

He raised an eyebrow at him.

"Nothing illegal."

"So, this is the only way I get you into the hotel business? Attached to a five-thousand-dollar string?"

Stuart wanted to tell him that he'd come work for him regardless, that he wasn't the sort to hold his loyalty over anyone's head, let alone his father's. But he kept quiet. Maybe he was the sort.

His father let the drapes fall closed, and the kite vanished from view.

"The hours are nine to five. Monday through Saturday. There are nights, too."

Stuart nodded his head in affecting agreement.

"I'll start you at the front desk. Rotate you through the restaurant and the bar. Maybe even have you do a stint in housekeeping. By the time you move up here, I want you to know every job in this place."

Stuart could tell his father had spent considerable time thinking about this, imagining what the proper instatement of his son might look like.

"This is really what you want?" his father asked him.

Stuart thought about it for a moment. Could he let go of the coaching? Easily. Florence's death had left him feeling less sure of himself, less willing to push the young women in the Ambassador Club to swim harder and farther than they'd ever swum before. If Florence could drown, anyone could.

It was the lifeguarding that would be harder to give up. From Stuart's stand, these last six summers, he had watched the whole world unfold. The wind traced ripples across the sand, sandpipers darted to and fro, and seagulls circled overhead in search of their next meal. Children laughed and fought and cried and fell asleep, sunburned and exhausted, in the crooks of their mothers' arms; young men used bad lines to romance girls who wouldn't remember their names come fall; and elderly couples marked the passage of time with the steady push and pull of the tide. Stuart was privy to it all, and when he pulled someone from the water and returned them to the world, he felt like a god. But then he thought of Anna, floating beside him in The Covington's pool. If she said yes, retiring from the ACBP wouldn't feel like a sacrifice, not really.

"Yes," Stuart said to his father. "It's what I want."

"Lou," his father called, in a loud enough voice to register with his secretary in the next room. A few seconds later, she popped her head inside the door.

"Bring me a check."

~

Stuart took the check directly to the Boardwalk National Bank and was halfway to the Adlers' apartment when he ran straight into Anna. The meeting felt fortuitous until he realized she hadn't even seen him. Her hair was wet and loose around her face, she'd skipped a button on her dress, and she was moving so fast, he might easily have missed her altogether.

"Hey!" he called to her, trying to get her attention, but she didn't turn her head, just kept moving past him down Atlantic Avenue. "Hey, Anna!"

She stopped suddenly, whipped her head around, searched the faces of the people around her until she realized Stuart was standing just a few feet away from her.

"What's wrong?" he said.

"It's Gussie," she said, a note of panic in her voice. "I can't find her."

"What do you mean?"

"When I got out of the bath, she wasn't in the apartment."

"Where are Joseph and Esther?"

"At the hospital. The baby's coming."

"Could she have gone to the hospital?"

"I called over and checked."

Stuart didn't think he had ever met a child who disappeared with the kind of regularity that Gussie did. "What about Isaac? Could she be with him?"

Anna shook her head fiercely. "He left yesterday on the four o'clock train."

"For where?"

"Florida, I think."

"For good?"

Anna nodded her head.

"Christ," said Stuart.

Anna covered her face with her hands, and her shoulders began to heave.

Stuart closed the remaining distance between them. He grabbed Anna by the shoulders but let go of her almost immediately, worried he'd overstepped. He'd yet to apologize for the way he had treated her on the beach the other night. It was quite possible she wanted nothing to do with him or his money but there was no use thinking about that now. "Where do you think she went?" he asked.

"I thought she might be looking for you."

Stuart pictured the rock, with the pair of painted sea horses on it. He'd put it in his pocket, and later found it when he was emptying his loose change into a small jar he kept on his dresser top. "I haven't been in the stand today. But let's check there first."

They took off at a run toward Kentucky Avenue. At the corner of Atlantic and Tennessee, Anna stepped off the curb and might have been hit by a speeding truck had Stuart not grabbed her by the hand and pulled her back onto the sidewalk. When the avenue cleared and they could safely cross, he didn't let go. They ran down Ohio Avenue, past the hospital and the junior high, and didn't stop until they were standing in front of The Covington.

The beach was unusually crowded for it being so late in the afternoon. Stuart let go of Anna's hand and checked his watch. Any minute, the lifeguards would lower their stands and come in for the night.

"What if she's not here?" Anna gasped.

From across the beach, Stuart could already tell the stand was vacant. Like Stuart, Robert was off for the day, so Stuart watched as two subs tipped the stand backward into the sand.

"Hey, guys!" he called as he made his way toward them. "You see a little girl this afternoon? Dark hair. Seven years old. She might have come around asking for me."

"She was wearing a yellow-and-white gingham dress," Anna offered.

The young men looked at each other, as if they were trying to do a quick inventory of the thousands of small children who had required their attention. One of them said, "The beach was packed today, so I can't say for sure. But no one came asking for you."

"Dear God," said Anna, moving a hand to her mouth. "What if she went swimming?"

"She hates swimming," Stuart reminded her matter-of-factly, and watched as Anna's face brightened.

"Where else could she be?" he asked her.

Anna listed off several places: the incubator exhibition, the plant, Fannie and Isaac's apartment—although she was sure Gussie didn't have a key.

They made their way from one place to the next as quickly as possible. "Does she know Isaac's gone?" Stuart asked Anna as they tried the door to the apartment.

"I think so," she said. "Isaac came to talk to her before he left."

"And he told her he was leaving?"

"He must have. She wouldn't talk to me about it, though."

"What about the train station?"

"Right, he took the train—"

"No, I mean, Gussie," said Stuart. "Could she be at the train station?"

Anna stopped, looked at him, and took off down the stairs at a sprint.

~

By the time they arrived at the station, the sun was low in the sky, and Stuart's heart was hammering in his chest. He paused in front of a newsstand to catch his breath and wait for Anna to catch up with him but when she did, she blazed past him, through the big front doors and into the station building. Stuart hurried in behind her and watched as she ran through the lobby to the waiting room. She scanned the wooden benches and luggage stands, then stopped to ask a depot agent if he'd seen a little girl matching Gussie's description. Stuart scanned the room quickly, then yelled to Anna, "I'll check the platforms."

He jogged through the station building to the train shed, where several hulking trains sat, ready to board. At the sight of them, Stuart's pulse quickened. The trains blocked his sight line, making it impossible to scan the platforms with any ease. He picked a platform and ran to the end of it, skirting waylaid luggage and clusters of passengers and standers-by. No Gussie.

Stuart tried another platform and was about to give up and turn around when he saw a small figure sitting on a bench at the farthest end of the platform. It was a girl, clad in a pale dress, clutching a leather valise. From this far away, he couldn't make out her face but he knew she had to be Gussie. He looked for Anna over his shoulder but she wasn't behind him.

"Harp-ave arp-I carp-aught yarp-ou arp-at arp-a barp-ad tarp-ime?" he asked when he had come to a complete stop, a few feet away from her. He gauged the distance between them—close enough to reach out and grab her, if the occasion demanded. She looked up at him in surprise and began to cry.

"I'm terrible at ARP talk," she said, between sobs. Stuart sank to his knees beside her and grabbed one of her hands.

"Not to worry, Gus," he said, switching to regular, old English. "You're fine."

She wiped her nose with the back of her free hand.

"I heard yesterday was a bad day."

She nodded her head vigorously and snorted several times. "Look," she said, staring over his shoulder. At the end of a nearby platform stood Anna. Her hair had dried in the late afternoon sun, and it hung in loose waves, which she pushed out of her face with her hand. God, she was glorious. Stuart and Gussie shouted and waved at her, and she waved back, excitedly, before disappearing behind a train and out of view.

"I bet she'll make it over here in record time," said Stuart. "She's very eager to see you."

"She is?"

"Sure, she's been a wreck all afternoon."

Gussie looked down at her hands, which were folded in her lap. She seemed embarrassed.

"What was your plan, Gus?" Stuart asked, glancing behind him to check on Anna's progress. She was already halfway down the platform.

"I thought I'd go to Florida."

"With your father?"

She nodded solemnly. "But it's tricky to figure out which train to get on."

"I agree, said Stuart. "That's why I rarely leave town."

Gussie looked ever-so-slightly amused. "That's not why. Adults know how to take trains."

Stuart stuck a thumb in his chest. "Not this one."

Anna flew past Stuart, nearly knocking him over in her urgency to get to Gussie. When she reached her, she squeezed Gussie's face between her hands and rested her forehead against hers. Together, they rocked back and forth, Anna muttering thanks to God and Stuart in equal measure.

"She was considering a trip to Florida," said Stuart, when Anna had released Gussie and returned to herself.

"Oh, Gussie," said Anna, stroking the child's hair.

"I didn't have enough for a ticket," Gussie said, holding out a handful of change, wrapped in Anna's handkerchief.

"I know this isn't easy, but you can't give up on Atlantic City," said Stuart. "Not when so many people love you and need you here."

"Nobody needs me," said Gussie as she hugged the valise to her chest.

"That's not true," said Stuart. "I do. And Anna does, too. Why else would we have inducted you into our secret society?"

"Because you didn't want me to tell my mother about Florence."

Stuart let out a short laugh. "Perceptive," he said, to Anna more than anyone. "Well, your mother's going to have that baby any minute, and then we're all done with secrets."

"No more Florence Adler Swims Forever Society?"

"I didn't say that," said Stuart. "Anna, wouldn't you say our society is stronger than ever?"

Anna nodded knowingly, as if the pair had just been discussing the society's state of affairs on the way over to the train station.

"But no more secrets?" said Gussie.

"None," said Stuart, looking at Anna. "Well, maybe just one more."

Anna

It was half-past seven by the time Anna, Stuart, and Gussie arrived at the hospital to find Joseph and Esther waiting in the lobby. Before Anna could get a word out, Esther caught her granddaughter up in her arms. She squeezed her, then turned to Anna. "Dorothy told us you called the ward, looking for Gussie."

Anna looked at Gussie, who shook her head ever so slightly in discouragement. "There was some confusion," said Anna, vaguely, before changing the subject. "How's Fannie?"

Esther relayed what she knew. Fannie had been moved to the labor room sometime early Tuesday morning, and her labor must have progressed accordingly because she'd been moved to the delivery room an hour ago. "It's her third baby. I pray it comes fast."

"You won't see her tonight?" Anna asked.

"No," said Esther, adamantly. "She'll need to rest." Anna wondered at the lot of them, sitting in the lobby. They might as well have been sitting in the apartment's front room, for all they were going to be able to do here.

"Do you want us to wait with you or take Gussie home?"

"Certainly, you should take her home," she said. Then, as if she realized that she wouldn't be able to order Anna around forever, she added, "Thank you."

"You'll stay?" Anna asked.

"Just until I know everything went all right." Esther's voice dipped, and Anna watched as Joseph reached behind his wife, rubbing his hand along her back. She was surprised to see Esther fold into the crook of his arm, as if the past several days had laid her bare.

"Gus, give your grandparents a hug and a kiss," said Anna. "You'll see them in the morning."

"Mrs. Adler?" said a deep voice from across the room. "Mr. Adler?" Anna looked up to find Fannie's doctor descending the stairs into the lobby.

Esther and Joseph stood to greet him, and Anna glanced at Stuart, who seemed every bit as curious to hear what he had to say as she was.

"You have a granddaughter."

Esther swayed, and Anna worried for a moment that she'd fall over. But Joseph was there, beside her, steadying her as she asked in a quiet voice, "Everyone's all right?"

"Better than all right," said Dr. Rosenthal. "Beautiful."

Esther's bottom lip quivered, and she sat down in her chair, hard. "She's fine? The baby, too?"

"Yes, perfectly fine."

Anna's eyes watered as she watched Esther let out a choking sob. It was as if, with this news, she were finally allowing herself to feel the full weight of her grief. Joseph bent low, grabbed his wife's hand, and kissed it, his own tears absorbing into the creases of her skin. "Bubala, you did it," he whispered. She buried her face in his shoulder. Esther had lost one daughter this summer but she would not lose a second.

Gussie wrapped herself around Anna's arm. "It's a girl?"

Anna looked Gussie squarely in the eyes. "You have a sister."

"She's named her Ruby," said the doctor, quietly.

Could Esther hear him over her own sobs? Anna could, barely, and at the sound of such an unfamiliar name, her heart lurched.

In ordinary circumstances, Fannie would have named this baby for Florence. It's what Jews did. They named their children for the dead, never the living.

Esther raised her head from Joseph's shoulder. "Ruby," she repeated quietly to herself.

Calling the baby Ruby—and not Florence—would be a kind of penance, a reminder that the child's life had begun with a lie.

"It's a beautiful name," said Anna, for Esther's benefit.

~

By the time their party emerged from the hospital, the sky over Atlantic City had turned a velvet blue, its edges singed with the glow of the Boardwalk's carnival rides and blinking marquees. The family moved in the direction of the apartment, and if anyone wondered at Stuart walking a half-dozen blocks out of his way to accompany them home, no one said anything. Not even Esther.

Esther seemed positively buoyant. And why shouldn't she be? Her plan had worked. Fannie was safe. The baby healthy. Esther held one of Gussie's hands, and Joseph held the other. Together, they swung their granddaughter into the air as they paraded down Atlantic Avenue. If either one of them were thinking about what the next day would bring—the conversation that would have to take place—it wasn't obvious to Anna. Even Gussie seemed to be in good spirits.

While Anna was extremely grateful for Ruby's safe arrival, she reminded herself that the baby's birth didn't actually change much of anything for her. Fannie would likely recuperate in the hospital for another week or so. By the time she was discharged and Gussie was returned to her, Joseph and Esther would be back in their house on Atlantic Avenue and Anna would be living in a boardinghouse in Trenton, still an ocean away from her parents but with little hope of seeing Stuart again. She doubted she'd be invited back to stay with the Adlers the following summer—not if Esther had anything to do with it—and she wondered if Gussie would miss her.

Anna glanced at Stuart. When the summer ended, would he resume coaching the Ambassadors? She assumed so. Would he think about her after she left for college? Likely not for long. She wished for one last swimming lesson, the chance to have him to herself in the clear, blue water of The Covington's pool. She wanted to thank him for helping her find Gussie and to apologize for being so forthright on the beach the other night. It wasn't his job to solve her problems. He'd already been abundantly kind.

As they neared the apartment, Joseph reached into his pocket and removed his keys.

"Anna, could I speak to you for a moment?" Stuart asked as they watched Joseph fit the key into the lock. Anna turned to look at him, gave him a nod so imperceptible that she was sure he had missed it entirely.

"Mr. and Mrs. Adler," Stuart said, without taking his eyes off her face, "do you mind if I borrow Anna? I'll bring her back very soon."

Anna was too embarrassed to make eye contact with either Joseph or Esther. What must they think? Instead she let her eyes rest on Gussie's face, which was lit up as bright as the Sherwin-Williams sign on Million Dollar Pier. COVER THE EARTH it read in bright lights. A nice sentiment, Anna had always thought. Gussie clapped her hands together several times before Stuart made a neck-chopping motion at her and she abruptly stopped. "I forgot!" she whispered.

By the time Joseph and Esther nodded their assent, Stuart had taken Anna's hand and begun steering her down Virginia Avenue, toward the Boardwalk. Anna could scarcely breathe. "Where are we going?" she asked.

Stuart laughed. "I have no idea. Somewhere where we can talk." They had walked less than half a block when Stuart pulled Anna into the entry alcove of a shoe repair shop, closed for the night. "This is going to have to do," he said. "I have to get this out."

He retrieved a slip of paper from the pocket of his jacket and pressed it into Anna's hand.

"What's this?"

"It's a receipt."

Anna turned it over in her hand and examined it.

"This afternoon I went to the bank and established a trust in your parents' names."

"A trust?"

"There's five thousand dollars in it. And it's all theirs. I couldn't touch it if I wanted to."

Anna didn't understand what he was saying. Nothing—not the receipt with all the zeros and definitely not the words coming out of his mouth—made any sense. "What?"

"For your parents' immigration visas," Stuart said. "You said they needed to prove they'd be able to support themselves. With this money and the twelve hundred dollars Joseph already put in the other account, I'd say they can more than prove it."

"You may never get it back."

"That's fine," he said. "More than fine. I just hope it's enough."

"I don't know what to say."

"I don't want you to have to marry anyone, including me, for a visa."

"Oh," said Anna, suddenly embarrassed. How had she so obviously misread him? On the beach, when she had so boldly outlined her predicament, she had convinced herself that he might *want* to marry her. Now she could see how naive she'd been.

"Anna? Are you all right?"

She was sure she looked stunned but she tried to find the words to reassure him. A rolling chair operator passed them by on his way to the Boardwalk, shouting "Five-cent rides!" and Stuart turned to look for the source of all the noise. Anna tried to compose herself but there was no use. Did this mean her parents really had a shot of making it to the U.S.?

"The money's theirs no matter what you decide," he said, returning his attention to her.

"Decide?"

"About me."

Anna raised her eyes to his for the first time since he had mentioned the money. His gaze was steady and sure. "You?"

"I thought that, if we were going to discuss marriage, it might be best to make it a separate conversation."

"Are we discussing marriage?" she asked, unsure whether to laugh or cry.

"I would very much like to."

A smile spread slowly across Anna's face.

"Before you say anything else, there is something I've been wanting to do all summer—"With one hand Stuart reached for Anna's waist and with the other he touched the soft skin of her neck. Her breath caught in her throat. He ran his fingers under her chin and gently guided her face toward his. Anna knew she should close her eyes but couldn't. The kiss was warm and tasted like all the best parts of the summer—the swimming pool at The Covington, salt air, sun-drenched skin, and saltwater taffy. As she sank into it, her eyes fluttered shut.

"Gussie will be heartbroken," Anna whispered when Stuart pulled away to look at her.

"Not true," he said with a laugh. "I asked for her blessing."

"And she gave it to you?"

"She did," he said, pulling her close once more. "She said that, if I'm unwilling to wait for her, she thinks you are the very next best thing."

~

The smell of coffee, percolating in the kitchen, lured Anna awake. Out her window, the sun—not yet visible in the sky—had turned the night a periwinkle blue. She looked at the clock on her bedside table. Five o'clock. This was early, even for Esther.

For a few minutes, Anna lay in bed, listening to the sounds of Esther's morning routine—the opening and closing of cupboard doors, the clanking of dishes removed from the drainboard. Everything sounded louder this morning, as if Esther knew precisely how little sleep Anna had gotten and was trying to summon her awake. Eventually Anna gave up all pretense of sleeping, wrapped herself in a robe, and wandered out into the hall and toward the kitchen.

"Morning," said Esther, the moment Anna crossed the kitchen's threshold. "I hope I didn't wake you."

"No, not at all," Anna said, stifling a small smile.

"Coffee?"

"Yes, please." Anna sat down at the kitchen table, tightened the belt of her robe, and readied herself for the interrogation she knew was coming.

Esther poured coffee into a mug and placed it in front of Anna, like an offering. "You were out late last night," said Esther.

Anna reached for the sugar bowl, already on the table, and scooped two heaping spoonfuls into her cup. She poured enough cream to turn the coffee a rich caramel color. There could be no easing into a conversation like this. She was just going to have to say it. "Stuart asked me to marry him."

Esther, usually so good at acting disinterested in Anna's affairs, pulled a chair out from the table and sat down on it—hard. "He did?" She didn't look entirely surprised.

"I said yes."

"What about Trenton?"

It was a natural question and one that Anna was going to get from her parents, too.

"New Jersey State Teachers College was as much about keeping me safe as it was about anything else." Was that true? She didn't even know anymore. If the Nazis hadn't come to power, she would undoubtedly have remained in Germany and attended college. But she wasn't the same girl she'd been then. So much had happened since.

"Stuart might wait," Esther said.

"He might. But I don't want to."

"What will your mother have to say?"

"About the fact that he's not Jewish?"

Esther cocked her head to one side, as if to ask, *What else is there?*

"She'll be disappointed, naturally," said Anna, wrapping her hands around the warm mug. She took a sip of the hot coffee, felt it find its way down the back of her throat and bloom in her chest. "They both will be."

Esther looked at her like she'd gone mad.

"I don't think it will be so bad as you think."

"No?"

"There are advantages to marrying Stuart," said Anna. "They'll see that."

"Visas?"

Anna nodded. She didn't want to give Esther the wrong idea, didn't want her to think that the decision to marry Stuart was a calculated one. But Esther was a shrewd woman. Surely, she could understand that this match had other benefits?

"His citizenship is one thing," said Esther. "But you know his father doesn't give him a dime?"

Anna took another sip of coffee. There was a small part of her that was going to enjoy delivering this next piece of news. "Actually, he's joining the business."

She looked suitably surprised. "Florence always said . . ."

Anna waited for her to finish but Esther's voice trailed off.

"I know this is very hard," Anna finally offered.

"I think about it sometimes," said Esther. "Whether I would have cut her off if she'd married him."

"He loved her very much. He's told me so."

Esther pressed her hands flat against the table and studied them carefully. Was she going to cry? It was difficult for Anna to tell.

"I do know," said Anna, slowly, "that Stuart wasn't what Florence wanted."

Esther looked up at her then, her eyes shiny. "What did she want?"

Anna recalled the way Florence had looked at her in bed, the night the letter had arrived, and shut her own eyes tight. Florence could have laid claim to them all but there was only one thing she had ever really wanted. Anna opened her eyes. "To swim forever."

A tear ran down one of Esther's cheeks. It hung at the tip of her chin before falling into her lap. Anna wished for more to say but could think of nothing that would do Esther any good. When the silence grew unbearable, she asked, "Will you tell Fannie today?"

Esther shook her head yes and exhaled slowly, as if she couldn't quite believe what she was about to say. "I have to explain Isaac's absence, so I assume I'll do it all in one go." She nodded toward her bedroom, where Anna assumed Joseph was still asleep. "Joseph will help."

"You'll feel better when you've told her. Everything."

"Will I?" Esther asked, looking Anna straight in the eyes. "Or will I just feel like Florence is really gone?"

Anna reached for Esther's hands across the table. Of course, Esther preferred to imagine her daughter was on a beach in Cape Gris-Nez. It was how Anna liked to think of Florence, too. Standing tall and proud, her arms stretched above her head, watching the water and waiting for a tide generous enough to carry her across the English Channel and all the way to Dover.

Author's Note

The character of Florence Adler is based on a real girl who grew up in Atlantic City. Her name was Florence Lowenthal and she was my great-great-aunt.

Florence was the fifth of six children. Her parents, Hyman and Anna Lowenthal, ran a jewelry and pawnshop at the corner of Virginia and Atlantic Avenues, and they raised their children—Ruth, Miriam, Grace, Daniel, Florence, and Joseph—in a house at 129 States Avenue.

Florence swam for the all-female Ambassador Swim Club and graduated from Atlantic City High School in 1926—the same year that Trudy Ederle became the first woman to swim the English Channel. In her high school yearbook, Florence's senior quote read, *Teach me how to swim*, and her *probable destination* was listed as *Swimming the Atlantic*. After high school, she swam for the University of Wisconsin, then transferred to the University of Pennsylvania. Her dream was, like Ederle, to conquer the Channel.

On July 3, 1929, Florence went out for a swim along the coast of Atlantic City. Two lifeguards, "Jing" Johnson and Neil Driscoll, saw her swimming along easily, just past the breakers at States Avenue. Only moments later, they noted that she had stopped moving. The guards deployed a lifeboat immediately, and when they had her back onshore, they rushed her to the Virginia Avenue Hospital Tent, where, for two hours, the chief beach surgeon, two additional doctors, and forty off-duty lifeguards alternated in performing artificial respiration. Florence's death was the first beach fatality of the summer. She was nineteen years old.

A front-page story, which included her name, ran in the *Atlantic City Daily Press* the following day. Reports blamed Florence's death on the ocean's cold temperatures but I think it is likely she suffered from hypertrophic cardiomyopathy and that her heart simply stopped beating. She was buried on the fourth of July in Egg Harbor's Beth Kehillah Cemetery.

My grandmother, Frances Katz, was six years old when she witnessed the Atlantic City Beach Patrol bring her young aunt's body back to the beach. For the rest of her life, she recalled two things about that day— Florence's red bathing cap and the echoing sound of her grandmother's wails as she realized her youngest daughter was dead. With Gussie, I hope I have done justice to both my grandmother and her memories.

In July of 1929, Frances's mother, Ruth Lowenthal Katz, was indeed pregnant and in the hospital on bedrest, after losing a baby boy the previous year. Like Esther, Anna Lowenthal made the decision to keep Florence's death a secret from her daughter. For the remainder of Ruth's confinement, Anna visited her in the hospital, never letting on that Florence was dead. Ruth's baby girl, whom she named Hermine, was born on the eighteenth of July, and only then was Ruth told the truth. Several years later, she gave birth to a third daughter, whom she named in her sister's memory. The story of Anna Lowenthal's gumption—really, of what we are willing to do to protect the people we love—is a story my family has never let go of.

That's as far as the similarities go. Ruth's husband, Harry Isadore Katz, was no Isaac. He was a devoted father and husband who eventually moved his young family out of their apartment and into a house on Atlantic Avenue. Unlike Joseph, Hyman Lowenthal never got the chance to mourn Florence's passing; he died the year before his daughter drowned. I hope Florence had a friend like Stuart but I don't know if she did. And Anna Epstein is a composite of several distant cousins my great-grandparents, Walter and Henrietta Hanstein, brought to the United States in the years leading up to the Holocaust.

Since this is a work of fiction, I have changed most characters' names. The exception is Florence, which I have kept as a tribute to Florence Lowenthal. May her name be a blessing.

Acknowledgments

I am grateful to so many people who supported me on this journey.

Carina Guiterman, thank you, first and foremost, for believing in this book. From our very first phone call it was clear that you loved Florence and her family as much as I do. Your edits, insight, and enthusiasm have made the book better in every possible way. To Marysue Rucci for your careful attention, and to Lashanda Anakwah for your work behind the scenes, thank you. I am indebted to Richard Rhorer, Elizabeth Breeden, Jackie Seow, Kassandra Rhoads, Margaret Southard, and so many people at Simon & Schuster for bringing this book to life.

I'm very lucky to be able to call my agent, Chad Luibl, a friend. For your thoughtful edits and warmhearted advice, and for taking me on this wild ride in the first place, thank you, thank you, thank you. To the entire Janklow & Nesbit team, thanks for rooting for Florence.

To the faculty and students at Virginia Commonwealth University's MFA program, and particularly to Tom De Haven, who launched and led the novel-writing workshop where this book was born. Tom, your encouragement made me believe *Florence Adler Swims Forever* would one day be a real book. Thank you. A special thanks to Matt Cricchio and Jake Branigan, who kept reading in Tom's garage long after the workshop ended. To Hanna Pylväinen, who generously allowed me to continue working on the manuscript the following year when I should have been writing short stories, and to Clint McCown and Gretchen Comba, who made sure I didn't get so dreamy-eyed about this project that I forgot to work on the next one. Thom Didato holds a special place in many, many people's hearts, and I am one of those people. Thanks for not only helping me navigate the program but for serving as an advocate of both me and my work.

In 2015 I was lucky enough to attend the Bread Loaf Writer's Conference, where I studied under Ann Hood. I had brought a creative nonfiction project to the conference but, on a beautiful Vermont afternoon, Ann and I sat in the barn and talked instead about a novel I wanted to write. Did she think I could rotate the story among seven characters, I wanted to know? Could I kill off the title character in the first chapter? I had so many questions. After we had spent an hour discussing the structure of this would-be book, Ann advised me to put everything else I was working on aside. "This is clearly what you're excited about," she said. "Go write it." You can argue that I shouldn't have needed permission to write this book but I did, and I thank her, again and again, for granting it to me. One day I intend to pay it forward.

A number of friends and family members read versions of *Florence Adler Swims Forever*, and the book is better for all their thoughtful comments. Thank you to Beverly Beanland, Ben Hanstein, Bobbie Hanstein, Blair Hurley, Tamsen Kingry, Debra Newman, Jenny Pedraza, Ruthie Peevey, Eve Shade, and Nicole Velez. Rabbi Andrew Goodman is a great friend and a careful editor who ensured I wasn't fumbling my Jewish prayers or traditions. Kristen Green deserves special thanks for giving me a front-row seat on her own journey to publication. She, more than anyone, showed me that manuscripts can indeed grow up to be books.

I was honored to share copies of the manuscript with my mother's four siblings, all of whom are as invested in Gussie and her well-being as I am. Thanks to Woody Hanstein, Judy Welsh, Joe Hanstein, and Jane Cunniffe for your careful reads and warm praise. A special thank you to Tod Simons for trusting me with this story.

To the staff and board of the Visual Arts Center of Richmond, but especially to Stefanie Fedor. While I was writing this book, I was lucky enough to work for a fabulous community arts center with an inspiring vision: *Art for everyone. Creativity for life.* I worked alongside potters, painters, printmakers, and photographers (not to mention writers), and the creative energy I felt in that space and among those people kept me going.

Thanks to the staff and volunteers at the Atlantic County Historical Society and the Atlantic City Free Public Library. My hearty thanks go out to the staff of the Knife and Fork Inn, who gave me a complete tour of the historic restaurant.

Growing up, I had several English teachers whose lessons and encouragement stayed with me long after the school year ended. Judy Bandy, Deborah Conrad, Elizabeth Mace, and LuAnn Smouse—thank you.

My grandparents, Frances and Walter Hanstein, did not live to see this book's publication. Before my grandmother died, at the age of ninety-four, I told her I was writing a "family drama" set in Atlantic City but I hadn't grown so bold as to tell her that the drama was inspired by *her* family. I owe her my deepest gratitude for sharing Florence with me.

I lost my father, Sam Moyle, to pancreatic cancer almost a decade ago. His absence in my life has been my greatest heartbreak. When he died, I was in my twenties, a young mother still trying to figure myself out, and I wrote my way through those early stages of grief. Even when the fog began to lift, the writing never stopped. In a very real way, this book exists because of him.

To my mother, Sara Moyle, who has always been my best editor and biggest supporter. She couldn't have known, as a navy wife raising four young children, that she was turning me into a writer. But, looking back, it's as if someone had handed her an instruction manual. Read to your kids constantly, take them to libraries and museums and theater, buy them plenty of blank journals, and traipse them through worlds that are not their own. Mom, without you I wouldn't be here. In more ways than one. For telling me Florence's story but also for raising little more than an eyebrow when I wanted to write it down, thank you.

To my siblings—Danny Moyle, Ruthie Peevey, and Eve Shade. It was a privilege growing up with you.

To my husband, Kevin Beanland, whose support and love has allowed me to pursue this dream. Thank you.

And lastly, to my children—Gabriel, Clementine, and Florence. You are my joy, my life. Without you, my world wouldn't be worth writing about.

Rachel Beanland is a graduate of the University of South Carolina and earned her master of fine arts in creative writing from Virginia Commonwealth University. She lives with her husband and three children in Richmond, Virginia. *Florence Adler Swims Forever* is her first novel.

Recommended Reading

Writing this novel required me to become an expert on historic Atlantic City, open water swimming, Jewish immigration, and much, much more. While this isn't an exhaustive list of the works I consulted during the research and writing of *Florence Adler Swims Forever*, it's a good place to start if you're interested in learning more about the time period or the place in which this book is set.

I was lucky in that some of the very old Atlantic City histories and travel guides listed below, which would have been difficult if not impossible to acquire, were given to me by my grandparents before they died. The books' pages are yellow and brittle and their spines have all but disintegrated, but in some cases, my ancestors' names and even their notes are penciled inside. Tucked between the pages of my grandparents' copy of A. L. English's *History of Atlantic City*, I found 1933 scrip, issued by Atlantic City and signed by Mayor Harry Bacharach, who was my great, great, great uncle. The past can feel ever-present.

Atlantic City

English, A. L. *History of Atlantic City, New Jersey*. Philadelphia: Dickson & Gilling, 1884.

Federal Writers' Project. *New Jersey: A Guide to Its Present and Past*. Saddle Brook, NJ: American Book–Stratford Press, 1939.

Funnell, Charles E. *By the Beautiful Sea: The Rise and High Times of That Great American Resort, Atlantic City*. New York: Knopf, 1975.

Heston, A. M. *Heston's Hand-book of Atlantic City*. Atlantic City, NJ: Self-published, 1900.

Irvine, Alexander Barrington. *Atlantic City: Its Early and Modern History*. Philadelphia: W. C. Harris, 1868.

Johnson, Nelson. *Boardwalk Empire: The Birth, High Times and Corruption of Atlantic City*. New York: Fall River Press, 2002.

Levi, Vicki Gold and Lee Eisenberg. *Atlantic City: 125 Years of Ocean Madness*. New York: Clarkson Potter, 1979.

Mauger, Edward Arthur. *Atlantic City Then and Now*. San Diego: Thunder Bay Press, 2008.

Ristine, James D. *Atlantic City*. Charleston, SC: Arcadia Publishing, 2008.

Schnitzspahn, Karen L. *Jersey Shore Food History: Victorian Feasts to Boardwalk Treats*. Cheltenham, Gloucestershire, England: The History Press, 2012.

Simon, Bryant. *Boardwalk of Dreams: Atlantic City and the Fate of Urban America*. New York: Oxford University Press, 2004.

Sokolic, William H. and Robert E. Ruffolo Jr. *Atlantic City Revisited*. Charleston, SC: Arcadia Publishing, 2006.

Wanamaker, John. *Rand McNally & Co's Handy Guide to Philadelphia, Atlantic City and Cape May*. New York: Rand, McNally, & Co., 1905.

Lifeguarding in Atlantic City

Fowler, Michael, Bernard Olsen, and Edward Olsen. *Lifeguards of the Jersey Shore*. Atglen, PA: Schiffer Publishing, 2010.

Garbutt, Robert. *Sand in Their Shoes*. Bloomington, IN: Author Solutions, 2003.

Jewish Immigration and Assimilation

Brandes, Joseph. *Immigrants to Freedom: Jewish Communities in Rural New Jersey Since 1882*. Pittsburgh: University of Pittsburgh Press, 1971.

Coan, Peter Morton. *Ellis Island Interviews: Immigrants Tell Their Stories in Their Own Words*. New York: Fall River Press, 1997.

Gillette, Robert H. *Escape to Virginia: From Nazi Germany to Thalhimer's Farm*. Charleston, SC: Arcadia Publishing, 2015.

Howe, Irving. *World of Our Fathers: The Journey of the East European Jews to America and the Life They Found and Made*. New York: Galahad Books, 1976.

Howe, Irving and Kenneth Libo. *How We Lived: A Documentary History of Immigrant Jews in America, 1880–1930*. New York: Putnam, 1983.

Rockaway, Robert A. *Words of the Uprooted: Jewish Immigrants in Early 20th Century America*. Ithaca, NY: Cornell University Press, 1998.

Shoffer, Leo B. *A Dream, A Journey, A Community: A Nostalgic Look at Jewish Businesses In and Around Atlantic City*. Margate City, NJ: ComteQ Communications, 2009.

Suberman, Stella. *The Jew Store: A Family Memoir.* Chapel Hill, NC: Algonquin Books, 1998.

Vernon, Leonard F. and Allen Meyers. *Jewish South Jersey.* Charleston, SC: Arcadia Publishing, 2007.

Zucker, Bat-Ami. *In Search of Refuge: Jews and US Consuls in Nazi Germany 1933–1941.* Chicago: Vallentine Mitchell, 2001.

Labor and Delivery at the Turn of the Century

Leavitt, Judith Walzer. *Brought to Bed: Child-Bearing in America, 1750–1950.* New York: Oxford University Press, 1986.

Wertz, Richard W. and Dorothy C. Wertz. *Lying-In: A History of Childbirth in America.* New Haven, CT: Yale University Press, 1977.

Swimming

Chaline, Eric. *Strokes of Genius: A History of Swimming.* London: Reaktion Books, 2017.

Mortimer, Gavin. *The Great Swim.* London: Walker Books, 2008.

Stout, Glenn. *Young Woman and the Sea: How Trudy Ederle Conquered the English Channel and Inspired the World.* New York: Houghton Mifflin Harcourt, 2009.

Wiltse, Jeff. *Contested Waters.* Chapel Hill, NC: University of North Carolina Press, 2007.

Florence Adler Swims Forever

by Rachel Beanland

This reading group guide for Florence Adler Swims Forever *includes discussion questions and ideas for enhancing your book club. The suggested questions are intended to help your reading group find new and interesting angles and topics for your discussion. We hope that these ideas will enrich your conversation and increase your enjoyment of the book.*

Topics & Questions for Discussion

1. *Florence Adler Swims Forever* opens with Florence's death and ends with the birth of Fannie's baby. In what ways do life and death frame this novel?

2. Early on, Gussie says that Florence always spoke to her like both a "beloved child and a trusted grown-up" (4). Apart from Florence, how do the other adults in Gussie's life treat her? Do you think it was right to send her to live with Esther and Joseph for the summer, or appropriate to make her keep such a big secret from her mother?

4. In the early 1930s, Atlantic City was seen as the "Jewish Riviera" of the East Coast. In what ways do you see Jewish culture celebrated within this community? In what ways do you see it under threat?

5. Describe Fannie and Florence's relationship. Do they have roles that they fall into? What do you think is gained by a seven-year age gap? What complications are introduced?

6. When Florence dies, Esther's first instinct is to keep Florence's death a secret to protect Fannie and her pregnancy. Discuss how others respond to this request. If you were in each character's shoes, do you think you could have kept this secret?

7. When Joseph and Stuart go to see Florence's ship sail out of New York, Joseph explains that "you give your children every possible chance" in life (188). What chances do the parents in this book give their children? Do these chances come with sacrifice? What chances seem to carry more weight—Anna's parents sending her away (financial), the Adlers supporting Florence's dreams (emotional), or Fannie staying on bed rest so her child can be healthy (physical)? Is one any more important than another?

8. When Anna visits Fannie at the hospital and reads to her from *Tender Is the Night*, she tells her that "we're all beholden to someone" (228).

Who are the various characters "beholden" to in this novel? Are they willingly so, or are they bound by structures that seem unshakable—like marriage, faith, or secrets?

9. Fannie is devastated by the death of her infant son, Hyram. Her mother, Esther, doesn't understand her grief, saying he doesn't need a gravestone because Fannie "didn't need a place to go and wallow" (33). What does it mean to Fannie to be pregnant again? How do these two mothers—Fannie and Esther—handle the death of their respective children?

10. The rise of the Nazi party and anti-Semitism in Germany, which had monumental effects on the lives of Jewish people in Europe leading into World War II, is a lingering threat throughout the book. Did anything surprise you about the experiences of Anna and her family? How would you have felt in their position?

11. How do you feel about Anna and Stuart's love story? What do they each bring to the relationship? Why do you think they are drawn to each other?

12. Near the end of the novel, Joseph strikes a deal with Isaac to entice him to leave the family forever. What do you think of Isaac's decision? Do you think—if he stayed—that he could have changed? Or was he meant to pursue something different with his life?

13. The novel ends without the reader learning of Fannie's reaction to the news of Florence's death and Isaac's departure. Based on what you know about Fannie, how do you think she took the news? What do you think her life looks like after these revelations? How would you have reacted if put in the same position?

Enhance Your Book Club

1. *Florence Adler Swims Forever* is based on a true story from Rachel Beanland's family. Share a story that is often retold and referred to in your own family. What does this story say about your family's understanding of its past? What has it meant to you in your own life?

2. A core theme of the book is that swimming is equated with freedom, power, and a lack of self-consciousness. Consider taking a trip to the local YMCA or to the ocean to swim as a group. Do you feel the same way about the water as Florence does? Or maybe you feel more like Gussie—preferring the stories of the water to the swimming itself?

3. Learn more about the rich history of Atlantic City, "The Queen of Seaside Resorts," at http://www.atlanticcityexperience.org.

A Conversation with Rachel Beanland

Q: Congratulations on publishing your debut novel, *Florence Adler Swims Forever*. How long have you been working on your novel? What was your process in writing it?

A: Thank you. Writing the book and seeing it published has been one of the most gratifying experiences of my life. I'd always considered myself a writer, but when I turned thirty-five, I decided that I needed to stop saying I wanted to write a novel and *actually* write a novel. I was working full-time, raising three kids, and I had no free time. I knew that the only way I was going to get a novel written was if I wrote it while the rest of my family was asleep, so I set my alarm for 4:30 a.m. and wrote for two-and-a-half hours a day, seven days a week, for two straight years!

For the most part, I wrote the book linearly. I have friends who write books in separate chunks and then move those chunks around until they've got something they're happy with. I much prefer to get page one right and then move on to page two. I didn't know how the book would end when I started writing, although I did always know that Fannie's baby would be safely delivered into the world and that Esther would play a large role in the final scene. I needed her to reckon with both her loss and her decision to keep that loss from Fannie.

Q: Florence Adler is based on the story of one of your ancestors, your great-great-aunt Florence Lowenthal. What was it like to grow up with this as a central story in your family?

A: I don't remember a time when I didn't know about Florence Lowenthal's drowning. It was a story that was told frequently in my family, usually by my mother. While she would give the details of Florence's death, her real focus was always on Florence's mother, whom I renamed Esther, and how tough she must have been to visit one daughter in the hospital, day after day, and never let on that her other daughter had died.

Whenever my mother retold the story, the moral was obvious. If you loved someone—your spouse, your parents, your children—it was your prerogative and even your responsibility to shield them from information that might cause them pain. My siblings and I took the message to heart. Over the course of our lives, we've hidden health scares, mental health diagnoses, and even deaths from the people we love most.

As a child, I can remember pushing back on this assumption that Florence's mother was right to keep her death a secret. I thought about my own brother and sisters and how I'd feel if anything happened to one of them. It felt important to me to be able to grieve such a significant loss in real time, and to make my own decisions about how I chose to mark a loss and mourn a death. Whenever I'd voice those feelings, my mother—and sometimes my grandmother—would come down firmly on the other side of my argument. I think the fact that we couldn't come to consensus was what told me I had the makings of a compelling novel on my hands.

Q: Did you ever consider writing the story as nonfiction? Was it difficult to fictionalize a story that was based on true events?
A: I never considered writing a nonfiction account of Florence's drowning and its aftermath because I just didn't think I had enough facts. What I had was a bare bones story, which had been passed down through the family like we'd been playing a giant game of telephone. With a little research, I was able to straighten out a few facts that had become skewed over the years and sketch in some more details, but it was never enough to comprise an entire work of nonfiction. Plus, my gut was that Florence's story would be enhanced by looking at it through the prism of other people's stories.

As for whether it was difficult to fictionalize Florence's story, I thought it might be, but because these events happened nearly ninety years ago, I found I was able—pretty easily—to treat everyone as the fictional characters they quickly became. I think it helped that, aside from my grandmother, I had never met any of these people in real life. And even in the case of my grandmother, I'd certainly never met her as a little girl! It was more difficult for my mother and her cousins to read the manuscript because they had grown up spending summers in Atlantic City with their grandparents—my Fannie and Isaac. In particular, my mother had a difficult time with Isaac because she knew her grandfather to be an extremely loving man. When she read the manuscript for the first time, I had to keep reminding her that what she was reading was a work of fiction. It took her about two hundred pages to forgive me for Isaac, but when she finished the book, in tears, she called me up and declared it beautiful. She's now the book's biggest publicist, so I think we're good!

Q: *Florence Adler Swims Forever* is set in Atlantic City in the 1930s and is a vividly rendered portrait of this place during a time of great joy (post-

Depression) and impending sadness (pre–World War II). What research did you do to bring this place and this time period to life?

A: While my grandparents grew up in Atlantic City and my mother spent significant time there as a child, Atlantic City existed for me only in my family's stories. When I decided to write this novel, I knew I needed to thoroughly research both the place and the time period.

I started by doing a lot of reading (you can find some of my recommended resources in the back of this book), but I quickly realized I was going to need more visuals if I wanted to make the city come to life.

What many people may not realize is that the Atlantic City of my grandmother's childhood no longer exists. Gambling was legalized in 1976, and in the decades that followed the majority of the old hotels were razed to make room for the casinos we know today. Many of the landmarks alluded to in this novel are long gone, including the storefront my great-grandparents owned at the corner of Virginia and Atlantic Avenues. I could—and would—make a research trip to present day Atlantic City, but the work I did beforehand was critical to understanding the city the Adlers, not to mention my own family, called home.

In its heyday Atlantic City attracted millions of visitors each summer, which means that—thankfully—a lot of souvenirs and related ephemera have survived. Visitors bought stacks of postcards depicting the famous boardwalk and piers, as well as restaurants, hotels, and even shops, and they mailed them to friends and family across the world. Now those postcards turn up in library archives and on eBay with some regularity. A quick Google search for "Hygeia Baths" or "Chalfont Hotel" almost always delivered me good results.

To help visualize how my characters moved through the city, I found and printed an oversized map of historic Atlantic City, which I mounted on foam core. With the postcards as clues, I used pins to mark the location of hotels and restaurants, boardwalk concessions and beach tents. It was a laborious process but it helped me tremendously. If my characters set off walking somewhere, I knew exactly what they'd pass along the way.

Q: In *Florence Adler Swims Forever*, the characters wrestle with grief and suffering (and these feelings are complicated by the fact that they must grieve in a very private, secretive way). Each character responds to Florence's death differently. Was it difficult for you to imagine how each character felt? Do you think the characters would have derived comfort from being able to share in collective grief (something the Jewish faith is known for)?

A: My father died of pancreatic cancer when he was fifty-eight. I reference the loss in this book's acknowledgments but I think it's worth mentioning again here. Had I not had that early experience with losing someone I dearly loved, I don't know that I could have written this book, or at least done justice to the grief associated with Florence's loss. What I learned as I navigated my relationship with my mother and siblings, and even my relationship with my husband and son after my father's death, is that we all grieve differently. I think rituals are hugely important, and when we don't find them in our faith, we look for them in other places. One of the things rituals do is teach us how to let go.

Before I lost my father, I never knew what to say to someone who was grieving. Afterward, I realized I wanted to hear people say his name aloud, to listen to them recall their favorite stories about him, to know they too were invested in keeping his memory alive. Writing this novel, I ached for the Adlers because I knew that in keeping Florence's death a secret, they were robbing themselves of a vital aspect of mourning. When we share our grief, we validate the fact that the person we have loved and lost made a lasting impression on our lives.

Q: The book contains many details about life in an American Jewish community in the 1930s. Was it easy for you to represent both the cultural and religious aspects of this experience? What did you feel was important to convey to readers about the Jewish experience at this time?
A: I was raised in a culturally Jewish household but I wouldn't say we were very religious. So, when it came to writing about the cultural and religious aspects of life in Jewish Atlantic City, I relied on a lot of research, much of which is outlined in the back of this book.

My grandmother always called Atlantic City a "Jewish town" but it wasn't until I started to immerse myself in the research that I realized the city did in fact have a higher percentage of Jewish residents than other cities of its size. This was due, in large part, to the fact that Atlantic City wasn't developed until the 1850s, when the Camden & Atlantic Railroad laid the first railroad tracks to Absecon Island. The city's boom coincided—quite precisely—with a spike in Jewish immigration to the United States. Jewish laborers, merchants, and professionals who had newly arrived in this country were looking for places where they might establish a foothold, and in Atlantic City everyone was hiring. It was exciting for Jewish immigrants to settle in a fledgling city with dreams as big as their own.

Q: Isaac could have been easily characterized as a deadbeat husband and written off as someone who readers would be happy to see leave. However, you depict him with a lot of empathy. What do you think of his ambitions and the decisions he makes?

A: It was very important to me to write Isaac as a complex character who—like all of us—has both good and bad traits. I didn't think readers would agree with his actions but I wanted them to appreciate or at least try to understand his motivations. We're all products of the world in which we grow up, and Isaac was deeply shaped by his early experiences and even the experiences of his parents. Isaac gets more backstory than many of the other characters in the book, and it's because I wanted readers to get some sense of where his ambition came from and how devastating it can be when that ambition is misdirected.

Isaac's decision to take Joseph's money and leave Atlantic City was in keeping with what I knew about his character, and it was also my way of offering Fannie a second chance. Women in the early twentieth century didn't have many options when they found themselves in bad marriages, but I—like Joseph—couldn't imagine leaving Fannie to live out her days alongside a man who could never be happy with her or make her happy in return.

Q: Your novel switches perspective between all of the major characters except the one at its center: Florence. Do you think Florence's story is well-told by those around her, or are there pieces that only she can tell?

A: I settled on the novel's rotating structure very early on in the writing process. Because I was dealing with family secrets, I knew I couldn't write an omniscient narrator. Each secret had to come out in its own time. By rotating perspective and only allowing the reader access to the mind of one character at a time, I was able to sustain tension and reveal secrets when it felt appropriate to do so.

What took me longer to figure out was when and how to make Florence's presence felt. I wanted readers to love her, so that they'd understand how greatly she was missed, and to achieve that end, I played around with the idea of giving her a prologue, and even inserting chapters that dealt specifically with her past. At that time, I was showing early chapters of the manuscript to a writing workshop, and I owe those first readers a huge debt. They convinced me that I didn't need to tell any part of the story from Florence's perspective but that if I interspersed other people's memories of her throughout the book, readers would come to love her anyway. Of course, this does mean that we won't ever know the full extent of Florence's feelings for Anna, or what happened to her during the final moments of her life, but I'm okay with that.

Q: What was it like to write from each character's perspective? Were there characters who were easier to write than others?
A: I love rotating perspectives because, as a writer, I never have a chance to grow bored with any of my characters. Each character has to work so hard and so efficiently during their limited time on the page, and for me, that presents a fun challenge. Also, every time I come back around to someone I haven't seen in a while, it's like reconnecting with an old friend.

As far as who was easiest or most difficult to write, it's hard to say. Each character presented his or her own rewards and challenges. Gussie was enjoyable to write because she's the embodiment of my grandmother as a young girl. Also, my eldest daughter was about Gussie's age when I started the project, so I was inspired by her. People say it's hard to write child narrators in adult fiction—that, as readers, we want our narrators to be capable of processing advanced thoughts and emotions. But I do think there can be this poignancy and humor in writing a child as he or she navigates an adult world; Gussie understands a lot but not everything, and what she is and isn't capable of translating is as much a reflection on the people around her as it is on her.

Fannie was a challenging character for me to write for a number of reasons. For one thing, she's confined to a hospital room. We're taught to write characters in action and, by definition, Fannie can't move, or at least not much! She's also the only character in the novel who doesn't know about Florence's death; the fact that she's being kept in the dark strips her of some of her agency. I wanted Fannie's chapters to be as robust as those of the other six characters, but to accomplish that I had to be creative. She needed visitors, obviously, but waiting around for people to appear in her hospital room couldn't be her whole life. I wanted her to form real connections with the doctors and nurses who cared for her, and I also knew she needed her own concerns about both the baby she was carrying and the baby who had died the previous year. When I discovered that the famous Dionne quintuplets had been born during the same time period as Fannie's confinement, I felt that the universe had handed me a rare gift. Of course she'd be obsessed with them!

Q: The book ends without us knowing how Fannie responds to Florence's death and Isaac's departure. How did you know when to end the story?

A: I get this question a lot. But the funny thing is, it never occurred to me to write that scene in the hospital—the one where Joseph and Esther tell Fannie that Florence is dead and Isaac is gone. Writers are taught that every scene needs to present new information, which will ultimately move the story forward. That scene, in which Fannie finally learns the truth, already exists in all of our heads. And it's devastating, right? I could have written a scene that captured some of that devastation, but the reality is that readers wouldn't have walked away with any new information.

I also think there's something about not sharing the scene that is in keeping with the ethos of the time. After the real Florence died and the family got through that terrible summer, my great-great-grandmother never uttered her daughter's name again. She even destroyed her photographs, which I find both fascinating and heartbreaking. In that post–World War I era, people dealt with tragedy differently. They didn't talk so much. Women like my great-great-grandmother put on a good face and moved forward as best they could.

Q: What do you hope continues to resonate with readers long after they've placed *Florence Adler Swims Forever* back on the shelf?

With Florence's story, there was this underlying assumption, within the family, that my great-grandmother wasn't strong enough to bear the simultaneous burdens of a dangerous pregnancy and her sister's death. That to protect her, essentially from herself, the family had no choice but to keep this terrible secret.

I still wonder whether, if I had been Esther, I would have told Fannie that Florence had died. I thought that, by the time I finished this novel, I'd have answered that question—if nothing else. But I still don't know what I'd do, in her shoes. What I do know is that women are frequently underestimated, and my experiences as a daughter, sister, wife, and mother contradict the narrative that we can't hold great sorrow and great joy in our hands at the same time. In fact, it's often the only thing we can do.

Q: What advice would you give someone who wants to be a writer? What's the best piece of advice you've ever been given?

Every writer is different but, for me, my breakthrough came about a decade ago when I started making myself write every day. I'd heard the old Flannery

O'Connor quote, "Sometimes I work for months and have to throw everything away, but I don't think any of that was time wasted. Something goes on that makes it easier when it does come well. And the fact is if you don't sit there every day, the day it would come well, you won't be sitting there," and I figured I couldn't control much but I could control the sitting.

I created a ritual out of my writing. I sat in the same spot each morning, wore the same ratty sweatshirt, and drank from the same coffee cup. Soon, my daily writing practice was a habit I couldn't break. Every page I produced wasn't perfect but it did bring me much closer to the book you hold in your hands.

Q: Have you ever been a part of a book club, and if so, what made it special? How did you decide what to read together? What makes for a good book club pick?
A: Before I went back to graduate school, I was a member of not one but two book clubs! I think they're a wonderful way to discover new writers and make new friends. Even when a book club is made up of your oldest and dearest friends, discussing a challenging book helps us better understand each other's differences. As a writer, I think it's especially worthwhile to belong to book clubs. I can get really in the weeds, thinking about a story on the sentence level. It's important to remember that everyone doesn't read literature the same way, and that people are reading in the bath or the carpool line or on an exercise bike, and that what they're looking for in a good book is both beautiful writing and a compelling story that keeps them turning pages.

One of the book clubs I belonged to adopted a really great selection process. The host chose three books she was interested in reading, and the rest of the group voted on their favorite. (They did all their voting in a shared Google document.) The system worked well because, when it was your turn to host, you were guaranteed a book you were excited about, but when you weren't hosting, you still felt invested in the selection.

I read a lot of literary fiction, and feel like book clubs work best when the novels under discussion have at least a few divisive characters and plenty of big unanswerable what-would-you-do questions. I love a good debate and there's nothing better than that moment at book club when the room erupts in conversation, everyone so excited about the book that they're talking over one another. I hope *Florence Adler Swims Forever* is that book for many of you, and I have faith that you'll enjoy many such moments as a member of the Barnes & Nobles Book Club.